BETTER EXPECTATIONS

BETTER EXPECTATIONS

The Estella Trilogy: Book II

A Novel
By

HUGH SOCKETT

Waterside Productions

Printed in the United States of America

First Printing, 2021

ISBN-13: 978-1-954968-80-6 print edition
ISBN-13: 978-1-954968-81-3 ebook edition

Waterside Productions
2055 Oxford Ave
Cardiff, CA 92007
www.waterside.com

To the memory of my mother and father

ACKNOWLEDGEMENTS

I am continually indebted to my friend and former colleague, John O'Connor for his constant encouragement as I work on this project, and his detailed and invaluable critique throughout the composition of this book.

I have been helped too by those readers of *Pip and Estella* who have been kind enough to send me their comments.

Josh Freel and Clay Cosby of Waterside have also been a constant support and I am grateful again to my proof-reader, Libby Sweeney for her attention to the detail in the manuscript, too much of which I miss in the writing.

As always, I could not have pursued writing as much as I do without the support of my dear wife, Ann.

Leesburg, 2021

CONTENTS

1874

1870

I

Philip, or Pip, Gargery arrived in Little Britain on a blustery March day to find Hamish Macdonald conferring with John Wemmick, the senior clerk. At the New Year Pip's uncle and namesake had passed away. The life-long sobriquet 'Young' Pip was now redundant.

After the usual courtesies and welcome, Macdonald took him by the arm and said:

"We have a serious crisis here, Mr. Pip. Mr. Wemmick tells me that, as he is now sixty-five, he wishes to retire. Since Old Pip's death I have been fretting over the need to find a junior lawyer and now I need a new senior clerk as well."

"I feel my age, Pip," said Wemmick standing by the window so that the light behind him made it difficult to see his face for any emotion he might be feeling.

"Maybe I'd work for another six months to help with recruiting a lawyer, but then I want to sit in my garden like my Aged P, and contemplate the wonders of Nature including Mrs. Wemmick," at which the three of them smiled.

"I miss Old Pip very much indeed," he continued, "and I think this practice once dominated by Mr. Jaggers now has to be managed by younger men. Have you heard how Estella is coping?"

"Quite well, I think," Pip replied.

"Estella is a strong lady and she will not let widowhood define her. Each day I think of Old Pip from my childhood, that wonderful calming voice as we walked on the marshes. I am no expert, Hamish, but on the matter of a clerk and a lawyer do I recall correctly that Mr. Courtisone recommended you, so why not try him again?"

"That is an excellent suggestion. I will walk by there this afternoon."

"However, I want to discuss seriously the purchase of a building in Clarendon Street by the Jaggers Trust for housing women prostitutes," said Pip.

At that moment Robert knocked on the door and gave Mr. Macdonald a gentleman's card, which read 'I. N. Klein' with a Paris address.

"What an odd card," said Hamish, showing it to Pip and to Wemmick, "I wonder what the I stands for? Ask him in, please."

"A foreign gentleman clearly, probably French," grumbled Wemmick.

"We will get rid of the gentleman, Pip, and then we'll talk about the building," said Hamish as the Frenchman came in.

He was tall with black hair, dark eyes, immaculately dressed and handsome enough, speaking English but with a strong accent and sporting a well-manicured black beard and a small moustache. Probably under forty years old, thought Wemmick, who looked at him carefully and had an inkling that there was a slight family resemblance to his former employer, the redoubtable Mr. Jaggers, something about the eyes, he thought.

"What can we do for you, Monsieur Klein?" asked Hamish.

"Thank you for your welcome," said Klein with a pronounced French accent. "I visit England as I wish to discover my lineage."

"Before you continue, Monsieur Klein," said Wemmick, proud of referring to a man as monsieur, "might we ask what initial is the name by which you wish to be known?"

"Isaiah is the first, but I use the name Nimrod as it is less common."

"A fine Biblical name, I must say," added Wemmick.

"A long way back in my searches I find a reference to a woman called Martha Jaggers, and I see in London reference books a lawyer named Jaggers at this address. There must be other Jaggers in the country, but I start with you."

"Ah," said Wemmick, now thoroughly startled by his recognition of the resemblance, "Mr. Jaggers was indeed a lawyer here and he died six years ago at the age of 80. I know he once mentioned a maiden aunt called Martha as he told our Mr. Pip of her existence, though he too is now deceased.

"Let me see, we are now in the year of our Lord 1870. Mr. Jaggers must have been born around 1785, so let us assume the said maiden aunt was born at least thirty years before him, say 1755, over a hundred years ago.

"I am not sure how we can help further. You would have to search parish records for details of her birth, anything after 1750, I'd say. I do know he was born in London but in which parish I know not. Are you somehow related to her?"

"*Peut-etre. Mon famille,* sorry, my family has a story handed down to me which I am searching.

"In the 1770s sometime, zis Martha Jaggers came to Zurich in *La Suisse* and gives birth to my great-grandfather, Henri. His father was unknown. *Ainsi,* I go to Zurich last year and after a long search I find there a very old clinic, *La Vierge Belle.* The owner of the clinic, though it was started by his great-grandfather, says he will look up the old records. I go home to Paris as he says the search will take two months.

"But then I get a letter last month from the clinic and *voila!* Martha Jaggers did give birth to a boy, Henri, who was adopted by Alphonse and Helene Klein, a childless Jewish couple, living in Zurich in 1785. Alphonse was a jeweler, with a specialty in watches, for which *La Suisse* is famous, and Henri then followed his adopted father into the trade.

"I wondered then why Henri, if he was a Protestant as I assumed, was taken in by a Jewish family?"

"That is certainly strange," said Hamish.

Klein continued: "In 1808, Henri, now twenty-three years old, married my grandmother Claudette, who was not Jewish, though

3

Henri had been brought up as a practicing Jew, so they were married in a synagogue. Then I think, h'mm, neither were Jewish by race, but by religion, *très intéressant, ne pensez-vous pas?*

"This pair, my grandparents, moved from Zurich to Paris and had several children, my father Jean-Paul being the eldest, born in 1810, but he was brought up as a Protestant. Jean-Paul married my mother Marie-Noel Raymonde in 1835, though I, Isaiah Nimrod, am the third son, and a jeweler which is now a family tradition, three generations. My older siblings died very young, so I am oldest one who survived."

Wemmick managed to conceal a yawn, though he was suspicious as well as bored.

"My goodness," said Pip, "this is a complex family history. But you are not married yourself, monsieur?"

"Ah, no, how do you say in English, I am a *bachelier*, bachelor, is that right? That is why I have the time to spend on these searches," and he smiled gently.

"Also, the Emperor of France is a foolish man and I dread a war with Prussia, so I take the opportunity to shut up my shop and renew my searches for this mysterious ancestor of my past, Martha Jaggers. France will lose if there is war, I fear, as that Count Bismarck is a very cunning man. If Paris were to be invaded, *mon dieu,* I could be left without money, for my shop will be, how do you say, ravaged?"

"My goodness," said Hamish, "that will certainly be bad for business."

"I think so," said Monsieur Klein. "As you see, I am a very cautious man, so I have come here with some of my stock of diamonds which are easy to carry and will last me years if need be. But I also confess that I am considering changing my name. France has, how do I say, a Jewish problem, though my trade is customarily Jewish. It is so complicated."

"I think you will have to stay in London for a long time to search out the records of Martha Jaggers," said Wemmick rising from his torpor. "I am sure you can find out by a diligent search of London churches, perhaps even of gravestones. As to whether she had Jewish blood, I have no idea. I know some lawyers used to think Mr. Jaggers was Jewish because of his looks, I never heard him countenance any such suggestion. To investigate his roots might be the best start to find more about your ancestor."

"This Mr. Jaggers would be a cousin of mine, would he not?"

"Your grandfather Henri and Mr. Jaggers would be natural first cousins, so you would be his third cousin as he was a generation or two above you, I think. This would be a cousin by nature, for once Henri was adopted by the Kleins, his natural origins would have no legal standing under British law. Of course, that only means there can be no legal ties, whatever friendships might emerge."

"Was zis Mr. Jaggers a rich man?"

"Yes," said Hamish as Wemmick tutted and turned his back in visible annoyance.

"He left a substantial amount of money for a Trust for the Relief and Education of the Poor which we manage, though the Trust's lawyer is a Mr. Courtisone. He was Mr. Jaggers' personal lawyer, so he might know more about this Martha."

Pip had been silent during this conversation, hoping the Frenchman would leave so that he could discuss the purchase of the building. But to be civil, he asked:

"Where are you staying, Monsieur Klein?"

"I stayed at Dover last night and I have not yet found a place in London."

"I have a room you can use for tonight," said Hamish eagerly, "then you can find a good hotel tomorrow. I have a small lodging at the moment just off Ludgate Hill."

Wemmick scarcely managed to restrain himself at this invitation as he had an inkling that this damn Frenchie was after Jaggers' money if he could get his hands on it. Pip mused that Macdonald would like a bachelor in his house.

"Was this Mr. Jaggers married? Did he have children?"

"No," said Wemmick, "he was not the marrying kind."

"Perhaps I am the only surviving relative then?"

"Of whom? Jaggers? I am not sure. By blood, perhaps, but not by law," Wemmick once again insisted.

"Perhaps, were you by any chance thinking that you might have a claim on his estate?"

"Oh no, my friend, I am not so crude as that," Klein replied with as much disingenuity as he could muster.

"Well, as I think about your interest in discovering your lineage, I think you had best talk with Mr. Courtisone who might know more, though I doubt it."

"Monsieur Klein," said Hamish, "I have to see Courtisone, so perhaps we can go there together now and, if you wish to use my spare room tonight, perhaps we can have dinner as well?"

"*Parfait, m'sieur.* I would be most pleased."

With much hand-shaking and good wishes, Hamish left with Klein.

Wemmick could hardly contain his anger once they had gone.

"Oh Pip, Mr. Macdonald is so naïve," he said scratching his head. "It is as plain as the nose on my face that this man is after a share of Jaggers' money. I am sure it is too late to enter a claim and if he does, it will drag on through the courts, draining the estate of money, though I'd bet Courtisone would know how to halt such an endeavor."

"Wait and see, my friend. Looking at this man's card," Pip said with a grin worthy of his father, "I think we should call Monsieur I. N. Klein "Steep."

"Why so?" asked Wemmick slightly startled by the change of subject.

"If you read his card as it is, I. N. Klein reads 'incline,' so that 'steep' would naturally follow as a nickname," at which Wemmick laughed heartily.

"Furthermore," Pip said with a smile, "this unmarried Steep perhaps shares Mr. Macdonald's other interest?"

"Goodness, a French sodomite," said Wemmick, "what is the world coming to! But then perhaps he is genuine. People do say that being a Jew in France these days is more of a liability than it is here."

Holding his hat on his head against the wind as he walked back to
Chelsea later, Pip was pondering the fact that he had not been able
to get the purchase of the building going, side-tracked first by the
search for a lawyer and a clerk on which he had no views, and then
by this damn Frenchman.

Meanwhile his wife Susanna had used her afternoon walk to
meet her neighbors.

"Excuse me, Madam," she had said in her Scots burr to a
woman passing her in the street, "we have been here in Cheyne
Row a few months, but we are not yet acquainted. I am Susanna
Gargery."

With a warm smile, the lady replied:

"How d'ye do? I am Sarah Bollaerts and my husband is James.
He is an artist, so we come here at exhibition times but otherwise
we live on our small estate near Thetford in Norfolk. Without children we can flit about as we please."

"How fortunate; we have two little ones, but have you lived here
long?"

"It must be seven or eight years now. I prefer Norfolk, but James
has his way as men do."

"Might we take tea together? Would you care to join me now?"

"Surely, I was just taking some fresh air, but that would be
delightful."

By the time tea was over Susanna had garnered a list of her
neighbors from Sarah and confessed that she planned a dinner
party and proposed to invite all on this impressive list of neighbors.
It was a long list.

Charlotte Mudge was the wife of a vicar in Norfolk who
remained in his parish. Staying with her was her nineteen-year-
old niece Elizabeth Fitzroy studying piano with a Monsieur
Pauer.

Near the end of the Row there was an architect, Frederick
Brandram, and his wife, Honora, and two doors up from the

Gargerys was yet another artist, Charles Meggison and his wife, Mary.

Two Italian gentlemen lived alone, Rizzio Campanile, an Italian professor of music, and Giovanni Fantana, another Italian, and a sculptor.

When Pip arrived home, Susanna could not contain her excitement.

"When she left, Pip, I rushed into my sitting-room to write down the names and house numbers of this group which I thought would do as a dinner party start and began to write the invitations.

"I need another man to ensure a balance, so I will invite Hamish Macdonald. We have to get along with him, whatever our views about his behavior. I will also ask Estella and Albert, but I doubt whether she will want to travel up to London from Kent. He is nearly nineteen, so he can sit with Elizabeth Fitzroy."

"I expect Estella will come. As I told Wemmick today, she is not one to surrender to widowhood."

"You are right, and we must do our best to make sure she is always wanted in our household."

"I agree. You're quite wonderful, my dear, constructing this party. But I didn't get time to tell you. There is a real fuss in Little Britain. Macdonald needs a lawyer, and Wemmick wants to retire. Then this damn Frenchman turned up, looking for news of Jaggers' maiden aunt, as he thought she was his ancestor!"

"After his money, I assume," said Susanna.

"That was Wemmick's thought too, though he tried to quash any hope of that by telling the man that as the ancestor's son was adopted, he would have no legal claim. But I think Klein, for that was his name, was more anxious to leave Paris than to find his ancestor. I thus got nowhere on our building. Anyway, Hamish offered him a bed for the night."

"So, the Frenchman is not married, I assume."

"How did you know that?"

"Oh, my dear, I admire your innocence, but Hamish is Hamish after all."

The wind had not relented as Macdonald and 'Steep,' as he was now known privately in Little Britain, hastened as planned to Courtisone's office. Once in the great man's sanctum, Macdonald went first and received the curt but helpful answer that he would give the matter of a junior lawyer some thought.

'Steep' introduced himself and repeated the story more briefly than he had explained it to Wemmick and Pip. Courtisone nodded sagely and said:

"I knew Nathaniel Jaggers from childhood, and we were the best of friends as adults, though we were private, even secretive. But now he is gone, I feel no inhibition about giving you some information about Martha Jaggers whom I met late in her life. Perhaps the most beautiful old lady you could possibly imagine, with translucent skin, bewitching dark eyes and long grey, formerly black hair.

"Nathaniel told me of Martha in the Jeffries Club one night. He wanted me to know in case someone came out of the woodwork, his expression, to contest the will. However, Monsieur Klein, let me tell you a bit more which may assist your search."

"That would be most helpful, sir."

"First, Nathaniel's parents lived for many years in the house in Gerrard Street, Soho. To the best of my knowledge, he intermittently attended St. Anne's Church. I am sure that the baptismal records will indicate Nathaniel's parents' addresses and his mother's maiden name, but Martha also worshipped there before she went off to Switzerland and afterwards.

"Nathaniel had a secular mind and he stopped attending church as he was mightily offended by Mr. Wade's introducing to the Parish some of the Romanist nonsense that had floated downriver from Oxford."

"Was there ever any idea with whom Martha consorted to give birth to Henri?" Asked Klein.

"Knowing the family well, it is unlikely to have been a man from below stairs. I am sure his identity will be impossible to discover."

9

"Can you tell me anything else about Mr. Jaggers?" asked Klein.

"I swore never to tell this but there are now no living relations at all.

"Nathaniel was an only child and Martha was his father's only sibling. Nathaniel's direct male ancestor, also a Nathaniel, was expelled from Wiesbaden in Hesse on the Lower Rhine as a young man about the time that terrible war started. That would have been 1630 or 1640. He came to London in the late 1650s and changed his name. Nathaniel Jaeger became Nathaniel Jaggers. So, our Nathaniel was a Jew by race if not religion, as were his male ancestors."

They returned to Little Britain and Hamish told Wemmick of the outcome.

"Well, I'll be blowed. He did have Jewish ancestors! That is a surprise. Perhaps not, though. I never saw him so angry, several years back, when a Jew called Fagin was apprehended running a group of pickpockets. He raged for several days about how the man could let down his race and was delighted that he was executed. Now I see why. At the time I was dumbfounded by his anger."

By the end of May, Pip and Susanna Gargery were well settled into their very comfortable Georgian style double-fronted house in Cheyne Row, fashionable in part because Mr. Thomas Carlyle was living at the other end of the row. Bought with Susanna's money, Pip reflected grimly, but not with a grumble.

Ornate railings guarded the front door with a few steps down to the street under a canopy with two Doric pillars. There was an elegant drawing room on one side of a capacious hallway with a library on the other. At the rear of the house was a splendid walled garden with cherry, quince and apple trees, and a blaze of roses in the summer, mainly on the walls, but a rose bed near the house had four Hadley rose-bushes with their deep luscious red color and a scent that would charm the birds off the trees. The basement with its separate tradesmen entrance on the front of the house comprised the kitchen and washing areas, and the cook and maids slept in the top rooms of the house.

At the last-minute Hamish asked if he could bring 'Steep' Klein to Susanna's dinner party which upset the balance at the table. Estella had sent a message to say Albert and she would come. Giovanni and Rizzio did not know each other so Susanna placed them close enough at the table not to dominate the conversation to meet her concerns that garrulous Italians would overwhelm it. Both Susanna and Estella noticed a mild glow between Albert and the young Elizabeth about which they exchanged amused looks.

"What are you two talking about?" asked Estella with a slight smile as the maid cleared away the soup dishes.

"We were talking about our studies. Elizabeth is studying piano, and I am studying art, but we were also talking about the war in France."

"My father is in the Diplomatic Corps in Paris, and I am staying with my aunt Charlotte for a term learning piano with my tutor. I have been hearing from Father about the possibility of a war quite soon. He thinks it may not turn out well for France if the Emperor gets trapped by this Count Bismarck into a declaration."

"Monsieur Klein will have views about that, I am sure. Why not talk with him after dinner?"

Estella let the two young people chatter to each other and surveyed the scene.

Here were Pip and Susanna's neighbors, a motley crew, she thought. Sarah Bollaerts was a plump, bespectacled woman clearly of good breeding, with a laugh that sounded more like a loud exhalation of breath, followed by a large intake.

Her husband James was a man of mild manner, sporting a large reddish-grey beard, and surprisingly well dressed for an artist; no smock and beret for him. He explained to Estella how much they enjoyed their small country estate near Thetford. They had some land which they rented out, but they loved to ride across the Chase.

Although it was apparent that the couple was childless, Estella was somewhat perplexed as to their intimate relations. Certainly, though a mild man, Estella saw James as a definite philanderer. He looked at her eyes closely as he spoke to her and once or twice shifted his glance to her lips which verged on the impertinent, though she was secretly flattered to be able to elicit unwittingly a man's interest. She also noticed he watched Susanna far too closely.

Susanna meanwhile was thrilled to find herself hosting such an artistic company, and she started dinner conversation about music, as Monsieur Campanile and Monsieur Fantana seemed highly interested.

"I am so delighted I brought my piano down from Edinburgh, and it is now tuned," she said to Campanile. "Is the piano your instrument?"

"Oh no, Mrs. Gargery," he began.

"Please call me Susanna, I am sure we will all be great friends."

"Susanna, then, a charming name! I can play the piano, of course, but I teach the violin. Do you play?"

"Oh, Rizzio, I learned the piano as a child, but with marriage and children and my other interests, I have no time. You are on your own, then?"

"I fear so," he replied, "for reasons I do not wish to share at this moment."

"But I must insist that we will have musical evenings," Susanna continued, eager to establish herself as the neighborhood hostess.

"Elizabeth here is learning piano with a Monsieur Pauer."

Meanwhile Pip at the other end of the table was engrossed in a conversation with Frederick Brandram, an architect, and telling him of the prostitution project, saying he would value his advice about the building the Trust was planning to buy. Brandram was clearly a professional man, tall, with a small goatee beard, impeccable clothes, fastidious in his remarks and his hands thin but immaculate.

Estella thought she detected something of an unhappy past in his gaze at Honora his wife, and indeed, she hardly said a word throughout dinner. Estella was not certain what the silence conveyed but she anticipated drawing her into conversation at some point. Her husband Frederick Brandram did not seem much interested in the project itself but clearly saw work for the Trust on building a real possibility.

It was Charlotte Mudge, however, who plied Estella with questions about the project and the Trust, and Susanna joined that conversation. Charlotte was younger than Estella, charmingly dressed, her hair in a tight golden bun.

"I am fascinated by your project, Estella. I know Octavia Hill quite well."

"Really?" said Estella. "That is exciting to know as she has an expanding reputation among social reformers for work on housing of the poor."

"Yes, she manages more than a thousand poor tenants."

"How did you know her?" asked Susanna.

"A family connection," said Charlotte dismissively. "I fear Octavia can be a dragon with a formidable determination."

"She sounds exceptional, don't you think, Estella? We need to learn from others, for all we have managed to do so far with the Trust in terms of housing is to help a farrier from the Crimean War become a blacksmith in northern Kent with his wife and family."

"That is most interesting," Charlotte replied, "for while I agree that most housing for the poor is dreadful, we do not place enough importance on the rural poor, though that does not seem to be a problem in Craynham, my husband's parish in Norfolk."

"My husband Pip has experience of both, you know," said Susanna.

"Really, how?"

"He was converted to Primitive Methodism as a child from the Kentish marshes and after being wounded in the Crimea, he became a full-time preacher working first in rural Kent but later in the industrial north. But when we married, he was asked to manage the Jaggers Trust and gave up his preaching."

"How interesting, Susanna, I noticed he walks with a stick, presumably from a war injury."

"He was a farrier, not a soldier, and was accidentally shot in the ankle while clearing up dead horses after the Charge of the Light Brigade."

"Ah" cried Charlotte, "my cousin Arthur was a Dragoons Officer killed in that ridiculous Charge. I blame Cardigan, that drunken fool."

"You must talk with Pip about it, as I know so little," said Susanna. Conversation then moved to personal matters.

"Susanna tells me you are recently widowed, Estella," said Charlotte. "I am very sorry for your loss."

"My grief comes and goes, you know."

"I suppose it does. I try to spend as much time apart from Oliver, my husband, as is decent. Nowadays I have Elizabeth as my excuse for being here. The house here is quite small but comfortable and owned by my brother-in-law, a well-regarded officer serving in India, and his wife is there too."

"So, no parish duties, I assume."

"My goodness no, and it is great relief, but I will call on you if I may?"

"That would be delightful," Estella replied anticipating a new friendship with this woman who had such a splendid voice, remarkable for its depth. If she was talking out of one's sight, she would sound almost like a male tenor.

After the dessert, the women retired to the drawing room and the men stayed for port and cigars. Susanna was anxious not to have her dinner parties spoilt by whist or other card games which she believed created only animosities, spoilt conversation and lengthened the evening. The six women, Susanna, Estella, Sarah, Honora, Mary and Charlotte moved to the drawing room. Albert and Elizabeth were given Susanna's permission to go to the library.

Pip was anxious to find out more about 'Steep' Klein than he had heard in the office. He first ensured everyone knew each other, so new introductions were appropriate: James Bollaerts, artist; Rizzio Campanile, musician; Giovanni Fantana, sculptor; Nimrod Klein, jeweler; Hamish Macdonald, lawyer; Frederick Brandram, architect, and Charles Meggison, also artist.

"Tell me, Nimrod," said Pip, "how do you find social relationships in Paris? I mean, we hear a little about how the Jewish community is distrusted there, and, in your trade, I am sure there are many Jewish traders."

"It is very interesting, Pip, I regard myself as Swiss and we have an instinct, how do you say, a calling for work with jewelry and fine things. I have many Jewish friends. But at that time, Jews were largely, how do you say, integrated into the Swiss population, perhaps because there were so few of them there, as most had become Germans in the Jewish diaspora."

"But are you then a Christian?"

"Oh yes, a good Calvinist, but I must confess to my religion being worn on my sleeve which is not difficult in France as the Church has none of its previous standing since the Revolution."

"How about you, Macdonald, are you a religious man?"

"I am a Presbyterian Scot, committed to "no bishop, no king" but without the wild extravagancies of some. To me, religion is good for keeping people in their place, for teaching them to accept their position but to urge them to find an individual relationship with God.

"As you know, Hamish, I have been a preacher and that was a wonderful calling but now I seek to improve the lot of the poor through practical action."

"Not possible," interjected Klein. "I am not a Communist as Karl Marx would have me believe."

Astonished at this, Pip asked:

"Have you met him?"

"Oh yes, he wandered around the 7th *arrondisement* where my shop is, but we met elsewhere."

"Ah, at the little shop in the Bois de Boulogne, I suppose,"

"How did you know that?"

"When I was preaching in the North, I met a very drunk Karl Marx with his friend Friedrich Engels in Salford and tried to preach them temperance," at which Klein laughed so much, he almost fell off his chair, spilling his port the while.

The others smiled at Klein's discomfort, though he soon recovered.

"My apologies. Trying to preach temperance to Marx is a task for Sisyphus which I am sure even he would refuse!" All the men laughed in their jocular way at this remark.

"I don't understand this temperance idea," said Bollaerts. "If people wish to drink themselves to death, why should they not?"

"The problem," Pip commented in a serious vein, "is that working conditions and poverty leave strong drink as the only pleasure in life."

"Apart from women," said Giovanni with that way some Italian men have of smirking when women are mentioned.

"Should we really be vulgar and talk religion, politics or women after such a wonderful dinner? Surely not," said Frederick, clearly dismayed by the professor of music's remark.

"Let's try art," said Giovanni. "What do you think, Meggison; you're a painter. What do you think of these painters who call themselves the Pre-Raphaelite Brotherhood?"

"Painting is a mode of expression. I paint what may be called natural scenes from daily life, mainly country life, but also portraits. The PRB seems to be evolving a different style, often focusing on classical themes, often of women with large eyes and sallow complexions. They focus on literary figures primarily, not nature as I see it."

"I don't know much about them," said Pip, "but Estella had her house decorated by one of them, William Morris, was it?"

"Ah yes, Morris," replied Meggison. "But they seem a rather louche collection of people at Kelmscott, especially that Simeon Solomon. Like me, he exhibits at the Academy, but he appears to favor the love of men rather than women which could get him into trouble."

At that remark, Hamish was on the verge of challenging the implicit criticism of men like him but drew a bow at a venture.

"Well, Charles, here we have a group of artists and musicians and I hope we can be tolerant of people who love men. Homosexual desire has been a feature of human nature since the world began, a commonplace in ancient Athens, but not unknown in earlier times, such as the story of David and Jonathan."

Pip could not bear to have yet another debate on this subject, so he stubbed out his cigar and changed the subject by suggesting they join the ladies.

When all were seated in the drawing room, Susanna asked if they enjoyed their port and there were murmurs of assent from the men.

"We ladies were just having a very interesting discussion about whether people who love people of the same sex should be regarded as criminals. Our sense is that men get more easily targeted by the law than women, so we really have two matters to debate: Love and desire on the one hand, and issues of equal treatment on the other."

Pip blanched at his wife's introduction of this damn subject yet again.

"I see," said Brandram, who had contributed little to the conversation so far. "How interesting we should all be discussing these questions. I was struck reading Mr. Mill's essay on liberty by its force. The only reason to prevent people doing what they want is if it harms others. That seems basically right to me. On that argument, I am not sure why adults, men or women, should be punished either in law or convention."

"From the viewpoint of a woman," said Charlotte, "I find so much hypocrisy at large in the nation: We are humiliated by our conventions which make us almost like savages. Why in the world would anyone care what people do with their bodies? Of course, my husband is an old-fashioned Tory in his Norfolk parish, so his job demands that he worship convention as well as God."

"I agree," said Giovanni, "but maybe we do not yet know each other well enough to declare our dispositions."

"Absolutely," said Susanna, "but either Charlotte or I will host another dinner in a month or so, and I do hope we can all meet again, as I am feeling there is much friendship around the table. I can see we have some radical notions afloat here which merit further discussion."

That last remark quietly infuriated Pip but he held his tongue. His religious commitments seemed to be under siege from the indulgent sentiments he had heard.

As she left, Estella pondered Honora's silence, speculating on its origins, and looked forward with pleasure to meeting Charlotte again.

II

Her curiosity about Honora could not sweep away Estella's memories of that day at the beginning of the year when she made the journey with Albert from St. Anne's Soho to Highgate Cemetery. She had promptly decided that there was no objection to his grave being only two places away from that of his first wife Beatrice and her born-dead daughter: Some mild comfort for her in knowing that her own mortal remains would eventually rest atop her husband's, but even now four months later, she had little relief from her misery.

She remembered that January afternoon as an unremitting struggle to put out of her mind the sight of his beautiful body lying in a white silk shroud encased within the oak coffin. With a supreme effort, her gaze penetrated the oak to see him asleep, not dead, his grey hair restored to russet, that slight remembered smile on his face just as he was before the cancer ravaged his body.

She heard the clattering of the door as Albert came in from the Art School, dropping his easel and paints on the hall floor. He came into the sitting room, this lively young man Pip's son, whose looks and manners reminded her so much of the lover in his grave.

"How are you, Estella?"

"Oh, I was just recalling your father's funeral which is my wont I am afraid."

"I think about it often too, as much about the good friends who came to support us as the burial. Young Pip and Susanna were as upset as we were, and I thought his mother Biddy would drown in her grief."

"True, she is anything but a stoic."

"It was good to see Herbert and Clara Pocket there. Remind me, how was my father connected to them?"

"Herbert was one of Miss Havisham's cousins and they used to visit her from time to time. I did not have much to do with them. I looked out of my window one afternoon to see your father punch Herbert on the nose and send him sprawling. I laughed then as I had never done before."

"But was there not some financial relationship?"

"I don't remember the details, but thereafter they became good friends and when your father had money from my convict father, he gave Clara money to get him a clerkship without Herbert's knowledge, I should say."

"I see. Father told me once about how Herbert and he had sheltered the old convict. They must have been very good friends by then."

"Indeed. Nowadays Albert, I think I have had a very strange life. I never knew my father, Abel Magwitch the convict murderer, yet he was such an influence on your father's life, for good or ill. That is so odd."

"I suppose we have no idea where the old man is buried?"

"I had never thought of that, Albert. I am not sure how we would find out. I don't even know which prison it was where he died and Pip never mentioned it."

"That is a pity."

"One other memory of the funeral sticks in my mind, though. Susanna came to comfort me after the burial and while I knew her parents had died when they were abroad, I had not known the details."

"What happened?"

"There was a freak weather, a tornado I believe, in the town where they were on holiday in Sicily. But she had to wait several weeks before their bodies were returned, and she was an only child of fifteen you know. Can you imagine the distress that must have caused her? Impossible to contemplate."

"She's a splendid woman, I think, quite beautiful and always so animated and lively in conversation."

"Yes, she is much brighter than Young Pip. Oh dear, I must get out of thinking of him as Young Pip, not Pip as your father is no more."

Estella then made her excuses to Albert, saying she was very tired and needed to rest and went upstairs to her bedroom. Albert too went to his room, lying on the bed as the conversation about his father had revived the misery of losing his best friend. Their shared grief would be everlasting.

The following day was a lovely April day with the inevitable shower, and they decided to go to the country, making the journey by train to Chatham and then by carriage to Numquam House. Albert missed a drawing class, but that was not a matter for concern. This house was Estella's country refuge close to the Kentish marshlands with its glorious garden, elegant rooms and its south-facing aspect giving sunlight all day, still a place of delight for them notwithstanding the murder of Estella's mother Molly in the garden and the killing of a man in the dining room, later deemed to be justifiable.

"For all that has happened here," she told Albert, "I still love this house and I must try only to think of the pleasures we enjoy here."

"I must say, Estella, I love it too. Just look at the flower beds, the rose arbor, the lawn, the oaks and ash trees beyond. It is quite beautiful, especially for a house near the marshes."

"It certainly gives me solace."

"Estella, I am probably too young to offer you counsel. You are beautiful and in excellent health. I know you miss my father desperately, but please keep your mourning period short; don't think you are gliding slowly to your grave."

"You are right, of course, so like your father. Long ago, he came to see me to tell me he was engaged to your mother, but he lifted me out of my depression then, much as you are doing now. Pip would want me to have better expectations than a drawn-out, lonely widowhood."

"Remember too that you are a lady of great privilege. Do what you want. Defy conventions if you must."

"That will be no novelty, but I will follow my wishes and desires untrammeled by convention, or, I might add, religion."

"You too are such a free spirit Albert, and you are such a comfort to me."

He then went out to walk in the garden, and she lay down on the drawing room sofa and wept some more at this sense of freedom which was a little frightening. As the sinking sun shone through the French windows in the dining room the maid called her to dine.

Spring was well advanced, and she was conscious that today, April 23rd, 1870, was exactly four months since Pip died. Albert had returned to Semper House after a week to continue his studies at the Kensington School of Art which he said was to include a visit to the British Museum.

For two years or more before Pip died, Estella had employed Nellie as a servant dedicated to caring for the finer ornaments in the house. They liked each other and chatted very briefly over the months, including the recent days of her mourning.

Today was no different. Nellie had come in through the kitchen door a half hour earlier and was bustling about cleaning, trying to do so quietly as her mistress was in the house.

"Come here, Nellie," she called as she came downstairs, "we need to discuss the future."

"Yes, ma'am, I'm coming."

Estella studied this one of her maid servants carefully as she came into the room and stood politely near the door to the hall. Nellie was obviously in awe of a house where there was elegant furniture and velvet curtains, doors with crafted brass handles and high windows, compared to filthy, low-ceilinged, dark and dirty hovels with vermin for company.

"Nellie, you look very relaxed and attractive this morning. When I first met you, you seemed to be like a cat scared of drowning, worried that danger and malice was ever-present. Now you seem more like a leopardess."

Nellie gave her usual broad grin, saying: "I don't feel like that big cat, but I do feel happy and settled with my Fletch, and my kids are luvly."

"What about this husband of yours then?"

"Horatio? I call him Fletch and he has put on so much muscle. I tease him about his getting 'eavy, cos he's so much bigger than he was when Mr. Pip and he was back from that war. Funny, really, now he's what I thought a blacksmith would be like, you know?"

"Yes indeed, with horny hands of toil as the saying goes. Tell me more about you?"

"Oh no, I was never like this, not ever in my life, Ma'am. What I loves most now is Fletch draggin' out the old bath, me heating the kettles, him having a real soak, and me washing his back, letting the warm water go around his body. Then out he jumps all fresh. You see, we's never had a bath afore we come 'ere."

As she said this, her eyes glistening with pleasure at describing her husband's nakedness, Estella startled herself a little at feeling more than admiration for this younger woman.

"How different your life has been from mine, though not so much in my first six years. You have your terrible experiences of men, including the one that tried to kill you, let alone the men in your family. I was brought up by a rich mad woman who taught me to hate men."

"Oh, I don't hate all men," said Nellie.

"How old are you, dear?"

"I'm not sure and I don't really know when my birthday was, sometime in October I used to fink."

"But don't you know, roughly?"

"I know I was thirteen when I started whoring in Chatham. I suppose I am somewhere around twenty-five."

"I'll tell you my life story someday," replied Estella somewhat guardedly.

"Is your muvver the one with the stone in the garden?"

"That's right. That's where she was murdered."

"O dear o' me, how awful for you. I hope they got the bastard, pardon my language."

"Two of them, in fact, but they were both dead before they could be arrested."

"Stone the crows! And you living here in this lovely house."

"Yes, life has been unkind and kind to me, but I am determined to live as well as I can with the time left to me. And I hope you two will now have charmed lives."

"Thank you, ma'am, I cannot believe how my life has changed, what with help we'se had from that Trust, though I'm not sure what it is or does."

"A very rich lawyer, a Mr. Jaggers, left an enormous amount of money in his will for the relief and education of the poor. Together, Susanna and I direct the Trust with Mr. Pip as the manager now that my husband is gone. Oh dear, there is now no need to call him Young Pip as he is the only Pip left."

"Oh, them Gargerys were so kind to us when we was starving, and old Mrs. Gargery though she's Mrs. Shoreham now, ain't she?"

"I remember. You and your husband have been the first to receive help from the Jaggers Trust."

"Yes," she said, moving into the room closer to Estella than might be thought appropriate for a servant, and with an intense voice laced with pride declared, "and Fletch wants me to tell you all that we don't need trust money no longer. We are right on our own two feet at last! We can pay rent to Mrs. Gargery, though she says she don't want it no more, neither."

"Well done, indeed, both of you. But my dear, I expect now to live here quite frequently, though I will probably try to be in London for two nights each week. You've met our son Albert, haven't you? He's been and gone and will come here only on occasion but will stay mainly in town as he still needs some care, even at eighteen."

"But he's not your son, is he?"

"No, my husband was married before to Beatrice, but she was a frail woman who had three miscarriages and then died in childbirth. Albert was her surviving infant, but we came to regard him as our son, though he lived with the Gargerys until he was nine or ten."

"Oh, that is so sad about his wife; but then I should not say this, for you and Mr. Pip would not have been married, would you? And you'se was so happy together!"

"Yes, that is true. Meantime, are you happy to continue to work here?"

"Oh, yes, ma'am, any fink, any fink, I can do for you, I will."

"Excellent. I meet next week with Mr. Macdonald to discuss how we will progress and Mr. Pip plans to look at buildings we might buy or use for our charitable work with prostitutes. I was quite shocked to learn that there were male prostitutes. I had never heard of such a thing with my sheltered upbringing. Have you?"

"Lor, yes ma'am, there was plenty of mollies where I came from, and there were places that they got together for, y'know, those were molly-houses, I mean they was taverns and so on, but places where those men go together. Not that I had anyfink to do wi' em."

With that, Nellie was in full flow:

"Cor blimey, that life I lived! Now I looks at it from 'ere, it was like living in a sewer; every bad thing you can imagine was there, murder, people thieving all the while, women and children getting beaten, everything, and men selling themselves 'cos they needed to live too. Mind you, it was usually gentlemen who came after the mollies. Women like me had to put up with all sorts.

"But your ideas is wonderful, ma'am. Lots of people would be very grateful. I'd like to help you wiv' your London work, though I doesn't know how. Of course, if you worked in Chatham, I p'raps could, but I ain't never going near London never again as long as there's breath in my body. Sorry, Ma'am, I'se talking too much."

"Not at all. Yes, Chatham is a possibility, especially as it is a navy port."

"Oh, yes, ma'am, when sailors has bin away for a while, that's all they think of when they get off their ships."

"Of course, so they would. The men in Parliament get very excited about controlling disease from prostitution to reduce its spread among soldiers and sailors. So, it has been intent on locking up women who carried it, but they paid no attention to the men who were also responsible for the disease spreading!"

"Them parliament men don't know their arse from their elbow, if you'll pardon the expression."

"Indeed, what a quaint metaphor. However, like Mrs. Josephine Butler, I think that Parliament should have extended the punishments to men, if they must deal out punishment for a disease. So, we will have to be wary that the police might raid any establishment where we might set up providing medical help but that is all for later discussion with Pip and Susanna.

"I am pleased you are so happy here at the Forge and, of course, your children will now go to school, won't they?"

"Yes, ma'am, my man Fletch takes 'em in the cart each morning to the village school which, they say, has twenty-three young'uns now. That's a blessing too, them learning to read and write wot I never did, but I miss 'em during the day."

"Can't you read and write? I am quite surprised."

"No Ma'am, we were supposed to go to school, but we never did."

"Oh, you must learn to read and write. I'll help you. I taught my mother years ago, and somewhere I will have the readers which we used. I'd love to teach you. Each time you come here we will have a lesson when you've finished your work."

"Oh, that would be wonderful, then maybe I can read to my young'uns."

"Reading lessons then. Next month, I will consider doing some Trust work in Chatham as well. To tell the truth, the Trust has so much money, we are going to have to think of new ways to spend it."

"Cor, I wish my life was like that."

"Yes, I suppose we all do. I've never had to worry about money, but I tell you this. Until I met my mother and married Pip, I was truly and seriously unhappy, though I hid it. Money did not make me happy, but love did, eventually."

"For a long time, I never knew what people really meant when they said they was happy till I started to live with Fletch, I think, then I knew it was love, too."

"That is exactly what I felt. I did not know what it felt like inside before I realized I loved my dear Pip."

"Ways I think about it is like this. My face looks quite different now. I used to be, what d'ye call it, frowning all the time, my face tightened up like a ball. So, when I look in a mirror nowadays, I sees someone quite different from the girl I used to be. Terrible, really."

"No, it's a wonderful change for you. My husband used to tell me in the early days how my face had changed to show my real beauty, as he put it."

"I can't imagine you'se ever being not beautiful, ma'am. I'se never seen a woman as beautiful as you. But I just wanted to say agin, ma'am, how sorry we are about your Mr. Pip. He was such a kind man, such a gentleman, a lovely person."

"Oh, thank you, Nellie," and without warning, she let loose a flood of tears.

Nellie hurried over to her hugging and comforting her, stroking her hair, something that Nellie found the natural response to Estella's distress, but Estella, still weeping for Pip, was surprised by just how comforting it was for her servant to hug her, let alone touch her at all.

Suddenly she turned around with her tear-drenched face and kissed Nellie warmly on the cheek, holding her in the embrace and feeling stirred by the warmth of this body close to hers.

"Thank you, thank you, Nellie," she said, "I find your touch so comforting."

"Oh no, ma'am, I'se just so sad for you, you'se being so kind to me and my family."

"I'm weeping like my mother, and I suppose I should not seek to control my emotions."

She took Nellie's hand and stroked it gently, saying:

"I am glad you got to know my husband here. He was a special man. Albert called him his hero, though I am never quite sure why. That young man is getting so absorbed in his painting and trying to do a portrait of his father from some drawings he made a year or so back, as I only have two small likenesses."

Nellie stood up from the embrace taking Estella's hand in commiseration, again a not unwelcome surprise to the older woman, but hardly a convention for a mistress and her servant.

"Oh, what a beautiful ring!' she exclaimed. "What a lovely blue."

"On my right hand?" said Estella. "But it is merely decoration, whereas my wedding and engagement rings are on my left. They're the important ones."

"Lor, I never really had a ring proper like, though we managed to get something cheap when we was marrying."

"I'd like you to have it, Nellie," said Estella suddenly overcome with the young woman's friendliness and compassion, pulling the ring off her finger.

"It belonged to my guardian, a Miss Havisham, but she rarely wore it, at any rate, after I went to live with her, so it does not carry any sentimental value for me. But, as you have no rings, this shall be the first in your collection."

"Oh, ma'am, I couldn't."

"I insist. You have been such a comfort to me today. Look after it. Wear it when you're going out, not coming here polishing the furniture or the silver. The color suits you, matches your eyes. It's a jewel called a sapphire."

"I don't know what my Fletch will say, I really don't."

"Tell him it is a ring that should be worn by a beautiful young woman. Here, take it."

They both watched as Nellie put the ring on her right hand, smiling proudly to herself and holding it out to look at it, gleaming back at her delight. Estella noticed how workmanlike her hands were, fingers bitten to the quick, though they might obviously have been slim and graceful if her station in life had been different.

She stood up to admire the ring and put her arms around Nellie's shoulder, gently ruffling her hair. Nellie turned and looked at her, then threw her arms around her in the tightest of clenches almost as if she would never see her again.

"Oh, ma'am, you fill my heart with such joy and love wot I never thought I would get from anybody like a mother or an auntie or a sister."

"Let us be sisters, then, Nellie," releasing herself from the young woman's embrace, but holding her hands and kissing her again on the cheek and being kissed in return.

"That will be our secret. And now you must be off or Fletch will wonder where you are. Goodbye, my dear, I will see you again soon."

Nellie closed the drawing door gently and left for home. When she got home, she went to the Forge, and Horatio put down his hammer to listen:

"Darlin' I just had a funny time up the big house."

"Really?"

"She was so warm and kind, not like other old hags I've come across. Look, she gives me this luvly ring."

"Now that'll be worth something, Nell. When are you going to wear it though?"

"I suppose I could wear it when we go to the Bargemen, but people will notice and comment. Maybe I'll just keep it as a treasure."

"If times turned bad, we've got that to fall back on."

"Oh, I'd never sell it."

"Course you would if the kids were starving."

"Yes, I would, wouldn't I?" she said laughing.

Back at the 'big house,' Estella collapsed exhausted in her chair after Nellie left, wondering how suddenly her servant had become so close to her. In fact, she realized, apart from the formal kiss or two with such friends as Susanna, she had never grasped any woman in a full embrace, certainly not her guardian Miss Havisham. To Nellie it had obviously seemed quite a natural response to her distress which demonstrated her concern. How strange, but how comforting.

She promptly fell asleep and dreamt of Nellie's arms around her. Outside it was now dark and she awoke to hear the housemaid preparing the table for dinner. As with many who dream of a mild wickedness, she smiled to herself at it, and pondered. What was that about? Was she missing intimacy and looking for it? Was this then a hidden desire for possessing that young woman? Perhaps she simply wanted to make Nellie her whore, jealous of all those men who had been there before her. Just a dream she thought as she roused herself to dress for dinner, though she felt a little elation at this manifestation of a trifling physical desire.

Notwithstanding the success of their dinner party for their neighbors, this Gargery-Urchadan marriage was proving a considerable challenge. They became engaged at their second meeting, he a lame preacher, she an independently wealthy educated young woman of strong opinions. Their love for each other was intense, even incandescent, and they now had two children, both boys, Lachlan age four and Malcolm age two.

Being a preacher for a large part of his life had given him a certain attitude to his beliefs—that they are a gift of God. It is an attitude of rectitude, the sense that one's beliefs must be right, not in Pip's case derived from an authority as with those in the Catholic faith. He was open-minded, but only up to a point. Some might regard him as pompous, though he was not a sanctimonious or even an over-pious man, but he was difficult to dislodge from a firmly held position. He would have regarded himself as a progressive liberal, not a Tory.

He found himself regularly launching an idea significant or trivial with Susanna only for her to disentangle options he had not considered which frequently led to action running counter, though sometimes parallel, to his original idea. To put it mildly, this was a source of some irritation to a man whose rectitude was under siege from his wife. Moreover, in his determination to treat his wife as an equal he was increasingly uneasy about her getting the upper hand if he was honest about it. She was right, he thought; she always was.

For Susanna had always been something of a free thinker, a startlingly clever intellectual, a woman given to questioning, to deep thought and to adopting radical ideas. Social conventions could be ignored, so she was thrilled by his declaration that her property rights would not be severed by marriage.

On this day, she was in her sitting room on the first floor distracted from trying to read *Das Kapital*, a difficult task at the best of times, by thinking about the husband whom she loved very deeply. They had clashed over several matters, none with quite the virulence over Hamish Macdonald's love for men, not women, where Pip rested his dogmatic argument on religious grounds.

Their most recent argument about their eldest boy, Lachlan, was a danger signal. What did it matter in the sum of all creation whether Lachlan wore a cap to chapel or not?

She knew that she was more intelligent than her husband, that she had a quickness of wit and phrase, analysis and argument that left him, if it were a race, in the dust. The problem was how to manage this difference as that would demand accepting arguments or plans or action she knew to be weak which would then signal a certain loss of independence.

Would she then be sacrificing, that strong word, her intellectual independence to mollify her husband, or because she loved him for his weaknesses? What might then follow? Precedents are always created in marriages, and so far, her influence was very powerful. On this line of thought she decided that she had to use her judgment more carefully about what was worth a struggle and what was not.

In this contemplative mood she put down her book and came down the stairs, crossing the hallway to his study. As she went in, he was hunched over the details of a large building that he wanted the Trust to acquire or lease. She determined to curtail her intellectual inquisitiveness with him, for sitting there was a man she loved so deeply and making him unhappy was the very least of her desires. She walked over to him and put her arms around his neck.

"Look at this plan, darling," he said, using a quill to point to its features.

"Let me explain. If we get this building, it is built around a private garden with a fountain, quite small, and only built twenty years ago. It was used as a monastic dormitory, so it has about twenty small rooms on the upper floors which can be used to house our guests from the streets."

"That looks splendid, Pip. I am sure Old Pip would have approved, and Estella will be delighted."

Continuing, she mused, "How is the building to be run? I think we might call it Jaggers House. We will need men to ensure its safety; it is a home for 'fallen women', and they will need to be upright men of sterling character, not tempted to take advantage of the women, will they not?"

"Indeed."

"But I have an idea, darling."

"Ah, I always get a little tense when you have an idea," and they both laughed.

"Now that we have had a large dinner party, we need to develop friendships. I don't mean that we should venture into society, though we could afford it, you know, with soirees and visiting times and all that rigamarole. Let's try to build a close circle of friends, preferably of people who are both like us and not like us. Variety in friendships is, I am sure, a welcome way of life."

"I agree wholeheartedly, my dear. Our neighbors were an excellent place to start, and we will need to be selective. This morning, I must go to Little Britain again to convince Wemmick and Macdonald we should buy this building. It's very grey and wet outside, and inevitably my damaged ankle can almost tell me what the weather will be like, dependent on the intensity of the pain. There will be a cab about, I am sure."

Had Estella been able to get inside Honora Brandram's mind that evening across Susanna's dinner table to investigate her silence, she would have encountered a complicated set of mental acts. For although she was physically at the party, Honora felt to be viewing everything that happened as if from the top of a tree.

Down there were those people talking with confidence, arrogance and ignorance in equal measure. The tones and the words, the gestures, glances and the asides were too distant, too far away and she was far too detached to catch any fragment of a discussion. Yet she felt everyone was noticing her, some with disdain, some with a slight embarrassment, and others with what she took to be compassion or simple curiosity, particularly by the men.

The structure, the dimensions and the parameters of her loneliness formed the geometry of her isolation in the midst of a company.

Her life was a living death without the quietus. Her husband Frederick would sit opposite her at breakfast reading a newspaper, drinking tea, wolfing down a muffin or two, and with a regular pattern of conversation including merely "Good Morning, my dear" and "Goodbye, my dear." Only on the weekend did he attend dinner of an evening as he visited his five clubs in order on weekdays. Evening conversation then was merely perfunctory, almost always on those minor details of keeping the house which concerned him, such as whether his boots had been cleaned properly.

Not that she found him a threat. Far from it, she was awash in gratitude for his rescue of her from the dreadful fate of a convent. The arrangement worked, though it was devoid of intimacy. He told her from time to time that she should want for nothing, but what she wanted was beyond his reach and hers.

When she thought about him, she would admit that she admired him. She had no understanding of his work, except that he was an architect, and he shared nothing of his design or planning with her. It was not that he treated her badly, he did not treat her at all. She felt that she was just there like a door handle performing a function in being turned from time to time as the necessary precursor to his satisfaction, but inert when not in use.

Yet the ordeal of her loneliness was insufferable because her lonely plight had been determined by others, by her being forced to endure extreme violence to her body, by the harsh unforgiving religious dogmas of her parents, and ultimately by the social convention that demanded that she be ashamed. Shame had been imposed on her, the cruelty and injustice of it all present each night in the charmless dry oasis of her bedroom where the walls seemed to close in on her as she sought to sleep.

Her nightly supplication was like an incantation, a medieval chant or a litany, never changing:

"Bring them back to me, O Lord. Please."

III

Pip was not so much baffled as confused. After the Gargery's March dinner party broke up, the couples walked to their homes along Cheyne Row, but the single men, Giovanni, Rizzio, Nimrod and Hamish stood talking on the street and then moved to Giovanni's house for a drink: Nimrod for anise, Hamish and Giovanni for Scotch whisky, and Rizzio for that almost unpalatable Italian bitters Fernet-Branca, which he thought of as a good *digestif.*

As Pip looked at them out of the window the dinner party conversation was in his mind. He knew about Hamish Macdonald, of course, but was this sodomite perversion really so common? He'd worked in Kent and the industrial north but had never come across it before. He realized he needed to pray to God for guidance.

The matter was constantly in his mind. Sitting in his study one day in high summer, he thought about his indulgence with Harriet on those delicious afternoons in Salford when he was a single preacher and she a free spirit, and he smiled at the memory of the pleasures. Surely, he was defying convention with her, but he did not then believe it contradicted God's law, however strict his colleague ministers might be about the sanctity of marriage.

If he could pursue his desires so freely, why not others? Provided, of course, as he was being told, they did no harm to others. Such a muddle, men and women, men and men, women and women.

One evening in July Estella was in London, and she took a walk with Albert down to the river from Soho.

"Did you like Elizabeth?" Estella inquired with discretion.

"Oh indeed, she is quite charming, and we have met three or four times since that party. Her aunt says she can always meet without a chaperone provided she has met the other person. The three of us talked and Mrs. Mudge agreed to our meeting."

"She's a beautiful young woman. Look, dear Albert, your father and I spent too little time making friends with the other sex when young. I hope you will become friends with Elizabeth. I am, of course, not trying to press her upon you as I hope you will have many woman friends.

"Please don't be concerned about inviting women to Gerrard Street. or, for that matter, to Numquam. Ask Elizabeth to come in the afternoon and she can stay for dinner. She can play our piano and you can show her your paintings. We will send her home in a cab."

"Thank you so much, Estella. I meet women at my art classes, but I have not wanted to make friends with them. I think Elizabeth is different. At the moment she is mightily concerned that her father may get caught up in what the papers seem to think is a war about to break between France and Prussia. He is in the Paris Embassy, of course, but it is still a worry."

"I am sure he will be safe."

They returned home and said their good nights, now with a kiss on the cheek. Now back in London, there was too much to think about. It had been a challenge to be in company without Pip who had always been close in any room of acquaintances or strangers, the husband to whom she would smile across a room, the husband who would come up behind her and put his arm around her waist and whisper some endearment. Two women had also come into her ken; Honora, whose silence and demeanor presented a challenge and Charlotte whom she was certain would become her first woman friend.

It was late August when a messenger arrived at Little Britain. Macdonald and Wemmick were concluding a discussion about the war in France, both believing the French would not have chosen to fight if they thought they could not win.

The message was addressed to Mr. Hamish Macdonald from Mr. Courtisone, and it contained the names of two men who might serve as partners with various comments, but none as effusive as he had originally written about Macdonald himself, a fact that did not escape Wemmick's attention.

Clarence Fotheringaye-Smythe was twenty-eight years old, unmarried, had his legal education at Trinity College, Cambridge and was working at the Eustace practice in the Inner Temple.

Stuart Twaddell, older at thirty years of age, was a Scotsman, married and working in Edinburgh for the MacLetchie and Tulloch practice.

"These both seem plausible, Wemmick, don't you think? Particularly another Scotsman."

"Perhaps. With Courtisone's reference, I am sure either of them would be satisfactory, but his comments about you were much stronger. Can we cope with another Scotsman?" He said, laughing, but with a degree of uncertainty.

"I am not sure but thank you for your nice comment. I think Twaddell was before me in Edinburgh. Certainly, the name rings a bell, but it is not an uncommon name in the Lowlands."

"Let us have both of them together for lunch and then talk privately with each afterwards."

"Oh, dear me, no, Mr. Macdonald. One at a time, I think, offers more opportunities. Meantime I will scout around my clerk friends and search for information."

"Perfectly satisfactory: I suggest September 5th, next Monday."

Mr. Fotheringaye-Smythe arrived at Little Britain bearing no more than a sense of his well-bred personality would allow. He gave the initial impression that those he encountered who were not in his social class deserved the utmost condescension. This complemented the sense of deference he would display were he to encounter the King on Earth or God in the Halls of Heaven.

Appearances deceive, however. For he was not a snob, in the modern parlance. He had simply inherited a manner which was the privilege of men like Mr. Darcy, whose stance and attitudes had so upset the Bennett girls but like Darcy, Mr. Fotheringaye-Smythe was an intelligent, thoughtful person with a social conscience.

"We have a description of your education, Mr. Fotheringaye-Smythe…"

"Please sir, Fotheringaye is a nuisance," interrupted the gentleman, "I'd be pleased if you just call me Smythe."

"Well then, Mr. Smythe, tell us something about yourself and your background."

"I know lawyers respect confidences. So, I do not mind admitting that through a family catastrophe in a previous generation which involved a pack of playing cards, I am obliged to find a respectable way to keep body and soul together since my dear widowed mother and relict of he who had brought disaster to her can offer anything but her love and best wishes."

"She is then a woman of reduced circumstances?"

"Indeed, which she bears with an admirable and enviable equanimity."

"We gather you work with Lord Eustace."

"Indeed, it is very grand in the Inner Temple and hospitable to me, but the position offers little opportunity for advancement to a partnership as partnerships will be filled by his Lordship's heirs, his three sons, James, Adrian, and Samuel Eustace, who is the youngest."

"You are fortunate indeed," said Macdonald.

"I am, sir. My father had been a chum of one of the old Eustace partners, Sir Michael Claiborne, and I suppose Lord Eustace took pity on me, though I have worked hard, and he is well satisfied. To be frank, I am looking here for both a challenge and a future."

Macdonald decided he would take the bull by the horns.

"As you know, Smythe, the laws on sodomy were changed in recent years in that those guilty of the offence were no longer to be executed. What sorts of punishment do you think such criminals deserve and if, asked to defend them, what would be your approach?"

At the boldness of this question, Wemmick winced inwardly though he knew that any putative partner would soon be cognizant of Macdonald's apparent proclivities, not that he flaunted them.

"What an interesting question. Two months ago, my Lord Eustace convened a meeting of his chambers to discuss this subject. Although I have no evidence, I suspect that that he thought one of his sons might have this perversion, and that he was endeavoring to scare the putative young man into abandoning that pursuit or at least temper it with sagacity were he to be so inclined which, in my considered opinion, was most unlikely.

"For my part, I am not in favor of punishment of such people, not least because I had two friends at Cambridge who revealed themselves to their very close friends of whom I was one, saying that they could not bear the continuing deceit. If one concedes that this so-called perversion is in fact natural and founded in love of some sort, the law should avoid it."

"But" Macdonald went on, "is it not a threat to society? If you were obliged to defend a man with this predilection in court, how would you handle it?"

"Truth to tell," replied Smythe, "I have had little experience of advocacy which is why I would wish to work here to gain that experience. I debated at Cambridge, but advocacy is different.

"The legal problem is complex. If the evidence is clear a lawyer cannot somehow twist it to its opposite. The challenge would be met, I think, by outlining both its natural origins and its historical prevalence, coupled with the significance of love in a society, followed by a plea for mercy, because such men are not usually vagabonds or murderers.

"Of course, *de minimis non curat lex*, (the law does not care about small things) so one might argue the triviality of the offence too, though that would depend on the circumstances pertaining to the individual's appearance before the law."

"How thoughtful," said Macdonald. The discussion then turned to another problem of significance, the treatment of children as criminals. On this Smythe took a harder line than Macdonald or Wemmick might have done, though he would be more lenient with what he called "children of the street" rather than those who had living parents.

After various other questions, Macdonald indicated the interview was finished, so Mr. Smythe rose from his seat and ventured forth at some risk to his future.

"May I set out those of my qualifications which would not be on any letters you might have received about me? First, I am an expert on the rearing of hunting dogs. Second, I endeavor to be an upright man. I dislike intensely men of my generation who flaunt their wealth or despise the poor. I am a liberal and hope, if I can further my career with Mr. Gladstone's party, to join Parliament for which legal experience, I believe, is a *sine qua non.*

"Finally, I hope to marry in the not-too-distant future. The lady in question is not yet aware of my intentions so I will not mention her name, but what we lawyers might call a preliminary discovery suggests she will be receptive to my approaches."

"Thank you very much, Mr. Smythe. We are going to meet with another man who has been recommended to us, but we will invite you to meet with us again if we to decide to come to an arrangement with you."

After their initial adverse reaction to Mr. Smythe on grounds of his superior class, both Hamish and Wemmick found themselves rather pleased with this candidate. He appeared an honest, conscientious man of ambition recognizing his own needs in terms of learning the practice of the Law. He might also attract a very different kind of client thereby broadening the base of the practice. His provenance was unsullied.

The other person of interest was Stuart Twaddell from Edinburgh, who turned out to be what Wemmick later described as a different kettle of fish. He was the epitome of the tough unbending Scotsman. In his reply to Macdonald's first question on sodomites, he sounded like John Knox in his blast of the trumpet against the monstrous regiment of women.

"Sodomites?" he asked in reply.

"It was a grave mistake in my view to abolish the death penalty for this behavior. As a married man, I would never allow my children near one, whatever his background or breeding. In fact, I would want to introduce castration as the only way for God-fearing men to be protected from these vile, unnatural practices and those who prosecute them. That is a somewhat strange question to start discussion of a possible partnership. Do you have a particular interest in this minor social problem?"

At this implicit challenge, Macdonald managed to stay calm, but Twaddell went on.

"There was a group of young men studying law, all juniors to me in Edinburgh who seemed to have sodomite tendencies in their behavior. They were fortunate not to be exposed and sent to prison."

Now Macdonald was both angry and frightened, but was, once again, resolute.

"We are advisors to a philanthropic effort to assist male and female prostitutes, which would involve your legal skills, were you to join us. How would you argue a case if you were to defend such a person, as might be incumbent on you in this practice?"

"Och, I could never do that as a lawyer. Others may choose otherwise, but I am strict in seeking guidance from the Lord. I would have to work on other cases."

"I see. What are your views on the punishments appropriate for children?

"I would defend any child and have indeed done so in Edinburgh. Those found guilty of any felony or assault on a person should undergo a strict disciplinary education and be obliged to join Her Majesty's forces for a period of five years thereafter. This is, I think, a merciful stance to punishing children. Their backgrounds are often so harsh, not helped by consigning them to Australia or throwing them in prison."

"Thank you, Mr. Twaddell, we appreciate your travelling down from Edinburgh for this meeting."

"Thank you too, but if your financial offer is unacceptable, I might as well leave for Scotland tonight. What is on the table?"

"What did you anticipate being your remuneration?" asked Macdonald.

"Fifty per cent of the practice income immediately, and a full partnership within six months, assuming mutual satisfaction. I'd expect to be able to charge all legitimate expenses, such as cabs to court or to meet clients, to the practice."

At this, Wemmick stepped in:

"As the Senior Clerk here for many years, I would not advise Mr. Macdonald to enter into any kind of commitment at this stage. To begin with, we would pay you a not ungenerous salary, but we could not commit to partnership for several months, perhaps even a year of working together to decide if a long-term partnership was desirable. This is a practice built primarily on the work of Mr. Jaggers followed by the formidable if not widely appreciated contribution of the deceased Mr. Pip."

"In that case," said Twaddell, "I bid you good afternoon and I am sorry to have wasted your time," at which he grabbed his coat, hat and stick and stormed out.

"What a relief," said Wemmick, "a thoroughly disagreeable character and his attitude to the money was, saving your presence, Hamish, what we might understand as not unusual for a Scotsman."

"Usual or not, totally unacceptable. I must confess to being surprised, but perhaps he is not doing as well as a lawyer as his references might suggest. Maybe his wife is a tough Scottish woman, like Susanna a little but without her wealth, telling him to get to London and not to come back without the right sort of bawbees, as she would call his salary.

"That was a most distasteful experience, and we can safely invite Mr. Smythe to join us, don't you think?"

"I do and I will be in touch with him directly. He can start immediately."

❧ ❧ ❧

Taking their coats from the stand in the hallway, Wemmick and Hamish then donned their hats and hastened to The Cheshire Cheese for lunch. At the far end of the low-beamed dining room, Estella, Albert and Elizabeth were slowly enjoying oysters in their shells, so they headed straight for that company and were invited to eat with them.

"My husband used to speak of this place as really more of a dining club for men, so I thought I would try it out and bring Albert and Elizabeth for safety."

"Yes, indeed; while women are not excluded, it is a hostelry more accustomed to men in the legal profession particularly." said Wemmick. "Eating here is so close to the Temple and it was Mr. Jaggers' favorite haunt, apart from his club."

"Which club was that?"

"The Jeffries, in a street off Long Acre. Mainly lawyers there too, as I understood it. It was named after the Hanging Judge, Judge Jeffries, who had a number of men executed after the failure of the Duke of Monmouth's rebellion."

"Excuse me, one moment," said Wemmick. "Shall we have more oysters and then the venison and claret? That's very good here." They all nodded, and he continued:

"Jaggers argued that Jeffries just followed the law of the time and so he was prepared to join a club with that name. He saw the judge as scrupulous in terms of the law and he said that there is little evidence that he was having them executed because he enjoyed it or because he thought it would please the King.

"Of course, Mr. Jaggers made a number of errors of judgment always outside the Law."

"As I know to my cost," said Estella.

"Come now, Mrs. P," said Wemmick, "would you have met your husband if you had gone as a ward to someone else?"

"True, life has its own way of doing things. But you know Mr. Wemmick, I think the time has come for us to call each other

43

by our Christian names, don't you? I think of you as John, not as Mr. Wemmick, and I hope you think of me as Estella, not as Mrs. Pirrip."

"I agree wholeheartedly with that, Estella," said Wemmick.

"Oh, good gracious, I have known of you for a very long time, and I have since come to know you properly after you met your mother. But you have always been Estella. Jaggers used to talk of you when he had been to Satis House to deal with Miss Havisham's legal affairs. He used to say things like 'what an intelligent girl she is,' and later, 'how beautiful that Estella has become.'"

"Yes, but he arranged that dreadful marriage for me. You know I told him at Molly's funeral once just how poor his judgments had been, and he admitted it."

"He did mention it. Your meeting with Molly changed his life, you know."

"Poor Jaggers, it was a coincidence from his worst nightmare."

At that moment, Pip and Susanna walked in.

"Goodness me," said Hamish, rising from his chair, "a gathering of the clans. How come you both are here?" at which those present all rose from their chairs for greetings.

"Susanna and I realized the other day that we had never visited St. Paul's Cathedral and I was curious to see Nelson's Tomb, having sailed with the Navy in the Crimean War. Then I remembered that Old Pip had mentioned a wonderful lunch with Jaggers here so we thought we would try it."

Estella then got up to embrace Susanna and shook hands with Pip.

"Let me tell you," said Estella, "how the work with prostitutes is going. Pip has almost secured the building, but that depends on you lawyers. Hamish and I plan to visit a Shoreditch neighborhood to observe, and then to go to Moorfields to see what happens on Sodomites Walk.

"Nellie told me never to go to those areas alone," she continued. "They are full of villains of all types, especially thieves. Indeed, some of the women who are apparently prostitutes are thieves and, indeed, murderers. But I think Hamish will afford enough protection."

"Certainly not," said Wemmick. "You should definitely hire a bodyguard. I will find a reliable man through my informants."

"On another matter," Hamish announced, "John Wemmick my friend and partner here intends to retire in six months after a lifetime of service to Mr. Jaggers, Mr. Pip and the practice in general. We will hold a celebration nearer the time, but he and I are searching for a partner and a replacement for John, though he is irreplaceable."

"Well, well, well, John," said Estella, "and I thought you were ageless."

"Say no more about that tragedy now," said Hamish.

"On a brighter note, John and I have interviewed two men as potential lawyer partners, one of whom refused our terms in advance. But the other is Clarence Fotheringaye-Smythe, a man whom we will invite to join us, and you will all meet him, I am sure, as I think he will accept."

"What did you make of that Frenchman, Hamish? Is he still staying with you?"

"You mean Steep?"

"Who is Steep?" asked Susanna.

"Oh, it's a silly joke," said Hamish. The name on his card read 'I. N. Klein', and we read it as 'incline,' and so nicknamed him Steep. He said English humor was very droll."

"I don't know whether this is of any importance," Hamish continued, "but Courtisone told us that Jaggers' ancestor left Germany in the early 17th Century, and that this ancestor was Jewish, named Jaeger, which was then amended to Jaggers after his flight to England.

"Of interest is that the said ancestor, also a Nathaniel, must have arrived after the Civil War of the 1640s when there was obviously great confusion, for Jews were banned from England until Oliver Cromwell changed the law in 1650."

"So Jaggers was Jewish?" asked Estella with surprise.

"Indeed so, but his immediate family were faithful to the Church of England attending St Anne's Church in Soho."

"Mr. Disraeli is Jewish," said Wemmick, "and thank goodness we are not like people in Russia who, I understand, force Jewish people to live in special districts, whereas here they congregate in London's East End voluntarily. Though I noticed in *Lloyds Weekly Register* the other day that a synagogue has been opened somewhere further north; Maida Vale, I think."

Before the party broke up, Estella informally described a couple of matters the Trust might formally consider.

"With my husband's death, might we consider enlarging the board, perhaps with another lawyer from the practice if Hamish engages one? Personally, I would like Albert to join the board too, but he would need to reach the age of twenty-one to do that."

"Excellent idea to have Smythe on the board if he joins us," said Wemmick, "as I think he will. Albert could attend as an observer, you know."

Albert's pleasure at this consideration was apparent in his smile from ear to ear, and Elizabeth too smiled to herself, noticing how solicitous Estella was for Albert's welfare and how highly he was regarded by the others.

"I will also be asking the board to consider operating a project for prostitutes in Chatham. You know the Chapel there; Pip and my helper Nellie might be able to assist."

"If I could offer a consideration," said Wemmick. "I think we have to be careful, as the old saying goes, about biting off more than we can chew. Let us get the London operation going first."

"I am tempted to agree on that score," said Pip.

"I am in solid support for Chatham," said Susanna. "Pip knows the chapel people there, and we don't know whether your Ministry position is filled, do we, darling?"

"I have not heard, and such a Chatham project would be desirable but, like John, I don't want the board to get ahead of itself."

"What will be important as we progress is to spend the money the Trust has," observed Wemmick.

"On the other matter, can we wait a few months before inviting Smythe as a lawyer?" asked Hamish. "I'd like to ensure that he is suitable for us, for there is always the possibility that our relationship with him might not work. Moreover, we cannot oblige him to work for the Trust."

The conversation ended, however, with Wemmick suggesting that Estella become Chairman of the Board, an idea that was unanimously accepted and graciously received, though it would still require a formal meeting.

"I realize that to have a woman in such a position is a breach of a convention, but I am honored to carry the torch for continuing the emancipation of womanhood," said Estella in response.

Then lunch was over, and to the surprise and unspoken delight of the company, Hamish paid the account, accidentally tipping his purse of sovereigns and half sovereigns out on to the table.

After their return to Semper House, Estella retired to her bed, and Albert and Elizabeth sat alone in the library. As they entered the room, he took her hand and they sat together hand in hand on the chaise longue, looking searchingly at each other. She was a very pretty brunette with soft curls and dauntingly brown eyes and a wide mouth that made her astonishingly attractive, at any rate, to Albert. He was now *trés gallant*, as the French would say. Elizabeth was older but only by six months.

"Tell me," said Albert, "and I have no experience in these matters, but are you as fond of me as I am of you?"

"Oh, Albert, I think of you night and day. Please kiss me."

He wrapped his arms around her, drew her to him, her head laid back as he kissed her guardedly and without venturing further than that. Then they heard the maid in the dining-room preparing to set the table for dinner, so they got up smiling at each other, still holding hands.

"I must be gone, or my aunt will be worried."

"What about your mother? Does she like Paris?"

"She is American by birth and rather rich. I have not heard from my father, though I expect a letter any day. After I finish my engagement with my piano tutor I will go back to Paris if this war does not upset my plans. If someone fires a shot near her, she will go back to Georgia.."

"I'd love to see Paris."

"Come with me and search out those painters you've heard about. I am sure my father would welcome you."

"Very tempting, but we must say good night. I'll send for a cab for you, darling, may I call you darling?"

"Of course," she said, as they embraced tightly.

"I will definitely come to Paris. That jeweler fellow Nimrod Klein has invited me to stay. Let's see what the conditions are when your piano lessons are completed. I am sure the embassy there will be out of trouble as England is not involved."

"Dare I say this, Albert, but I think I love you."

"I love you, too, my dear Elizabeth."

Eventually the cab arrived, and Elizabeth left for Chelsea with promises to meet again soon showering the hall at Semper House like confetti.

IV

Rain had come in from the west as Pip and Susanna walked down Fleet Street and up Ludgate Hill to St. Paul's. Although Pip was still formally a Primitive Methodist, he could appreciate great beauty with religious symbolism. He admired St. Paul, who, when all was said and done, was an itinerant preacher like himself. After walking with Susanna around the cathedral and the crypt to see Nelson's tomb, Pip noticed that visitors could go up the stairs to the Whispering Gallery, where one could lean against the wall and a whisper could be heard around the inside of the cathedral's dome.

His venture in the Gallery was almost a catastrophe.

Susanna decided to sit quietly in the nave appreciating the beauty of holiness rather than go up the numerous stairs for the experience. She wondered whether Lachlan and Malcolm might appreciate this building, as her own religion was far too austere, bereft of such tributes to God as this cathedral.

Leaving his silk hat with Susanna, Pip climbed up the stairs to the gallery, his gammy leg a mild hindrance. What a grand view, he thought, briefly waving to Susanna sitting down there in the Cathedral nave, though the height quickly made him retreat from the balustrade.

He put his head to the wall, as did other visitors and heard a voice whisper: "Praise be to God." There were two children with a nanny on the other side of the dome, and a well-dressed man, whose voice it clearly was. But then he heard another voice say, "I am watching you," but looking around the Gallery, he saw no one else as the other visitors had left. He put his head to the wall again and heard the same voice. He dismissed it but was unnerved enough to want to get down to Susanna.

He began to have an increasing sense of vertigo and stumbled back along the gallery deciding to go down. He went through a door which he thought was the one that led to the stairs.

This was not the way down from the Gallery. He had entered a passage inside the dome, but after several yards, he tripped on a piece of stone, one of many littering the floor, fell over, knocked his head and his stick fell right down to the outer wall of the dome. Bending down in this narrow passage to pick up the stick he could just glimpse the Tower of London away in the distance through a tiny window at floor level.

Now very confused, he gathered himself together, got up and pressed on for a few minutes, stumbling on the uneven surface as he went. His unwelcome presence disturbed a colony of bats that swirled around his head, releasing white dust from their perches that settled on his coat. He moved giddily along the passage anticipating that it must lead to the way out and the stairs. He slipped again, and a bat landed on his arm which frightened him into falling again, this time clinging onto his stick but bruising his damaged ankle on a stone. The passage seemed narrower and tighter, and a sense of claustrophobic panic rose in his throat.

He stopped moving, standing back against the inner wall to collect himself. His panic began to subside as he wondered why he had not turned back earlier rather than blundering on. After several minutes, he turned back, having traversed at least a quarter of the inside perimeter of the dome. Covered with the dust let loose by the swirling bats and his fall, he steadied himself once more, stopped and sat down on a block of stone, glad that although it was nearing twilight outside, at least another tiny window offered some light.

It took him some time slowly to retrace his steps, but he found the door because it was ajar, got back to the Gallery, and realized that somewhere along the passage he had dropped his gloves when he slipped. At that point he was far too anxious to get down to the nave to Susanna than stumble around in the cathedral's attic to find them.

Once back in the gallery proper, he sat down next to the wall, only to hear the mysterious voice again. He looked around carefully, but he could see no one. He got up, brushed himself down, found the proper door to the stairs, treading down them with care with his bruised ankle, and met Susanna at the entrance to the stairs.

"Goodness me, what has happened to you?" cried Susanna when he appeared. "I had just decided to come up to look for you. Oh, look, your coat is covered in dust."

"I was so disoriented," he said, clinging to her, "I lost my gloves and bruised my ankle. I nearly lost my stick."

"You look as though you have seen a ghost."

"Not exactly, but I heard a voice whispering when I was alone in the gallery, and I could see no one."

"Was it a man's voice, and what did it say?"

"You know, I am now not certain whether it was a man or a woman. It just said: 'I am watching you.'"

"Did you think it was God, then?"

"I don't know, I don't know. I want to go home. Let's get a cab."

Together they walked as hurriedly as they could out of the Cathedral into the dusk light of smoky London, as he told her more of his adventure. Once on Ludgate Hill, they hailed a cab and were soon back in their living room, the log fire blazing away merrily, both shaken by Pip's experience, but in different ways.

Pip was still not quite ready to accept that there was no one there and that he had imagined it. Did God whisper? Or was it simply his conscience, though it was not laden with burdens, notwithstanding the tensions in his marriage. Stumbling about in the rafters of the Dome of St Paul's Cathedral was perhaps an analogy of his marriage, or perhaps a signal that he should not treat his infirmity lightly.

Susanna on the other hand was very perplexed. Was this a problem with his mind? He was a brave man for he had been in great danger in the Crimea but was somehow disoriented with this experience. She wondered too, being a believer herself, as to whether the Almighty was not issuing a husband a warning, but of what kind?

He was certainly not a philanderer, a spendthrift, a bully or a wastrel, but a good-hearted man, albeit with one or two limitations. He had certainly not heard a ghost. Though a good Presbyterian Scot, she knew the Anglican Litany that included the plea to the Good Lord for delivery from 'ghoulies and ghosties and long-legged beasties and things that bump in the night." He'd had a few oysters; perhaps they were the problem.

On his return from lunch, John Wemmick's immediate thought was how much he enjoyed the company of these people, all indirectly or directly connected to Mr. Jaggers and Mr. Pip the elder. What interesting people they were to meet regularly. He reflected on how full his life had been at his work and, although he was ready to retire, if he was honest about it, he did not look forward to too much time at home, or indeed degenerating into deafness or some other infirmity like his Aged P.

As the determined date for retirement approached each day, clouds of uncertainty billowed through him and he shared his thoughts with his partner, the former Miss Skiffins.

"I'd really like to retire soon," he said as they sat in the cozy living-room after their supper.

"Really? I'm not sure I could do with you around the house all day," she said, with a smile.

"But I am not sure Macdonald can really cope without my advice."

"He will have to start sometime."

"I know, I know. Of course, I'm a board member of the Jaggers Trust so I won't lose touch with the family, but that's only twice a year. Maybe," he continued with a degree of whimsy, "I could work with Mrs. Gargery and Macdonald on a project."

"That would take you into London all the time. Aren't there things you could do here in Walworth? I mean, this is not the countryside it was when we was children."

"That might be a good idea, but I've just come from a lunch today and they are all such nice company I'd like to keep in touch with them. "

"I don't know about that, as I only meet them at weddings and funerals."

"And then there's Estella," he went on. "Mrs. Pirrip, I mean.

"I've told you, haven't I, Mrs. W., how much she has changed. She must have been quite rootless and lonely after her disastrous marriage and that Miss Havisham going up in flames. Then there was that mad creature, Molly, her mother. In some ways she was more like her mother than she knew. Odd really, that she should then have come together with Pip after all those years."

By now, Mrs. W. was fast asleep in the comfort of her chair. With the fire going down, Wemmick was none the wiser about retirement, but he jogged his wife awake and they went to bed.

Estella came downstairs after her rest and sat down in the Library where she found Albert doing nothing. "Now then, dear, what's the matter?"

"I am somewhat enraptured by Elizabeth, but I know we are still too young to determine any kind of future together. She too is very receptive to me, or rather it was the other way around in our encounter today."

"She is a charming girl of great talent too, I believe," said Estella. "Now, you know my past, how I found myself in love with your dear father, so I am not in the best position to advise you young sprigs of nineteen years old. All I would say is this. Trust your instincts, although they may become unreliable in that you may change your affections.

"But signs of mutual regard and love should never be put aside. You should enjoy each other wisely, but not too well. You should take each month or year as it comes, get to know each other profoundly and commit yourself to love, even for ever, but wait to commit yourself to marriage as that is a step that is very painful for both parties if it were to be broken."

"I see and I do agree in principle. Right now, of course, I just want to carry her away with me! But I know that would not be efficacious."

"No, indeed."

"But tell me, now that my father has been dead awhile, what is it like to be alone?"

"Oh, my dear Albert, what a tender question. I knew for a year or so that the day would come when I would be alone, and we were lucky to have that time after his surgery. Trying to go to sleep is probably the worst time of the day when all the different kinds of memories flood through my brain. Just being by myself, almost anywhere, is also a struggle. I cannot tell you how grateful I am to have you living here with me, for not only are you such a living reminder of your father, but you are also so solicitous for my welfare."

She got up from her chair and went over to put her arms around him, and they both wept silently for a few minutes.

"Would you come with me to Highgate Cemetery tomorrow, Albert? I have not been for a month and that is the part of my loneliness which connects me back to him. For you, of course, there is also your mother to contemplate."

"I'd like that. Could we do this together each month or so? It would certainly help me, and I think it would help you too."

"Let us see after we have been there tomorrow. On another matter, will Elizabeth come to Numquam for Christmas?"

"I doubt that if her father is home in Norfolk."

From July to September, after the outbreak of war between France and Prussia on July 19th, Elizabeth was to be seen every morning rushing downstairs in Cheyne Row to get *The Times* reports on the War. That newspaper printed correspondent Russell's portrayals of this fast-moving enterprise with great skill, just as it had done in his reports on the Crimean War.

The Ambassador to France was Lord Lyons, and the Honorable Henry Fitzroy, her father, was Head of Chancery in the Embassy of the United Kingdom at the Hôtel de Charost, 39 rue du Faubourg Saint-Honoré, Paris. Not only was the embassy one of the most splendid buildings in Paris, bought by the Duke of Wellington, but the street was the most famous of boulevards in one of the most beautiful cities in the world.

Henry was born into one of England's more significant peerages, the baronetcy being created in 1601, and his oldest brother now being the 2nd Earl of Camberley. Diplomacy and public service were in his blood. Elizabeth was his only child, and with his aristocratic background Henry hoped that this wonderful young woman would find happiness, preferably with someone of her ilk, but *noblesse oblige*. He was full of regret that her mother probably would not give a damn.

Elizabeth was haunted by the possibility that he would be caught up in the mayhem. If the French Army was unable to prevent a siege of Paris, what will happen if the Prussians invade? What does an embassy and its staff do when a capital is invaded?

She need not have worried, for Bismarck had learnt from Napoleon's debacle in Moscow. No occupation of Paris for him. From the defeated French, he only wanted cash in the form of reparations and two French provinces, Alsace and Lorraine. She did not know any of that yet, of course, nor did she know that negotiations were proceeding with Bismarck for a *carte de passage* that would make it possible for her father to come out of Paris safely.

"Aunt Charlotte," she said over breakfast, "why do you think mother had disappeared?"

"She was a strange woman and, I thought, totally unsuited for Henry, my dear. I must be careful, for she is your mother."

"Please say what you think. I could bear nothing else."

"She was a rich American woman, growing up as a pampered girl, with slaves in her early life, and an attitude to people which I think your father eventually found detestable. She found the South a rather different place after the Civil War, and her 'daddy' took the whole family to upstate New York to Grandma's home, so she followed them there.

"I am sure your father thought that life in England and Europe would modify those attitudes when they were married, but after his first posting to Paris, she turned nasty about all things French, which was hardly the most desirable attitude for a diplomat's wife."

"I had very little to do with her," said Elizabeth. "She spent a lot of time at parties, not often with my father as he was so busy. I expect she's gone to Monaco or some other dissolute place."

"I think your father thought she was a fine catch, though I guess her family wanted her out of their hair too."

"It is odd, though, Aunt, I really do not know her, and she is my mother."

"I talked with Henry about it once when you were younger. One child is enough with Mary-Lou, he said, and my daughter is everything a father could want—beautiful, talented, loving and with a mind of her own. Strange, really, that neither he nor I have been happy in our marriages."

"I miss him, though," Elizabeth continued. "A piano can be a very lonely instrument and we used to play quite difficult duets."

"Oh, yes, I remember you at Wymondham last Christmas, playing that gorgeous Mozart piece."

"Yes, the D Major Sonata, we were very excited by that. It was then he told me that he thought the Emperor might want a war with Prussia at some point and that, if it broke out, he wanted me to come to London because I needed more expert piano tutoring anyway."

"That is true, but as he is without your mother, I hope you'll be able reunited soon."

"I have been so fortunate in meeting Albert while I am here, but my father is very special, full of kindness and generosity, so I must care for him above all if my mother is not with him."

The Prussian army swept all before it, so Henry was intensely busy throughout the autumn. He had more time after the capture of the Emperor, the defeat at Sedan and the declaration of a Republic at Bordeaux in early September. He tried throughout these events to jot down notes, attitudes, or conversations for what he hoped one day would be his diplomatic memoirs, but he did not forget his daughter, writing her long letters about what was happening to her great delight.

My darling,

You will have read about the defeat and the capture of the Emperor, and I confess I would rather have departed for England then, for it is too sad here; the spectacle of these poor people trying not to look humiliated is sorrowful beyond belief, and besides they look very suspiciously at all foreigners and are fearfully irritated against England — all the doing of the English newspapers. I spend my time with passports and other work, and we work from morning till night, but it is overall a good thing as there is nothing on earth else to do; the Bois closed, the Tennis Court is shut, and no one seems to like going to the clubs or into society of any kind where one meets the despondent natives. But I'll be home soon, if only for a short while and we can discuss your returning with me, depending on the situation. (September 3, 1870.)

Henry knew very well his daughter's concern for him and that she would be searching the newspapers for information so he wrote as often as possible.

Darling Elizabeth,

I now have a little time to be able to write. My Chancery posting makes me the person responsible for British subjects. The Embassy is constantly besieged by Britishers, male and female, in a most agitated state, asking what they are to do, and what will become of them and their property in the event of the Prussians, or, what seemed to me then quite as likely, a revolution.

They were told of the dangers and urged to leave. No one knew whether trains to Calais might stop. This problem continued without ceasing: We were beset all day by British subjects in great distress. But Lord Lyons has announced that the Embassy servants will be allowed to wait at dinner in trousers, not the formal livery! What would we do without such condescension to the war? (September 5, '70)

In these letters to Elizabeth, and he wrote frequently, Henry often mentioned Lord Lyons as the embodiment of aristocratic British mien, a pillar of stability in those turbulent months. Elizabeth laughed at his description of the man, driving in his open carriage with its stepping horses and she regularly read out the letters to her aunt Charlotte, and to Albert and to Estella if they were there. However, from Henry's letters, Lyons was good in a crisis, keeping the embassy staff in good humor but also making sure to visit his niece in her Parisian convent. That piece of news was a surprise to Aunt Charlotte as she thought the family was Protestant to the core.

The Ambassador had to be near wherever the new French Government happened to be, but because the Prussians might attack Paris, Lyons moved most of the embassy to Tours leaving Henry, a younger man he greatly admired, in charge in Paris while Prussian armies continued to march on the city.

The Honorable Henry Fitzroy was an exemplar of those members of the English upper class who saw it as their responsibility to serve the nation, rather than lead a life of leisure on a country estate. He was a handsome man in his early forties, tall with brown hair, now showing some greying at the temples. He had high cheekbones and a very strong forehead. His sight was not good, and though he hated spectacles and his monocle, pouring over papers made both a necessity.

Habitually he'd sipped his whisky of an evening, gazing out through the embassy garden at the Rue du Faubourg Saint-Honoré where the leaves were falling from the young plane trees now everywhere in France. He remembered his predecessor's interesting comment that these planes were recent. Oak trees were symbols of the monarchy and were felled across France in the years after 1789.

He had begun to accept reluctantly that his marriage was a disaster. His main disappointment was that to him loyalty was a paramount virtue, but also he liked to pretend that keeping his marriage together would be a blessing for Elizabeth, the daughter he loved to distraction. In many ways she had already begin to replace his wife, and his letters to her were precisely what, in a different marriage, he would have written to his wife.

Those letters brought great comfort and laughter to his daughter and his sister though they implied consistently that it was far too dangerous for Elizabeth to go there in the immediate future.

Early in the war, after intense and long negotiation with Bismarck and his officials, the British and Belgian governments agreed to be neutral in the conflict. That was all very well, but then there were constant complaints from Prussian authorities about the sale of arms from England to the French, specifically from the Birmingham Small Arms Company, which Henry recorded.

Darling Elizabeth,

I intended to write yesterday but my life has become even more complicated as there have been accusations that English manufacturers continue to supply the French, although HMG is neutral. This means I must pay attention to bills of lading, counterfeit materials, cases supposed to be containing guns revealed to be packed with material that in inspection did not turn out to be contraband. I told Washburne, an American diplomat, it would do the French little good anyway.

I was dining yesterday at Cafe du Helder talking with Basil Linkman, a Daily Telegraph correspondent. The poor man was suddenly dragged from the table being accused of spying, but more importantly, his expensive glass of Chateau Margaux was knocked over in the process. He was released today but it shows how jumpy everyone is. I spend my time getting Britishers out of prison. One poor man, arrested a second time, was convinced he was about to be shot and had written an adieu to his wife in the lining of his hat!

Of course, I am hoping to come out of Paris very soon and be with you, certainly for Christmas. I assume from your letter that you will wish to bring this young fellow Albert to Wymondham with you. (8 December 1870)

Elizabeth read that letter with great delight, as Christmas was now only two weeks ahead.

In mid-November 1870, a letter arrived from the rejected candidate, Mr. Twaddell, asking for a private meeting, not in Little Britain, as he had some information to impart.

Macdonald showed the letter to Wemmick, who was alarmed. He advised Macdonald to reply that any information he had could be given in the office and that, while it was fine for him to meet informants privately, lawyers should avoid clandestine meetings. Wemmick said he would go in his place to any such meeting.

Macdonald did not view this letter with the alarm that Wemmick attributed to it, though he recognized Twaddell was a rather unpleasant man.

"Why the alarm, Wemmick? Maybe he feels embarrassed by his behavior and wants to reopen negotiations?"

"That I doubt. I do not trust that man. But you must make your decision. Perhaps you could suggest that he come to the office, but after hours, so that you would meet privately."

"That will work splendidly, I am sure."

"Then, I will place myself behind the door slightly ajar leading to the pantry with your permission, so that if anything untoward were to occur, I would be on hand."

"H'mm, I am uncertain about that, but let us try it."

It was a dark, damp evening around seven o'clock when Twaddell knocked at the outer door and Hamish went to let him in.

"Good evening to you, Mr. Macdonald."

"Good evening, Mr. Twaddell. How can I help you?" asked Hamish as they walked into his office.

"Och, I wanted to know if you had filled the vacant position?"

"Yes, I am afraid we have."

"Are you really sure that I am not an appropriate person to have working with you, Mr. Macdonald? I have been doing some research in Edinburgh and found that you were a member of that sodomite group I mentioned at our last meeting.

"Now I would not want this information to be spread widely around London, nor would you, I am sure. But, on the other hand, if it is quite impossible for you to employ me, then perhaps you would engage me as a part-time legal adviser at a salary of, say, one hundred pounds a month and then your secret will be safe with me."

Behind the pantry door, Wemmick was seething with rage, but careful enough not to betray his presence.

"Ah, Mr. Twaddell, both your offers might be possibilities, but as you know from our last meeting, the financial side of the practice is run by my senior clerk, so I could not possibly make any commitment at all without his knowledge and agreement. We have no secrets and I do not intend to embark on that course now.

"Were you to join us, given what you have said, Mr. Wemmick would necessarily be a party to the arrangement, so I am sure you do not expect an immediate answer, so give me a few days to consider with Mr. Wemmick regarding your employment here as a regular or a part-time lawyer?"

This careful reply pleased Wemmick immensely as Hamish had totally ignored the comments about Edinburgh.

"Nay, I did not anticipate an answer tonight. I will stay in London for forty-eight hours at the Majestic Hotel where you can contact me. After that, need I say more?"

"Good night, then, Twaddell."

"Good night, Macdonald,"

Once Twaddell had left, Wemmick burst into the room. He kept his righteous anger well-hidden and simply said:

"So, this fellow is a blackmailer too."

"I fear so. What should we do, Wemmick?"

"This needs the utmost care. A nasty business. You see how the advice given you by Old Pip was so sound."

"Yes, indeed, and I am very careful."

V

When they arrived in Little Britain the morning after Twaddell's letter arrived, Hamish told Robert the clerk not to admit anyone and then called in Wemmick, who had been sitting brooding at the desk in his office since his arrival half an hour earlier.

"I am so sorry, Hamish, that you should be confronted with such an evil man. Of course, it is quite out of the question for you either to employ him or to pay him. With blackmailers, there is no option but to call their bluff and risk the consequences, for otherwise you are in thrall to the man forever."

"That's right, of course."

"Drawing on the little experience Mr. Jaggers had with such people, I'd say we cannot contemplate surrendering to this. Moreover, his moral character is such that he should never be a lawyer anyway, and we might seek ways to end his career."

"I have lain awake all night, Wemmick, wondering about the appropriate way to proceed. I have simply no experience. I agree with what you say. I simply cannot become a pawn in a blackmailer's hands."

"Indeed, and not just for yourself, but for the practice and its legacy."

"That is right. Imagine the damage that man would do if we had him here. I am aghast at the hypocrisy of the man who stands on a religious high horse and then resorts to these threats. But I do have to confront a fact about myself."

"Yes, I fear so. You will never be out of dangers of this kind, given social conventions and the law as it stands."

"After a sleepless night, I have decided I must marry."

"Gracious me! But would that be fair to the woman?"

"Yes, in that I will tell her of my desires. I need to find a woman whose main purpose in life is not marriage *per se,* but children. We could live as friends, indeed as a married couple, and I would be delighted to bring up children, for that would have nothing to do with my desires.

"I have never been in the company of women. My education at university has always been with people of my own sex. Growing up, I had no female near me except my mother, so as I matured, I was always in male company."

"That is sad, so you don't really know what it would be like to be close to a woman, Well, well, Hamish, I suppose it possible to find such a woman.

"For my part, I am sure that this evil Scotsman has absolutely no proof that illegal acts were performed by your Edinburgh group, and certainly no proof of your crime. The law refers only to actions, not to companionship. I do think it is an option to sue him for blackmail."

"I suppose, so, but it is enormously high-risk, is it not? To be honest with you, Wemmick, I have never committed any illegal act under these laws. Frankly, I am too frightened. I have been waiting to see if I could find a man with whom I might share a life. I am not a promiscuous person. Indeed, I shudder at that aspect of life."

"Then we can consider going the legal route if your conscience is clear, Hamish."

"Yet might I then be involving my friends in ways I would not wish?"

"I doubt it."

"Let me think about this," said Wemmick. "Remember we have twenty-four hours to devise a strategy. I heard nothing from him sufficiently strong in law for you to be concerned. He is guessing that you have broken the law. Might we be able to show him he is wrong? He will need some proof. Searching for a woman to marry is strong enough to deter him. If we were able to supply that, somehow, then we could find a way to punish him, legally or otherwise, for his behavior."

"That might bring him to heel, I suppose, but it does depend on our convincing the man that his threats are groundless. How about this as a strategy?" said Hamish tentatively.

"I'll invite Twaddell to my office tomorrow. We will tell Robert to delay him in the hall. Meantime, we have a woman of marriageable age in this office. She then leaves, passing him. When I call him in, I say that I am sorry to have delayed him, but I had urgent business with my fiancée. I then tell him I am unable to appoint him to a permanent position or an advisory one and wish him good day."

"Then we could seek Courtisone's advice on how to proceed with him."

"Now that, sir, is a very deft strategy. Would it convince him?"

"I don't know, but it is worth an attempt."

"But who is the woman?"

"Who else but Susanna?"

"My goodness, do you think she would participate in this deception?"

"I am sure of it as she has always shown me the utmost sympathy."

"Hmmm. I noticed that you did not respond in your initial conversation in any way to his implicit accusations?"

"No, I was careful not to, not least because they are unfounded."

"It is a gamble, of course, if he is really set on your destruction. Then he might return to find out whether you were in fact married."

"That is my intention, anyway. But if Courtisone were to act, that might make him wary of further attempts at blackmail, but were he to be dismissed, I suppose he might be more vengeful. We would have to take that risk."

"Then you must go to Chelsea immediately and discover whether Susanna would take part."

After Hamish left, Wemmick went to his office and sat at his desk, musing on Hamish's circumstances, though he was more surprised at himself. He had never had any close contact with someone like Hamish before. Indeed, he had not thought much about the perversion.

But he was above all a realist. Hamish was a nice young fellow, a good man, a sensible man and a promising lawyer, just trapped by his own desires which mattered not a jot to Wemmick, however much it might upset the neighbors. After all, he had seen far worse aspects of human behavior in the many years he had spent with Jaggers.

Hamish arrived in Cheyne Row flustered but determined. A maid opened the door. Pip, fortunately, was away in Shoreditch. Susanna was looking quite flushed as she had just returned from a walk with her children along the river and Lachlan was sitting with her, playing with the Solitaire marbles on the table.

"Hamish, how good to see you."

"Thank you for seeing me, Susanna."

"And why would I not?" she retorted.

"Oh, I don't know. Truth to tell I am in an extremely unfortunate situation, and I have come to ask for your help."

"Oh, my goodness that sounds bad, but we Scots must help each other in this world of Sassenachs."

"Indeed. The facts are these. You know we have invited Mr. Smythe to join us, and he has accepted. I didn't trouble to mention at lunch that we had decided not to invite a Mr. Duncan Twaddell, the unsuccessful candidate."

"Why, because he was Scottish?" and she laughed.

"Oh no, he behaved as though he were a reincarnated John Knox, breathing fire and fury on sodomy."

"These people are so self-righteous."

"He tried at the interview to demand compensation and terms which were quite unacceptable, and he left not wanting to waste his time, but he has since returned to London and asked to meet with me. The man has now resorted to blackmail.

"He has said that if we did not use him, he would let it be known about my proclivities as he had done some research about the group of my friends when in Edinburgh. He has given me forty-eight hours to respond. Of course, I admitted nothing when I met him after hours in my office, with Wemmick listening from the pantry."

"But that is monstrous."

"Indeed, Wemmick and I have been discussing alternative ways to proceed. Telling him to go away. Telling of his behavior to his seniors, even entering a civil suit.

"But this is where I need your help.

"Would you come to my office at an appointed hour? When he enters the office, he will be asked to wait by my clerk, then I will say goodbye to you, and you will walk past him in the hall to your cab. When he comes in, I will apologize for keeping him but say that I had important matters to discuss with my fiancée. You would pose as she.

"I will then meet him and say we are unable to meet his requirements."

"An interesting strategy. Where was this man Twaddell working?"

"MacLechtie and Tulloch, in Edinburgh if I have the names right."

"Ah well, that's a coincidence. They were my father's lawyers, but I have changed to a firm here in London. I knew Sandy Tulloch quite well. He's as upright a man as could be on God's good earth. I think your idea is a good one and I am happy to assist."

"Let me also say this, Susanna. I have decided that I must marry and have children. I need to find a woman, as I told Wemmick, who is more interested in having children than in romantic love for her husband, though I would hope we would be good friends. I simply do not see how I can survive as a lawyer without it. Of course, I would tell whoever became my betrothed so that there was no risk of future misunderstandings."

"Well, that is a different matter, and I may just know someone who would agree to that arrangement, but I must think carefully about approaching her, so it will be a few months before I feel confident of introducing her to you.

"But on the Twaddell matter, let us proceed as planned with this addition. When I come out of your office, I will engage him in conversation, briefly— find out his firm and tell him I know Sandy Tulloch. Would that be effective?"

"I am sure it would. How could he then proceed knowing that my 'fiancée' is a friend of his senior?"

"Indeed, but if he persists even after that, your marriage must occur soon and be announced not merely in London but in Edinburgh."

"Thank you so much. I hope Pip will not be upset by this arrangement."

"Oh, I am sure he will be," she said with a grin, "but doing a favor for a friend is just a good thing to do."

"Excellent and thank you. I will send a message to Twaddell giving him a time to appear and perhaps you would come a half hour earlier."

"I will."

Hamish told Wemmick of Susanna's agreement after hastening back to Little Britain.

"Splendid, though I don't think Susanna should engage this fellow in conversation. Perhaps as she is leaving, she can call back to you 'I will write to Sandy Tulloch about the property, or something like that.'"

"Excellent. Let us hope it proceeds satisfactorily, though I must confess I am very nervous."

Estella meanwhile had visited the building Pip had identified and found it an excellent base. She returned to Numquam later that day, intending to stay a while and investigate the Chatham possibility. Nellie appeared as usual and Estella simply could not take her eyes off her when she was in the room—this beautiful woman who, she thought, would be so elegant were she dressed in the fashion.

"Nellie, I have floated the idea with the Trust of doing some good work with prostitutes in Chatham. I wonder whether you would accompany me and with your husband too if he were able, to show me the districts used and perhaps, while we were there, I could get you some dresses and hats, for if we are to conduct a project here together, you will have to be well-dressed as my companion, won't you?"

"Oh, Ma'am, I'd love to do that. You'se so kind to me, I wish there was something I could do for you."

"Fiddlesticks, Nellie, this will be our adventure. Oh dear, I will be sixty-five years old next year."

"Maybe," said Nellie, "But you'se still as lovely as when you was thirty!"

Nellie came to Numquam at ten o'clock the following day wearing the best clothes she could find. November was often a very cold month near the sea, but that day, the sun shone just enough to keep the chill at bay. On the ride to Chatham, Nellie chatted non-stop about life at the Forge and the Cottage, how well Fletch was doing and how they were growing their own vegetables and how the children could read, and she read to them, an incessant flow of whatever came into her mind.

Estella watched her, bemused.

Yet suddenly the uncanny became the obvious to Estella as she listened.

My mother, Molly.

Nellie was Molly.

Their childhoods were initially different, but then the same. Molly took a year or two to have a proper conversation rather than just chattering on. Both Molly and Nellie were passionate, unguarded in their desires. Estella had been through all this before with her mother and now, she realized, she was educating a younger woman whom she loved, no two ways about it. Whether that love would become desire was another matter.

Perhaps Nellie was a reincarnation of her murdered mother, for had not Nellie almost been the victim of a vengeful killer too? She could not take her eyes off the younger woman's mouth and the incessant movement of her lips as she spoke, so full of passion and promise. Like Molly, here was a woman brimming with native intelligence and overflowing with compassion and relief at the changes in her life.

Oh God, Nellie is Molly, Estella realized. *Am I then Nellie's child?*

Her carriage stopped outside an old posthouse inn where they had an early and brief lunch. Both were acutely aware that Nellie might encounter men who had visited her in her days as a whore, so Estella guided her to the dress shops at the fashionable end of town. An hour later, Nellie was in a fine satin dress with a bustle, a simpler but fashionable hat, and white gloves, at which she whispered to Estella she had never worn a pair ever. Two other outfits were acquired and ordered to be delivered to the Cottage. Nellie immediately fell in love with her new persona as exhibited through her garment.

"Oh, ma'am, I feel a different woman, almost a lady now. Cor, look at me," she said looking at herself in the shop window as they left.

"You look as you deserve to look, Nellie, but now let us take a cab to see what Chatham is like as my carriage is too ostentatious for our task. We'll begin with a ride around some districts you would choose, as a preliminary expedition."

Nellie then instructed the driver to ride the streets close to the dockyard, Wood Street, Cottage Street, Manor Street and along Dock Road, the place where Nellie had first accosted Pip. There they were, often in groups of two or three, obviously dressed for their profession.

"See, Ma'am, that used to be me."

"How distressing. How could you stand it?"

"I had no choice. See, that's the thing when you'se poor. You get what you can, when you can, where you can. Otherwise, you starve. Then I'd have loved to be a skivvy in a big house, but I couldn't find one. So, I was on the game."

"What game?"

Nellie chortled, "Oh Ma'am, being a whore is what we call being on the game."

"Oh, I see."

Nellie then explained how most of these women sent their earnings to a man who had control of them, either as a husband which was most common, or to some villain or other who 'owned' women of the street as if they were a pack of horses.

"I knew in general of these practices, though I have never seen it in action. I suppose soldiers and sailors are their customers from different areas of the world, China, Africa and elsewhere."

"There are taverns and place for them where they sleep. But often after three weeks or months at sea without a wife or a woman they are desperate for, well, you know what."

They returned to the Inn, Nellie with a certain kind of nostalgia, Estella with a sense of shock, but now armed with a new determination. As they sat next to each other in the carriage on the way back to Numquam, Nellie reached out with her gloved left hand and took Estella's right hand in a relaxed but firm grip. They were silent each looking out of their side of the carriage, astonished, both basking in their growing friendship.

Two weeks later and on an apparently fine afternoon, Nellie took the cart to Numquam, a mere one and a half miles along a beaten grass track. She was always happy when she went there, especially if Estella was there. It was a mild autumn day when but about a mile from the house, a small storm blew in from the Estuary and by the time Nellie reached her destination, she was utterly drenched.

Estella had gone to the window to watch the heavy downpour and was surprised to see Nellie racing the cart to the kitchen door. She hurried into the kitchen where Nellie was standing with water dripping on the floor from her clothes, her long blond hair pressed tight on her head and they both laughed and laughed. The cook and the maid had their day off, so there was no one to help.

"Oh ma'am, what shall I do? I am soaked to the skin."

"Come to my bedroom, then, and we'll get those things off you and find something dry to wear while your clothes dry out."

They hurried up the stairs to Estella's room, water dripping on the risers, and Estella found a towel. Nellie started to undress, rubbing her head furiously and then drying the rest of her body while Estella went to her dressing room to find clothes for Nellie to wear.

She selected several garments and returned to the bedroom to see Nellie standing naked, having finished drying herself. Estella's eyes burned at this wonderful sight, this beautiful woman, looking just like the Botticelli Venus. Nellie looked at her flaunting her nudity and she saw the lust in Estella's eyes which she could easily identify given her background. Seductively she said:

"So, what do you think, Ma'am?"

"Oh, you are quite lovely, Nellie. You remind me of the painting of Venus, the goddess of love being born out of the sea," she said, trying to keep calm while desire rattled her whole psyche.

"Now look Ma'am, I feel so sad for you, 'cos I know you won't have another man," she said, stroking her hips, reveling in her nakedness, taking a small step towards her.

"You loved your husband too much to start off with another one.

"Yet I knows you. I've noticed how you look at me, sitting close to me, teaching me to learn, giving me dresses and hats. And you gave me that ring and then I knew we was special, calling each other sisters.

"But loving is loving and I loves you. The way I've been most of my life is like this. I've just got this thing in my head about giving myself to anyone who wants me, that's what someone with what they say is a whore's heart. That's what I did with Fletch.

"The difference with you is that I do love you which don't mean I don't love Fletch, 'cos I do. I gave him all the money I got whoring to him after I married him, well, soon after, anyway. And we's good together. I feel so safe with you, unlike with a man. I want you to have me and love me.

"Please touch me," she said moving ever closer to where Estella was standing in bewildered silence.

"You can have me in secret whenever you want, as I won't stop coming here to help and to learn. I've never loved a woman before, so this is all new to me."

"And to me too," said Estella, trembling with desire and edging slowly toward this beautiful naked woman, the likes of which she had never seen. She could scarcely understand this intense lust-filled thrill running through her, searching this enticing female body up and down.

"Now, come 'ere," said Nellie, reaching out and catching Estella's hand which she placed on her breast.

"I want to be your whore, cos I know you need loving, and I do love you. I want to serve your body too, 'cos you're so gorgeous.

"Let me take those clothes off now."

"Oh, please, darling Nellie, do as you wish, and I will submit."

Estella then put her arms around this sensuous naked body, her fingers trembling as she ran her hands down Nellie's back. Nellie undid the satin dress and the various undergarments, and they stood looking at each, smiling and thrilled by this change in their relationship. They kissed deeply, their arms around each other.

Later it was past the time Nellie was due home.

"Will Fletch be annoyed that you are late?"

"I don't think so, and you know, I am sure he would not mind if I told him about you."

"No, please don't, please, please don't, Nellie. I could not bear anything which risked making us unhappy. You didn't tell me, by the way, what he thought of the dresses."

"He was so shocked and said at first he didn't like it, but when I said we was going to do some good work in Chatham with whores, he relaxed.

"Don't worry, darlin'. I'll keep mum, my clothes will be dry by now and I'll leave this towel in the kitchen. Cook will have left supper for you, I know. I'll see you day after tomorrow."

They kissed gently and Nellie left.

Estella lay in bed for a long time, and did not trouble to eat supper, but slept deeply for hours. She had not thought much at all about the Sapphic life but, oh god, she had enjoyed herself in ways she would not have thought possible.

She was nevertheless very puzzled by Nellie. *Why would the young woman really engage with her if she was having the kind of loving she had with Fletch? Was she just being a whore with me, being paid in rings and dresses? Or was she somehow able to enjoy her husband, but also enjoy me? She said she wanted to help me.*

Perhaps such women like Molly and Nellie treat bodily intimacy not as some treasured gift from God or somewhere, but just as what Molly once called 'a bit of fun.' Coupling with someone you fancied, a new term she learnt from Nellie, was just what one did unless there was some obstacle, like a husband or a wife. She remembered how Molly had offered herself to Wemmick in the very early days, which simply baffled her.

"What would the neighbors think?" she said aloud and giggled for a while at the thought.

But as she gathered herself to get up from her bed, her illicit pleasure made her look at her own body in a different way. She rehearsed the moments when she had brushed Nellie's long blond hair down her back, brushing out her own long hair as she did so.

Now she must find some literature about women in love with each other, and she'd read it to Nellie as a child might read to her mother. Dimly, she remembered some mention of poetry by Sappho which she determined to search out.

Word had been sent to the Majestic Hotel that Mr. Macdonald would be glad to meet him at his office at noon the next day, which pleased Twaddell immensely. He dressed in his somewhat elderly frock coat and slightly battered top hat, dreaming of the handy income which awaited him. This route to solvency seemed very promising to him, especially since he had blotted his copybook with his Edinburgh partners on a matter of unprofessional behavior. Parting from them would be acrimonious to say the least, so there was a spring in his step as he left for the encounter.

He was an obstinate, selfish, slightly cruel man, with a dash of religious fervor to make him a thoroughly unpleasant character to most who met him except his domineering wife, a woman of guile and even more thorough-going dishonesty than her husband. She would be delighted were he to find himself a London position, but he had kept silent on the blackmail he was seeking to achieve with his putative partner, hoping to regale her later with his success.

When he arrived at the office Robert showed him to a seat in the hall, saying:

"Mr. Macdonald is expecting you, but he is presently delayed."

"That's all right, my boy," he said with the surety of arrogance, "I am sure we will get to know each other well."

Robert was a young man of great integrity, so although Twaddell continued to seek to engage him in conversation, the clerk was mute and continued with his work on accounts.

Inside Pip's office there was great excitement with minor changes being made to the earlier plan and it was now time to implement it.

Readying themselves, Hamish opened the office door, and an elegantly dressed beautiful young woman came out. Twaddell heard Hamish say, "you won't forget to write to Sandy Tulloch, will you, dear?"

He was also stunned by the reply in a distinctive Scottish voice:

"Of course not, darling."

Twaddell heard this exchange as if it was the prophet of doom. His eyes blurred, his palms broke out in a sweat and to use an old phrase, his timbers shivered. In the moment he had while this woman passed him by for the door, he could not decide whether to flee, excuse himself or even get up from the seat to which Robert has assigned him.

"Ah, Twaddell," said Macdonald as he came out of the office to meet him, "I am sorry I was delayed, but I had some business to complete with my fiancée."

The color fell from Twaddell's face reflecting the other varied forms of physical distress he was already suffering.

Thunderstruck, he saw immediately that he was now in serious legal jeopardy having attempted blackmail for which there were conspicuously no grounds on which he could enter any claim, as Macdonald had this beautiful fiancée and between them, they obviously knew his senior in the firm of MacLechtie and Tulloch. He was struck dumb, a rare occurrence in his tangled life.

"Do come in," said Macdonald. Twaddell entered almost like a schoolboy being called to task by a master, his malicious heart in his boots.

"I have considered your request of the other day and I must decline. The basis on which you spoke to me has no basis in fact or even in theory. Wemmick and I considered the position carefully, as he was at our meeting listening to you from behind that pantry door there. Unlike you, my conscience is completely clear. So, we propose to turn the tables.

"We will not offer you any kind of appointment, permanent or temporary and you should know that we would be able to give evidence to any interested party about your illegal attempts at blackmail. We suggest that you return to Scotland, thinking carefully about your employment as a lawyer, given your propensity for blackmail.

"We will not let this particular sword of Damocles fall on you, however, unless we hear of some other egregious acts which would persuade us that we should inform interested parties. I do not wish to have any further contact with you, and I do not require any sort of explanation for your conduct. Good day to you, sir."

At this, Twaddell turned and shuffled to the door hanging his head in shame, and unsurprisingly, without so much as a goodbye or a thank you. While he was clearly in danger, that danger seemed for the moment was stilled, for which he should have been deeply grateful, but then his character was such that he did not properly recognize it. Once out of the office, he sped to the street, hastening down the pavement in search of a cab.

Wemmick once again appeared from behind the pantry door exultant. "What a triumph of ingenuity and skill we have. How Mr. Jaggers and Old Pip would have loved it all."

"I hope so. Susanna was wonderful, and I shall go to see to Cheyne Row to thank her promptly. After all, she is my fiancée," at which both men laughed so hard and long that Robert put his head round the door to see what the fuss was about.

"However," said Wemmick, "an evil man deeply wounded is a clear and present danger. He may well seek revenge in some other way. I think I will have him watched for a month or so. I think we need to bear that expense."

"I agree wholeheartedly, and it may well be worth the money. I think we should keep all this between the three of us, and I am sure Susanna will not tell Pip, given his religious inclinations."

"All in all," said Wemmick, "a splendid end to the year. I'd thought of wishing him a happy Christmas," and they both laughed heartily.

"That's all over, thank God, now we can enjoy our own Christmas, and I see it has started to snow."

1871

VI

Estella's friendship with Charlotte had grown apace, not least because her niece Elizabeth was in love with her step-son Albert. After a long afternoon tea spent discussing almost everything that was common to them, Charlotte got up to leave. They walked together to the Hall for her to put on her fur coat, hat and gloves against the cold of a January morning.

"Dear Estella, that was such a good conversation about Elizabeth, and I am comforted by it. I hope we will become fast friends."

"I share that sentiment," said Estella primly.

"It is also of special comfort to talk about my dear brother Henry. I know him to be a man of good judgment and I was delighted at his return to England when it appeared Paris was to be sacked by the Prussians. I missed him, of course, as he immediately rushed off to Scotland to shoot grouse or some other innocent bird.

"Poor man; his despicable wife Mary-Lou disappeared at the first sign of war, God knows where, but it was a great advantage for Elizabeth who had him to herself at the family country house in so far as that is possible at a family occasion."

"Do you think Albert was part of their private conversations?" asked Estella.

"He was invited to Wymondham, of course, but I think she planned to ask Henry if she could invite Albert to come to Paris with them."

"That would be lovely for Elizabeth," said Estella "though I suppose it all depends on the Prussians.

"I fear so," Charlotte replied with a grimace.

By the end of 1870, indeed, it was clear that the French had been decisively beaten and that Paris would be attacked. The embassy closed. Lord Lyons the ambassador left for Tours and Henry packed his bags, and since he had already obtained a *carte de passage* from Bismarck, he left for London carrying his gun-case and immediately went north to Yorkshire. He returned to the family estate in Norfolk well in time for Christmas where the Fitzroy family gathered and celebrated with their usual enthusiasm.

On New Year's Day 1871, Elizabeth sat in the blue drawing-room at Wymondham holding hands with Albert, reminiscing about their splendid Christmas. Her father had gone off for what was to be his last shoot before returning to Paris.

"I think your father likes me, darling. I will always remember him saying, 'young Albert, tomorrow we must find a tree to cut and bring in for Elizabeth to decorate with your help.' It was the first time we had talked properly, sitting with a brandy after you had all retired."

"I told him that would be exciting and asked him about Paris. I said that you had given me stories from your letters, but even reading *The Times*, I couldn't get a full picture of events.

"I find his letters so fascinating. Reading them is like sitting in a theater watching a play develop."

"Did he tell you anything when you were on your tree adventure?

"Oh yes, especially about Parisian reactions to defeat which he found so unlike the English"

"Please tell."

"A mixture of disbelief and resolve, as he described it, flooded the city with its voices. '*Les armées doivent être victorieuses*,' '*Vive Thiers*,' '*a bas les Prussiens*' people shouted, as if they were denying what had happened. Paris was very grim, so he said, and the city shut down as if in grief that night.

"I asked him about the cafes, as they are so famous.

"Unfortunate,' he said. He remembered dining with Colonel Claremont, the military attaché, at the *Café des Anglais*, but they were the only people there, and the Boulevards were empty."

"Is he not such a brave man, my father?" said Elizabeth.

"Oh, indeed. He certainly thought that it was the end of Paris as he had known it, because he expected the Prussians to invade and smash the place to bits as they did at Strasbourg. I think he had told you, or so he said, that patriotism had begun to show its ugly side across the city, with all aspects of life having accusations of treachery and spying continually cast around with abandon.

"I was particularly shocked by one of his comments, Elizabeth. He said he thought that in the popular French mind, England had contributed to their defeat, and some of these ignorant brutes had even gone so far as to say and to believe that English and other foreign armies came in to assist the Prussians in the last fights which riled up the mob."

"That's ridiculous."

"Yes, indeed, and he had quite a funny story about the mob. They had forced their way into the *Tuileries'* gardens one day and who should be there but De Lesseps, you know who I mean?"

"Yes, he designed the Suez Canal," said Elizabeth.

"Your father reminded me that the fellow knew all about canals and suggested that it would be advisable to open the gates in the center of the palace, which was done, and the stream of angry people passed through accordingly into the *Place du Carrousel*, and no injury was done."

That evening, Henry returned with several pheasants, a few partridges, a woodcock and some pigeons, all of which were taken to the outer kitchen. After dinner that night, puffing on the remains of his cigar, Henry was in contemplative mood:

"We must join the ladies soon, Albert. You know, we British really do have a stiff upper lip.

"In the midst of the excitement when the people were trooping back from the *Corps Legislatif*, I found Lord Lyons engaged composing a dispatch on Tunisian finance, and all the while the looting and pillaging was becoming common place and most people were dirty and demoralized."

"How could he concentrate in the midst of that noise?"

"It baffled me too. But you must come to Paris and spend a month with us. I anticipate getting a wire to get back any time soon."

"Thank you, sir, I'd be delighted."

The following afternoon a snowstorm kept the company indoors. After dinner the family sat in the drawing-room of the Wymondham Dower House listening to Elizabeth play Beethoven sonatas. After the blazing third movement of the Moonlight sonata, she got up quickly and walked over to her where her father was reading and sat down next to him. Albert joined them.

"Tell me, Father," said Elizabeth, "how do women with children cope with an impending invasion? It must be terribly frightening. How much of a commotion was there as the Prussians approached the city?"

"Overwhelming," Henry replied. "The Britishers were anxious about getting a train to Calais, while the Parisians were going about chaotically trying to prepare for the anticipated siege. Men and women were in the same boat, I fear. I had interminable correspondence with Count Bismarck, and with various French and Prussian officials trying to get permission for British subjects to leave. Of course, I could do nothing for French people."

"Were there no others to help?"

"Yes, there was an American general, Ambrose Burnside. He was such a nice man, a veteran of the Northern Army, known for the way he wore his hair down his cheeks which his soldiers imitated and called him 'sideburns.' He was very helpful in these negotiations."

"You never mentioned how did you get out; was it on foot, in a carriage, by train?"

"One or two brave souls got out by balloon, which we used at the time only for diplomatic messages. I left by carriage with my pass.

"My dear, by then the turmoil in Paris had become unrelenting. Boulevards were packed with people shouting and yelling, poor devils quite unprepared for the shambles to come. Volunteers for the defense of the city were just an armed mob at the best. Some had no arms at all, others only rifles. There were only four French generals in Paris, and one was a cripple. Several waiters I knew joined the National Guard."

"I hope it all quietens down before we go back."

"We will be quite protected, my dear, have no fear on that score."

After Elizabeth and the others had retired for the night, Henry reached his bedroom just as his brother Freddie came down the corridor.

"How's your personal life, my brother?" Freddie asked.

"Diplomatically fine, domestically absurd."

"Why such venom?"

"Mary-Lou is not planning to return for a while until peace is certain. There seems to be nothing whatsoever in common between Elizabeth and her mother. Her letter contained nothing at all about her daughter."

"I don't want to say I told you so, but I will."

"I know, I know. I increasingly think her not returning very desirable."

"Anyone else?"

"Good God, no! I am far too busy to pursue women. Paris society had been abandoned and I am not a man to pick women off the street, or in a fancy salon for that matter."

"I think you need the comfort of a woman in your situation. But then you were always rather prudish, even a risqué tale will shock you."

"Indeed, especially from diplomats of the Hapsburg Empire who seemed to have something of a fetish for the profane and the louche."

"Do you miss her?"

"I do. I miss Mary-Lou for all her faults, and I will write to her to say so. Then it would be up to her to decide, but that will also be influenced by conditions there after the Civil War and the effects of the Civil War and the Lincoln assassination."

"Are you likely to be posted elsewhere?"

"Probably, but not Washington, and I doubt she will go anywhere with me apart from Paris. If I were to go to another embassy as had been mentioned, she would decidedly not come, especially to some god-forsaken part of the world."

"If I can be of help while you're here, my ear is at your service."

Early the following morning, the gorgeous sounds of the Tempest Sonata being played with great verve and mastery resounded through the Dower House, an appropriate piece with which to recall Paris and its nadir. Elizabeth had also been experimenting with recently published Schubert impromptus and with Franz Liszt, whose reputation as a pianist and composer had spread across Europe since the 1840s, all of which made her father gaze at her with unbounded admiration.

One morning in the New Year, Pip was returning from discussions about the building and decided to stroll up Bond Street first, vaguely looking for things to buy for his children, as he was quietly upset that all their Christmas presents had been chosen by Susanna. He had it in mind to find something special for Lachlan and Malcolm from their father only.

He did not want to admit to himself that he was not rushing to go home. His marriage was not nearly as happy as it had been at the outset. He blamed himself for not coming to terms with the fact that Susanna was an independent thinker and tough as old boots, a feature of her Scottish background.

These days they seemed unable to agree on any matter, however trivial. It was as if she was fixated on controlling the household, himself included. She was quite strict with the children but was unable to keep a nanny for more than six months because she would not give them a smidgen of independence.

But marriage vows were sacred, and it was a matter now of trying to find a middle way. He planned to offer to take her to Paris or Dieppe in the spring for a few days together to be outside the growing pressures of Cheyne Row and the family. They had become irregular in their loving time together, and Pip had learnt enough from her to realize that any talk of his rights as a husband would be folly in the extreme. After two children, he thought, she seemed to be reaching the limits of her need for physical satisfaction, a further cause of his distress.

He turned into an arcade off Bond Street and there was Harriet looking in the window of a jewelers. She had not noticed him, so he approached her from behind stealthily and almost whispered in her ear: "Fancy seeing you here."

She turned and threw her arms around his neck to the surprise of passers-by.

"Oh, Pip, how wonderful to see you again after all these years. How are you? You must be married by now, I am sure, so how are your wife and family?"

"We cannot stand here, Harriet, let us walk to the restaurant around the corner and have some lunch. I was about to buy presents, but meeting you is the best present I could have! How many years did we have together?"

"Three, four maybe, and do you know, my dear, I have not been able to take a serious lover since."

"How come? You told me you were so free with your affections."

"I don't really know, and it has not been for want of an opportunity. You spoiled me, Pip; the memories of our love have persisted with me. But what of you? Tell me all."

"I married a rich, strong independent young woman of considerable intellect."

"That sounds perfect to me."

"Yes, and it is still so. We have two splendid boys and hope to have a girl next time round. But here I need your counsel, wise as you are. I find life with her difficult, really because she is so

intelligent. I don't know how to proceed. Indeed, I am mightily confused, a strange state for one with my previous certainties."

"After lunch why do we not walk to my lodging in Long Acre, if
you are not promised forth elsewhere?"

"For an hour or so, but I should be home well before dark."

It was a fine but cold day, and both were well wrapped against
the wind. They walked to Long Acre, though discussion about Pip's
marriage was not part of the conversation. The lodging was a small
room, comfortably furnished, and Pip looked around it as he had
never seen her room during their Salford liaison, since she was
boarding with her grandmother.

Harriet took off her coat, hanging it in a small closet near to
the window.

"Why are you here in London, not Birmingham?"

"I am trying to study the art of the Renaissance and I plan to
go to Florence quite soon, perhaps for a couple of years, but I have
started my studies here."

"I see," he said quietly, and then turned to look at her, all the
desire for her welling up inside him like a volcano.

"Before you go, will you make love with me?"

"Now? But, Pip, you are married."

Ignoring that comment, he reached out and pulled her to
him, kissing her with every remembered passion. They knew each
other almost too well, remembrance of their four years together in
Salford swimming into their minds. Their hands knew what to do.
Their heads swam with lust. They found that shattering strength of
purpose and desire that marks renewed love.

Not a word of contemplation but of action fired by greed for
each other. Bodies turning over and back. Fingers clawing at flesh.
Commands issued, answered and repeated. Grunts of pleasure.
Moans of ecstasy. And then, an eerie silence as both lay back. Not
sated, however; animalistic demands were again engaged until, an
hour later, she murmured,

"Oh, darling, I have missed you so."

"I have thought about you often, but when I saw you, I knew I could not live another moment without making love to you. I must go now, but I will send a message here tomorrow. I have an idea that would enable us to spend a little time together."

When Pip got home later, Susanna was immensely cheerful, and he dissembled by explaining what a splendid time he had working on the building.

"I have been thinking about Biddy," he said. "I have not seen my mother for a while, and we had no plans to visit at Christmas. I want to be sure that she has considered what to do with her ownership of the Forge and the Cottage, so would you mind, darling, if I went there for a few days soon? Perhaps you could come as well, but it does not seem that necessary. Perhaps I can invite them here?"

"Of course, of course, though the children would love to see them. No, I have plenty to do here, and I have been mildly concerned that we have not been in touch with them. If there were problems, I am sure we would have heard. I have had some thoughts, by the way, about our working much more closely with politics—the Liberals, of course. Who knows, we might get you into Parliament."

"I don't think I am ready for that."

"But my dear, you were a marvelous preacher, and you could speak on behalf of causes you supported."

"Well, perhaps, but let us discuss that when I return. I will write to Biddy and ask if she has a room for me; if not, I'll stay at the Blue Boar and take a trap there daily. Goodness me, she must be sixty-six this year. I am glad I remembered her birthday last year."

The next morning Pip wrote to Biddy asking to come and stay for a few days, and he wrote to Harriet too, saying that he anticipated being able to spend a day and a night with her shortly. Biddy replied by return of post telling him not to come 'in this weather,' so he sent a note to Harriet about the delay.

To say that his conscience was rattled would be an understatement, for after they had dinner on Thursday, Susanna came across the living room with two glasses of whisky and sat by him. He had never ever refused her invitations and now was not the time. They went to bed, and mutual enjoyment followed, for the first time feigned by him.

"I am going to miss you, darling, even for such a short time."

"Me too," he said with as much conviction as he could muster.

"You are so generous to go off to All Hallows, so upright and so gentle."

"Thank you, my dear," he replied, now without a feeling of guilt.

"I am sorry, you know, about the arguments we have had but which I never really enjoyed."

"Nor me."

As they lay in each other's arms, she continued to say how much she loved him and their children and what a happy marriage they had. At that remark he started to shiver with guilt, but if he was honest, little remorse. They fell asleep in each other's arms afterwards, she almost immediately. He awoke early relishing the predicament he had chosen, and quite unable to break out of it.

His plans were thwarted again by a letter from Biddy saying that she had thought about it and would prefer him to come nearer the Spring with the result that further meetings with Harriet were curtailed. Indeed, it was well into February on a Friday morning that Pip left Cheyne Row in a cab, apparently headed for Charing Cross station, but in fact going to Long Acre. Amid the almost twenty-four hours of passionate love, they talked of their future, its possibilities and dangers.

"I am so sorry it has been so long."

"No matter, Pip, but I really do want to go to Florence," she said over a late breakfast, "but I would be away for three months at least."

"I'd put up with that," said Pip, "and when you return, we can still have the commitment we had in Salford."

"Perhaps, but our consciences will come calling," she replied. "For you the problem will be guilt at the deception; for me, jealousy, envy, call it what you will. I want you more deeply now than in the North, but it would break your marriage, you know."

"But why?"

"It will be impossible to keep it from your wife."

"Surely not, if we are discreet."

"But would you be prepared for that? Could you leave your children?"

Then he glanced at the clock and saw that he would miss his train if he did not leave immediately. They kissed goodbye and he left for the train confused, guilt-ridden but happy.

But, as he sat watching the Kent countryside pass by, the question was whether he could sustain an intimate existence with two women, even though he really did love both of them. He was steadily convincing himself he could, given his prowess as a lover with both wife and mistress within thirty-six hours.

However, his time with Biddy was a treat. She pampered him, questioned him, wondered when he would bring her grandchildren to All Hallows at which he asked her to Chelsea which she promised to do in the summer, especially now there were steam-trains that went so quickly.

"I need to ask you, Mother, about the Forge and the Cottage. What will happen to them when you're gone? Have you made any arrangements?"

"Oh, no, Pip, I've made no will if that's what you mean. I've just assumed everything I had will go to you, my dear boy. Harry and I are agreed on that."

"Well, that is sweet of you, but I would like to get this worked out with a lawyer. I will have Hamish Macdonald draw up a will and you can sign it when you come to London, or I come here."

"Oh, I think I'll survive till then."

"But what will you do with the property, Pip?

"I don't know. I will talk to the Fletchers some time I am up here."

"No time like the present, and you should see Estella as well."

"I will take a trap to see my old farrier mate Fletch, and then go to Numquam tomorrow."

The following morning, he went over to the Forge and there was Fletch hard at work, the children at school. They chatted for an hour and eventually talked about Fletch's plans.

"I'd prefer to continue paying rent to Mrs. Gargery, Pip."

"Biddy is happy with that. You all seem to be very happy here, making a good living and your wife with her job at Numquam. Bit of a change from Balaklava, eh?"

"Oh God, I should say so, and I cannot thank you enough for this opportunity."

"Small thing to do for someone who saved my life," said Pip, putting his arm on Fletch's shoulder.

"Nellie's doing some Trust project with that Estella, too, which she is excited about."

"Ah yes the Trust's work in Chatham, I know about that. I have also been talking to Biddy about her will and when she goes, I will be the owner."

"That will be fine, I can pay the rent to you."

"Let's hope that's a long way off. I want you to know it will always be yours to use. Maybe there's a time when you'd want to buy the Forge?"

"Maybe," said Fletch, but no conclusions were reached by the time Pip prepared to see Estella before going back to London.

"Nellie's over there now, so you'll be able to talk about that project," said Fletch.

They hugged each other as former comrades-in-arms, and Pip left.

The maid answered at Numquam, and Estella came out from the living-room to greet him. When he entered the drawing room, he was taken aback to see Nellie languishing in a chair, a book in her hand, and not dressed as a maid, but as a lady about town.

"How are you, Mr. Pip?" she said, getting up from the chair, "Mrs. Pirrip is teaching me to read."

"And she is doing so well, the poor darling," said Estella. "I think she will be able to read Dickens' books soon."

"I hope so," said Nellie, "and it's fun reading to my little ones."

After a cup of tea, some cakes that Nellie fetched from the kitchen and some conversation about the projects, Pip made the excuse to get back to Biddy. He could simply not understand how Estella and Nellie seemed more like old friends than mistress and servant. The poor darling? That was a very odd phrase for a maid servant, especially for a gentlewoman like Estella. He needed to talk to Harriet, and he almost forgot to send a note to Susanna saying when he would return.

"You are going to enjoy this, Mr. Wemmick, sir," said a middle-aged man in a cloth cap and a raincoat that had seen better times.

"I'm glad to hear that, Sidney; I like being entertained, especially as the New Year is well advanced, and Valentine's Day is just around the corner."

"No, but from what you've told me about the target, I'd be surprised if you didn't not get a good laugh out of this."

"I am on tenterhooks, Sidney, on tenterhooks. Reveal all."

"It were like this, see. Your target, Mr. Twaddell, went back to Scotland to his missus. I followed him there and waited."

"Well done, Sidney."

"It was over Christmas, too, though them Scots have a good time at New Years. I was then thinking I should just give up and go back home, but then what's he do? He leaves his home and goes to the station, looking to board the train for London, so I had to hurry to get a ticket and get on board too, though I had promised myself to return to London with nothing achieved. What's all this, I ask meself?"

"You stayed in Scotland all that time?"

"Weren't your instructions to follow him, Mr. W?"

"They were, but pray proceed."

"He comes to London, me following. The other evening, he leaves his hotel in the city just as it was getting dark. No cab, proceeding to walk east, yours truly keeping out of his sight but following close behind. Biting cold it was.

"Crikey, he was careless of the traffic and the roads, in a hurry, I s'pose. He only went and stepped in a horse's business on the road, didn't he? I was dying laughing! He had to scrape it off on a low wall, cursing something foul in Scottish, he did."

"What on earth was he doing?"

"I'll come to that, Mr. Wemmick sir. I had no idea where we was headed after we walked through Shoreditch, but he was obviously up to no good as he would turn round sometimes to see if anyone was following him. You know, shady like."

"Get to the point, Sidney, please."

"Then blimey, Mr. Wemmick, if he didn't head for Sodomites Walk when we's got to Moorfields."

"He what?" cried Wemmick, starting up from his chair astonished.

"Yes, he was there talking with some of them mollies for at least half an hour. I was getting cold, I tell you. I stood a good way off watching, just far enough away not to be seen or to be thought to be part of that gathering. Oh no, not me, sir.

"He was on the edge of the group, ooh, there must have been about thirty of 'em, and he started to walk away with his consort, if I may use that word, when out of nowhere constables arrived and your target was hustled into the back of one of their Black Marias!"

"Goodness me, how extraordinary!"

"Yes, I guess he'll be up before the beak in Bow Street later this morning."

"Well, thank you, Sidney. Here's an extra two pounds for excellent work," at which Sidney thanked Mr. Wemmick profusely and left with the sense of a good deed well done to be soon shared with the long-suffering Mrs. W.

As Sidney left, Hamish walked into the office.

"Who was that Wemmick, one of your men?"

"Indeed, and he brought very surprising and interesting news. Mr. Twaddell was arrested last night at Moorfields and will no doubt today be charged with lewd and immoral behavior."

"Och, no. I canna' believe that; now that is a wee surprise!" said Macdonald, shocked into a Scottish brogue.

"Shall we go to Bow Street to witness the proceedings?"

"It will be a pleasure, not a duty."

Their trap hurried from Little Britain to the Bow Street Magistrate's Court where His Honor Hubert Crampinghorn was sitting. Various thieves and vagabonds were summarily dispensed with, and then the men from Moorfields appeared one by one in front of His Honor.

In due course, it was the turn of Twaddell, looking as downcast as is humanly possible to be. Hamish suddenly felt quite sorry for the man with whom he apparently shared something.

"Wemmick," whispered Macdonald, "when the time comes, I want you to go down and post bail on my account."

"Oh, no, you must not do that."

"But, poor man, he is such a sorry sight, for this will break him and his family."

A short while later, Twaddell protested his innocence saying he was a married man with children and was a lawyer searching for clients, which was greeted with hollow laughs from those watching, and a slight smile from the bench. He was allowed bail in the amount of five hundred pounds after pleading with the magistrate that he not be kept in prison awaiting trial, although he had no idea whether he could raise the money.

Underneath the court, where constables and prisoners mingled in unhappy congress, Twaddell had broken down completely, when Wemmick appeared in front of him to post bail.

"We suggest you go back to Edinburgh promptly," said Wemmick. "You won't be in court till the next assizes."

"Did Macdonald do this for me?"

"Yes, unwisely in my view, Mr. Macdonald took pity on you."

"Tell him, I beg his forgiveness. As his fiancée knows Mr. Tulloch my senior, I hope he can put in a good word for me."

"A good word, sir? Did you not try to blackmail him? Get back over the border, you scoundrel."

As Hamish rode with Wemmick back to Little Britain, he remarked on how extraordinary that man's view of the world must be to ask for forgiveness in his situation.

"At least now we are sure that he is no longer a threat to the practice or to me in person. I must tell Susanna about this. I wonder whether what he pleaded is in fact true. It is certainly a line of defense, is it not, except that he would have to rely on the man he walked away with to give the right evidence.

"It gives me little pleasure to suggest it," continued Hamish, "but perhaps we can get Smythe to defend him when he is tried."

Wemmick laughed out loud. "That would certainly be good practice!"

Then Wemmick turned to Hamish as they walked into the office.

"I have been thinking that I would postpone my retirement, Hamish. After Old Pip died, I was very depressed and wanted to break all my connections here. But now I realize that, though I don't have children of my own, I do regard the Pip family as almost mine, and I feel I can give you another year or two, certainly until Smythe is settled."

"I cannot think about anything I would like to have heard more than that. Thank you, John, thank you. I am a novice lawyer. You have already helped me more than I can thank you for, and another year or so of your incalculably valuable wisdom and experience gives me hope I will survive."

"I am fortunate to be in good health, Hamish, and while contemplation of nature sounds attractive, I think that I would get tired of birdsong and barking foxes, even though Walworth is not what it was."

"That is such good news. I must now hurry. I am invited to dinner at Susanna's tonight. She hinted that she might have found a woman that might be suitable to marrying me, knowing my present proclivities."

"I hope that works for you, and for her if it is to be her. Perhaps you will find it impossible. Do you really want the responsibilities of fatherhood?"

"You know, I had never given it much thought, but since this Twaddell affair I think I could warm to it. Perhaps I should spend some time with Lachlan and Malcolm to test the waters."

"Ah well, a good month's work, I think. There is nothing more satisfactory to the law than exposing a hypocrite."

"I agree profoundly."

VII

It was St David's Day when an apprehensive Hamish arrived at Cheyne Row with a bunch of early daffodils for his hostess as Susanna had invited him to meet a prospective wife. How does one have a serious conversation with a woman on personal matters? Perhaps it will be just like talking to Susanna, he thought as he rang the bell. The maid opened the door and Pip appeared from the living room with a broad smile on his face.

Hamish asked if he could talk privately with him first. In the library, he told him the whole story about Twaddell, which left Pip thunderstruck. They would talk about it more fully later.

Hamish went into the living room with his nerves jangling. Susanna rose from her chair and introduced her old friend Mary Hamilton.

Hamish saw before him a woman of palpable distinction, her dark hair cascading over her shoulders, her eyes a brilliant blue, but clearly with an inoperative left arm which hung sadly down her left side.

"How d'ye do, Miss Hamilton."

"How d'ye do, Mr. Macdonald."

"Now," said Susanna, "Mary is my oldest friend. Our families were close, very close. We have known her since we were in swaddling clothes, and she was a considerable help to me when my parents died."

"Let me get to the point, Mr. Macdonald," said Mary in some haste.

"Susanna has told me of your situation. Once that discussion is over, we can enjoy the evening, whatever the future."

"Miss Hamilton, let me say I am as nervous as a kitten at meeting you. So, forgive me if my behavior reflects that."

"I am sure it will not.

"However, I was married to David, a dear man whom I not only loved but liked. We were young, we had splendid times together, but he found the intimate side of our marriage very difficult.

"Before I married him, I sensed that he would really prefer the love of a man to a woman, but he was so kind, so gentle, so good a friend that I was prepared to allow him to make what close friendships he wished. With a paralyzed arm since infancy, I was not in a position to have a wide choice."

"I can hardly believe that is true," said Hamish.

"Believe me, Mr. Macdonald, Pip's leg is the mark of a hero. My arm is the mark of something awry in my ancestry which can frighten even the best of men.

"That apart, I don't think David would have found our intimate life impossible. Indeed, for what it was I enjoyed it, thankful that at least there might be the prospect of children, which I feel is my destiny. But then, exactly two months after our marriage, David was crushed in the street by a runaway horse and carriage.

"Oh Mary," cried Hamish, "how dreadful."

"Indeed. That was four years ago now, and I have spent some time recovering from the shock. I have now decided I will marry again. I am here because Susanna, who is quite the dearest person I know, thinks that you and I might form a friendship which could lead to marriage. I could have children and you might be discreet about your lovers, though that is something we would need to discover."

"My dear Mary," said Hamish, "I have rarely heard such a tragic tale of sadness and I give you my most sincere commiserations. I do know what it is like to lose someone one loves whatever their strengths and weaknesses. I admire you for your courage and I would like to spend some time with you to see whether a friendship might grow. We need not, I think, take this discussion further now, but let us arrange to meet. I am sure our good friends here do not want to be burdened with our endeavors."

Pip smiled benignly and then intervened.

"This is a wonderful beginning which perhaps may blossom for both of you. But now, let us have some dinner."

They went into the dining room, which was carefully furnished with heavy dark Victorian furniture, an immense sideboard, and a candelabra glowing in front of a large mirror. The carpet was deep red, and the walls fashionably dark blue with white doors and heavy, velvet dark green curtains. A large mahogany gate-leg table was furnished with wedding presents of silver cutlery and Susanna's family dinner service with a small thistle in the middle of each plate, produced by a potter in Stoke-on-Trent. The main table had several leaves removed to make the occasion more intimate with just the four of them. The boys were not introduced, as they were being prepared for bed by Nanny Hopkins.

"What a charming room," said Hamish, "but I must tell you first of developments in the case of Mr. Twaddell, Susanna."

"You mean, I am no longer your fiancée?" she said with a smile.

"No, I fear not," he said returning the smile.

At that point he rehearsed the story's origins, the blackmail threat and Susanna's role as his fiancée. He then explained how Wemmick's informant had watched the arrest, Twaddell's appearance before the beak, how he arranged for bail, and how he intended to offer the scoundrel legal counsel for his trial.

"Now that kind of generosity impresses me greatly," said Mary.

"Me too," said Pip and Susanna in unison.

"Well, thank you," said Hamish.

"I am something of a sentimental man, Mary. I find myself ashamed when I see another human being in distress. Frankly I think Twaddell is a cruel man, obstinate, opinionated, and Janus-faced. I really do not know why he should court disaster in that way. Old Pip, bless his memory, warned me before he died about the consequences of unwise affiliations and meetings."

"How like my uncle, Hamish my friend," said Pip. "I regret I have been somewhat arrogant in the past about the fact of sodomy. I confess to being confused by my religion and indeed ignorant about what I will call the condition, but you have shown me that, while the condition itself is not a trivial matter, human beings are capable of great love and goodness. I thank you for yours."

"My husband, darling. How kind you are," cried Susanna, "and Hamish, how generous, how loving."

"Indeed," said Mary.

Conversation then spread to other topics, notably the work with prostitutes which was still not truly off the ground.

Pip was still concerned but amused by his recent experience at Numquam, and he thought he would share it first with Harriet, but with a couple of glasses of claret inside him, he opened his experience to this company."

"I went to see Estella the day before yesterday before coming back from my mother's. She was immensely cheerful, but there, looking very comfortable in the best living room chair, was her servant Nellie, my comrade Fletcher's wife, dressed in fine clothes.

"My astonishment was because when I first met her, she was a whore in Chatham, and she accosted me. Susanna and I helped the family to take over my father's forge and we later gave them counsel following the Whistler killing after Estella had hired her.

"Estella called her 'her poor darling' and, frankly, I was shocked and unable to grasp whatever it was going on, so I left somewhat hurriedly and rather impolitely."

"Presumably they are now lovers," said Mary, with a directness that Hamish admired but the remark took Pip aback.

"Really?" he said, his voice rising in temper.

"What on earth would my uncle have said about that? It can't be true. He has hardly been dead a year! What extraordinary disloyalty to this his memory! I am an innocent in these kinds of affairs. If it is true, it is monstrous, and I will not be in her company ever again.

"Think of the disgrace! Yet there is also her husband, my dear old comrade Fletch. How can Nellie so betray him?"

"It is certainly a great surprise and indeed somewhat shocking," said Susanna.

"I suppose she is very lonely after Old Pip's death," she continued. "Maybe Nellie is not quite the nice little abused woman we thought of her as, but a scheming she-devil after Estella's money. I'd guess she did the seducing, as it beggars the imagination to envision Estella initiating such a liaison."

"What completely foxes me," said Pip, "is that you ladies assume that their relationship is physical. I for one cannot grasp how she manages to turn to Sapphic love after such a strong intimate relationship with Old Pip.

"How can a woman, so to speak, switch from a man to a woman?"

"I have never been that way inclined myself," said Mary, "but I have been lonely since my David died, and I know the depths of depression that make one feel as though one is drowning.

"I do not know either of these women, but I can imagine a young woman with a whore's heart reaching out to a lonely older woman, compassion leading to contact and then to physical love. Then I suppose too that if one is in a disastrous marriage, one seeks love where one can find it," a remark which went like a rapier to Pip's heart, and he could not control a slight blush.

"A whore's heart?" Asked Hamish quietly, "good gracious, what is that?"

"I surmise that if one grew up as a whore," said Mary, "offering one's body for money to simply buy food and drink, one would become used to offering one's body to another if one recognized the light of desire in the other's countenance, particularly, as I said, if one became a whore at a young age. It becomes more than just a way of life.

"Of course, it would be a habit engendered in a woman after years of being abused by men, especially if it began at an early age so it is not a condition that is natural to a woman, far from it."

"Oh dear, I cannot imagine how dreadful it must be then to have this so-called heart of a whore," said Susanna, surprised by this analysis.

"On this account," said Hamish, mildly astonished by the quality of Mary's mind, "Nellie simply wanted Estella to enjoy affection, and noticed her distress at her husband's death. How indeed could one not?"

"Maybe," said Susanna, "but I am sticking to the she-devil account. Obviously, Pip saw an affectionate relationship quite different from that of a mistress to a maid servant."

"Yet what astonishes me," said Pip, "is that Estella as I have come to know her, that genteel, somewhat haughty lady, should risk her reputation by engaging in a Sapphic relationship. It is not that I disapprove of it, though I do, but I recognize, as I have been forced to recognize myself, that social conventions in such a matter can be overwhelming."

"I suppose it is easier for two women to keep their secret," said Hamish, "but it does occur to me that with Old Pip's death, she sees in Nellie a replacement for her murdered mother, a person she can look after, educate and love."

"Now that, dear Hamish," said Mary, "is a very acute observation. I recall Susanna telling me all about that killing.

"It does offer us a perspective on their relationship which, if one accepts the whore's heart notion, makes the affair not a matter of sheer lust or even waywardness, but a thoroughly understandable liaison."

"On that view," she continued, "one would sympathize with each of them and certainly not ostracize them, the remaining difficulty being the status of the relationship, given the presence of the husband. One must assume that they are comfortable with it. It is quite another matter whether he knows about it or tolerates it."

"I talked with him when I was there last week. He said Nellie was spending time with Estella, and that they were planning to work on prostitution in Chatham. But he did not seem upset at that engagement."

"Estella did say something of the sort at our lunch recently," replied Susanna.

"I think we should invite Estella to dinner so we can really plan to get this London work off the ground. Maybe that will give her the opportunity to explain Nellie to us. Not that we have any right to know."

"Perhaps, but Albert surely does," said Pip.

"Who is Albert?" asked Mary.

"Her nineteen-year-old step-son."

"H'mm, I am not sure it is any of his business," said Mary.

As he went home, Hamish was full of hope for a relationship with Mary. He was astounded by her frankness on several occasions, displaying a woman of great intellect, charity, spirit and good sense.

The following afternoon, however, Pip went to see Harriet and over the afternoon, he told her of seeing Nellie dressed as a lady at Numquam. Like Mary, she was not at all shocked, regarding the situation as quite natural.

"I am not a person to submit to conventions of almost any sort, not that I know either of the women involved either, of course."

"Hamish suggested that Estella has found in Nellie a replacement for her mother, and that Nellie was simply a whore at heart, responding to anyone who looked at her with desire."

"That is a satisfactory notion, said Harriet, "except for the little matter of the husband."

"When we first met them," said Pip, "Fletch told me that when they were starving, Nellie went back on the streets to get money for the pair of them, though not after the children were born of course."

"Maybe he knows but does not care about his wife's liaison with the lady at the big house. Positively he may value her freedom. God knows women need it."

But matters then turned more serious.

Sitting next to him on the sofa, stroking his coat with her hand while lying on his shoulder, Harriet continued, "I am afraid, my darling, that I am in love with you, besotted with you, and I want you for myself. Realizing this, but also being unable to face wrecking your marriage, I am leaving for Florence as soon as I have made the arrangements."

"I hoped we could continue as we are."

"No, Pip, this is not a good arrangement. You will be, no—you now are, a married man with a mistress in the eyes of society. I will not let you become a man living a lie. Deceitful. Packing lie upon lie to cover your immoral behavior. You are too good a man to get swallowed up into that rigmarole of conflict.

"Indeed, let us suppose that your marriage really did break down over me. Do we think we could enjoy a future with the guilt and remorse that would inevitably bring? I do not see you abandoning your children and, indeed, being able to give up the intimacy of your family.

"I do understand," said Pip quietly, "and I have started to feel already the burdens of deceiving Susanna as with my visit to Biddy. I simply ignored my conscience and, at the time, thought the deceit was very enticing.

"What could be easier, even if ever so slightly corrupt? Yet I so desire you, I need you so much," at which tears came to his eyes and he sobbed and sobbed while she ran her fingers through his reddish beard.

"Oh, my dear Pip. Ours has been such a delicious intimacy, like nothing else I have known. We must end our loving to retain our integrity as people too, but also as lovers. Ours is a love which respects boundaries, I think. The freedom we had in Salford now has such boundaries. That we will continue to want each other, I have no doubt."

"But one more time," said Pip, "please."

"No, my dear, we must resist that temptation and begin as we mean to carry on."

They got up, put their arms around each other and murmured goodbyes with friendly kisses. "Promise me one thing," said Pip. "If you are ever in real distress, you will call on me for help."

"I promise."

He walked out into the rain a chastened man, determined now to heal any breaches with Susanna and to appreciate his good fortune that this wonderful woman had such moral character, even if it seemed to have been a little shaky from time to time, but to his benefit.

Early that March when her chores were over, Nellie sat on the large settee with Estella's head in her lap, purring like a kitten as she stroked and caressed her lover, a hand running through the older woman's hair. They had not been to bed together for some weeks, each content to bask in the other's affection. Not that their desires were sated, but that they had reached this relaxing level of comfort with each other. No longer mistress and servant, but lovers and companions.

"I've been thinking," said Nellie. "We've been sort of together for a few months now, and I really think I must tell Fletch about us. As I told you, he was fine with me whorin' so as we could live, so I don't see why he wouldn't be alright with me lovin' you."

"But maybe he is missing you around the house, though, you don't come every day and then, only for afternoons."

"Oh, I know he don't mind me coming and he's pleased I have rings and dresses, but he don't know we have been bedding together. So, I think, my love, I must tell him where we are and if he objects, well, I suppose I'll have to stop going to bed with you."

"Oh dear, really? You are so sensuous a creature, so alive with passion and we have worked out how to really enjoy ourselves? Some nights I am simply aghast at loving you as I never dreamt that I could make love with a woman, yet it has felt so natural, so easy, so delightful."

"It's fantastic, and it is quite different from Fletch and me."

"Oh, no, don't talk about you and him, my imagination is quite enough."

"Oh, go on, I'd love to tell you'se what we do," she said, giggling.

"Sometime, then, but not today."

"You tell him whatever you want, my darling, and I'll hear all about it when I come back."

As she approached her cottage in the cart, Nellie was trying to decide how and when to tell Fletch, the man of her heart. She decided with her usual guile to wait till they had slaked their passions and were lying quietly together, exhausted, but immensely fulfilled.

"Fletch,"

"Yes, my love."

"Can I tell you something?'

"Of course," he said sleepily.

"I've been to bed with Mrs. Pirrip."

"Really, that must have been fun."

"No, seriously, we've been lovers for a while now."

"Really, what do you do?"

"Oh, you know, but it's very different from you and me."

"Well, she gives you rings and dresses, so you'se go to give her something back and I expect she enjoys a bit of your lovely body."

"You don't mind?

"Why should I mind?" he said, turning over toward her.

"Now if it was a fellow, not some rich old bird whose husband has just died, I'd be livid, probably beat you and chuck you down the stairs. No, of course not, but why would I be jealous of her? And if you like it, I don't see no problem.

Anyway," and he yawned loudly, "just don't stay out too late as I need my supper on the table, same with the kids. Night, night darling, 'fun tomorrow' as my mum used to say."

He turned back on his side and was asleep in an instant.

Surprised at this completely unexpected response, she turned over, wrapped her arms around her husband's waist warming her body against his and fell asleep.

When she awoke, she could hear the anvil being assaulted, so she threw on a slip and went downstairs to make some breakfast.

When the children had been packed off to school, Fletch came in and sat down for his breakfast.

"I was thinking this morning about you and the old lady."

"What about it, Fletch?"

"Like I said, I'm not really bothered, not least because I thinks you'll get tired of it. Or she will."

"That's happening already. I mean, we like each other's company and we're fond of each other, but we haven't done it for weeks."

"There is one thing that would really upset me, Nell, and that is if anyone else knew.

"If anyone knows, everyone knows. That's just how it is around here. Imagine going into the Bargemen and everyone knowing about you and her. Think of the jokes, the looks we'd get. What would folks say about me?"

"Blimey, you're right, ain't you? I'd never thought of that, I don't know whether any of her London set know, but Mr. Pip what was your comrade called in the other day when I was there, and he might have suspected something."

"Oh, Christ, Nell! See, that's what upsets me. You must tell her it's over and stop going there.

"Well, I can go to work when she's not there, can't I?"

"Yeah, I suppose so, but I'd rather not, make a clean break. But you must tell her why. I don't care what you do with her in bed, but I do care a lot whether people knew and gossiped. I mean, does her maid know? Does her cook know?"

"Oh, no, we've never done it when they're around. She don't want anyone to know either, she don't. Well, she's gone to London today and I must go up there and clean this afternoon."

But when Nellie arrived at the house, Estella had not gone to London but had decided to delay her visit for a day. She was in her library reading and she heard Nellie arrive. Estella was immediately charged with lust and desire, and called Nellie in.

"Darling, come here," she said, and pulling the younger woman down on to her knee, began to kiss her passionately, loosen her hair and bury her head in her breasts. Nellie could not help but respond, in part because it had been so long. They got up and, holding hands, hurried up to the bedroom, their passions over-whelming them.

"I've got somefink to tell you, Estella," Nellie said afterwards.

"Oh, how lovely, you've never called me Estella before."

"I know, but this is serious. We must stop. That was the last time."

"But darling…"

"No, it's like this, see.

"I told Fletch last night and he is fine with you and me making love as he would not be if you was a man. He said he'd throw me down the stairs! Have fun is his attitude. But this morning he said that we should stop because, if anyone found out about us, it would become common talk and he would have all the jokes and nonsense thrown at him.

"He couldn't go into the Bargemen even alone or with me if it was well known about you and me. We would have to move some-where else if that happened. He's a proud man and he don't want people knowing his wife is sleeping with a woman."

"He is right, of course. I never gave him any thought."

"I mean, he's real worried that Mr. Pip saw us the other day as I was not there like a servant, was I?"

"No, that's true, but I will be meeting him shortly and will gauge his reaction."

"You see, it is fine for you. If anyone found out, you could go and live in London or move somewhere else. We can't do that with-out upsetting everything we have built."

"You're right. I am just going to have to bear the loss of you."

"And me too, you know, and he wants me to stop working here."

"Oh, surely not, does that matter?"

"He just thinks it should be, what did he say, a clean break."

Estella turned over and looked at this beautiful woman, her hair all askew, her body white and clear, and gently ran her hands all over her, touching her sorrowfully tip to toe, as if saying goodbye to every nook and cranny:

"I do love you, my dear Nellie. You have brought me such comfort, pulling me away from the grief of losing Pip. We will see each other from time to time, I am sure, and look at each other and remember. You must go now."

Nellie hurriedly dressed, had one last lingering kiss, and got in the cart and rode back to Fletch, who came out from the Forge to greet her.

"Well?" he said.

"It's all done, it's over. She took it very well, saying she'd never given you a thought and she saw what a danger it would be if anyone knew. I'm not going there again," at which she burst into tears, howling like a spoilt child making a demand.

He tried to comfort her, but she pushed him away and walked to the other side of cottage, continuing to weep copiously, sitting on the stump of an old tree. Fletch left her alone and went back to his anvil.

Half an hour or so passed and she appeared at the Forge door, her face flush with her drying tears.

"I do love her, you know. She's given me so much. But I do love you, too. You are my real love," and she kissed him deeply, pulling his face down to hers and rubbing her hands on his neck.

"I know, sweetheart," he said, as he comforted her, "but this is for the best."

Estella too wept some tears after Nellie was gone. Yet she soon pulled herself together quickly, accepting such a turn of events, as she had always done since she met Pip. Hurriedly she prepared herself to travel to London where she arrived at Semper House the following afternoon. On the hall table among other correspondence was a message to go to Susanna's for dinner. Life was nothing if not full.

She had sent a note by post to Hamish, saying she would call the next day and hoped he'd be free. He had not yet left for Scotland as Mary wanted to stay a bit longer with Susanna, partly because of her curiosity about this woman Estella, whom she would meet at Susanna's.

VIII

Estella was at breakfast with Albert after his month in Paris at Henry's invitation, but he returned as he did not want to show any impropriety. It was now early April and Estella could tell that Albert was anxious, though whether about Elizabeth or about his wish for adventure, she could not say.

"Sadly, Elizabeth has had to stay in Versailles with her father," Albert said. "As a diplomat's daughter she could have a safe conduct to come here, but it would be safer to postpone it. Much of France is in German hands and Paris will be under siege if *The Times* is right. I would like to go back there to be with Elizabeth, but I cannot ask for accommodation in the embassy again. I lack adventure, Estella, I want to go back and I hope I have your blessing."

"My dear Albert, our experience of war is that of Young Pip, but he was an active participant, not a voyeur. I am sure you can get some diplomatic protection. When do you plan to leave?"

"As soon as possible and with your consent, but it will be difficult if the Prussians have attacked Paris. Then I would have to go south out of the city."

"Well, you have all the money your father willed to you but visit your bankers and see how it is best to carry the wherewithal these days. I am sure that sovereigns will make sense but ask them. What is your real purpose here: adventure or being with Elizabeth?"

"Both, but mainly the latter. I am just nineteen, she's a year older and we do plan to marry soon. I anticipate asking her father for her hand while I am there. But I have been reading about groups of painters in and around Paris who are painting, as they say, *en plein air.* I think that is a wonderful idea and would like to see them in action."

"That would be thrilling, but I do hope it's not dangerous. I like her aunt Charlotte very much, by the way, and Elizabeth is a charming girl of great talents. Your father would have been excited for you, too."

"I think so too. Can we visit Highgate again together before I go? I found that last visit so comforting. The stone should be in place now too, shouldn't it?"

"Yes; indeed, let us go there this afternoon."

As they rode north to Highgate Cemetery in Estella's carriage, Albert asked:

"Are you happy, Estella? You were at Numquam a long time and I was preoccupied with my painting and with Elizabeth, so I fear I have not been attending to you."

"That is very kind of you. I am so pleased that you show your concern for me once again. I have been content at Numquam, but now I must get on with the project. I continue to mourn your father, but I am getting accustomed to my widowhood. But I must also tell you something which I hope will not shock you."

"I have found I am not easily shocked. It seems that artists exist to break boundaries of convention. You will not believe some of the behaviors I hear about. However, please tell me."

"I formed a strong loving acquaintance with a young woman that is now over."

"Excellent; so you have not been lonely down there in Kent."

"No, indeed. My lover was Nellie Fletcher."

"Yes, I think I met her once; she is really beautiful, though she had a hard life, I think."

"It does not upset you?"

"Why should it? My father once told me all about Hamish and pointed out that we should find love where we may, provided we do not risk our other obligations. But you and Nellie Fletcher had no such obligations, so you were free to love as you wish."

"Well, we have ceased to be lovers, even companions for the moment, aware that any gossip would badly affect Mr. Fletcher's business."

"That sounds very wise to me. But do you like Elizabeth's aunt, Mrs. Mudge? Perhaps she could be your new lover."

"Good heavens, no."

"She certainly is a strong person. She had asked me so many questions, grilling me like a lawyer, but now is fully supportive of our eventual marriage."

"That is a relief, as she would be a formidable foe."

It had become a very cold day, even for April. Arm in arm, they walked closely together down the path to see the two graves, those of Pip her husband and his father, and Beatrice, his mother. An elderly man was standing near Beatrice's grave after laying flowers there.

"Excuse me, sir," said Albert as they approached. "I am Albert Pirrip, and Beatrice was my mother."

"Oh, Albert, how wonderful to meet you after all these years. I am Algernon Pocket, Beatrice's father."

"How d'ye do, then. This is Mrs. Estella Pirrip, my father's second wife."

They exchanged greetings.

"How come," asked Albert, "we have lost touch?"

"Your father brought you as a young child to see us in Hackney and my wife Sybilla, now long dead, saw him as a villain who had brought about Beatrice's death by getting her pregnant so frequently, but your mother just had physical difficulties resulting in her miscarriages.

"But Sybilla was very rude to Pip in her distress at her favorite daughter's death, and she swore she would never see him or you, Albert, ever again. Since she died in 1865, I have not thought further about meeting you as I did not know where you were. But you look a fine young gentleman, and I must say, with a look of your mother. Let me put my arms around you. This is quite overwhelming."

He held Albert fast in his arms, murmuring "my boy, my boy" as Estella stood by.

"Tell me about yourself."

"Shall we complete our separate visits here," said Estella, "and then have some refreshment elsewhere so that we can talk?"

"Of course, of course," said Mr. Pocket and he wandered away toward the gate, stumbling on his cane as he went.

"What a coincidence, Albert. Here you now have a new family connection. He is your grandfather."

"I can hardly comprehend this. I have not thought about him for years!"

"I am surprised his cousin Herbert has not been in touch since Pip died. Good lord, how complicated relationships are," she said, touching the new stone memorial.

They found a small cafe to have a cup of tea and some cakes near the gates.

"Tell me, what is in your life, Albert?" asked Algernon.

"I want to be a painter, so I am going to Paris to be with my dear love Elizabeth, whose father is a diplomat there.

"What a wonderful adventure."

"When did my grandmother die—1865, did you say?"

"Yes. After Beatrice died, she seemed to go into a steady decline and found little comfort in her other children, now both married."

"I am sorry, but I would like to visit you when I return from France, and I will keep in touch."

"Excellent. Are you financially secure? Might you consider later joining me in the family business, as neither of my own children have shown any interest? The expansion of London has made me quite a rich man and I was considering opening a design business to which your artistic flair might contribute."

"It's early days, grandfather, but I will consider it carefully."

Throughout this, Estella was silent. She felt great pity for the man, who seemed a gentle sort, obviously finding widowhood difficult. She briefly thought she might meet him just because he was so lonely, but then thought not.

"How very odd," said Albert, as they were driving back. "My grandmother on that side was clearly uninterested in seeing me, the child of her favorite daughter, just because she blamed my father, and quite wrongly I am sure."

"Yes, there is an expression about cutting off one's nose to spite one's face which I think fits her attitude. How could she not want to meet a fine young man like you and clearly destroy her family happiness in the process? But you will meet him again."

Hamish had heard about Estella's relationship with Nellie from the party at which he met Mary. She entered his office looking exceptionally beautiful, immaculately dressed in the height of fashion.

"Good morning, Hamish."

"Good morning, Estella, you are looking radiant this morning."

"Yes indeed, we need to get on with this project. Nellie and I investigated Chatham, but it was not really possible until we had something going in London, so I will stay here for a while to work. Have you got anywhere with the male side of the project?"

"Not really, as there have been some major developments of which you are unaware.

"First, we have appointed a lawyer whom you will meet later, but we rejected a candidate who then tried to blackmail me and we were able to kill that endeavor with Susanna's help."

"Goodness gracious, tell me more about that, it sounds exciting."

"In due course but let me go on. Second, I realized that my sexuality was a threat to the legacy that Jaggers and your husband left, and that the only way to circumvent that would be for me to marry."

"Marry? Great Heavens, why on earth would you do that?'

"It is a complicated matter. Whoever I marry would have to know of my desires, and I have been introduced to a widowed old friend of Susanna's who was married to a man like me."

"Wait, this is getting too much for me. You have been introduced to a woman who would marry you, knowing you were a sodomite? My head is spinning."

"Yes, and you will meet her at Susanna's, and we are then going to spend several days in Scotland exploring each other and seeing if there is any compatibility."

"What? Surprise on surprise yet again."

"But that is not all."

"You mean there is more? I am going to have to lie down after this onslaught of news."

"The blackmailer I told you of, one Twaddell, was spotted by one of Wemmick's informants consorting with male prostitutes and the police arrived just as he was leaving with a young man. I bailed Twaddell out and sent him back to Edinburgh. He told the beak he was looking for clients."

"I should never have buried myself in the Kentish countryside with all this going on. But surely you will not defend him when he comes to court, as he is a blackmailer?"

"Ah, the milk of human kindness? Wemmick and I think we might give our new young lawyer that opportunity. But to our project. Wemmick has located the identity of the young man whom Twaddell was talking to. Not a difficult search as the man was also arrested."

"Wait. Wait. Please. This is all too much for an old woman. First, who is the new lawyer?"

"Well, he is not yet a partner, though that will no doubt come. I'll call him in, you must meet him. His full name is Clarence Fotheringaye-Smythe, but he likes to be called simply Clarence or Mr. Smythe."

Hamish went to the door and told Robert to ask Mr. Smythe to come to his office.

Clarence duly appeared and Hamish introduced him:

"Smythe, this is Estella Pirrip, Mr. Pip's wife, he who was a bastion of strength in this practice until his untimely death. She knew Mr. Jaggers very well indeed and, believe me, if she were not a woman, she would be an adornment to the English Bar. Her advocacy of causes is unrivalled."

"Stuff and nonsense, Hamish. But I am delighted to meet you, Mr. Smythe, and I am sure we will have much to share as we start this project."

"It is a pleasure to meet you, ma'am. I have heard so much about Mr. Pip, and I offer you my sincere condolences."

"Thank you, Mr. Smythe. Tell me, which part of the country do you hail from?"

"Ah, I have been working in London, but the family properties are in the Kentish Weald, at least such as remain. It is a pleasure to meet you."

Smythe then left and Hamish continued:

"Twaddell's consort, if I can call him that, will prove of great value in getting entry to the male prostitution community, just as Nellie has given us ideas about the females' activities. The man is a mere sixteen years old, called Jack Masham."

"Well, well, well. What a catalogue of events. Indeed, I am nothing if not flabbergasted. Shall we now go to look at the building Pip has found for us, while I digest all of this news on the way?"

"The building is a first step and perhaps we can survey the streets as well, though, as you will recall, Wemmick advised us to have a bodyguard."

They arrived at the Jaggers Building, now so-called as it was the property of the Trust, to find Pip there discussing furniture with a merchant. Pip told them that most of the beds were ordered, and a large room had been set aside for medical help. There were a couple of offices and while the project would be directed by Hamish and Estella, there would be two full-time people doing the basic work.

"How about nurses?" asked Estella.

"I think we need to find a couple of doctors to give us advice on that. I have sent out a query to all London hospitals asking for volunteers. But I am anxious to put together the staff before we get out in the streets. We need to be properly ready for clients before we recruit."

"Of course," said Estella.

Nevertheless, Hamish and she tried to take the carriage nearer the area, but the conditions were impossible, as they observed from the end of the street they had proposed to traverse. It was not only too narrow to accommodate the carriage: Conditions were hellish. Filth in the street which seemed to be a sewer. Semi-naked young children playing in mud. Women hanging around the doors of hovels. A drunken sailor came up to the carriage and banged on the door, screaming obscenities.

"This is going to be more of an effort than we thought," said Estella. "Let us retreat now and plan different ways to engage with the women when the building is finally ready."

"Yes indeed," said Hamish. "I wish I were a brave man."

"Fiddlesticks," Estella replied.

Charlotte Mudge had long planned a dinner and her invitation thwarted Susanna's own plans for another party on St. George's Day, but they amicably decided it was Charlotte's turn, though it was not an arrangement to satisfy the conventional in terms of a balance of men and women. Her niece Elizabeth was there, and Estella had been asked to bring Albert; the Gargerys, of course, as well as Mary and Hamish.

Estella had warmed to Charlotte as a most gracious lady who was now a true friend. She offered her guests whisky before dinner, which surprised Estella since she had not drunk whisky since those evenings with Molly. It was so delicious and so calming, and, as an acquaintance from Aberdeen had once told her, whisky is cheap at any price.

After dinner, Albert and Elizabeth headed for the small music room, leaving just Charlotte, Susanna and Pip, Estella, Hamish and Mary.

"Susanna," Charlotte asked, "have you seen the book by Mr. Carroll, *Alice in Wonderland?*"

"Oh, yes, is it not marvelous? Though Lachlan prefers something more adventurous or practical."

"That is very interesting, and this Mr. Carroll is somewhat of a mystery," Charlotte continued. "Carroll is a pen name, I am told, he is actually a Dr. Charles Lutwidge Dobson who studies and teaches mathematics in Oxford. But he is also a keen photographer, particularly of young girls, and the stories are written for the daughter of the Dean."

"Tell me," said Hamish quizzically, "he takes photographs of young girls only?"

"It appears so, Hamish."

"Oh," Mary interrupted with her usual candor, "perhaps he finds them of sexual interest."

"Really?" said Estella. "I am learning so much about the ways of the world these days, blackmail, male prostitutes, and now little girls. I must be an innocent abroad."

"Oh, Estella," said Mary, "people seem to find all manner of ways in letting their desires flow free. Perhaps there are some prostitutes who not only enjoy the life but develop the sense that they are there to please men who want them. I am offering an explanation, of course, not a seal of approval."

"Do you plan to meet with whores before offering your project's services?" Charlotte inquired.

"I have been very lucky in that respect," said Estella.

At that response, Pip and Susanna listened very carefully.

"I have a quite beautiful young woman who works for me. You know her, don't you, Pip, Susanna?" They nodded.

"I have been teaching her to read and write, and she is such a lovely person that I have bought some dresses for her. She used to be a whore in the Chatham docks, and she has the most terrible history as a child, abused in ways that beggar the imagination. In fact, she accosted Pip when he was a young farrier, didn't she, Pip?"

He nodded.

"I have learnt a good deal from her about conditions for prostitutes. It was she who suggested we concentrate on medical services and on accommodation, primarily for women who have been beaten up either by their husbands or their customers. Over the months she has become more of a companion to me rather than a servant, and there is a mutual respect and love between us."

"That sounds delightful, Estella," said Mary. "Are you lovers?"

The room fell silent. Estella gazed at the ceiling. Charlotte looked shocked. Pip looked down, but Susanna intervened:

"Mary, I really do not think that is any of your business."

"I am terribly sorry if I have caused offence. It was not my intention, but Estella seemed so close to this young woman that my question seemed a natural one. After all, in this household we have not been shy about talking on matters of sex and love, have we?"

"Indeed," said Pip, "I think we are all close friends just because we can talk openly about these matters, but I would certainly not push Estella to declare one way or the other."

"But Mary dear," said Hamish, "the question did sound more prying than sympathetic. Now you all know about me but Estella has had a long and happy marriage, so she will want to keep private her relationship with Nellie, whatever it is. She was only answering Charlotte's question about how she comes to have knowledge of prostitution."

"Alright," said Estella, "Alright. Let me gather my wits about me."

She hesitated.

"Before I fell properly in love with my husband, Pip, I trusted no one, no one at all. I was proved right to be circumspect. For instance, Jaggers, my lawyer, had concealed my natural mother from me for over twenty years. Now I am an old woman, nearer the end of my life than the beginning.

"There are six of us here. I don't really know Mary well yet. I know Charlotte and Hamish of course, but I am prepared to trust you all just as I trust Pip and Susanna, but I must swear you all to secrecy and a promise that you will not discuss what I am about to say with anyone, including between yourselves. Do you all promise?"

There was a unison: "I do."

"I was very lonely indeed after my dear Pip's death. I particularly missed his warmth in bed and our intimacy. You see, such intimacy, its excitement, its delirious experiences, was new to me until I met him in my early forties, though I knew him from childhood.

"Now I had known Nellie for a while as she came regularly to clean the formal rooms of my house and she was almost murdered in my drawing room, so we had a close bond. In that period, she was an immense comfort to me, being very solicitous for my welfare, and I came to admire her. She was very upset for me at Pip's death. I think she is a beautiful woman, and when I broke down from time to time, she would hug and hold me which I found delightful.

"I gave her a ring that belonged to my guardian which I did not want.

"I bought her dresses when we were thinking of starting our project in Chatham and I needed a guide.

"One day she arrived to clean the house and she had been caught in pouring rain. She was absolutely drenched, and I took her to my bedroom to change her clothes.

"While she undressed, I searched for some clothes and when I returned to my bedroom, she was naked, as if she had risen like the Botticelli Venus from the waves."

Charlotte clapped her hands to her mouth at this, and Susanna gasped. Pip blushed. Both Hamish and Mary looked quizzically straight at Estella, showing no emotion.

"Quite simply, she sensed that at that moment I wanted her and that, as a whore from childhood, when she saw someone wanted her she offered herself to me. We became secret lovers. It was an overwhelming delight for me, for it was not until my reunion with my mother ignited my passion for Pip that I had felt properly about my body. This experience with Nellie was new but intensely desirable. I am in fact very proud of our love."

Mary stopped her.

"Estella, that is the most tender and loving story I think I have ever heard. Thank you so much for trusting me. I will not let you down."

"Thank you, Mary. But the end of the affair is of particular importance. This week we have agreed to halt our close relationship. Her husband was at first quite happy for us to be lovers as it was not a threat to him, but he then realized, as I had not, that if anyone got to know of our relationship it would spread like wildfire in the community, and he could well be a laughingstock and lose his business.

"Neither Nellie nor I want that and in any event in recent weeks we agreed we would not see each other which is immensely sad, but necessary. More than that, if it were to become common knowledge, Nellie would also be damaged through her husband's suffering.

"So, there you have it. It is not me that you would damage were you to gossip about Nellie and me, but first and foremost her totally innocent husband."

"Mary spoke for all of us, Estella," said Susanna. "You have had the most interesting, even dramatic life so far, and your secret is quite safe with us. Pip and I talked about his visit to you, and we speculated that Nellie was not really some kind of replacement for Pip, but for your mother."

"Quite so," said Estella. "The similarities were extraordinary and what I was able to do for each of them were very similar: Filial love for my mother, and Sapphic love for my Nellie, my lovely, beautiful whore."

The room was silent once again.

"How about you, Hamish?" asked Mary, anxious to hear his views on everything if she were to marry him.

"Oh, Mary, I am a sentimental man, and this is such a splendid love story. Its end makes me want to weep, however. For is it not tragic that two people who love each other cannot satisfy their longing because of the social dangers we may note, not even because the husband prohibits it? Gossip is so damaging an evil."

"I agree with everything that has been said," said Pip, the picture of Harriet burning in his mind. "I have one question. Do you intend to tell Albert?"

"I have told him, and he was undisturbed, remembering that his father had taught him about the importance of love."

They all smiled at this.

"But thank you all for your understanding. I now realize I have no need to feel lonely with such friends."

"Estella, my dear," said Charlotte, "this is an evening I will always treasure as I have never witnessed such bravery—bravery because opening yourself up to your very close secret was a very high risk. You courted significant danger with style."

IX

When they met later on May Day, Hamish said, "I cannot decide, Mary, whether we should plan to walk from town to town, say from Inverness to Fort William, deep in the Scottish Highlands, or whether we should stay at an Inn somewhere and undertake walks from there."

"You are very ambitious, Hamish, I like walking in Hyde Park, but I am afraid a walking holiday would not be comfortable for me. Why don't we stay in Edinburgh as we originally planned for three nights, and then we can see where we are?"

"I think that will suit us very well, Mary."

After several such meetings where compromises were made, Mary told Susanna of their gist and the two friends discussed the marriage possibilities.

"I suspect poor Hamish is terrified at the prospect of getting to know you, though he obviously likes and admire you."

"Well, we both have infirmities, but as it is his first time, he may well find marriage a daunting prospect."

"What about you, dear Mary?

"I have no qualms whatever. He is thoroughly delightful, interesting, compassionate and well-mannered to a fault. He's handsome, of good Scottish stock and I can imagine beautiful children I would bear with his parentage."

"Is it not a terrible risk?" asked Susanna. "might such children come to know of his proclivity? Would he change? Is that even possible? I doubt that."

"It is a risk, of course. If it comes about, the dangerous side of a marriage like ours would be his falling in love with another man such that our married life would just be an empty shell, his thoughts constantly being elsewhere, the children neglected, let alone me."

"Did you not experience this worry with David?"

"No, Susanna, but threats exist in every marriage. Perhaps I should wait to find a man who loves women, and me in particular. But enough of me, tell me about Estella."

Susanna then said what she knew about Estella. She had discovered the whole story of her life from Pip, as he had heard it all from his mother years ago.

"Goodness gracious," said Mary on hearing the story, "what strength and yet what weakness, and this sublimation of desire only to be awakened by her mother and, my oh my, what a story that was too. Do you think I was too abrupt in asking her directly about her lover?"

"I was dumbfounded when you asked, but your question yielded such frankness, such truths, such courage."

"It might not have done. I have often been criticized, especially by my parents, for this quirk of being straightforward and inquisitive. My brother Cecil loved me for it and enjoyed provoking me frequently into some indiscreet remark when I was young."

"Where is he now?"

"Pioneering in America raising cattle with Maggie his wife. I miss him. I wonder what Hamish would make of Cecil, but I know he would be fascinated to discover what Hamish thinks about me for my rather direct way of conversation. I will write about that in my quarterly letter.

"By the way, Susanna, do I sense that you are expectant with a child?

"Indeed. I desperately hope it is a daughter this time."

"Congratulations to you both, the world needs more strong women."

"I don't want to tell Pip yet."

❧ ❧ ❧

Hamish went to the office with a certain glow about Mary, and Wemmick greeted him with a shoal of briefs. Smythe was called in and the briefs were spread out.

"I have told Mr. Smythe of the Twaddell case and I think he is excited at the prospect, eh, Mr. Smythe?"

"Yes, indeed. Let me put it like this. I will call on the young man Masham after I have found out from him what one hopes will be the truth. Of course, prosecuting counsel may get there first. Masham is himself to be tried, so it might make sense for me to defend him as well.

"Merely gathering as a group is not an offence, and the police rounding up suspects without proof is like trout-fishing with a net, not a fly. The whole business strikes me as rotten. I may well have to refuse to defend Twaddell once I talk with Masham."

"Hmm," said Wemmick. "Be careful about anything that could be interpreted as an attack on the police. Use the 'we all make mistakes sometimes' argument about them if you must whilst praising them as defenders of our women's honor, etc. etc."

"That is essential, Clarence, but talk with Masham," Hamish added. "He has not been bailed, so it will be easy to meet him."

"I will do that now," he replied, "unless we need to talk further."

Clarence Smythe left the room full of energy for this assignment.

"When are you off to Scotland then, Hamish?" asked Wemmick.

"Quite soon, I think. We plan to have two nights in Edinburgh and then go over to Loch Lomond, I think, but we spend time tossing around options."

"You'll be taking the Flying Scotsman, then?"

"We will, but a daytime journey, not overnight."

"It sounds wonderful. I am taking Mrs. Wemmick to Brighton on Saturday. We have not been on a train, so it will be an excitement and we hope our aging hearts can stand it.

"But how is your courtship going with Miss Hamilton?"

"Good, I think. You know her history, of course. She is extremely outspoken, which I both admire and fear. Not that I am frightened of her opinions, merely her questions. She can ask the most provocative questions out of genuine interest, but they can sound aggressive, rude or just plainly offensive."

"Oh dear, no doubt with your lawyer's guile, you can temper that tendency."

"Perhaps, but you will appreciate that it is all something of an adventure for me."

"I can see that. Of course, being a lawyer's clerk these many years and witnessing all kinds of human foibles, nothing really surprises me, though I must confess that yours is a dilemma I have not previously encountered."

"Her worries are obvious, I am sure. For me, I could see her putting my children against me if I deviated from my marriage. I could see myself, in my worst moments, becoming extremely unhappy, trapped like many a woman into an unhappy marriage. In such circumstances, leaving her would expose my proclivities to people and if she decided to divorce me, such a legal affair might eventually land me in jail."

"Come, come, Hamish, your Scottish visit will blow the wind out of such dire possibilities, I am sure. But in your case, as *Punch* recently had it: 'Marry in haste, repent at leisure.'"

"There too, I am very mixed. In one mood, I would marry her tomorrow. In another, I will wait years. Very provoking."

"If you are truly uncertain or not prepared to take the risks, please don't marry her, as you would end by hurting her as much as wounding yourself."

"Yes, that is true. Thank you, Wemmick, as ever for your sage advice."

"At least you are both old enough not to need to travel to Gretna Green."

"No indeed," said Hamish, "I love that place, as a symbol of Scottish obstinacy. It was only recently that I discovered its origins. Before 1774, girls could marry at 12, boys at 14 with or without parental consent. Scotland did not comply to the more English restrictive laws, so Gretna Green became the destination for elopers. Perhaps we will visit there just to see what the fuss is about, and perhaps even witness a wedding or two."

Pip and Susanna were returning from their walk to Chiswick along the river, greeting the Meggisons and talking briefly with them. It was a beautiful autumn day with its mists on the river, and the stench of London being blown by the west wind toward the North Sea. The mid-day post had arrived and with it a note from Harry Shoreham to say Biddy had fallen ill 'with her heart' as he put it.

Reading this to Susanna, she agreed that he must get down to Kent forthwith. He boarded a later afternoon train at Victoria Station and got a carriage to take him to Blue Boar Inn where he left his luggage, and then on in a trap to the Shorehams' small cottage in All Hallows.

She was lying in her bed, asleep.

"What's wrong, Harry?" He asked.

"I don't rightly know, Pip. She was fine yesterday, but then she had a funny turn in the night, saying she had a pain in her chest. My neighbor, Mr. Hardcastle, sent a message to a doctor in Chatham and he came this afternoon, but he said there was nothing he could do, and there was something wrong with her heart. Just to rest and keep her quiet. I asked him if she would survive, and he said he thought it wouldn't be long."

"Is that Pip?" said a very thin voice from the bed.

"Coming Mother, you don't seem well."

"No, Pip dear chap, I think I am going to meet my Maker, praise the Lord. But you mustn't be sad for me, Pip, I'se had a wonderful life, and you were my blessed little chap we loved so much. But I've something to tell you before I go."

"You just rest now, and we will talk about it later."

"No, I need to get it off my chest. I loved your father very much. Joe was a good man. But I was first in love with Old Pip wot you called your uncle, and he promised he would be my husband but then he went off to be a gentleman. We was all looking after Joe's first wife, Georgina, when she was attacked. So Old Pip and me, we was very close in them days."

"Oh, yes, I remember his saying as much."

"I was so pleased because I hated Estella, his going to Miss Havisham's and all. When he was 'prenticed, we went for a walk one afternoon. I suppose we must have been about fifteen, and we was walking along that track to the Battery, you know, don't you, and he said, now as he was 'prenticed, he asked me to marry 'im when we were older and had some money. I said yes and we kissed.

Pip smiled and said, "now that surprises me, Mother," in a vain effort to cheer her.

"But then all of a sudden, he were gone to London. It were very painful to me when he came back to see Joe, though it weren't often. He hadn't forgotten, I'm sure, the way he looked at me. But then that convict came back, he lost all his money, Joe helped him, and he was off on his travels.

"Yes, he has told me all about that. Not too good as it turned out."

"Anyway, I married your father, as I thought about it at the time, to always be near my beloved Pip. But Pip was gone, Joe courted me, and I came to love him so dearly, and I knew my love for Old Pip was just something that can happen to a young woman. We never talked about it, Pip and me, because when he got back, you were three years old and Joe and me were happy."

"Well, Mother, I don't see that that is something to have kept secret. I think everyone knew you had been sweet on Pip."

"No, it was more than that. We was going to marry. So, what I mean is this. You know he treated Joe bad when he became a gentleman because he told you, didn't he?

"Yes, he did."

"Well, now you know it was not just Joe that was on his, what d'ye call it, his conscience, but me, Biddy, and he never admitted that he had made me that promise."

"I see."

"And I worshipped him as a young woman. Now it's all old history, and times have moved on, haven't they? You've been a preacher and now, you're a family man with children. But thank you for coming to see your old mother.

"Now I must rest."

Pip bent down and kissed her, and she responded. "Be happy, my son," she said.

Pip slept in the back room at the cottage and Harry woke him with tears in his eyes saying that she had passed away in the night without waking. They talked later for a while and Harry said he did not want a big funeral. So Pip sent a wire to Susanna and stayed on until after the funeral. Biddy was laid to rest with her Joe under the old oak in All Hallows Churchyard. Harry, Pip and a few friends from the village attended the committal.

As she was laid to rest Pip wept for his mother and for his father Joe, the dear old chap, who would have been eighty-six that day.

The hearing in the case of *Regina v. Twaddell* was to open in London on May 6th, Mr. Justice Comely presiding.

Beforehand, Clarence Smythe had consulted with Wemmick first on how to handle his meeting with Jack Masham, a prisoner in Wandsworth Jail, as he had pleaded guilty in the Magistrates Court and received a lighter sentence, a mere four-month hard labor whereas Twaddell had been sent for trial.

"Mr. Masham," Smythe said as they sat in the prisoners' meeting room at Wandsworth, "I would like you to give evidence about your meeting with that Scotsman, Mr. Twaddell, though perhaps you may be called by the prosecution anyway."

"What's in it for me?"

"How do you mean?"

"Are you going to get me out of 'ere?"

"No, I think you must serve your sentence, and I am sure we can do something for you when you are released if you cooperate. Tell me what happened. You were with Mr. Twaddell for only a brief time, I think, and I need to know of your discussions."

"Yeah, 'alf an hour, I guess. He'd talked to Alfie, another rent-boy first."

"Was Mr. Twaddell talking to you about the law and how he could help you?"

At this, Masham started to laugh.

"Lor, of course not. Is that what he told you? Load of rubbish that is."

"What did he say then?

"He started off by saying he'd never been with a man before and I seemed a very pretty boy, which I am, of course," he said smirking.

"Then he said he'd like to take me somewhere so as I could show him what to do. That got me interested in him and he said he'd pay me a lot."

At this, Smythe had to restrain himself, so disgusted was he with Twaddell's deceit.

"You're not making this up, are you, Jack?"

"Why should I? He was going to give me good money. He had some lovely ideas about what he'd do to me which I will keep to myself. But I would like some help when I get out."

"What would you want?"

"God's truth, I hate what I'm doing. When I was a kiddie, I don't know, six or summat, this man next door came on to me and started to use me, regular, like I was just a puppet. My dad was dead, my mum was working as a skivvy, and this man started to give me money but only if I went with other men. So, they paid me, and I gave it to him, and he paid me. Then my mum died of the fever. But I need to stop doing that with men and try to have a normal life."

"I understand. We can help you. Just come to our office immediately you are released next year. We will find you proper work and a lodging."

"Oh, gawd, I'd be so grateful. I'll give myself to you for free if you wanted it."

"Good lord, no! That won't be necessary."

When the interview ended, Smythe returned to the office to tell Hamish and Wemmick of the outcome.

"I am sorry, but I cannot appear for Twaddell," he began.

"He's a first-class liar. Masham told me Twaddell wanted him, how he had not been with a man before, and how he thought Masham would serve him. There is more to it than that, which you don't want to hear, but I believe him as he has no reason to make it all up. He has a sad history, of course, brutalized by a neighbor as a child, and I mentioned to him the possibility of accommodation in a Trust building.

"So, what should we do about Twaddell?"

"Leave him to stew in his own deceptions, I think," said Wemmick.

"I'm afraid so," agreed Hamish. "I don't see any good reason now why we should offer him any assistance at all. Masham will be called as a prosecution witness, I'm sure, given what you've told us, so I suspect Mr. Twaddell will be Her Majesty's guest for some long time. Of course, the Crown may call other young men too."

"But go to the Bailey if you will, Mr. Smythe, to retrieve that bail. We will send word to Twaddell that you will not be defending him, and he must appear on his own."

As she had heard about it from Hamish, the fascination for Estella about the case was that it gave her insights into male prostitution, so she came to the Old Bailey the following day. She was there early and sat patiently in the gallery when Clarence appeared and sat next to her.

He whispered to her about his earlier meeting with Jack Masham and his later conversation with Hamish all of which she heard about in amazement, hardening herself against such depravity, and thinking that Masham might be recruited as a male to the Trust's project.

"All rise," barked a stentorian voice, as Clarence whispered, "I am very anxious, Mrs. Pirrip, as to how Twaddell will behave here."

"I look forward to it, too," Estella replied with a smile.

"Silence in court!"

Twaddell was brought up, and immediately looked around from the dock to see his wife in the gallery. He also noticed Smythe up there in the corner. Both Masham and Alfie were called to testify by the Crown first, and the barrister, Humphrey Godspeed Q.C., extracted from Masham more of the sordid details that Smythe had not heard. Estella was appalled.

Twaddell then rose to defend himself and to Smythe's utter astonishment, he was called to the witness box from the Gallery. He descended quickly into the body of the court and then into the witness box.

"My lord," said Twaddell to Sir Francis Comely, "this is Mr. Smythe, a lawyer from the Jaggers practice whose clerk posted my bail. I am sure he will give evidence of my probity and my declaration that I was merely seeking clients that evening."

Clarence promptly interrupted Twaddell. He was acutely aware as he descended to the court that Twaddell would drag Hamish into this charade if he could.

"M'lud, I fear I can only appear as a hostile witness for the defense."

"Mr. Twaddell," said Sir Francis, "I will need to hear privately from Mr. Smythe to ascertain whether he can be allowed to be a witness, hostile or otherwise."

"I would like to call him," said Twaddell with an evil smirk.

"Then I will ask you the defendant, Mr. Godspeed and your junior, and Mr. Smythe to accompany me. The Court will stand down but not be adjourned," at which the clerk in a very loud voice repeated what the judge had said so that no one in the gallery, or for that matter in the neighboring courts and the street outside, need be in any doubt that that was indeed what the judge had said.

The group sat around a large leather table in a room replete with law books and a desk with a large armchair emblazoned with the royal coat of arms.

"M'lud, my name is Clarence Fotheringaye-Smythe, lawyer, formerly of my Lord Eustace chambers, but now of the Jaggers Chambers in Little Britain."

"Good heavens," said the judge, "Clarence Smythe. I thought I recognized you. My warm regards to your mother. Pray, continue."

"It grieves me greatly to state my position as a hostile witness. I was not informed by the defendant that he proposed to call me, and I was a spectator only because my practice decided to provide bail for Mr. Twaddell on the grounds that he was a recent candidate for a position in the practice. I anticipate being able to collect the bail money at the conclusion of this case."

"Ah," said the judge, "so the defendant might have been appointed to the practice?"

"Indeed."

"Why was he not appointed? Were you the successful candidate? Is this why you are appearing as a hostile witness?"

"No, m'lud. As I understand it from the Senior Clerk in Chambers, he was not appointed because at the close of Mr. Twaddell's interview he made excessive demands on remuneration and partnership which were declined, so he withdrew his candidacy. However, he later approached my senior with a demand to be appointed, accompanied by entirely unjustified threats referring to my senior's behavior.

"In short, Twaddell tried to blackmail my senior, but at the meeting where he expected to have those wishes granted, he realized just how unfounded and vicious his threats were, and he hurriedly withdrew them. The Senior Clerk was a witness to these claims and is prepared to testify should that ever become necessary."

"Is this true, Mr. Twaddell?"

"Yes, m'lud, but...."

"No buts, Mr. Twaddell, is this true?"

"Yes, m'lud."

Smythe continued: "We saw from that moment just how immoral and deceitful Mr. Twaddell was, but when he was apprehended at Moorfields we could not help but believe his defense and that he had been mistakenly arrested.

"It was appropriate to assist a fellow lawyer in such a circumstance. The bail was an act of generosity, but it was not a high risk, as indeed it has proved. I spoke with the witness Masham recently and he told me in less vivid terms what he has told the court this morning. I thus declined to offer myself as counsel for Mr. Twaddell."

"So, Twaddell, do you still wish to call this witness?"

"No, m'lud," said Twaddell, now broken and dejected.

"Then let us return to the court."

On coming back into court, Smythe spoke quietly to Mr. Godspeed saying that the practice did not intend to pursue the blackmail charge, though he had admitted it before the judge. Twaddell's wife had disappeared from the gallery when the judge and party returned to court. Then Mr. Godspeed briefly summed up the case for the prosecution. Twaddell offered nothing in the invitation to sum up his defense.

The judge then summed up the case for the jury which included a devastating analysis of Twaddell's character, the vile act of his procuring a minor to practice sodomy, and a recommendation that he should be struck off immediately. After a speedy return of 'guilty' from the jury, he concluded:

"I sentence you, Stuart Twaddell, under the Offences against the Person Act of 1862 to two years hard labor to begin forthwith. The Court is adjourned."

"Congratulations, Clarence," said Estella as they descended the marble stairs from the Court.

"I suppose so, but what do you think? Does the punishment fit the crime?"

"Of course not. My husband once told me of an expression Mr. Jaggers used quoting some 17th century playwright: 'The Law is an Ass,' and it is certainly true in this case. I know that my husband was solidly against such punishment, though I don't recall his defending anyone so charged."

"I do feel sorry for the poor devil," said Clarence.

"My sentiment precisely. I am as anxious as anybody that the man who tried to harm Hamish be punished, but these laws are senseless. What, in God's name, does it matter if men want to play with each other?"

"I am very concerned about his family too," said Clarence.

"Yes, indeed. He is manifestly a thoroughly unpleasant fellow but imagine their fate. How would the mother tell her children, how could she live with him when he is released, how would she get support when she had no income?"

"Perhaps the Trust should examine possibilities with convicted prisoners' families."

"Now that would be an excellent project, would it not? Did you tell the young man to be in touch with the Trust?"

"Indeed, I did."

"I have been calling you Clarence. I hope that is not presumptuous. Call me Estella, please."

"Not presumptuous at all. My names are a handicap, but I am proud of them.

"Let me call you a cab, Estella," and they smiled broadly at each other.

As Smythe returned to Little Britain with the news, he contemplated the reactions of Mr. Courtisone on whose recommendation Twaddell had been invited to interview. He was very puzzled indeed as to how Twaddell had found out who he was, not that it mattered much as he was also very grateful indeed that a nasty attack on Hamish had been defeated. Maybe his senior's marriage to Mary would obviate any further risk or danger. He chuckled to himself as he walked home at Estella's description of sodomy as men playing with each other.

X

As was their custom at breakfast, Pip and Susanna were bent over their individual copies of the *Daily Telegraph* of May 9, 1871. Susanna was getting increasingly irritated by Pip's constant exclamations of "Good Lord' 'I don't believe it', and "Oh, goodness, won't Karl be excited!" that she pleaded with him to allow her to read in quiet.

"But don't you realize, my dear, these Communards in Paris are doing what those German philosophers I met in Salford wanted. Government by the proletariat, though the French army seems determined to crush it from what I read here.

"I am really shocked and surprised. I never thought those wild ideas of Karl's would get anywhere. How strange. And, of course, he is right. The capitalists with their army will seek to smash it."

"I suppose," said Susanna, "that when you have a war like that with people killed, displaced, hungry and without leadership, revolutionary ideas seem more attractive. There will obviously be a vacuum in which the question 'what do we do now?' invites radical answers, rather some kind of restoration of the *status quo ante*."

"You sound like a member of the Foreign Office. No, my dear, I jest. You are absolutely right! It is great pity that this experiment in new ways of governing is not able to be tested and found wanting. Smashing it with troops won't kill the idea. The French have lost their Emperor, though he is no great loss, and have established their Third Republic under a man called Thiers. I suppose the Communards seized their opportunity."

Six-year-old Lachlan then entered the room, a 'bonnie laddie' as his mother called him. He came over to her and she hoisted him up on to her lap. His young brother, 'wee' Malcolm, followed behind and went to sit on his father's knee.

"Why is Father so excited?" Lachlan asked her.

"Oh, some news from Paris."

"Isn't that where Albert went?

"Yes, but there is a war," explained Susanna. "The Emperor of France was very upset with Count Bismarck and the Prussians, so he decided to fight them. But he lost the battles and he was captured.

"As the Emperor was gone, the French got themselves a new President, not a King, and he made peace with the Prussians after giving the Prussians lots of money and some French land, so the Prussians didn't smash Paris."

"What happened to Paris then?"

"Well, Father was excited because many people in Paris decided they did not want a President. They wanted to govern themselves more like a family, or a commune as they call it."

"Did the Emperor die?" said Lachlan, uninterested in the politics.

"No, he is living in exile near London I believe."

"Did Albert go to see the President?"

"No," said his mother, "he went with Elizabeth— you remember Elizabeth? She came here two or three times. Her father works for our Prime Minister in Paris."

"Is Albert doing any fighting?"

"Oh, no."

"So where is Albert, then?

"We don't know, but we could ask Mrs. Mudge, Elizabeth's aunt. She might know. We'll find out."

"It must be very exciting to be a soldier and fight people."

"Ah," intervened Lachlan's father, "Albert is not fighting, and being a soldier is not very exciting. Indeed, it is terrible."

"Have you been a soldier, father?"

"Not a soldier, but I did look after cavalry horses in a distant land where there were terrible battles. I had an accident and a bullet landed in my ankle, which is why I am lame."

"I didn't know that is why your leg is like that, Father. Did you kill anyone?"

"No," said Pip, laughing, "I just looked after the horses."

"I want to be a general when I grow up."

"We'll see about that," said Susanna. "If women ruled the world not men, maybe there would be fewer wars. Now run along for your lessons."

The boy walked to the door of the room, strutting like a soldier, followed by Malcolm, who had recently graduated from toddling to walking.

"How on earth can we help our children realize that war is the most dreadful thing human beings do?" asked Pip.

"We just keep on telling them how dreadful it is, I suppose, and then decide whether we support a government that goes to war."

Since mid-March, the French Government had lost its authority over the radicals in Paris who had set up the Commune. The Prussian army had occupied Paris for only two days early in March, and the new Republic made no effort to control the city leaving the Commune to take over. An invasion by the government's army was now anticipated. As a result, all but a small skeleton embassy staff remained in the city.

Henry and Elizabeth were having breakfast at the embassy's temporary location in Versailles.

"You know, my dear, the extraordinary thing about this whole affair is that these French people will fight their own countrymen but not the Prussians."

"But surely the new government, whatever it is, will take charge."

"You would have thought so, but this new Republican government is taking a devil of a time to get the game in their hands. It will be increasingly difficult to disarm the National Guard inside Paris the longer they hold back. The Communards have seized their opportunity and are holding an election. But enough of that, tell me more about your life with Aunt Charlotte."

"She's a wonderful person. I had seen her before I went to London as I had visited her at Craynham Vicarage. She is making friends with Estella Pirrip, a very beautiful woman for her age, and she is wonderful with Albert.

"I think Aunt Charlotte and she will become close, and I am not surprised why she chooses to be in Chelsea as often as possible. That vicar husband of hers is the most remarkable prig and my presence gave her an excuse to get away from him, which I hope she will often use."

Henry laughed loudly and smiled at his daughter. "Now then, you should not speak with such ferocity at one who is, after all, your uncle. I have no idea why she consented to marry him."

"I don't know either, I never understood their mutual attraction."

"Well, you have several uncles and aunts, you know; perhaps she was short of opportunities. She did not discuss it with me, which was a disappointment at the time."

"I suppose that must be it. I don't know how he manages to run an agricultural parish with such attitudes. I am surprised anyone would go to his church. His sermons are always about accepting our situation, what God has intended for us. Do you think that a man laboring in the fields really would believe that?"

"Of course not, though they may behave as though they believe it just for peace and quiet. That is what is so interesting about France, my dear. The Revolution came about as much because of the priests as by conditions. Village priests in France were drawn from the poor people.

"Of course, the aristocrats held all the high positions in the Church, but down there in the villages across France, these priests knew what poverty meant. One way to understand it is to conjecture that the priests in the villages gave the people permission to revolt, not being prepared to see the monarchy as a gift of God.

"Our English clergy are different, usually minor members of the genteel classes. Your uncle is not rich, but he comes from a good family. I doubt whether he has ever lifted anything heavier than a claret jug in his life."

They laughed together gaily at that idea.

"Oh dear, I do so dislike the man, but Aunt Charlotte is quite a radical in her way."

"Yes, and you are a lot like her, my favorite sister, as she is."

"We discuss the Revolution and the conditions of the poor, about the Chartists and so on, but she also knows women, like that Miss Hill, who are helping the poor. She is very well-read, too, and her particular favorite philosopher is Mr. Mill, who lives nearby."

"That's Charlotte. Tell me, my dear, I am still not sure why your young Albert wanted to risk coming to Paris. Why has he not stayed with us here rather than going off to see painters and some jeweler or other?"

"He wanted adventure, Father, though he does have radical views. He is determined to find this group of painters he has heard about, and to get to know a man called Gustave Caillebotte. Albert grew up first in a blacksmith's cottage in Kent, you know. His mother had great difficulty in bearing children, as I understand it, and she died giving birth to a daughter, who also died."

"Oh, how tragic!"

"Yes, but his father became a lawyer with a very famous practice in London, headed by a Mr. Jaggers."

"Oh, I know of Jaggers! He did a wonderful thing in defending an old friend of mine, Dingleberry, my tutor at Cambridge, against that blasted man Binding who beat his wife."

"I don't know anything about that, I am afraid. Albert was only a year old when his mother died, so his father asked his very close friends in Kent to care for him rather than hire a woman in London. His father died and his step-mother Estella has become very fond of him and she encourages Albert to be independent, as she says she never had it at his age. I want you to meet all my new friends, by the way, when we get back to London, when we do."

"Of course, you shall tell me about them directly. But first, tell me about your feelings for Albert."

"Oh, I love him dearly. Most of all we are very good friends. We enjoy each other's company greatly, going to concerts or art exhibitions, learning from each other."

"I could tell that at Christmas, but you are very young."

"Oh, we have not yet talked about marriage, though I think he thinks we have. We are prepared to get to know each other. I do admire his bravery in wandering around in Paris outside embassy protection."

"I think it foolhardy, my dear."

"I know, Father, but I still admire his spirit of adventure."

"I am glad you want to get to know each other better. I think your mother and I were in too much of a hurry, and we wanted different things. She loved the society life here, but her American background leaves her too insensitive to others, especially of a different race, creed or color. That's what being brought up in the old South will do.

"Of course, her father was rich enough for her to get to England when the South was obviously losing, and their Georgia estates were ravaged when General Sherman marched through the state. Fortunately, her "Daddy," as she called him, had married a northern woman who is your American grandmother and she had huge properties in the state of New York, so they escaped the fighting and went north.

"I am now sure your mother prefers to live away from me."

"I am not sure that is a bad thing, Father."

"Perhaps not. I suspect I will continue to be posted to Europe after this French experience. I have indicated I would like to go to Greece or one of the Italian states next if my health permits."

"Oh goodness me, are you really ill?"

"No, but I had a sort of return of my old attacks on Monday night, I suppose in consequence of the fatigue during the day and being rather out of sorts since that rough passage we had across the Channel."

"Did you see a doctor in London?"

"No, I am sure I will be well when these events come to a close."

"Mother should be here to help you. Are you unhappy about her behavior?'

"I'm neither happy nor unhappy because my work is demanding, but you are simply the light of my existence. I am so proud of you; it makes my heart ache."

"Oh, Father, you are so generous and kind. I will be your companion now. I will live with you and support you and, if that means several years before I get married, whether to Albert or someone else, I would be enormously happy to do that. I suppose I am half-American but, as I have never been there and Georgia sounds terrible with that slavery business, I don't see myself as anything but English."

"Let us see where life takes us. I so dislike being split like this, with the Ambassador in Tours with the new Republican government and my having to run things from Versailles. We must both hope for a speedy resolution of the chaos in Paris."

Finishing a letter two days later, Henry went into the drawing-room in his quarters to find Elizabeth.

"The news from Paris is dire. I hope you are not too frightened thinking of Albert's fate."

"Not really, as I believe he will survive. After all, I am not like the wife of a soldier; he is just an itinerant painter, but I am most displeased with him. He should have attempted to contact me."

"Oh, I am sure he has, but my information is that conditions there are very fraught, you know, with the army ready to take control of the city, now the Prussians are gone. I expect we will see him soon. He did have his British identity papers with him, did he not?"

"Yes."

She was about to go to her piano when a M. Nimrod Klein was announced.

"Will you meet him, Father? He dined at Aunt Charlotte's last winter, and he may have news of Albert."

"Of course," said Henry.

Klein came into the room, no longer his immaculate self, but filthy from head to foot, unshaven and apparently very hungry, though not quite starving. Nevertheless, he greeted Henry with due deference to a member of the British Embassy, but Henry did not offer to shake his hand, not sure whether he was a spy, a reprobate or a lunatic with his wild looks.

"Who are you?" asked Henry.

"I am Nimrod Klein, a jeweler in Paris, m'lord. Before the war started, I go to London in search of an ancestor of mine, a Martha Jaggers."

"Oh, Jaggers again, are you related to him?"

"I do not know, but I went to London to escape the war which I saw was coming, but I could find nothing about my ancestor. I could see we were going to be beaten, so as the war ended, I go to stay with friends in a small village, Montreuil-le-Gast near Rennes, far away from these battles and from those Prussian devils.

"Once the armistice was signed, I rush back to Paris to see what had happened to my shop. I was there only a few days when the Communards took over, and let me see, it must now be sometime in April, but the radicals have changed the weeks and days to the Revolutionary Calendar and I am very confused.

"My shop was not touched, but it was small, and people knew I would have taken my valuables with me. I was in hiding in Paris recently as who knows what these vandals would do? But some weeks ago Albert come into my shop. He did not know I was back in Paris, but we were very glad to see each other. He has had many adventures, I think."

"But he *is* alive and well, is he?" asked Elizabeth.

"Yes, but he is hungry like everyone else and he spends his time listening to groups of painters in cafes, such as are open, avoiding the Communards. He told me you would want to know where he was, and I had decided to leave the city anyway to see my mother, but I then go back. He will stay a little while longer, even though the fighting gets worse daily."

"Why is he staying there?" asked Elizabeth. "Does he not know how worried we are?"

"He told me to send you his love and he would come to Versailles soon."

"If he can get through the army blockade," said Henry.

"Of course. I had to give an officer a large diamond to get through, and I thought he would shoot me there and then. But now I go to my mother in Bordeaux, I think."

"You are welcome here as an acquaintance of my sister. You look as though you could do with a wash and meal, but perhaps not in that order?"

"*Merci beaucoup*, m'lord Fitzroy.'

After lunch that day, Henry sought out Elizabeth for their afternoon walk, trying to keep her spirts up.

"Still no word from Albert himself. Our difficulty, my dear, is that we do not know where he is, do we? So, we can't send a message and I can't easily send a messenger to get one individual out, as we have responsibility for all British citizens. We must just wait and see.

"I have another topic to broach with you. I now have serious intimations from the Foreign Office that a position as Counsellor may be open to me in Athens at the beginning of next year, now only a few months away.

"I would return to England in July, and then do the preparatory work in London before sailing for Athens. I'd prefer to sail, not go by train across Europe. Now, would you come with me if their suggestion becomes a reality?

"When the offer is made formally, I will have to state who will be with me. So, I need to know what you would prefer to do. I doubt whether your mother would want to come to Athens. Its recent history is most unlike the Athens of Plato and Aristotle."

"If Mother does not return, of course," said Elizabeth, "I told you I would look after you. I know you are sometimes quite ill. You work too hard, being a very conscientious man as a public servant."

"But what about Albert?"

"We will see, won't we? I think it is now too early for us to marry and, besides, who knows what may be happening to him in Paris?"

"Well, the new French government is settled in Tours for the moment but the situation in Paris with this self-appointed Commune cannot continue. I suspect that by the end of May we will be back in Paris, probably to spend months cleaning up the building which I am sure will have been used by the Communards."

"It would be very exciting to go to Athens. I visited the Museum in London with Albert and we saw the marbles Lord Elgin brought back. Thank goodness they are here, as the Greeks do not seem to know how to look after their treasures."

"Tell me, Father, do you think all this could happen in England?"

"Chaos originates in war: Everything civil gets out of control. We are protected by the Channel, as Napoleon found. Here the Emperor simply made a fool of himself, unleashing all kinds of pent-up furies.

"In England we see both parties in government seeking more or less quickly to answer public needs. My concern is with London where the extraordinary growth of population makes it a tinder-box. Yet we must also be concerned with the industrial north. We had Peterloo, Chartism, and working people want to decide their own fate."

"I must say that I think we might find better ways to help the poor than we have. Albert said that Pip had met a revolutionary once, a German, Karl Marx I think his name was."

"Great Scot, really? You won't know this, but we get regular secret communications about troublemakers in France, and a Karl Marx is on that list, though the report said he spent much of his time in London."

"I will ask Albert more about him when he finally comes to see me."

"Frankly, my dear, I doubt he can get out of Paris.

"I heard an interesting story yesterday which will amuse you as it is about a piano.

"The Prussians were excellent at pillaging. In one case, they took just the insides of large clocks, as the cases would be too difficult to load on their wagons or the trains. A Frenchman near Metz returned sometime after the famous battle near his house and found everything in perfect order in his house, even the piano in good tune.

"He expressed his surprise to the officer billeted there.

"'Yes,' said the latter, 'I have taken the greatest care of the instrument, as it was such a good one. I fear, however, that it may suffer by the journey.'

"'What journey?'

"'The journey to Berlin. We are going to have the things packed to-morrow.'"

"Oh, my goodness," cried Elizabeth, "how dreadful. Why can they do that?"

"The French lost the war, dear. To the victors, the spoils. If we want to buy anything of quality, I think we will have to go to Berlin!"

"How sad, the ruin in France must be something awful."

"War creates all manner of confusion. Now the French government has lost control of Paris, Versailles has become a focus for every non-French refugee, even though there was nothing there in the way of amusement, except rides and drives in the environs. Then the damn British tourists arrived—Anson, Brackenbury, Colonel Baker, Campbell of Islay, and others."

"I thought the town seemed crowded."

"Indeed, but my admirable superior, Lord Lyons, braved it and went back to Paris just before the radicals took over, as he wanted to visit his niece in her convent, and that gave rise to a rumor that ce vieux aristocrat had a harem of nuns at the embassy!"

"A brave man, I think," said Elizabeth. "What happened to clergy during the war?"

"They got it in the neck, I'm afraid.

"The ecclesiastical community had to leave Paris en bourgeois; dignitaries of the Church, monsignors, vicars and such, dressed in very vulgar, dirty clothes, and with their beards half grown, looking, I thought, like very low billiard markers!"

At Semper House one evening Estella sat down for a whisky with Charlotte, putting off writing a letter to Albert.

"You will know this, Charlotte. If I send a message to Albert c/o Fitzroy at the Foreign Office, will it reach him even though as the newspapers suggested, the country is under Prussian control? These last few days I just can't stop thinking about Albert."

"That's inevitable," said Charlotte, "but he does not strike me as the sort to engage in battles, though he will relish a Parisian adventure. I am sure Henry would have someone look out for him, so I don't think you should worry unduly.

"Tell me, Estella, changing the subject, would you take on another man?"

"Good Lord, no, but this widow label is such an affront. I am not so much lonely as morose. After Pip's death I realized what a responsibility Albert would be for me. Loneliness, however, is the characteristic of the single life but he is wonderful company. He became my child very gradually, not at all when he was living with Joe and Biddy, but then, as he was so well brought up by them— polite, inquisitive—he needed an education and I have grown to love him profoundly. But another man? No, I have Nellie to love for that side of my emotions."

"What does Albert think of that?"

"He is my only close relative and is happy for me and I think he would see me as a close friend, but I hope that you and I too will always be good friends, Charlotte, not just because of the attachment of our youngsters."

"I am sure we will, my dear and I look forward to your dinner party tomorrow."

"As do I, it has all been such a rush to arrange, especially as I have a surprise."

"Do you mean Italy? Rizzio has asked me about it and I told him to ask you."

"Oh dear," she said laughing, "my secret is out."

The following evening, Estella hosted a small dinner party. Rizzio had visited her the previous week to suggest that the Cheyne Row friends might take an excursion to Italy. Estella was immediately excited at the prospect, so she had invitations hurried to her guests: Hamish and Mary, Rizzio and Charlotte, and Pip and Susanna. After the usual greetings, Pip asked:

"What news of Albert, then?"

"Well, at least something," said Estella. "I am not sure whether he does not choose to write or whether communication is impossible. I had one message dated March 2, 1871, brought out of Paris by a trader who had got a *rite de passage* somehow. I'll read it to you:

> 'My journey was not at all like that in January when I came across with Elizabeth and her father, when the sea was terrible, and I was very sick.
>
> I am all right. I met M. Caillebotte the painter I wanted to see, but he then left Paris. Klein's accommodation is satisfactory.
>
> Elizabeth's father who is the Head of Chancery has been very kind. If the situation gets worse, he said, they will move to Versailles, though he is not sure when the Ambassador will return. Anyway, everything is up in the air. I must go now. I hope you are well. I send you much love.
>
> *Ever your obedient servant, Albert.*'

"The rebels are still in charge but not for long if the papers are right. I don't know whether that Frenchman Klein is there. It is all very confusing but let us go into dinner."

"It must be very difficult for you, Estella dear," said Susanna as they began to eat and talk.

"Yes, but let us talk of happier times, past and future. We can do very little.

"Now Rizzio is here for a reason. He came to see me recently as he is offering to organize a tour of Italy for people who might like to see Florence, Venice and Rome, and Pisa, I think; was that not right, Rizzio?"

"Yes, indeed. I had already talked with my friend Charlotte, and she suggested I talk with Mrs. Pirrip. So, I wondered whether other people might be interested in taking part."

"Everything will depend on whether it is safe to go, I assume," said Susanna.

"Oh, I think it is now very safe. Italy is now unified under the King. If we go next April, we can enjoy the countryside and the famous cities. I know all these cities well and I would conduct a tour and arrange for the hotels once you have decided how much you want to spend. As everywhere in Europe, the quality of the hotels is very varied."

"Och," said Susanna, "no time like the present. We would love to do an abbreviated European tour, wouldn't we, Pip?"

"I am sure we would. Why not this summer, say July? I would love to see Florence. It seems to have magic about it, I am not sure why."

"We will be able to see whether it is true that Italians love children," said Charlotte, with a somewhat mocking tone of voice.

"Please, Mrs. Mudge," said Rizzio vehemently, "please not to speak badly of my country and its people."

"I apologize," said Charlotte, taken aback by Rizzio's reprimand.

"We'd love to come," said Mary, quickly changing the subject.

"Rizzio, are we limited in number?"

"Let me see, Estella, but I think if we were twelve altogether, that would be excellent."

"Then make the arrangements and invite the others."

Discussion then passed to the prostitution project, in which Rizzio had little interest, though he still seemed to be smarting from Charlotte's ill-judged comment.

"We have a doctor prepared to come regularly to the building," said Pip, "though only one nurse. They are in short supply.

"We have now talked with some twenty women who had come for shelter and their stories were so harsh and gruesome that I cannot retell them at the dinner table. Nevertheless, it is money very well spent. Only eight of the twenty have some form of syphilis, which was an indicator of why the government has been so fierce in trying to combat the disease.

"I think the Project is now doing well, though it is only a start. What is your overall impression of our work, Pip?"

"I am very pleased with the progress, Estella. We might revive your Chatham Project, but I am also wondering whether we might find whores in our building who are married with children and have a husband with a trade, whom we might be able to set up in a business of some kind. It would be a matter of character, and of course, other capabilities.

"We must think about that," Pip continued, "but we must spend Mr. Jaggers' money soon. The more we think broadly about possibilities, the better. We could try other ports—Liverpool for example."

"There is this core problem," said Estella. "How would we oversee activities outside London? But enough of whores!

"Charlotte, tell us more about Elizabeth's father, your brother."

"He is inevitably my favorite brother as we are closest in age. The eldest son is John, and he is heir to the title and takes that very seriously."

"Which title is this?" asked Rizzio, rejoining the conversation.

"My father is a baronet, the 6th or 8th, I forget which. He is a public servant and a politician, but since my marriage, I see little of him. But my brother Henry is a splendid man, plagued with ill health, but working as a diplomat in the family tradition.

"Might we meet him if he is in London?" said Pip.

"I earnestly hope so. I understand his wife fled to America or somewhere else when the war broke out; whether she returns remains to be seen. Of course, she married Henry long before their Civil War started there, so she may have returned to different conditions."

XI

Hamish and Mary eventually embarked on the Flying Scotsman the last day of May as Hamish had been delayed by the trial and other matters. They arrived at the Waterloo Hotel for dinner. This was a splendid Georgian building and the largest hotel in Edinburgh with fifty rooms and granite exterior walls, the grey color so familiar in that city. It had immense ballrooms and was very well located, just beyond the north end of Princes Street near Calton Hill. Their adjoining rooms were well furnished, but to their great surprise, a water-closet had been already installed in the bathroom which served their rooms, and the precise details of its operation were posted on the bathroom door.

The sun was up when they met for a truly Scottish breakfast with eggs, Ayrshire bacon, sausage, Stornaway black pudding and tomatoes, but beginning with the traditional porridge that Mary tasted but could not take more. Then they sat quietly in contemplation, both surprised by their situation:

"Did you sleep well, Mary?"

"I did, though I am accustomed to a maid assisting me."

"Ah, this would be a requirement for you, a maid to help you as a valet would?"

"I'm afraid so. I have chosen dresses and clothing for this journey that do not require buttons or other objects that I cannot handle, as I have only one hand. It is such a problem for me, Hamish."

"I would be more than pleased to learn how to help in these kinds of situations where we would not bring a maid."

"Thank you, David and I established a procedure which worked. I dispensed with my dress maid when I married as he wanted to help me dress and care for my clothes, though that might be regarded as unmanly."

"Nonsense, I would be only too happy to help you in that way. I would like to dress you, not merely in the morning, but assist in choosing clothes and hats and other garments."

"What were your sleeping arrangements with David?"

"We had separate but adjoining rooms, and we rarely slept together all night. My problem is that my arm is such an inconvenience. I am obliged to lift it with my right hand to be able to turn over at night. It is quite heavy. I learned long ago how to get in and out of bed without assistance."

"If I were to find a man I wanted to engage with, which seems increasingly unlikely, I would not invite him to our home for purposes other than, perhaps, to meet you," said Hamish, "a marriage bed would never be shared."

"Good. David was very solicitous in that regard, though I never met any of his lovers, although he can have had very few as our lives together were so curtailed."

"Poor man. Let us take advantage of the weather and explore the castle, though we will need very warm clothes today. You have not visited Edinburgh before, have you?"

"No, indeed."

"I used to come to the castle as a child, though it always seemed terribly forbidding to me."

"Let us take a trap."

From just inside the castle gate, they could stand and look at Princes Street down below, a magnificent concourse of horses and carriages and people out walking or going about their business.

"How did they get water up here?"

"I think there was a well down there," said Hamish, pointing to some ruins, "and they had a crane to bring the water from the spring there up to the castle. Of course, you know, the place was a prison for many years. After that a search was made for the Crown of Scotland and a chest in a sealed room was broken open and there was the Crown, the Scepter and the Sword of State which we can look at over there in the Crown Room."

"How romantic. Of course, English-Scottish relations have always been turbulent."

"Oh, we are a patient people. I am sure Scotland will be independent again someday."

Mary was astonished to see the brilliance of the gems and pearls in the Crown of Scotland. They were very important objects to the people of Scotland as they signified its rich history, though, as Hamish told her, the clans then were too warlike for it easily to become one unified country.

They came out of the castle by the same gate and took a cab back to the Waterloo Hotel. They went to their separate rooms and came down for dinner.

"I have wondered," said Mary, "where might we live together?"

"That depends on what we could afford."

"Presumably you have an income from the practice," said Mary, "and I have a small amount from my family and more from David's estate. I live comfortably, as people like to say."

"I would like to live near friends, Mary. There is something comforting about having neighbors who are friends, not merely acquaintances. One can feel very lonely indeed cut off if one does not choose a home wisely."

"I would love to be close to Susanna," she replied.

"I agree, and she has been such a good friend, as you know. I must say I find Pip pompous at times."

"Oh, that is just his preacher background getting in the way of his humanity," said Mary with a sniff.

"You know, Hamish," she continued, "I like our possible arrangement. For I sometimes think that the very idea of 'love' is just a ploy to entice women into emotional subjection. Women fawn and swoon, like the young girls in that novel by Miss Austen, who have been taught to imagine that they will be in love with a man. But that just makes them the man's plaything."

"H'mm, I suppose that is possible, especially for young women who have been constrained in their upbringing to anticipate 'love' and the bodily feelings of desire that grow with it as a way out of that constraint. Yet that means—out of the frying pan into the fire for most of them, too?"

"Indeed, but with regard to us, I do not know," she said, "whether if we were to marry I would come to love you in that romantic sense and have those types of desire. Of course, if our arrangement matures, it will not be just a business arrangement. I suppose I regard love as the consequence of a relationship, not a foundation for it."

"How interesting your views are, Mary: Love as a trap for women. What an idea, but with an implication that love should be free, that we should do what we want with our bodies and with whom. Perhaps my revulsion against promiscuity is an indication that I too have been in that trap. Yet as far as we are concerned, we would become equal partners, respectful and fond of each other, and eventually if we achieve that closeness which is the symptom of love, then that will be most desirable."

This conversation quietly pleased both of them.

Hamish had a challenging encounter the following afternoon when Mary had retired to rest. He was walking down Princes Street and he met a member of his University group, Walter Mackenzie, with whom he had a close and an almost intimate understanding several years before. They shook hands, avoiding an embrace, and slipped into a small bar for a whisky.

"Och, Hamish, how is life treating you?"

"I am well settled as a London lawyer."

"What brings you to Edinburgh? If you've a friend here, bring him along tonight and I'll gather some of the auld gang together for a wee dram."

Hamish was thrown by this invitation, not knowing how quite to respond but decided it was best to tell the truth.

"Oh no, thank you very much but I don't think the lady accompanying me would relish an evening of drinking and carousing with all of you?"

"A lady? How come?"

"It's a long story, Walter. The gist is this. I was the victim of an attempted blackmail in London."

"What for?"

"For loving men not women, what do you think?"

"Who could do such a thing?"

"A Scotsman, a lawyer, and a John Knox Presbyterian and a former member of this University."

"Oh my God!"

"Though we have erased that problem very successfully, I realized I must get married. I would like to have children. But I am only going to do so, if the woman understands me fully, d'ye ken?'

"Oh, Hamish dear, don't give in. Please don't. Move back up here where most people are more tolerant."

"I can't."

"Are you committed right now? When do you have to go back to your lady?'

"An hour or so."

"My lodging is just round the corner. Come with me and I will show you what you are missing. I have always desired you. You look badly in need of some good physical entertainment."

Hamish blanched at the invitation, his mind racing and his body brimming with desire. He looked at this handsome man, willing to surrender himself to what he wanted.

"Oh, Walter, you don't know how much you tempt me, but I am not looking for a quick outburst of lust and desire, but for a steady companionship with soft gentle loving."

"But who is this woman, then?"

"She is young, widowed and her husband was like me. We are here talking and seeing whether we could marry."

"Will she give you your freedom?'

"Yes, but now I must return to the hotel. I do thank you for the opportunity and I am sad to have to decline it. But it is good practice. Give my regards to the group."

"I will, I will. You are sorely missed."

Mary looked very serene and lovely when she came into the dining room to meet Hamish for dinner.

"How was your afternoon, Hamish?"

"I hope you will be proud of me."

"Proud? Why?"

"I met an old friend from my university days. We were in a group of young men of like minds, and I liked this friend Walter a great deal. I explained to him why I was in Edinburgh as he pressed me to know, and I told him our circumstances."

"Good gracious, what did he say?"

"He implied that it was my tragedy and invited me to his lodging nearby."

"Did you go?"

"No, he offered, indeed practically begged me to go with him, I think because he thought that would end my interest in marrying you."

"But you refused."

"Yes, and I was glad to. Months ago, before I met you, I confess that I would have gone with him, but now? I have to take the prospect of marrying you very seriously indeed and acknowledge that with it come all sorts of new obligations."

"My dear Hamish, I have spent the afternoon in my bed, not sleeping, but coming to a decision. If you so wish, I will marry you with the understandings we have reached. I see no special reason to delay, and I hope we can be married quickly.

"But I need to be sure that you do not find me, as a woman, impossible to love physically. If that were the case, and we were to marry, I could not have the children I so desire. So, would you come to my bed this night, and see whether my having your children is a real possibility."

"I am slightly stunned by being invited to bed by a man and a woman within four hours of each other! I would love to come to your bed. I have not bedded man or woman so I will need your guidance. I do find you attractive, and I mean sexually, but that originates in my admiration for you as a person. You are beautiful and intelligent, and I would be proud to be your husband."

Hamish woke up suddenly the following morning. Mary was asleep on his left shoulder, her paralyzed arm lying on her. He picked it up, knowing she could not feel it. He fondled her atrophied fingers, so tiny, almost like a baby's, her wrist almost so small you could put a ring from a finger around it, and the flesh of her arm white as white can be, without a freckle or mark, but reed-like thin.

Whatever happened in his future with men, he loved this woman. He pondered the experience he had just had and how satisfying it had been, yet he felt some guilt about seeing images of Walter beneath him occasionally when he was in the throes of his making love to her.

As he lay there before getting up, he felt confirmed that he was a man who wanted to love one person above all else. Whether that was a man or a woman was not the point. Besides, he had a chosen a profession which would be impossible to pursue had his love fallen on a man. A lawyer cannot live a double life of upholding the law and simultaneously being in breach of it. Put all that aside, he thought, this Mary was a sweet lovable companion.

"Let us marry immediately," she said over breakfast, "in case I am pregnant. I don't know what happened to you last night, but I need no further proof and now I think I should not have asked for it."

"Not at all, and it was lovely, Mary. Let us return to London tomorrow secretly. Come to stay with me. I have the room now Klein has gone back to Paris. We will find a Registry Office and send a message to Pip and Susanna, Estella and Albert, and of course John Wemmick and Clarence Smythe."

On Saturday June 24th, 1871, Hamish and Mary became Mr. and Mrs. Macdonald to the great joy of their friends. Estella was especially thrilled as she liked Hamish and wanted him to succeed in the practice her dear Pip had helped to grow in esteem. Susanna was beyond delight at her success as a matchmaker.

❈ ❈ ❈

After the wedding, Estella took the train to Numquam for the week-end and then returned to spend a week interviewing prostitutes in the Jaggers Building, as it was now called. Among the five women she talked to, Fanny Filby seemed to be a woman they could help properly. She was a pretty woman with long black hair and blue eyes, probably Irish.

"How is it that you are whoring, Fanny?" Estella asked.

"My husband's a sailor, Ma'am and I haven't heard from him for over a year. His ship came into port a while back and I went and asked the captain where he was. He said there was a group of his men went ashore in a place called Rio, and they never returned to the ship. He hired some other foreign men there to bring the ship home. So, my Fred has just disappeared, and I never heard from him, so I got no money."

"Don't you have any family to go to?"

"Lor, bless us, they's worse off than we are. I've got my two kiddies to look after. My dad was a drunk and he was killed in a fight just after I was born, see. My mum, well, she then got married to a sailor, too. They looked after me for a while, then I was on my own."

"How old are you?"

"Cor blimey, I don't know, eighteen, I suppose."

"With two children?"

"Well, I know I was fifteen when I had Johnny, so yeah, perhaps I'm eighteen or nineteen."

"What would you really like to do if you had the chance?"

"Settle down, running a nice quiet pub in the country with my hubby is my dream with a nice place for my kiddies."

"Well, in the meantime, Fanny, the Trust is going to give you a living wage for you and your children. You can stay here in your room in the building. You'll do some cleaning, but you will get food supplied. If you start whoring again, you will have to leave."

"Oh, no ma'am, thank you, ma'am, thank you, 'cos, unlike some of my friends, I never liked whoring. I was dirty enough, but that made me feel so dirty like I was the dregs of something, I don't know."

"I understand, Fanny. Let's see how you get on. We will also give you some money to buy clothes for your children."

Estella thought carefully about Fanny when she got home. How striking was Fanny's dream! It had never appeared to her with such clarity that everyone and anyone could have a sense of something which would yield happiness away from the ghastly situations in which they were trapped. She had needed Pip to get her away from her dire situation.

Here were these poor women, living constantly on a knife-edge of disaster. What on earth could have happened to Fanny's husband? Those men at sea, she thought, what a frightening life it must be, no wonder they wanted a woman when they came into a port, whether for solace or just to get rid of pent-up frustrations.

By the end of May, the government led by M. Thiers had recaptured Paris and their army was restoring order in a city wrecked by violence and brutality. Henry and Elizabeth were back in the embassy. One afternoon in late May 1871, Albert struggled into the grounds, wounded in the left eye and the right leg. Elizabeth was both thrilled and horrified and Henry sent a wire to Estella with the news.

"How are you, Albert?" she said, a week after his arrival. "You have slept and rested for over a week now and surgeons have treated you as best they can."

"A week, is it? I lost track of time, but oh, my darling Elizabeth, it is so good to see you."

"I am glad it is only your left leg that is broken and it has been set, but the damage to your eye looks much more serious."

"Maybe so. I can't see from it with the patch but let us wait and if I am blind in that eye, well, I still have the other, so I can still paint."

"I'll fetch Father now so he can hear more about it."

Albert was in one of the palatial guest rooms in the embassy. At the far end from the ornate double doors was a colossal bed with a canopy emblazoned with the royal coats or arms, fit for a prince, as Elizabeth thought of it. Elegant chairs were brought to the bedside as Henry said:

"Albert my boy, you have been through these terrible two months of the Commune. You looked starving when you struggled in here but tell us again about your experience."

"At first, when the rebel Communards took over, they went wild. I witnessed two French generals—French, not Prussian you should notice—being executed in the most brutal fashion in front of a cheering mob."

"That must have been Lecomte and Thomas," said Henry, "Go on."

"Barricades were put up everywhere, trains stopped, I saw telegraph wires being cut, paving stones were piled up with barrels, ladders and ropes to stop people moving around, I suppose. I kept my British identity papers close to my skin in case I needed them and tried to keep away from the centers of violence, but it could erupt anywhere."

"Yes," said Henry, "I remember Lord Lyons saying at the time that the Parisians were bringing about their own ruin. That election was the signal."

"I saw there was an election of course and there were some proclamations by the Communards. I waited in lines for ages to buy food. But I was excited one evening when I was wandering around in the *Rue de la Folie-Regnault*, for rebels brought out the guillotine from a store and set fire to it, to the delight of the crowd."

"Ah yes, that was the hated instrument of justice used by the Jacobins for aristocrats first, but dissenters later."

"I read on a wall a new decree which said that all between seventeen and thirty-five should enroll in the National Guard and I did not know whether this would apply to me as a British citizen. But it seemed too that anyone who was not a real Red was being imprisoned, butchers especially, for some reason. Men were getting out of Paris as a result, dressing up as girls, using ropes down the ramparts, which must have been very dangerous. I heard of two young men who followed a funeral outside the walls and then ran off.

"I hated most the shelling of the city, presumably by the French army. Beautiful buildings were being destroyed."

"Were you searching for your painters all this time?" Asked Henry.

"Yes, when I could. But the atmosphere was so charged and so exciting, I was enjoying myself. I thought I could never be hurt, fool that I am. I stayed in the center of the city, venturing occasionally to Montmartre but not going to the outskirts like Neuilly, which were hotly contested."

Henry interrupted this narrative.

"We think that this insurrection was driven by Reds who turned the real wish of Parisians to govern their own city into this movement. Possibly it is directed by an International Society in London. It was a third, if very limited, French Revolution."

"It was certainly brutal," said Albert.

"Cannon roared all day, it seemed." Albert continued. "I heard bullets crashing against stonework often, Cafes were shut, and it was everyone for himself except for the ruling group. The red flag floated over the Hotel de Ville, and I saw a printing works being burnt and the following day a bank was attacked and looted."

"I blame Thiers and his government for not being prepared to get at Paris earlier by invading with French troops rather than lobbing shells into the city," said Henry, "as that gave the Communards time to organize and to wreak their vengeance on individuals and institutions."

"There was a period of truce, though, and I found my friend Gustave with another painter, Pierre, in a café off the Bois, very depressed. It was eerie when all the noise of firing stopped. Communard soldiers looked very depressed, too, and fortunately none of them tried to recruit me. But they seemed to me to be just a mob by the time of the truce as food was so short, and anyone with anything was a target.

"I went with all Paris to the *Tuileries* when it was opened to the public—goodness me that must only be about six weeks ago. You cannot imagine the luxury, Elizabeth—a bath carved out of marble. Sold silver taps. Like me, the crowd was very curious, but also quietly very angry, for most of them were just very poor people gazing at such riches but caught up in this political chaos.

"Somewhere in my clothes is a piece of the *Colonne Vendome* which I saw being brought down."

"What was that?" asked Elizabeth.

"It was the column with a statue of Napoleon I at the top. I had been one evening in a café a few days before in a large group listening to the painter Courbet, who was the leader of some organization of artists, arguing that it should be smashed. I didn't know artists would have such influence, but politics were different in the Commune."

"But I later saw the *Tuileries* had been set on fire, and various other buildings burnt. I was told they had burnt the Library at the *Louvre* too. I suppose I got so used to the pandemonium of war that I was like a ghost, flitting from building to building.

"They were completely mad. Wanton destruction everywhere, petroleum being thrown about so that everywhere seemed on fire. Worst of all, the rumor had it, hostages were being murdered. But then the French army descended on the city and it was just like hell must be."

"I got caught up in a mob which suddenly surrounded me, not to attack me but it was as if a wave was sweeping everything in front of it. The mob suddenly started to dissipate as French soldiers were coming down the street firing at them, and I am not sure how I got this bullet in or very near my eye, but I felt blinded, stumbled and fell down some steps and hurt my leg. I had no idea it was broken.

"Two soldiers helped me, and I knew enough to say '*je suis anglais*'. I struggled with immense pain, but they abandoned me. Eventually I got myself to the gates of the embassy, which were open as French troops had occupied the gardens.

"Here I am now, in this gorgeous bed, safe and sound."

"I told Elizabeth some weeks ago," said Henry, "that you were brave but exceptionally foolhardy. We must get you back to London to get that eye attended to. I will be coming to England shortly, too, as I have now been told my next assignment is in Athens. Elizabeth can escort you to London and either your stepmother or my sister will care for you. I will have a wire sent to your step-mother in London."

Estella received the news of Albert just before she was to meet with Hamish, Pip and Wemmick each month to assess the project's progress and its financial situation. She was immensely relieved that he was still alive, though worried about his injuries, but she could do little to help, except send him a message hoping he'd recover soon. But then, both Elizabeth and her father were there to take good care of him.

Every half year, the formal meetings of the board were held with Courtisone as counsel, and Smythe as an observer. At the June meeting, Estella was worried at what she saw as a slow pace of activity, and she was now anxious to discuss how they could bring their guests, as she called them, out of prostitution and into a worthwhile living. She explained Fanny Filby's situation, and Hamish brought up Smythe's offer to John Masham as another possibility, which Estella strongly supported.

"Why don't we also help those who have been convicted when they are released?" asked Pip.

"Why don't we help the wives of the convicted? What will happen to Mrs. Twaddell?"

"Wait. Let us assess then what we have so far," said Hamish.

"We have the Jaggers Building with accommodation for twenty souls and it is well staffed, two on permanent basis and a doctor on call. The security is good."

"It seems to have started well," added Pip.

"Secondly, we have a provisional proposal for a Chatham Project, but that is now abandoned?"

"Yes," Estella agreed.

"Third, on finding housing and employment for individuals. We have completed the arrangement with the Fletcher family as they are now able to fund themselves.

"Fourth, we have the suggestion to find occupations for people like Fanny Filby already in the building, and for John Masham, now released from prison, and where appropriate, provide for their families as well."

"I for one am delighted with this progress after only five years," said Estella. "Jaggers would be thrilled."

"Indeed," Wemmick added, "but we must be careful that the lawyers do not spend too much time on the work of the Trust at the expense of working on briefs. We must get the balance right between our anxiety to pursue philanthropy and the bread-and-butter cases which keep us going."

"Mr. Wemmick is correct. That is important," interjected Courtisone.

"As usual," said Hamish, "your counsel is invaluable. Estella, I don't know how much time you wish to spend on these projects."

"Hamish my dear man, a widow like myself always has time. I hope to visit other projects, such as Miss Hill's, which offer housing.

"We'd need to clear the Filby-Masham proposal with our legal counsel. Mr. Courtisone?"

"I see no objection. Indeed, I am mightily impressed with your progress so far. I will at some point suggest one of my younger partners to take my place on the board. I have Philip Hardyman in mind."

"Right, John, we don't need to visit him. Would you draft an invitation letter?

"Of course."

XII

Pip asked Estella to have lunch with him after the meeting.

"I was thinking the other day about my uncle Pip and my mother. I know she taught him some of the rudiments of reading and writing when they were both quite young and before he became a gentleman. But did he ever talk to you about his friendship with her as a child or a young man?"

"Why do you ask?"

"I sat with her just before she died, and she said Pip and she were sweethearts and had agreed to marry before he went off to London and that she felt as much betrayed as he had betrayed Joe."

"Wait, my dear Pip, this is a very severe accusation about my husband, bless his memory. He went through with me how he felt he had let Joe down, far too often in fact, and he probably told you. But I never recall his mention of your mother in that circumstance."

"How did he regard Biddy? As a child, I remember his coming to the Cottage frequently and even when I was grown up and after my injury, but there never seemed then to be any source of friction between them. I thought they were more like brothers and sisters."

"Exactly. Now I can imagine Biddy and Pip as youngsters tramping around those marshes on a sunny summer afternoon, then sitting on the grass, picking buttercups and shining them under their chins, laughing and rolling around, which led to a bit of kissing. Then she says she loves him, or the other way round, and he says they will be married one day, and she says how lovely and gives him another kiss.

"Then they hold hands and get up and run back to the Cottage, embarrassed but very cheerful. So perhaps Biddy was remembering something like that in her old age. Pip would have mentioned it to me, I am sure."

"It is certainly not difficult to imagine, and that does offer an explanation."

"People are so perplexing, aren't they?" said Estella.

"We all have our secrets," she continued, "and we have memories that make us squirm, things we did that were either out of character or downright disgraceful. I find it so difficult to assess others, especially those we love. I think of Miss Havisham my guardian in this respect.

"It could be that, while we think of her fiancé Compeyson as a villain in jilting her, perhaps he saw in her something he could not stand, albeit at the last minute. Maybe he saw she was a controlling woman who would have made their marriage hell. He felt he could not face it. Sometimes I think there are as many ways of interpreting her life as there are birds on the trees."

Pip laughed at that.

"It is interesting, is it not, as with Biddy. My mother might have been in love with Pip all along and married Joe as a substitute!"

Chuckling again, he commented: "No, I don't believe her either."

"To change the subject. Are you both coming to Italy on this Rizzio trip next month? I hope so.

"I think it will be fascinating. There are three couples whom I don't know that well from your neighborhood: Sarah and James Bollaerts, Frederick and Honora Brandram, Charles and Mary Meggison, with the Mudges, Charlotte and her husband, Oliver the Vicar. I should not say this, but I thought at that dinner party that James Bollaerts was a philanderer, and that Frederick was a brute to his wife. Charlotte's husband is rather reactionary in his views, I am told. As for Rizzio, he is a closed book."

"We will obviously have an enjoyable time examining character then as well as art with these people for company."

"You are right, Pip. I am very interested to return to Italy. Rizzio should provide entertainment for us, rather than spending all our time in galleries, some of which I expect I have already visited."

"I hope to enjoy myself too. Susanna has arranged for Lachlan and Malcolm to be cared for and my understanding is we will be away one month, is that correct?"

"Three weeks or maybe a month. Rizzio will need to examine carefully whether we can go through France, which is still a war zone."

At that point, they shook hands warmly and departed. Estella wanted to check the building before setting off for Italy.

The inhabitants of the Jaggers Building comprised women between seventeen and thirty years old, half of them with children under six, and they lived in the same rooms as their mothers. There was what might euphemistically be called a dining room. Pip had furnished the women's rooms, so needed were wooden tables and chairs which Estella had persuaded Algernon Pocket to provide. He donated the oak and poplar and had two of his carpenters assemble them, so they were sturdy and with luck able to resist harsh treatment. The kitchen led off the room to two large stoves where large pots seemed always to be on the boil.

Prowling the floors were three cats, Tinker, Tailor and Soldier, as Pip had seen a rat when viewing the building and thought that these animals would solve any vermin problem and might prove to become pets for staff and guests. Cats were easy to find and these three were no more than overgrown kittens, but they behaved themselves and only once did Tailor bring in a full-sized rat which was immediately buried, as the cook said they carried disease.

That cook was Mrs. Eliza Potenger, whose demeanor, dress and attitudes were familiar to anyone who had worked or lived in an institution where food was made available. A metaphorical rod of iron was wielded by Mrs. P. as her weapon of choice, especially when children crept in to steal food. But she was no tyrant as she had had three boys of her own, now gainfully employed in Billingsgate Fish Market so her own home had a constant whiff of the sea.

The women guests were used to mental and physical combat.

Whores on the streets who lacked a degree of toughness usually did not last, either because they could find no work or because, as with Nellie and Whistler, brutal men savaged them and theirs were the bodies fished out of the Thames, some of whom had been murdered and others who had found the river as the only solace in their miserable lives. Nellie had told her about Nancy Sykes a woman she knew and how her man killed her.

Inevitably, too, groups formed and alliances were made. Those with disease were often shunned, and some longed to get out to regain their independence, dreadful as it might be, though they were not ungrateful.

Sissy was one such woman pining for her soldier husband, now stationed in India, thinking of him belching and farting in a chair by the fire on his return from the nearest hostelry. In his absence she had to stand on a freezing street corner, wind howling round her bare legs and midriff, being a tart, hooker, harlot, succubus or gay, whatever was the abuse term of the culture, month or generation.

Rarely had she used her own room, so she endured lascivious sailors, drunk policemen, or intrepid louts, bitten on the neck or arms and always desperate to clean herself out after two or three such engagements of an evening. 'Three bob standing up' was what she offered, more often than she could count, money in her hand to get something for her children to sup on, before she curled up on a sofa where mice had once made their homes.

But now she was safe in the Jaggers Building.

Pip had appointed a former constable as security who had been badly wounded months before in a fight down Cheapside. He had recovered but his left shoulder was damaged but he could use his left arm and his hands so he could sustain this job. Pip and Estella were pleased to provide an occupation for a brave man as they did not anticipate women engaging in fisticuffs, their ignorance of which showed the distance between the classes.

In any event Mr. George Holditch was strong enough with his right hand to restrain any woman, though perhaps not a horde if ever that happened. Yet his great advantage was that, as a former colleague, police were always on hand if needed and always ready to turn a blind eye too if that were required. Yet the Jaggers Building would always be a target, located where it was and for its distinctive purposes.

Estella took a cab down there before leaving for Italy and arrived just after pandemonium was reaching a crescendo. Crying children and angry women were shouting in the dining room, some screaming, everyone very upset with Mr. Holditch, as it seemed to her. Lying on the floor was a young woman, her dress in tatters, a huge black eye and her bare legs bruised and cut.

"What on earth has been going on, Holditch?"

"I don't rightly know, ma'am."

Estella turned to one of the less excited women, Polly Horsant.

"What's being going on here, Polly?" she asked.

"I fink that's Ethel Coldheart on the floor there, and her man came in somehow, dragged her down 'ere from her room, shouting he would take her away and she was fighting back, so he knocked her down and did her, if you know what I mean, at least that's what they say.

"There were this bangin' and screaming, somefink dreadful and George here, he tried but he couldn't do anything, this man were so strong. Then all the women set on him, dragged 'im off 'er, but then they all said it were George's fault for not stopping him."

"But how is Ethel now?"

"She'll be alright. She's a tart wot's been knocked about before. She'll survive."

"I don't like it though, how could he have got in?"

"Well, I don't like to tell, and I doesn't know whether it's true, but you see that older woman over there, Maud's her name, I think he paid her to let him in."

"How could we have prevented that incident, Holditch?" Estella asked him later.

"I don't know. We can't keep the women as prisoners, like, if they choose to go out, though most of them don't want to 'cos it's so safe here, but if they do, like, then they's going to meet trouble. But that Maud Armstrong is a wrong'un, I think. I know she's done time and for more than what she'd for whoring. Burglary, I think, with a fella, and there was assault there too. Some poor maid got badly beaten up."

"That won't do. We must find a way to discipline her."

"Throw her out, ma'am."

"I suppose so," said Estella, aware that she was not looking after these women, who were not angels who had been defiled and desecrated, but many were women hardened by background and perhaps villains of one sort or another, almost like her mother, Molly.

Yet as she looked forward to Italy, she felt the building was in safe hands.

The journey to Venice took five days on trains, beginning in London, and while the seats were comfortable enough for long journeys, overnight sleeping accommodation was arranged by Rizzio in hotels at four different locations across the continent.

After the long sea journey from Tilbury, a small hotel in Rotterdam proved comfortable for everyone. There followed a very early start for a long journey to Innsbruck with one night en route in Munich where the party stayed at the *Hof Laime* near the Nymphenburg Palace. Then on to Innsbruck where the Grand Hotel, opened only a couple of years earlier, provided them all with luxury accommodation. Rizzio had chosen to travel through Germany and the Austrian part of the Austro-Hungarian Empire rather than through France as the Tyrol rail line was now open and no one knew whether France would be safe.

The final stage of the trip to Mestre and Venice via Verona engendered soothing and staccato conversation as everyone had enjoyed a good night's sleep.

"These mountains are sumptuous, are they not?" offered George Meggison as the train rattled south. "Well worth painting."

"Where are we now?" asked Charlotte later.

"Near Trento, I think," said Rizzio.

"This is really glorious weather, and I am so looking forward to seeing the Colosseum in Verona," said Frederick.

"Now I remember Verona was the site for Shakespeare's *Romeo and Juliet* which I am sure we all know," said Charlotte, "but I have completely forgotten what *Two Gentlemen of Verona* is about."

No one, not even Oliver her husband, could come up with a reply.

After settling in the Hotel Accademia in Verona, the party enjoyed a balmy evening's walk around the city. The warm weather generated a feeling of soporific comfort, though all were apprehensive being in a foreign land. The city was viewed with interest, perhaps more so as it was but a short distance from Venice.

The journey had not occasioned much debate, discussion or controversy on serious matters. At each stop, Brandram the architect would look for houses and major buildings whereas Vicar Oliver Mudge would look for the churches or cathedrals. The women chatted about clothes, lederhosen in Munich being a particularly interesting topic since bare legs were not a feature of men's clothing in England. Estella still saw Honora as a target for her compassion noting her almost total silence, broken only by monosyllables but could not yet see her way to engage with the lady, who seemed to be locked within an invisible carapace. She constantly shared with Charlotte her worry about Albert's condition and received plenty of sympathy.

After Verona, their train passed through Mestre across the causeway to the station at Venice. It was a late summer morning and vapor-filled clouds were dissipating over the Serenissima, billowing their way off the top of the Campanile. Porters scrambled around them and wheeled their cases to the canal where they hired three gondolas, including one for the luggage.

Rizzio was proving an admirable guide with only one rule: Don't ever drink the water. However, the Reverend Oliver Mudge had become thoroughly irritated by Rizzio for reasons that were apparent to no one else that he decided he was not going to be told what to do by some greasy Italian musician.

Questions about drinking the water and whether it was healthy were matters of authority for Oliver. While Rizzio might be competent enough at arranging travel for a party, the vicar determined he could not be regarded as an expert on water. Indeed, he was arrogantly, not blissfully, ignorant of the fact that in Italy it was a matter of luck whether the water was poisonous or not, as towns and village had different systems, usually well water, where the quality depended partly on how much unhealthy material had come out of goats or cows' rear ends.

Contaminated water could yield cholera, the 'blue disease' that Pip had experienced on the ship taking Fletch and him to the Crimea. Hotels and cafes were very careful about boiling water as only a few years before the party arrived over a hundred thousand Italians had died in a cholera outbreak.

Yet the Reverend Oliver Mudge was not daunted, however much others counselled him. He drank from taps near wells when they had wandered around of an evening on the journey. Nor did he suffer, believing that God was on his side. His long-suffering wife Charlotte suffered this behavior in an angry silence.

Walking to the steps where three gondolas were tethered awaiting their human cargo Oliver was thirsty. It was a beautiful warm day. He was dressed in his straw hat, a casual college blazer, shirt and college tie. He walked away from the party to get a drink from a tap on the wall watched by several gondoliers.

"*Signor, signor,*" called a couple of the men, "*Fermati, fermati, quell'acqua è sporca.*"

Oliver turned on the tap and cupped his hands, then paused to look around and see who was calling. Since he did not know any Italian though still could handle some Latin, he realized he was being asked to stop. The two men rushed over to him, leaving their straw hats in their gondolas and grabbed his hands so that the water spilled.

"Who do you think you are?" he shouted to the alarm of the party, but especially to Charlotte and Rizzio who immediately rushed over to the remonstration.

"Sir, they are telling you not to drink the water," said Rizzio firmly.

"I am not going to be told what to do by a couple of rowers," he replied.

"Then you will become ill and die."

At this point, Charlotte arrived and told Oliver he was keeping everyone waiting, which appealed to his sense of decorum where concerns for his mortality had no influence. The gondoliers shook their heads in disbelief, though they were used to the vagaries of tourists.

After settling into their hotel near St. Mark's, the party sat outside the Café Florian after dinner, watching pigeons and people. Next day, in the *Scuola di San Rocco*, Oliver challenged the elderly guide saying that a particular painting was not a Tintoretto, as it was not like the others. That mildly upset everyone except Susanna who got very angry indeed.

"Mr. Mudge," she said in a loud hectoring tone, her Scottish background audible in her excitement: "You know nothing whatsoever about this painter or his work. Tell me, before you continue to insult this guide, have you ever seen a Tintoretto painting before you walked in here half an hour ago?"

Silence.

"I thought not. You are becoming rather objectionable, you know, with this attitude that you know everything about everything, except about the fact that you yourself are an opinionated silly old man who wants to be noticed."

"Madam, I must protest at the violence of your language."

"In which case," Susanna retorted, "you had best change your behavior and with it, the way you think about yourself and your effect on others. You are very close to destroying the happiness and companionship of this expedition and you will never be forgiven if you do. Or is this kind of disruption your real aim?"

Pip whispered to Susanna to be careful not to be too excited and took her hand as they moved around the room, examining with care the paintings that had hung there for three hundred years or so. Rizzio walked to the other end of the room in tears, certain that this stupid man would break up the party for which he had labored so long.

Charlotte ignored her husband's argument with Susanna and talked quietly to Estella who held her arm, commenting that the soft, dark light from the candles made it difficult to see the paintings in all their glory.

"My dear," said Estella as they went from the building into the square, "I am sure we will see some of his work in other better-lit rooms. But why is your husband so contrary?"

They sat down on stone seats around a plane tree.

"I wish I knew, Estella. My marriage has been a great trial. Oliver is a pious man, but not an intelligent one. I knew this before I married him, but what I did not realize that his frustration at his own inadequacy manifests itself in a truculence. I did not really want him to come but come he would.

"He is just intelligent enough to see that he is not gifted in any way, intellectually, emotionally, perhaps even spiritually which is why we are stuck out in the wilds of Norfolk. Yet he persists in thinking of himself as being the next person to become a bishop! I tell you this in confidence of course, but I gave up loving him some years ago, and caring for him only a few months ago."

"Was there an occasion for that?"

"Yes, and this really is a secret," she said as they moved out into the sunshine.

"I had been in London for a few days but returned earlier than expected. It was a fine evening and the trap put me down at the gate as I wanted to wander up the drive to the Vicarage, both to look at the garden and to steel myself to being with him again. I went into the house, opening the front door that was on the latch, put my bag down, called out to him, and went into his study.

"I heard him talking. He was sitting there half naked, bare to his waist. With him were two young boys from the choir, sitting on their haunches on the floor, both completely naked. There was a group of candles burning in the middle of the floor.

"I just called out 'what on earth are you doing?'"

"Alright, you two," he said to the boys. "We will resume our lessons at another time. Go now," and the children gathered their clothes in a hurry and fled for the door.

"I was more than astonished. It was obvious to me then that he was well on the way to some sort of perverted practices about which I wished to know nothing. I went to bed, sleeping in a room reserved for guests. When we met at breakfast, he apologized sincerely. I had to ask him what it was all about, as if I didn't know. He said the boys were taking confirmation instruction and he wanted to find out what ways would attract boys into the true religion, how they could face God 'naked and unashamed.'"

"Oh, my dear Charlotte, what a terrible thing."

"Complete nonsense of course. Goodness knows where that sort of thing might have led, though I doubt it already has, as far as I know. As you know, my dear, it is quite impossible for a vicar's wife to divorce, let alone the problems for the laity. I therefore spend as much time as I can get away with in London. I could not really stop him from coming on this trip but our marriage is now an empty shell. My worry is that he is beginning to be even more bizarre, and I even think he might be going mad.

"It is so difficult. By the way, I am going to have to leave my Chelsea home as the officer and family will be returning from India."

"Then you shall stay with me at Semper House until you decide what to do."

The party spent four days in Venice before heading off to Florence. Their most interesting excursion, apart of course from the Palace of the Doges, the Church of St Mark and the Friary Church, was a trip on three gondolas around the lagoon, stopping for lunch on Murano to watch men blow glass and then on to a scarcely inhabited Torcello, but with the extraordinary mosaics in the church which seemed to come from both Roman and Byzantine traditions.

Brandram, the architect, was lost in wonder at how that could have been achieved in the eleventh century. Estella and Charlotte, arm in arm, spoke of the passions that had made men build such churches, and how few such new ecclesiastical structures were being built in Christian Europe, which, of course, Oliver overheard and attributed to living in a heathen culture. Pip and Susanna walked hand in hand around the Church of Santa Maria Assunta thinking of their own chapels so bereft of decoration.

"I wonder," Susanna said, "have we nonconformists gone too far? Should not people be inspired by such beauty, the beauty of holiness?"

"When I think of our Queen Street Chapel in Salford and this magnificent church and all those who came to both, worshipping the same God," said Pip, "I wonder why we have allowed our differences to take charge of our similarities? I know the history of nonconformity: Luther, Calvin, Zwingli and the Wesleys recently. But we need to think again and just imagine what it would be like, my dear, to preach in such a building, one's voice echoing around the paintings and the mosaics speaking of God's love for us."

"Perhaps we should think more carefully about our children's religious upbringing, perhaps showing them the worship of God in different traditions."

"Let us not discuss this in front of the Reverend, darling."

"Dear me no, though he does seem to have been quieter since I admonished him yesterday."

"Brilliant, as ever my dear, very well judged, to the point and expressing what everyone else would have been delighted to have said."

Estella and Charlotte were also impressed by the Church and its beauty, but they resumed their preoccupation with Honora whose silence had concerned Estella for months. She seemed a sad creature, her husband's fashionable clothes in contrast to hers which, while quite in the fashion, seemed to take on a dowdy appearance as if influenced by her manner. The pair decided to try to make Honora their project for the rest of the expedition. They began by insisting that she join them in a gondola for the long journey back across the lagoon to Venice.

XIII

That last night in Venice Estella lay thinking about Albert and then about Charlotte and Oliver and wishing she could share what she had heard about them with her beloved dead husband Pip. It was Charlotte's last word about her husband, 'mad,' that occupied her thoughts, though she had not encountered madness since her last years with Miss Havisham. Then there was Honora, poor woman. Yet what pleased her was how her own friendship with Charlotte was developing, here indeed was a stable woman friend.

She liked Susanna, but they were just friendly, not real friends. Why could that be? How come Miss Havisham had not wanted her to meet other women of her class? Thinking of her past with that woman as she drifted toward sleep, she mused about just how evil her guardian was—well, perhaps not quite evil, but damn close.

Rizzio marshalled everyone to leave for Florence, the train passing through Padua and Bologna, a mere hundred and fifty miles, so the party would arrive in Florence without feeling tired. Gondolas had brought the party hurriedly and late to the station, primarily because Oliver had left his Bible in Florian's where he went for coffee early each morning. The women gathered in one of the two compartments as the train was preparing to leave.

In the other compartment were the men. A division arose because two of the men, Bollaerts and Brandram, smoked cigars on a regular basis. Rizzio found the tobacco difficult, but not wanting to upset the men, made his excuses to wander around outside on the train.

"Why does he not want to be with us?" asked Oliver, whom the two smokers had privately dubbed "The Mad Vicar."

"Oh," said Meggison, "some people find cigar smoking difficult."

"I don't see why you should give up the pleasure of smoking," said Oliver, "just because some greasy Italian objects."

"Wait," said Meggison, "please do not refer to my neighbor Rizzio in such a derogatory tone."

"That's the trouble with you fancy artists," Oliver replied, "you just think people should be free to do what they want, even if they come from an inferior race. Italians are the scum of the earth, and as they are inferior they should put up with what we want."

"What are you talking about?" asked Bollaerts angrily. "Don't you know that Italians are the descendants of the Roman Empire, a great and prosperous people who conquered the known world?"

"Huh," said Oliver disapprovingly. "They engaged in some terrible practices. They had Christians slaughtered in their colosseums. They were drunkards who vomited their suppers to have more wine. They crucified men and slaves. Their armies enslaved thousands. They stood by while Christ was crucified. Crassus alone crucified five thousand men lining the route into Rome with this spectacle as he came in triumph! Let alone Caligula who bedded every woman in his family, and one of Claudius' wives had over a hundred men sequentially. They were beasts and Italians are their descendants."

"And, of course, Englishmen are pure as the driven snow?" said Brandram, "You talk nonsense most of the time, Mudge, goodness knows what sort of rubbish comes out of your mouth in the pulpit!"

"I preach the word of God."

"Does God think Italians are inferior? What is all this then about loving your neighbor?"

"Don't you lecture me about religion, you heathen!" he said loudly, his eyes bulging as he jumped up from his seat, getting increasingly irate. In the corner the sleeping Pip stirred.

There was a brief silence.

"I object, I object," screamed Oliver, foaming at the mouth and wagging his finger in Brandram's face.

"Sit down, you silly man," said Bollaerts.

"Are you mad?" asked Brandram.

"I can't stand this. I can't stand this. You are all heathens!" shouted Oliver so loudly most of the train could hear, just as it was stopping at the station in Padua.

Oliver opened the door the moment before the train halted and stepped out, landing with a crash on the ground, much to the surprise of sober Paduan matrons awaiting the train for Florence. Pip awoke with a start to find his companions all trying to get out of the train to attend to the aberrant vicar, now sprawled on the ground with a bloody face.

"Where is Charlotte?" Pip asked.

In the next compartment the women were deep in conversation, ignoring what was happening outside when Rizzio burst in:

"Mrs. Mudge, your husband, he is wounded!"

"Has he been in a battle?"

"No, he jumps off the train," Rizzio getting his tenses muddled in the excitement.

Various Italian railway employees were now on the scene with their gesticulations arguing whether the vicar should be moved, whether an ambulance should be called, whether he should be fined for trespassing, whether the train should be disembarked and, had they gone on much longer, whether God exists.

Pip and Bollaerts lifted the poor man off the ground. He was much shaken by his self-imposed ordeal, God apparently leaving the vicar to his fate. Charlotte had dismounted and walked to him, peering down at her husband's blood-stained face and asking in a kindly voice:

"Why did you jump off the train, my dear? You were not pushed, were you?" at which Brandram whispered to Pip that it was a close thing.

"I am hurt, Charlotte. I think I may be dying."

"Stuff and nonsense. I expect you lost your temper again."

"No, I did not. I was merely expostulating with my heathen companions about the vices of the Roman Empire."

"And that caused you to jump off the train?" asked Charlotte incredulously.

"You know, Oliver, I think you should see a doctor when we get back to London. Your tempers are becoming increasingly bizarre."

By this time, Oliver had recovered somewhat and was standing up. The Italian employees, with more exaggerated gesticulations than heretofore, were demanding that they all get back on the train as it was now running late, a not unusual occurrence in that country. The members of the party clambered up the steps, Oliver assisted by Pip. The train's whistle sounded. Oliver was attended to by Charlotte and Susanna and brought into their compartment. Bollaerts was amused by the whole exchange and commented to Brandram that he would remember Padua with sorrow, and they giggled like schoolboys.

Pip signaled to Estella in her compartment, for she had sat quietly through the brouhaha and they walked to an empty compartment.

"Does religion really drive men crazy?" asked Estella, at which Pip could not control his laughter and she joined in. The noise of their laughter could be heard along the train and Oliver immediately sensed that the laughter must be directed at his escapade which unsettled him, though Charlotte managed to quieten him in much the same way as one might seek to quiet a dog which had been suddenly frightened.

Susanna was thinking of that possibility and wishing she had a muzzle.

"No," said Pip, still giggling, "but people can get very confused. Seriously, I suspect that the vicar is suffering a brain problem of some sort. He seems to lack self-control which is not the best quality for a man of the cloth. Actually, I do think he is ill."

"He is indeed very strange. Charlotte has confided in me about some of his behavior, and I suspect she thinks he is going mad. You know, some people who are very religious are so distant from reality that they do go mad."

"I met some strange elders when I was preaching. The problem with a lack of self-control is what we have just witnessed. A person can inflict severe injury upon themselves because they lose sight of the world as it is."

"You are right, but Oliver cannot be committed to an asylum, surely. He is not that lunatic, yet."

"It may come to that, but poor Charlotte. It must be a terrible responsibility."

"Yes and no. If he is just a very unpleasant person to live with and will not change his behavior, then she would just have to accept that and live her life independently."

"But don't the bonds of matrimony demand otherwise?"

"No Pip, they do not, if a woman is to be treated as an equal in the way that you committed yourself to Susanna. If one is an equal, but in a loveless decrepit marriage, I see no reason why a woman, or for that matter, a man, should not just move away. Of course, were there children to be cared for, another whole set of obligations and questions would arise. But in the Mudge marriage, there are no children."

"I was about to say, 'what about convention?' when I realize that is precisely the point. Modern conventions assign an inferior place to the woman whereas that must be changed. Yet she must also pay attention to her vows, must she not?"

"Do I hear the pot calling the kettle black? I must not make fun of you, dear Pip. Of course, convention forbids independence, and with that comes new relationships like that lady you communed with in Salford, the lovely Harriet."

"What do you mean?" He asked in surprise.

"Tut, tut, Pip, my apologies for the use of the adjective, though it was correctly applied, was it not?" and she smiled.

"As a matter of fact—" and here she interrupted him.

"Oh God, don't tell me."

"Please let me confide in you. As with my dear uncle, I have things on my conscience, not all of which I share with Susanna."

"Please, Pip, do not go on. I hate having secrets, especially close to home. Let me ask you just one question. Are you still in contact with Harriet?"

"No."

"Then I care not about your past and I do not wish to have the burden of knowledge of any of your indiscretions."

"But I do need a confidant."

"I can understand that, but on this matter, I wish to remain utterly ignorant. Anyway, needing a confidant is just a sign of weakness. Keep your sins to yourself. Tell God if you wish, though I am sure He already knows," she said again with a friendly smile.

"Well, don't worry, it is quite finished. Though she did say when I last saw her that she was going to Florence to study the Renaissance."

"Pip, really, you are incorrigible. So that's why you were keen to see Florence and not Rome."

"No, I was genuine about that, but I last saw her months ago and who knows where she might be? But to return to Oliver, we will just have to see how he behaves. He is going to see a number of paintings of women which will occasion his disapproval, and I'll be interested to witness his reactions."

As the train trundled toward Florence, Oliver went to sleep and the two compartments fell silent. Susanna continued to struggle with *Das Kapital,* both with the argument and the weight of the book. Bollaerts gazed out of the window. Brandram lit another cigar, and the turbulence at Padua was soon put aside, though not forgotten. Honora pretended to sleep, seeing all that had happened as a very bad omen.

The Grand Hotel Cavour had been chosen, and everyone admired this magnificent hotel, tracing its history to the thirteenth century and it proved a delightful, if expensive, place to sojourn for a few days. Rizzio rejected several pleas to go to Rome, citing the current Italian political turmoil and, whatever its ancient monuments and buildings, its reputation for filth on the streets, beggars on the pavements, and, as Rizzio had put it with a smile, too many nuns, so Rome was not on the itinerary. Nothing to do with Pip's enthusiasm for Firenze, as the Italians call Florence.

Albert and Elizabeth arrived back in London in July under diplomatic protection, and they hastened to Semper House. Albert was in great pain and after a disturbed night they went to the Moorfields Eye Hospital the next morning. His leg had suffered a clean break, had been well set, and would heal in due course. Crutches helped his perambulation. His eye was a different problem, and Mr. Nettleship, a physician specializing in treatment of eyes, came to examine it.

"It looks to me," said Nettleship, wielding an immense magnifying glass, "that the bullet struck you a glancing blow on the cheekbone just by your eye, but it looks as though there is a tiny metallic splinter there which won't be bone, but maybe a piece of the bullet? Hopefully that is embedded in the eye's surface, what we call the cornea, without penetrating the interior of the eye. Certainly, your eye is full of blood. The splinter may wash out but if it has gone into your eye, that is unlikely. I take it you cannot see much if anything out of that eye. Let me put my hand over your right eye."

"What can you see?"

"A dark haze."

"H'mm. I will be delighted if you recover any sight in that eye, but I am not confident that you will, I am afraid. Keep the patch on and come and see me in a month. Meantime, I see you have someone to look after you."

On their return in the afternoon, Albert went straight to bed and slept. Elizabeth took it upon herself to send a wire to Estella as she knew she would be worrying about him:

'BACK IN SEMPER HOUSE STOP RECOVERING STOP HAVE SEEN EYE DOCTOR STOP LOVE ALBERT STOP'

She then lay down next to him on the bed, weeping slightly, and holding his hand near her lips and kissing it from time to time and dozing. They were both awakened later when the maid tapped at the door, saying there was a Mr. and Mrs. Macdonald coming to call. Neither Hamish nor Mary had wanted to join the Italy trip. His work was very demanding, and she wanted to be by his side.

"I'll be there directly," said Elizabeth. She hurriedly composed herself and went down, followed by Albert negotiating the stairs.

"Now that the fighting is done in Paris we thought to come, and that there might be news of Albert," said Hamish.

"You are a very brave young man," said Mary as Albert appeared, "though I expect Estella is worried sick about you."

"I am afraid she is," said Albert, recovering somewhat but speaking in a low voice, "and the party is supposed to be in Florence this evening. Elizabeth sent her a wire as if from me to say I am fine."

"What do the doctors say about your eye?"

"I am hoping for the best but expecting to be blind in one eye or, at any rate, have only a little sight there. But it will take some time before I know. But how are you both? Now that you are married, I heard."

"We are quite well," said Hamish, "but we do have some excellent news. Mary is expecting our first baby."

At that Elizabeth jumped out of her chair and put her arms tightly around Mary.

"Oh, how wonderful for you both."

"Estella will be thrilled," said Albert, "as I am sure will Charlotte. I will send another wire directly."

Two wires then arrived from London at the Grand Cavour. At the first, Estella's relief was palpable, but it was still disquieting about his eye. Tragic if he was blind, even in just one eye. Charlotte provoked mild amusement from Estella by saying that a painter with one eye and a patch would need only a smock to look the part, whatever his work was like! But the second wire announcing Mary's baby was cause for a bottle of champagne for the party.

"Goodness, we are beset with news," said Charlotte. "I've a letter from Henry forwarded from Chelsea. His marriage is virtually over as Mary-Lou shows no sign of wishing to come back to Europe, but most important of all, he is expecting to move to become a counsellor in Athens or Secretary to the Legation."

"He does not say what Elizabeth will do, though he does say how much he has valued her being with him through the trials of Parisian uproar. He also hints, somewhat vaguely, that his health has suffered, though he does not say why, which is hardly a good basis on which to venture to Athens."

"Oh dear, it will break Albert's heart if she goes with her father."

"An interesting problem is it not, Estella. If she comes to me for advice, what am I to say?"

"It may depend on how she phrases the question. If it is 'do you think it is my duty to stay with Albert and not go with my father,' or of course the other way round. My point here is whether she will talk about the problem in terms of duty, rather than love."

"Her duty will clearly be with her father, Estella, will it not? He will need a woman as his hostess in that environment. He is not well, his wife has left him, and she does not owe Albert anything, does she?

"Except of course that Albert is also now unwell," she said quietly.

"That is true, but I will be there to care for him and I would be confident that father and daughter have discussed the absence of the American mother and I would also be confident that she has told him she would care for him."

"Those are my thoughts, too, Estella. If Albert is well, he could go to Athens, too. They do know each other from their adventurous times in Paris."

"I think we have common ground here as the young people talk to us about it. We will say to each of them: Elizabeth must go, and Albert can visit, assuming he wants to, and she wants him to!"

They laughed together heartily and left the dining room arm in arm to prepare for the day's excursion to the Uffizi.

They walked down the streets toward the Arno River, gazing at the historic center with the statue of the fearsome Lorenzo di Medici and Michelangelo's David, which excited Oliver. He had joined Charlotte and Estella on the walk and when he saw that magnificent marble creation, he went into a muttering mood, realizing that his previous outbursts had not been well received.

"How awful, how terrible," he said to no one in particular, "how typically Italian to have a nude man where women and children can see it. David wasn't naked when he killed Goliath. Saul had given him his armor, but David felt it was too uncomfortable. He had his pouch on his garments so he couldn't have been naked."

"What are you muttering about?" asked Charlotte as they wandered across the square to the Uffizi.

"That statue is disgusting. The Bible clearly says David was not naked when he killed Goliath, so why is he like that? It is both a mistake and an affront."

"Oh dear," said Charlotte.

"Oliver my dear, why don't you take a quiet walk down to the river, just go down that street there. We will go into this museum, and you can meet us back here in a couple of hours for lunch. We will wait for you. I think you need some peace and quiet."

"Yes, alright. I am too disturbed to see paintings and sculptures. I will go to the river. You are right, my dear. I do need peace and quiet. Goodbye."

As he walked off slowly, Charlotte said quietly to Estella:

"I really think my husband is going mad. Here is one of the most celebrated Biblical heroes which one would have thought he would have loved, but instead he gets bothered by nudity."

"Let us see some paintings. I particularly want to see the Botticelli *Birth of Venus*."

Getting directions from a guide, they went through various rooms, stopping occasionally, but finally stood in front of the painting. Surrounding it were various couples of different ages. Estella was transfixed by Venus' beauty, and she remembered her being born full-formed from the foam of the sea.

The image was not what a woman could have looked like, she thought, with that long neck, but she eschewed the realism that had been all too apparent in Oliver's mutterings earlier. The face was extraordinary in its calm, pale gaze. She could not help the comparison with Nellie's nakedness when she had emerged from that downpour, another goddess out of water. That now seemed a long time ago, but it was still fresh in her mind.

"When was this painted?" she asked Charlotte.

"As I recall, toward the end of the fifteenth century, probably for a rich Medici decorating his house."

"It is surprisingly fresh after all those years. I hope they can continue to look after it. Let us sit down and take it all in."

The crowds had thinned out and they sat down on the bench next to a woman who was writing and drawing.

"I wonder what the men will think of it?" said Charlotte. "I am glad Oliver didn't come with us. He'd be preaching, telling us we'd all be damned if we looked at it."

"Of our party," said Estella, "I think the men, apart from Pip, will look at it with a prurient eye. Honora will be embarrassed. You know, we must get hold of that woman; she seems like a ghost most of the time."

The woman next to them seemed startled by overhearing this conversation and began slowly to put together her things as if she were about to leave.

"I hope we didn't disturb you," said Charlotte.

"Oh no, I was just preparing to leave."

"Are you a student of the arts?

"Yes, I am staying in Florence for several months. I have looked at the important churches, Santa Croce, the Cathedral and one or two others and am now exploring famous paintings. Are you here long?

"A few days, yes."

"Then you must see the leather-workers next to San Croce. They are astonishingly skilled. Let me introduce myself, I am Harriet Middleham from London."

"And I am Charlotte Mudge from Norfolk and London, and this is my friend Estella Pirrip, also from London."

Estella almost trembled as she shook hands with Harriet and said nothing but a how d'ye do, though her mind reeled with images of this beautiful woman in ecstasy with Pip. She had great difficulty containing herself.

Harriet also was recalling Pip's mention of a woman called Estella married to his uncle, perhaps.

"I hope we will meet again. We could learn from you. We are staying at the Grand Cavour," said Charlotte.

"Oh, I am in a lodging almost next door. I will seek you both out one evening soon and show you some of the nicest places tourists don't visit."

"We'd like that," said Estella and then to Charlotte's surprise, "and by the way, I believe we have a mutual acquaintance."

"Really," said Harriet. "Who could that be?"

"Were you not a friend of a preacher, Pip by name, in Salford?"

"Indeed, yes, we were great friends. Do you know him?"

At that moment, Pip and Susanna with Honora close by entered the gallery, though they seem not to have yet noticed Harriet and Estella in conversation.

"That's him and his wife over there."

"I would like to stay and meet them again, but I really do need to see my tutor," and she walked away briskly to a far door.

"What was that about?" asked Charlotte.

"I'll tell you anon," she whispered, as Pip and Susanna came across the gallery toward them.

Later that morning, Estella and Charlotte stood waiting for Oliver by the David. They finally gave up, found a small café for lunch, and went back into the Uffizi for the afternoon. There was no sign of Oliver at the hotel either, but Charlotte was not disturbed by his absence, though when she was dressing for dinner, she was increasingly alarmed.

When she went downstairs, the party was gathering for an aperitif.

"Have anyone seen my husband?" she asked.

"No, was he not with you?"

"Oh dear, I should not have let him go off on his own. He is probably lost."

As she said that, two policemen came into the hotel and went to the desk. The receptionist pointed over to where Charlotte was conversing with the men.

"*Scusi*," said the older man, and he held out Oliver's pocketbook, soaking wet.

"That's my husband's pocketbook. Where did you find it? Where is he?"

"I am so sorry, signora," said the man in halting English, "a body was drawn out of the river this afternoon with this pocketbook in it."

XIV

Charlotte burst into tears and Estella reeled in shock. Honora scuttled away, weeping copiously. Bollaerts, Meggison and Brandram all stood up almost involuntarily to express their sorrow to Charlotte. Pip and Susanna hugged each other as they rose to sympathize. Rizzio too was in tears, seeing his whole expedition collapsing in ruin.

"Signora, we like for you to come and see the body," the first policeman said in broken English.

"Of course," said Estella, "Charlotte, dear, you will need to identify Oliver, but any one of us could do that."

"No, I will do it," Charlotte said firmly.

Meggison took the second policeman aside and asked about the corpse, because he wanted to be sure for Charlotte's sake that the body from which the pocketbook was taken was in fact the mad vicar's. In broken Italian, he asked quietly for the deceased's appearance, hair color, anything that would distinguish him trying to make sure it was indeed Oliver before subjecting Charlotte to the particular dispiriting exercise of post-mortem identification.

"I did not see him closely, but he did have very blond hair."

"Are you sure," asked Meggison, "because her husband, the man whose pocketbook that was, had dark hair?"

"I ask my colleague. You wait."

The senior policeman was then taken aside, and he confirmed that the dead man had blond hair.

At that moment there was a crash at the main entrance to the hotel sending the buttons boy flying and knocking the liveried doorman off balance. Oliver appeared staggering, wild-eyed, his clothes in total disarray, with no hat, his spectacles awry and he promptly collapsed on the marble floor. Charlotte and Honora screeched in unison and Estella and Pip rushed towards him.

Now the whole hotel lobby was showing interest in what was clearly a man of the cloth lying spread-eagled on the floor of the foyer in the main entrance to this very grand hotel.

"Is that pastor drunk?" asked an American woman sipping a cocktail, with a bosom not merely noticeable for its size but for the clusters of diamonds which decorated it.

"I guess so, Honey,"—for that was her name—"probably German," said her husband, puffing at his cigar as they got up to walk to the dining-room.

Pip and Estella helped Oliver to his feet and walked him to a quiet corner with the rest of the party following. That itself was a task, as the huge marble floored centerpiece of the hotel lacked many quiet spaces. However, a nook was found with several small seats.

"What on earth happened to you, Oliver?" Charlotte asked, "why have you lost your pocketbook?"

"Have I?" he said feeling all his pockets.

"For goodness' sake, tell us what happened," said Charlotte.

"I am not sure," he said, starting to recover from what seemed to have been an ordeal.

"Let me think. Yes. When I left you with that obscene statue, I saw an interesting building across the river, the Pitti Palace. I was not feeling very well by the time I got to the river, so I rested, and two young men sat down beside me and started talking in German about me, I am sure."

"You didn't cross the Ponte Vecchio bridge, then, to get to the Pitti Palace?" asked Rizzio.

"No, no, I saw the bridge when I was sitting there, but I didn't cross."

"What happened?" asked Charlotte. "Tell us slowly, don't hurry."

"I sat for ten minutes and then got up to walk along the riverside pavement, and the two young men from the bench got up following me and we got into conversation as they spoke enough English."

"Were they well-dressed?" said Meggison.

"No, but then one of them said they would find a woman for me further along the river. I did not at first understand what they were talking about, so I asked them, and they said the vilest most disgusting things, making signs with their hands, and I got very angry," at which Bollaerts and Brandram exchanged a smirk.

"They then began to bump into me. I was trying to get away from them, but they were on either side manhandling me. I don't remember what happened properly, but we turned into a street where there was a little canal running into the river. They began to hit my back and my front, and I lost my hat, fell over, got up and as I am quite strong, I then pushed one of the men very hard and he fell backwards into the canal. The other man immediately ran away. I stumbled and fell over on the way back here, whilst hurrying back the way I had come."

"Great heavens," said Charlotte, "did you not stop to see what happened to the man in the canal?"

"Of course not. Why should I? I expect he got a bit wet," said Oliver laughing.

"More than wet," said Meggison, "He's dead."

"He's what?" exclaimed Oliver. "Oh, my goodness, I am very sorry."

"Yes," said the first policeman, "he was pulled out of the river this morning and your pocketbook was found on him. Here it is."

"What a tragedy! The poor man. I didn't mean to hurt him, but he was pestering me. He must have taken my pocketbook somehow in the struggle."

"But you found your way back, so well done," said Charlotte, looking carefully at her bedraggled husband, "though your clothes are a mess."

"Ah," said Bollaerts, "they must have been pickpockets as well as pimps."

The first policeman spoke in a severe tone.

"Signor, you may stay here tonight but you must promise you come to the *statzione di politia* at 10 o'clock tomorrow."

"Oh dear, my head aches. Why should I do that? I am the one who has been hurt?"

"Because the man you pushed is dead."

"It was his own fault if he could not swim," and he laughed loudly, though no one else did.

"I will make certain he is there," interjected Charlotte, "and Rizzio will accompany us so that we have an interpreter."

"This is more than merely bizarre, all of it," said Estella.

"I will take Oliver to our room so that he can wash and compose himself so that he can eat. He looks famished as well as dirty."

"We will wait for you," said Estella, and Pip and Susanna concurred.

Honora asked her husband Frederick Brandram if she could stay too and he waved his hand saying, "Do as you wish, my dear."

Hamish and Mary's plans to go for a vacation that August were abandoned, partly because Wemmick became ill and Hamish felt he could not possibly leave Clarence Smythe holding the fort over a few weeks. He went across the Thames to Walworth to see how Wemmick was faring. He found a rather sorry sight.

Mrs. Wemmick opened the door, obviously very concerned.

"He's not been well for a while, I'm afraid. He had this 'orrible 'eadache about ten days ago, and then he got this rash on his stomach. Since then, he's not been breathing very well and I'm afraid he may have pneumonia, though the doctor doesn't."

"Can I see him?"

"Yes, of course. The doctor has given him some medicine which is helping with his chest, but he is very poorly."

Hamish was shown upstairs into a bedroom with a nice view of the garden at the back of the house. Wemmick was lying in obvious distress, breathing poorly.

"Hamish, thank you for coming. I was going to write. This disease is called shingles by my doctor, and I have to be very careful to rest completely. I wanted to say that you should go ahead and get a clerk to replace me immediately as I am going to take months to recover."

"My dear Wemmick, you have been such a pillar of stability in this practice that a position is always open to you, even if you can only come in for a morning when you want, just to dispense your advice which is always so welcome. But I do agree, and I will begin a search promptly, though I will come, if I may, and share the diligence with you on any individuals we meet, if, of course, you are well enough."

"I will try, Hamish, I will try. I had a conversation with one of the clerks at Courtisone's office when we were there, and I think he might well be amenable to coming to Little Britain. Try him, he is Adam Masterson. Now, before you go, tell me about Mary."

"Ah, now we do have good news; my wife is pregnant."

"Oh, that gives me great pleasure. You'll find fatherhood a wonderful experience. That privilege has not been granted to me, nor was it to Mr. Jaggers, but Old Pip enjoyed it greatly, when he had time."

"Thank you. I will come and see you again soon. Rest now."

He got up to go straightaway as John Wemmick had fallen asleep. Mrs. W. was crying softly at the bottom of the stairs.

"He is a strong man, Mrs. W. I am sure he will pull through this."

"Oh, I do hope so."

From there, Hamish went to Courtisone's office in the late morning, not expecting to meet with him, as he was so often in court. He was fortunate, however, and was able to see the great man immediately.

"Ah, Macdonald, how very good to see you. I heard all about this disgraceful case with Twaddell. I wrote to Sandy Tulloch earlier and he was not effusive, but rather he said he thought Twaddell was not very happy and that he wanted to be in London. So, as you will have noticed from my letter, I reflected Tulloch's assessment."

"Indeed, we wanted to interview each of them, but he astonished me by his demands on remuneration and partnership. The first time we met him he was making exorbitant demands which Wemmick scotched, and the blackmail you will know about."

"The blackmail? What on earth do you mean? I only heard about the sodomy."

"Let me explain. Twaddell was under the impression that I am a sodomite. He asked to see me and threatened to expose me if I did not offer him a partnership or at least employ him as a part-time consultant. This was just before I became engaged.

"I consulted Wemmick and I met the man later, and he saw his mistake. Twaddell had the effrontery to summon my junior, Clarence Smythe, from the Gallery of the court to be a witness. He was there as we needed to recover our bail for Twaddell."

"You bailed him? That was generous."

"Well, yes, we were in some doubt about the accusations because at interview he behaved as a latter-day John Knox," at which Courtisone roared with laughter.

"I thought we should help him in that way which carried little, if any, risk."

"But when called from the Gallery, Smythe told the judge he could only be a hostile witness as he had met with the other young man being accused and with whom Twaddell had consorted."

"Yes, that part I heard about from Francis Comely the other night at the Jeffries Club. My goodness, for a young man leading a practice you have not been short of excitement, have you? How is Smythe getting on?"

"He is first class, absolutely first class. He will improve his advocacy, I am sure."

"I knew his mother well years ago. She was, still is, a fine beauty and we young men all had to take our turn trying to attract her attention, but she married Hugo and they have been happy all these years though he has been profligate with money. But what did you wish to see me about?"

"Ah, yes. My clerk, John Wemmick is seriously ill, and I need to replace him. He suggested that I ask one of your two senior clerks, Adam Masterson, if he might be willing to join us. I thought it appropriate to ask your permission to talk with him first and indeed invite any comments you might have about him."

"That is very wise of you to ask me, and I greatly appreciate such old-world courtesy which seems to be on the decline these days."

"That is most kind of you," said Hamish. "I am concerned, very concerned, that without Wemmick, life is going to be very hard."

"Now that you are here, I want to open up a prospect for you which has been on my mind for some time," Courtisone said. "When my friend Nathaniel Jaggers was alive, we used to talk from time to time about how we wished we had set up our practice together. But, as you may know, mine is a very old established family practice dating back to my forebears, and Nathaniel in truth wanted to be on his own.

"I am getting old, in fact, far too old. I have three younger partners, none of whom are members of my family as my wife and I were blessed only with daughters. Abigail, my oldest, would love to have joined me but as a woman she is ineligible.

"So, my question is whether we might merge our practices creating a *Courtisone and Jaggers* firm, as I am sure you intend to keep the Jaggers title for your practice. I have no doubt my partners will be agreeable."

"What an exceedingly interesting possibility, Mr. Courtisone. I am taken aback and will need time to think about it."

"Of course, it will take several months for us to align our financial arrangements and you will need to consult your friends and, I presume, John Wemmick. I feel a responsibility for you and the Jaggers practice. Now I am sure you two young lawyers will do very well, but you may be able to serve your clients more easily within such an arrangement. I am sure that Nathaniel would approve. I hope that we can finalize the arrangement early in 1872."

"Indeed. Thank you so much. Perhaps I will delay asking Masterson until I have sounded out opinion about our union."

"If it were to be effected, I would think Masterson would work for you anyway."

"My most sincere thanks, Mr. Courtisone. I will let you know before the week's end."

Hamish went straight back to Walworth without considering lunch.

Mrs. Wemmick was surprised to see him again so soon, but she said John was a little better after his lunch.

"Have you had lunch, Mr. Macdonald?"

"No, I have some exciting news for Mr. Wemmick, so I came straight over to Walworth."

"Then I will cut you a piece of the game pie I made and fetch you a glass of ale."

"That would be delightful. May I go up to see John?"

He went quickly up the stairs.

"Good heavens, you again?"

"John, I have the most exciting offer which we need to consider. Courtisone is offering to bring the two practices together as *Courtisone and Jaggers.* He said he had often talked with Mr. Jaggers about how they would have set up together, were it not for his having this old family practice. What do you think?"

"Blow me down with a feather, I don't believe it. You know, I think Jaggers would have liked it. That way, a consolidation makes everything more imposing. It saves you the worry of finding my successor, whether Smythe will work out or not. It's wonderful."

"I think so too, but can I ask you to think about what we should ask for and what would be the disadvantages of such an arrangement? Courtisone thinks it might take place after due discovery in the New Year, and I am inclined to agree with his timetable."

"Yes, that's seems right. This is the tonic I needed to get me better!"

It was getting late, and Hamish went home to tell Mary. She was very excited for Hamish, as she had always worried about whether these two young men could sustain such a huge responsibility as the Jaggers practice. She wanted the very best for her loving husband.

The Italian party did as much as it could to soak up the wonders of Florence and included a day out to Fiesole. They bought leather purses and boxes from Santa Croce, put lire in the boxes at the Duomo, heard the echo in the Baptistry, and spent a dinner evening regretting they did not have more time, especially to go to Pisa to see the Leaning Tower. Estella bought a painting from a street seller of a rather poor copy of the Botticelli she so admired, and a small card of a better copy.

She was relieved that Harriet had not called at the hotel, but she received a note on their last evening saying that she was having to return to England as her grandmother had died. She added that she would value meeting her in London and left her address asking her to write if she would like to meet, which slightly perked Estella's interest.

"I am becoming immoderately frustrated at my husband's behavior," said Charlotte when she was drinking coffee with Estella in the hotel foyer. "He is occupying too much of my attention."

"I assume the visit to the police was satisfactory."

"Yes, no blame on him, but he seems to be imagining things. He complained vigorously to the waiter at breakfast that the butter knife was dirty, a complaint that was not supported. He then claimed he had seen two cats in their bedroom and when I challenged him, he became angry."

"I wonder if being away from his parish is disturbing him?"

"I don't know. Matrimonial vows apart, I really do not want to be responsible for the rather odd man he has become. I am going to have conversations with his older brother and his sister, both of whom are married with children, but they keep their distance.

"I recall a well-known case of a committal to an asylum which entails first petitioning the Lunacy Commission with evidence and they would appoint a Committee to manage the individual's estate, but, separately, having a person examined by two doctors who would certify lunacy and only then that committal to an asylum would take place. A dreadful procedure.

"That is his future, and you have seen him. What do you think about it?"

Estella was both helpful and not helpful at all.

"Charlotte dear, I do not know whether these bizarre behaviors are evidence of an unsound mind or just craving attention from everyone. You won't know that until he is back in the parish.

"I am afraid you are going to have to live with him for a while to see but continue to live with me of course. I will be glad to come and stay with you in the Vicarage, so that I can be a witness to behaviors which might lead to a committal."

"I can imagine nothing worse than living alone with this man, but if you were there I might be able to cope, at least for a while."

"It is in the conduct of his calling that the problems may reveal themselves; his treatment of parishioners, his preaching and conduct of the services, including weddings and funerals. Moreover, that will also be a source of evidence. Yet, if he just does his work normally, then it will be difficult to prove."

"I will return with him to Norfolk and hopefully you will come there after a while. I will need to come to Semper House with him when we get back, as I must get some fresh clothes. If he settles down in the Vicarage, I will come back to London, of course."

"Of course, and I will join you in Norfolk at some juncture."

"Let us see how he behaves on the train."

The final evening dinner had been a source of great jollity. Pip, Susanna and indeed everyone were excessive in their praise of Rizzio who spent most of the dinner with a broad smile on his face.

Oliver stayed slumped in his dining chair, playing with his food and drinking more wine than he had been accustomed to. Before dessert, Charlotte took him to his room and returned to enjoy the rest of the evening.

The party finally arrived at Victoria Station on Saturday afternoon and they all shook hands with each other, mightily pleased with the holiday. The Bollaerts were off to their country house. The Meggisons, the Gargerys and the Brandrams took a brougham to Cheyne Row, and Rizzio went to see a friend, still beaming at the plaudits he had received for the trip.

Albert was rested and delighted to see Estella. Elizabeth was staying there, as the Cheyne Row house was no longer available, and she greeted her aunt with a bubbling excitement. She was taken aback by the state of her uncle Oliver who waited quietly in the Semper House study, staring into space while Aunt Charlotte rushed around with her maid collecting her clean belongings for the journey to Craynham.

After they left, Estella then sat down on Albert's bed and he told her about his adventure in Paris and how he got in the way of a bullet.

"I am getting used to the possibility that I might be blind in one eye."

"I won't hear of it. We will find the very best doctors."

"I think I have already been attended to by one of the very best. I am told Mr. Nettleship is very famous. But I will just have to wait and see how my eye heals. At least my leg will recover."

"And how are you, dear Elizabeth?" said Estella to the young woman.

"I am so glad to have my Albert back, but we have decisions to make soon. My father is going to the embassy in Athens in a few months. My mother seems to be staying in America and he is not well, so I feel I have to accompany him, in fact, as he put it, to be his hostess."

"What do you think of that, Albert?"

"I am resigned to it. I cannot go to Athens and, if Elizabeth must care for her father I want to support her in that. Her father has first claim on her."

"That is most generous."

"Not really, Estella. In the meantime, I will return to Paris and meet with these painters. Elizabeth and I are both still young. We love each other and we will be together again."

"I want Albert to paint, not mope around Athens where painters are not thick on the ground," said Elizabeth.

"You are both independent souls, not prisoners of your families," concluded Estella.

"Indeed," said Elizabeth, "freedom is our treasure."

Pip and Susanna arrived at Cheyne Row where their children greeted them with abandon and were given the various small items that their parents had found from each of the cities they visited: Toys from Venice for Lachlan and Malcolm, clothes from Florence and maps for Lachlan of both cities. While they had very much enjoyed their visit, there was still an atmosphere between them which neither liked.

Pip had spotted Harriet just briefly in the Uffizi and was dismayed that she hurried away. Susanna noticed that something attracted his attention which he did not reveal, or perhaps did not want to reveal, but she did not press it. Thinking about it later, there was something about his manner that worried her, not the problem of his character and her reaction to it. However, now they were back in England, she would see how things progressed.

She was pleased to discover her pregnancy before they went to Italy as that would cement their relationship. She longed for a daughter to cherish and she knew Pip would find a girl very special. She did not see how there could be another woman in his life, as he was never unable to account for his movements nor did she have any real suspicions about his fidelity.

Yet it remained a worry. She was a strong woman but as she played with the idea that he might be unfaithful, at times she would feel like an angry wolfhound, and at others as sad and regretful as a moping spaniel that she might not have been able to discover his preoccupation if, of course, it was not just a figment of her imagination.

For his part, Pip knew his relationship with Susanna had changed, but it was not the arguments over Hamish that rankled. Just as his uncle Pip had once confided in him about Estella, his problem was that he simply could not get Harriet out of his mind. He loved Susanna deeply, but he also loved Harriet, and the strictures of his religious oaths were a constant in his thoughts, but secondary to his desires.

Harriet had discarded him, and the break was mutual, yet he knew if the circumstances were right, he would bed with her again, as her love was free. He simply must share his problem with someone, and Estella was the only possible confidant that he could trust.

Susanna shared with him at breakfast a letter she had from Mary asking them to come to dinner, as she had some news.

"That would be excellent," said Pip, "I like them both very much."

"I do too. I also have some news. From the way I am feeling this morning, I may be with child again."

"Oh, my darling, really? He immediately got up and rushed round the table to kiss her and congratulate her.

"That is wonderful. I know we will have a daughter. It is written in the heavens. We will have a little girl to spoil and adore, a little Susanna who will be just as beautiful and adorable as her mother."

She glowed with pleasure and all her doubts about him disappeared in a puff of smoke as his endearments surrounded her.

"Now, Pip darling, we do not know it will be a daughter, do we? We must be prepared for both."

"I am convinced it will be a girl and I have a name for her already."

"Really?"

"Florence, of course!"

"No, I'd prefer Hannah," she said, mildly startled by the name he chose, but she got up and they held each other tight and jumped for joy.

"When do you want to tell the boys?"

"I think I will leave it until I begin to show, and I know a baby is really on the way. At this juncture, it is just the typical early morning feelings I had with them that I am now experiencing."

"Tell Mary we will be thrilled to come to dinner."

"I wonder whether marriage might convert Hamish or, at least, allow him to keep his feelings for men dormant which, I suspect, will depend on whom he meets."

"Perhaps. We must tell Estella too as I am sure she would want to know, and we need to find out how Albert is."

"Next month I want the Italian party to come to dinner again, probably without Oliver and Charlotte who I gather were bound for Norfolk anyway, but I would like to know if Oliver really is mad."

1872

XV

Throughout the autumn of 1871, Hamish had discussed with Clarence the possibility of the arrangement with Courtisone, and he was thoroughly in favor. Clarence then made arrangements with Hamish for them both to have a discussion with Lord Eustace, which took some time to arrange. Afterwards the indication from the experienced lawyer was not merely enthusiastic, but whole-hearted. Wemmick had made a list of the requirements for the Jaggers practice including the location of offices, the different needs of partners and the distribution of work among the clerks, especially the placement of young Robert. Courtisone invited Hamish and Smythe to his office to meet the lawyers in his practice.

Michael O'Grady was an unusual phenomenon, of Irish descent, though his father had been a Dublin lawyer who sought to come to London. Hector Billington was an older man, probably fifty years old who specialized in wills and transfers of property. Philip Hardyman was the youngest, near Hamish's age, and Courtisone's designee for the Board of the Jaggers Trust.

The meeting on the details was eventually held in December of 1871 and all agreed the proposed arrangement would be dated January 1, 1872 and be of great benefit. Hamish and Smythe agreed to generous terms, so Courtisone said he would draw up the papers for all to sign. *Courtisone and Jaggers* would be a fine law firm, but they would begin to concentrate on their work as solicitors, rather than as barrister advocates, foreshadowing the general division of labor among English lawyers.

They toasted to the union in Courtisone's dining room with a sirloin of beef and good French wine to celebrate the imminent partnership in the first week of the new year. Hamish sat next to Philip and during the conversation, it became obvious to them both that they might share more than a future partnership in the practice.

Philip was married with two young children, but his wife was older and preferred her own company. Hamish talked about Mary and their expectations, but the mutual acknowledgement of their real desires was apparent, though not to others around the table. Philip decided to take a risk, and as dessert was being served, he put his left hand on Hamish's thigh, and said how good it would be for them to meet at some point. Quivers of delight went through Hamish's body as he said how interesting that would be.

As lunch finished rather late in the afternoon, Philip made a suggestion:

"Why not come for a drink in my club, Hamish?"

"Delighted, where is it?"

"A stone's throw, quite near the Courtisone office, The Gavel Club. It's relatively new, comprising professional men and I suppose I am a founder member, though we keep the membership small, not more than forty, carefully vetted."

As they walked into the foyer Hamish noted a glass-fronted case on a table, displaying a large mahogany gavel with a thick fairly short walnut handle set in bulbous hammers on either side, standing upright on a velvet board, where a small plaque told the legend of the donor and founder of the club, Lord MacAlready.

"Come with me," said Philip after he had talked to the porter.

They walked down a long corridor with rooms or either side and went into one at the far end. Philip closed the door behind him as Hamish turned toward him. They looked away from each other and moved apart in silence, each wondering what might happen.

Philip spoke first.

"My dear Hamish, we have a great deal to talk about, don't we? We need both to be clear about what we are doing before going further. I get my pleasures whenever and wherever I find them, and there are three different members of this club with each of whom I have spent a happy afternoon. I love my wife and my children, but neither of us ever ask questions, although I am sure my wife does not know of these interests of mine. It is the only style of living that makes sense for my desires."

"You are fortunate, Philip, but I really am only interested only in a long-term committed relationship with a man," said Hamish quietly.

"I think I have more experience than you, so I'll let you into a secret, Hamish. This is an utterly private club for professional men built for our enjoyment. I will lock this door now, and open this panel and, hey, presto, look, there is a small bed for us to use. You must become a member."

"But as I just said, I really don't want the occasional experience, attractive as you are."

"That will be very difficult to find," Philip replied, "I know of several couples who thought they could just be committed to each other, but there is something about our style of life that makes fidelity very difficult."

"In my university group, we were all very timid indeed, perhaps more terrified of the law than we should have been. I am perhaps a rarity, for not only does my wife know of my desires, but several of my friends, a widow, another woman and a couple know too."

"Oh, good God," said Philip, giving Hamish a piercing look. "You are risking everything!"

"Even my senior clerk, John Wemmick, knows."

"What? Did you just come out with it?"

"No, I was blackmailed by a man we were interviewing for appointment, but that is a long story which ended with his being sent to jail for two years hard labor."

"I see," said Philip, "but the problem about fidelity for couples like us is this. It is extremely difficult for two single men to live together without creating suspicion, scandal even, though that is quite conventional for two women. Being unable to live together on a permanent basis removes the concern for fidelity. Relationships are here today and gone tomorrow.

"Might we have dinner with our wives and see what happens?"

"That would be interesting, but my wife Mary has a very sharp intuition and a very candid tongue. She would ask us directly, I know."

"In that case, we should postpone what I thought we both had in mind for this afternoon."

As they were leaving the club, Hamish asked Philip why it was called the Gavel Club. Philip led him to the glass case and said:

"Look at this gavel and how it is placed, upright with its bulbous double-headed hammer, Hamish, remind you of anything?" Hamish gasped and they both laughed heartily.

"But that really is utterly disgusting," said Hamish, as they walked out into the street.

On his way back to the office, he was in two minds about telling Mary of this encounter. She might be able to hold her tongue, but Philip was now a colleague and the risks were considerable, as Philip had indicated. Let it rest for the moment, he thought, though he disliked keeping a secret from his wife.

Oliver seemed to have become more settled when back in Craynham, and Estella went to Numquam deciding that not seeing Nellie was laughable, notwithstanding the clean break. Each knew where they now stood after breaking off their relationship as companions and lovers.

She was very glad to be home, noticing the very poor condition of many of her precious ornaments. Nellie had always been very efficient in irregular house needs, such as cleaning delicate silver or dusting china ornaments, but the house now looked uncared for. Nellie's successor, no more than a young girl, was not used to handling anything delicate. To be sure, she could mop a floor, but there were far too many fine artefacts in Numquam for them not to be kept in pristine condition.

The next morning, taking the reins herself, Estella rode her trap to the Forge and the Cottage. On the short journey, she felt there was something wrong with one of the trap's wheels, so she now had a proper reason to go there.

She drew up in front of the Cottage and the Fletcher children came running round to see who it was, and from the Forge Fletch appeared in his leather apron wielding a hammer.

"What can I do for you, ma'am?" he said politely.

"Mr. Fletcher," she said, using his title to show that she was not going to lord it over him, "I am worried about the wheels on this trap."

She got down as Nellie came out of the cottage, rubbing her hands on a towel.

"Estella," she cried, "it's so really nice to see you," and, ignoring Fletch who was inspecting the wheel, she put her arms around Estella in a hug which was reciprocated. They stood for a moment, looking closely into each other's eyes with remembered longing.

"Yes," said Estella, "It's so very good to see you all again. Let me see what Mr. Fletcher here has found before I ask you a question."

The two women stood very close to each other as Fletch looked at the wheel.

"Good thing you came here when you did, Mrs. P. That right wheel's about to come off and you'd been thrown out if it had collapsed on you."

"That's a blessing, at least. What does it need?"

"Well now, I'm going to have to keep it for a while. The shank is worn badly, and I'll make a new one, and the pins is all worn too, and I will take a closer look at the left wheel. We can't have you tumbling into the marsh now, can we?"

They all laughed.

"Fiddlesticks," said Estella, "that will take a long time, I suspect."

"I'll need a couple of days with it."

"Is it worth repairing? It is quite old."

"Oh, yes ma'am, it's a very fine trap and after years of use, these parts do wear, thank goodness, or I would not be in business."

They laughed again.

"Then I will leave it with you. But I came about another matter. I was so grateful, Mr. Fletcher, for your kindness and help in resolving the matter of the companionship which Nellie and I had developed."

"That's alright, ma'am, we didn't want no trouble now, did we?"

"No, we did not, and your thoughtfulness and generosity were of great importance," at which Fletch smiled at Nellie and drew himself up as no one had ever before said that he had done anything of importance, especially as the compliment came from a fine lady.

"All that was several months ago but I find myself in a difficult situation. I have employed a young girl from the village, but she is only good enough for mopping floors, whereas your Nellie was superb at handling all the precious artefacts I have—silver, fine china, which I dare not let the girl touch. The china is not properly dusted, the silver is badly tarnished, and I wonder if Nellie might resume her work with me, but only for dealing with the objects I have mentioned."

"That's up to Nellie," said Fletch, "now we know she won't be doing that with all those complications."

"What do you say, Nellie?"

"Oh, I'd love to come perhaps of an afternoon every two weeks. I'd have time just to do the silver and the china and keep it sparkling."

"That will be very good," said Estella, trying to contain her great pleasure at this.

"Why don't you come over when the trap is ready, and I can come back with you to bring it back? Today, I will borrow a saddle if I may and ride home, it is no distance."

"Oh no, Mrs. P. I'll ride you over there in my cart," said Fletch.

Estella and Nellie shook hands and after a brief embrace Estella got up into the cart with her own horse tied behind.

"You know, Mrs. P," said Fletch as they trundled along the track, "I never myself got to thank that there Trust properly for all they have done for us. When I think back just four years to where we was then and where we are now, I can't believe it. I'se doing so well, I'se going to be looking out to take on an apprentice, maybe two."

"That is interesting, Fletch, may I call you Fletch? I can think of one or two of these women we care for who have boys of twelve and thirteen who need to learn a trade."

Estella got herself down when they arrived at Numquam and she turned to thank him.

"Tell that Pip I thinks of him often. I saw him before Biddy died but he hasn't been down here since. Oh, and afore I go, one thing. My Nellie loves me, but she does love you, not that way, but because you have been so kind to her, teaching her to read and all."

"I love her too, Fletch. You see, my mother was just like her as a child, and I see in Nellie so much of what I saw in my mother."

"Well, I doesn't know anything about that, but I wanted to say that I is very comfortable with her loving you as long as there's no gossip."

"I understand, to be sure. I look forward to getting my trap back safe and sound."

"A couple of days will do it," said Fletch, detaching Estella's horse from the cart and leading it around to the stable. Then flicking the reins and turning his cart around in the driveway, he called out, "Good day to you, Mrs. P."

As he was about to leave a message boy came up the drive with a wire for Mrs. Pirrip.

'JAMES IRVING MACDONALD ARRIVED SAFELY THIS MORNING STOP MOTHER AND BABY DOING WELL STOP HAMISH STOP'

"How delightful," said Estella. "Tell Nellie that Mary has had a boy."

Early in March, Estella finally came to stay with Oliver and Charlotte Mudge at Craynham Vicarage and she shared Mary's news to Charlotte's great delight. Nowadays, Oliver was so calm that someone who had seen this bedraggled man crawling into the lobby of the Grand Cavour would not have recognized him as the same man. Charlotte and Estella walked in the countryside each day and each found the other's company quite delightful.

A fortnight passed and Estella said she must return to London. Oliver had seemed to her the model of a good country parson, out visiting the sick, preparing his sermons and, while she was there, conducting the funeral of a well-known elderly shepherd Ebenezer Basham, wool being the trade that had made Norfolk such a rich county and Norwich such a great city.

Confident of his restored health after the return from Italy, Charlotte told Oliver that she too would go to London with Estella to see how Elizabeth was coping with Albert's injuries and whether she was still preparing to go to Athens with her father. On the train to London from Norwich, Estella and Charlotte returned to speculations about Honora Brandram as it seemed to them that this was a woman with a secret.

"She hardly talks, only smiles a little," said Charlotte. "One could see only a face with a mask of great sorrow and underneath is a singularly attractive woman."

"Honora seems to show most of the problems confronting so many women in her face, married or not," said Estella, "though Frederick appears to dominate her."

"I agree; in my case, Oliver is a problem but any attempts by him to dominate me would fall flat."

"I wonder about Susanna, too. Susanna seems at times to be battling her way into an independent life and she had been promised that by Pip, though I am sure that is not easy."

"For myself," Estella told Charlotte, "I was fortunate to be independent, financially and emotionally, albeit with the Havisham curse but when I was badgered by my mother, I broke out of that shell into a free life with my Pip.

"But think of two more, Nellie the reformed whore and Harriet, the free lover. Nellie's life changes have been extraordinary, and she and her husband have about as sensible and loving relationship as is possible for a man and a woman."

"From what I have heard," said Charlotte, "that transformation is due to the Jaggers Trust. Whether that would have happened without their support does not bear thinking about."

Charlotte returned to the Honora topic.

"I am going to call on Honora when I know her husband is not there as she lives only four doors from my former house."

"It would be very good to make her feel comfortable with you on several occasions before I join you. You can see what might be possible."

When they got back to Semper House from the train, Estella told Charlotte that she could not resist writing a note of invitation immediately to Honora but, standing firmly on her two legs with her arms akimbo, asked in a mildly censorious tone:

"Charlotte, precisely why are we so anxious to help this woman?"

"Why do you want to help the whores in the building?" was the counter, and Estella immediately relaxed her aggressive stance.

"It is a puzzle and I think sometimes it is entirely Pip's legacy for me. I realize I was once a haughty cynical self, but now after Pip I am both more compassionate and determined."

"I did not know you in your earlier condition, my dear, but you are not compelled to help women less fortunate than yourself? You are not a religious person, are you, though I think you have only the vaguest of belief in God as some person out there, not a Creator as such, maybe just the embodiment of goodness."

"You are quite correct, but before the Trust was established, my husband and I were very self-absorbed."

"Perhaps the Trust is as much a godsend to you as it is to the recipients of its charity."

"Yes indeed, and, my dear, I am so very pleased that you are living with me when you do not have to be in Norfolk."

"Indeed, it is such relief. Thank you so much. My relationship with my husband continues to be so perplexing.'

Honora eventually arrived wearing that mask of sorrow, and as she spoke her greeting, Estella realized that she had hardly ever heard the woman's voice properly and how rich it was, like Charlotte's, quite deep for a woman, but so attractive. They talked over lunch.

"Honora," Estella said, "we have both been concerned for your welfare in Italy as you seemed so unhappy and withdrawn."

"Yes, that is true, and it has become my way of coping with the world since I was married ten years ago. My husband Frederick is a distinguished architect, and I am fond of him, but he does not want me to have any sort of independence, not for his own benefit but as a protection for me."

"I am not sure why I decided to marry my bizarre husband," said Charlotte, anxious for Honora to feel she was not alone in an odd marriage, "how did you come to marry yours? Was it arranged, a love match or what, for he does not seem to treat you well?"

"It is a very long story," replied Honora, "and I have never told anyone. No one thus knows except those who were involved at the time."

"What was it, then?" asked Estella softly. "You clearly have some great sorrow, my dear, and as it is clearly your secret, I would not want to press you to reveal it."

"No, for the first time in years and especially after the Italy holiday I am beginning to feel able to talk with women and meet other people."

"Why was that?"

"My husband married me as an act of pity. He was a friend of my father's and agreed to look after me."

"What on earth is this about, Honora? How did that happen?" asked Estella, her curiosity mounting.

"Oh dear, I have never told anyone. I am so ashamed."

"Come, come," said Charlotte. "If you have been hurt, there is no need for shame."

Bracing herself, Honora began, "I was nineteen years old and I went with a small church group on a pilgrimage to Lourdes. I was a Catholic then, and news came to all Catholics that the Virgin Mary had appeared in a grotto to a fourteen-year-old girl Bernadette.

"All my friends at the church were very elated and wanted to travel to the holy place. Of course, my father was then wealthy enough to finance such an expedition. I have since abandoned my faith.

"The six of us stayed in a small *pension* called *La Petite Arbre*, in a village called *Argeles-Gazost*, run by an older couple, the Mitterands, and their children, Jean-Marc and Philippe who helped the management of the inn. They were twins about twenty years old and we all thought they were very nice boys. They seemed very friendly and helpful to their parents and we ate well."

"Could you tell them apart? Or were they not identical."

"They were identical, so it was difficult."

"The night before we left, it was a lovely evening and I decided to take a walk in the village, and none of my friends wanted to come. I got to the village center walking on the grass between a line of plane trees where the village market was held on Wednesday mornings. As I was nearing the end of the line, Jean-Marc and Philippe were on the other side of the trees on the road and they wandered over to me and we began to talk.

"I had chatted with them only once before that evening in the *pension*. They were just as they were in the *pension*, quite friendly, asking me about England, and Jean-Marc suggested that we walk out of the village to a well which supposedly granted your wish.

"I knew these men or thought I did. But once away from the village," she said, her voice sinking to a whisper mixed with gasping for breath and tears flowing, her whole body shaking in her distress, "they started to put their arms and hands on me and quite soon we were in a derelict shed with straw on the floor. I protested, not really believing that they were doing anything more than being over-friendly.

"O dear God, the memory is so terrible," she continued, gasping to get the words out through her weeping, "but then Philippe put a filthy rag over my mouth and tied it round my head. I was simply unable to resist them. They forced me down on to my knees first to pleasure them, then took off my under-garments and each of them raped me twice and violated me, laughing all the time, insulting me, fondling me, hurting my breasts, treating me like a puppet doll," her howls of distress now audible throughout the house.

"Oh, my dear, how simply terrible," said Estella rising from her chair in a fury. "This makes me so angry I could scream."

"Let me go on," said Honora, getting a mild degree of composure, "I was in terrible wracking pain. They made me put my clothes back on, took me back to the *pension* and told their parents they had found me outside the village, and it looked to them as though someone had raped me. Monsieur Mitterand went to call in a policeman who was his cousin. I was taken to the station where I said it was the twins that had raped me."

Her tears stopped as she went on quietly, "I was not believed of course, and as we were all leaving for the train early the next morning, there was little I could do. Of course, my friends would not believe that I had indeed been raped, as opposed to finding some young man to dally with and I was in no mood to show them my bruises as proof."

"Was there no older person with you to help?"

"No, we were just a group of young women of the same age from our church, the idea being that as a group we needed no chaperone. There was really no leader and when I had finished with the police, I went straight to my room where my companion was asleep."

"So, nothing was done in France to pursue this crime."

"No. Of course, once home I confessed to Father O'Malley, our priest, what had happened, and he advised me more than strongly to tell my parents, both devout Catholics."

"They were appalled, but also in two minds about the level of my responsibility in the rape. My father somehow would not believe that two young Frenchmen would do what they did to me and blamed me for being such a harlot."

"Why is it," said Charlotte, her eyes blazing with anger, "that women who are raped are not believed? I simply do not understand that. Please go on."

"Then, of course, I realized I was with child. My parents were then further appalled, as I could not disguise it. They began to accuse me of wanton behavior, of being a whore. I understood, of course. They could not bear the shame, any more than I could.

"I was sent to a Welsh village to live with my elderly grandmother whom I loved dearly to await the birth of my baby and, of course, adoption was the only solution. Fortunately, they did not dispatch me to a convent."

At this point, Honora faltered, starting first to weep, and then to howl in anguish again and was hardly responsive when held in the arms of both her new friends. That continued for several minutes, Estella wondering whether she would be heard in the street, so great was the pain and hurt being let loose by the conversation.

"What happened to the baby?"

Inconsolable, Honora continued to howl again in grievous despair.

"Tell us, tell us," said Estella, sensing that there was some further secret to be revealed.

"Oh, good lord God, help me," she cried, "I had beautiful twin boys whom I nursed for four weeks before I gave them up. Oh Jesus, Mary, mother of God, forgive me. What could I do, sweet Lord?"

Charlotte and Estella both dissolved into tears as well, all three women consumed with grief and sorrow at Honora's terrible experience. Tears flowed for a long time before gradually, there was silence which none of them wanted to break, Honora continuing to sob gently to herself.

"Neither of you have had children, have you?" She asked, so softly as to be close to inaudible.

"No," they replied.

Between sobs, she continued,

"The pain of birth gives way to utter joy and relief as a child is put to one's breast. It is quite inexplicable to someone who has not experienced it.

"And when," and she broke down again, "and when there is one child on *each* breast, the joy is unfathomable. I can feel it now. I would have done anything within my power to raise my children. They will be almost twelve years old now, and I have never been told where they were dispatched, except that I understood a family was prepared to raise both children," and her tears flooded down her cheeks once again.

"Presumably you then left your grandmother's and returned home when they left you."

"Yes."

"And then?"

"My father and mother told me they wanted nothing more to do with me, that if anyone knew, they would die from shame. What do I do? I cried.

"Then my father said he had told a confirmed bachelor friend Frederick Brandram of my story, and, unlike my parents, he felt sorry for me. He suggested to my parents that he would marry me assuming I could keep his house, but he did not desire to have children. In other words, I was being condemned to a life looking at the outset as gloomy as the worst kind of prison."

"Stick to the children now, Honora. Did you name them?"

"Oh yes, and my grandmother helped me have them christened, two saints betraying my Catholic upbringing, Simon and Jude, as their feast day was my birthday, October 28th.

"We have to track those twins down," said Charlotte.

"And those devils in France," added Estella.

There was silence once again broken by a knock on the front door. The maid answered it and Frederick Brandram's voice was heard to ask:

"Is my wife here?"

XVI

Honora dried her tears and the Brandrams left without further conversation. Estella and Charlotte sat quietly, almost numbed by the cruelty the poor woman had endured from the rapists, her priest and her parents. Yet it steeled their resolve to help. After many a discussion on how to proceed, it was a month later in April that they invited Honora to Semper House again.

"They must be found," said Charlotte to Honora as she walked into the drawing room.

Honora smiled and laughed at the very idea that she might see her twins again. Estella and Charlotte laughed with her and began to probe further. Estella thought it was like watching a butterfly come out of a chrysalis for the older women, watching Honora becoming so relaxed.

"What was your grandmother's name?"

"She was Blodwen Evans, about as Welsh as you could be. She came from a village called Llanfairfechan near Conway in north Wales. She had been married but her husband was killed in one of the slate quarries nearby. Two of her children emigrated, and she never remarried, but she was a very kindly soul. She was not a Catholic. Her daughter, my mother Mary Evans, married Cyril Madden, a devout English Catholic, so she converted. I have no siblings."

"Did you give birth in her house?"

"Yes, and with neighbors agog to find out whether I was having a boy or a girl. I was told it was an easy delivery, though it did not seem like it at the time. Thank God I was nowhere near my parents."

"So would your twins have been adopted there?"

"I suppose so. I cannot think how that might have been done. I am sure my grandmother knew, but she died five years ago. I nursed them and my grandmother looked after me and she helped me to cope with them leaving me. I had to agree not to know where they had gone. The parting is completely gone from my memory. It was so very hard."

"Charlotte and I have decided firmly that we must find them," said Estella.

"We'd have to be very careful as they may not know they are adopted," added Charlotte. "Village communities are very close and people there will know of them."

"Yes," Charlotte repeated. "We really must be careful, Honora. You do not have any legal rights over them. Do they know they are adopted? Might they hate you because you gave them away? We must carefully work out what to do. There is also Frederick to consider."

"That's all very wise, but it gives me a sliver of hope," said Honora, becoming more subdued.

"You know, Frederick does not dominate me. I am so indebted to him for rescuing me from my parents that I am cowed by his presence."

"Are they still alive?"

"I don't know. I suppose Frederick would know but since they arranged my marriage, I have never seen them, and they did not attend my wedding."

"I can scarcely understand your attitude to your husband, mine being almost entirely the opposite," said Estella, laughing so loudly that the others joined in.

"I am much more interested in finding those evil French twins who assaulted you so dreadfully. I am intent on going to that village near Lourdes to confront them."

"Oh, my goodness, please don't. I could not bear to have anything to do with them."

"I am sure, my dear, but they must face up to their evil behavior and I propose to go there this summer."

"Wait," said Charlotte, "Estella, dear, what are you thinking about? We have discussed this before. What will you do if you find them? They are now probably both married with children, running that pension or another like it? Perhaps they have confessed to their priest?"

"No, Charlotte. It does us little good as women not to oblige evil men to answer for their sins. If the Law won't do it, others should. If that means embarrassing them in front of their wives, so be it. They should not be allowed to get away with such depravity.

"I intend to go and confront them, not tomorrow, but later in the year. You could both come with me? What was the name of the village and the pension, Honora?"

"The *pension* was in *Argeles-Gazost*. It was a pretty house, quite large, though only two floors and the Mitterand family lived in the cottage next door. They were very excited by the stream of visitors coming to stay, not so much by the vision. Oh, Estella, I am unsure, but I will come with you if Frederick allows?"

"What's Frederick go to do with it? We won't ask permission. We will just go."

"But I have no money of my own."

"But I do."

"Then you must let me come too," said Charlotte, "then we will have two French speakers."

"I must speak to Frederick, though. I now feel much more confident in doing so. I don't think he will care one way or the other. You know, in all these years, he has never touched me."

"Does he prefer men?"

"Oh, no, he despises men like that. I just think he is a good man of business, and enjoys male pastimes, cards in his club, shooting pheasants, partridges or grouse, though for some reason he won't shoot pigeons, perhaps because he hates pigeon pie," she said, smiling. "Anyway, with your wonderful support I feel strong enough. I can always say I want to visit Lourdes again. He can hardly refuse a religious pilgrimage!"

"In that case," said Estella, "I will see to arrangements; let me see, it is now April 12th, perhaps July will be a good time."

"Meantime, I will interview some private investigators to go to Llanfairfechan," said Charlotte, "it is important not to rush this inquiry and get it right, so getting the right man will take time, I am sure. We need to think this through with great care and not involve the lawyers, as they might discourage us."

"True enough," said Estella, "at least we know them well enough that they will not oppose our visit on the grounds that we are mere women," which brought smiles of recognition to the other two women present.

Courtisone decided that the settlement of the partnership called for a splendid occasion at his country house, a dinner with several courses, excellent wine and all the new partners and clerks and spouses together, and he began in January to plan for a summer's day. With his wife now long since dead, he had not been often to Crockett Grange, their country retreat in Hertfordshire.

He initially decided not to ask any of the partners to stay in the house as he did not want to appear to be a person inclined to favoritism, but he invited the Wemmicks as the oldest couple in the group to spend the night there. His eldest daughter Abigail was delighted to be his hostess, as his wife had died of an internal complaint when still quite a young woman and was disinclined to find a substitute. Like her sisters, Abigail owed so much to her father, and he had no son to carry on his legendary law career.

Indeed, Courtisone's daughters were a particular kind of problem for him. They were all thoroughly independent young women in a deeply affectionate and loving family, so he could no more tell them he wished they would find a lawyer husband to work in the practice than fly to the moon. As they all grew older, none of the three seemed yet inclined to want to be married as the family seemed to fulfil their emotional needs.

Courtisone walked around his office one morning outlining his plans for the celebration to Hamish. He was in no hurry and wanted the new arrangements to settle down first, so the event would probably be next summer.

"This is exceedingly generous, Mr. Courtisone, and a wonderful idea. We will be working together for years, and an event of this kind will facilitate fellowship, a necessary ingredient to a working practice."

"Thank you indeed, Hamish. I will accommodate everyone in local hostelries except the Wemmicks, who are too elderly to travel in a carriage to an inn after dinner."

"That is very thoughtful, and I know John and Mrs. W. will appreciate it enormously. Without it, I expect he would think twice about coming. With the offer of accommodation, he will be delighted. I wonder, however, if you had thought about inviting Pip's widow, Mrs. Estella Pirrip? I don't think you have ever met her, have you?"

"Only at meetings of the Trust, where she holds her own with gusto. But I know almost every detail about her, as Nathaniel used to regale me with many stories of her eccentric guardian, and then how Estella met her mother, Jaggers' servant, and how he had to confront the damage he had done.

"To tell you the truth, I became rather bored listening to his remorse. It did not suit him."

"Of that I know very little," said Hamish, "but she is very much engaged with the work of the Trust now and her husband was of course a mainstay of the practice before his untimely death."

"I think we can accommodate her, and I will ask her to stay at Crockett Grange as well. I do really want the members of the practice to be together. And with Smythe as a single, that will make the party an appropriate balance of men and women. Masterson will bring his lady, I am sure, as will my more senior clerk, Jonathan Greenberg. Abigail and I will consider dates.

While at the Courtisone offices, Hamish called in to Philip Hardyman's office. They had not met since their encounter at The

Gavel Club, but Hamish sent a message to say that they should postpone any thought of a meeting with their wives until the partnership dinner was over.

The more Philip considered it, the more frightened and worried he became about Hamish. Hamish himself was taken by surprise at the studied vehemence with which Philip told him of the dangerous situation any relationship between them might have, apparently ignoring the fact that Hamish had already ruled it out.

"Who knows," Philip said, his voice rising, "your wife might ask out loud some damn fool question like 'What it's like being a sodomite?' so that everyone could hear? I'll have to steer my wife away from both of you at this party of Courtisone's when it occurs. I'm certainly going to have us returning to London that night. The more I think about it, the more foolish and dangerous it would be for us to develop a liaison as you are so obviously very naïve about the complexities of being gay. There is also the consideration that working in the same environment almost certainly means that someone will guess and expose us."

"Wait, wait," said Hamish, but Philip ignored him.

"Any development of our relationship is thus quite out of the question. Imagine, Hamish," he ranted on, "say that Adam or Jonathan thought they saw something between us and began to gossip. That would spread like wildfire. Imagine that your wife Mary spoke in a semi-public place, such as the forthcoming party, with the candor which you credit her with. What could be more disastrous?"

"Wait, wait," said Hamish again, "you assume I want to begin a relationship with you. I don't."

"Oh, oh, I thought you did," said Philip calming down, "I am sure we can work together without rancor," and he was abruptly back to a normal conversation as quickly as he had left it.

As he set at his desk thinking afterwards about the conversation, Hamish was confirmed that he did not want to join Philip's world of deceit and high risk, whatever physical pleasure it might bring. He thought that Philip's angry rant was probably because he,

Hamish, had rejected him, perhaps an experience to which Philip was unaccustomed.

Yet what do I want? He thought. *I want someone to love, to be faithful to, to build a cocoon of love and friendship, something that is pure, never sordid and promiscuous. I am surprised and deeply grateful for the satisfaction I find in my intimacy with Mary. Now that is established, it is love and fidelity I cherish. That could have been with a man or a woman.*

Charlotte had now been several weeks at Semper House interviewing investigators, none of whom she trusted and meeting them only increased her determination to find the right person. She decided to return to Norfolk in May to check on her husband. She thought it best not to continue the search for the moment, as Estella and Honora had not even left for France at the end of July. It was a chore living with her husband as he always seemed so busy with services, sermons, wedding, funerals and pastoral obligations. She eventually arrived in the vicarage one September afternoon before to find Oliver in a state. Of quite what kind, she was not sure.

To begin with, he was not wearing his dog collar and to her certain knowledge he had never dressed without it. Then he was drooling slightly at the mouth and babbling away about a dog that he had found in his study, something she could not comprehend at all. So, she took him by the arm and led him into the garden, lovely in the summer, but a sorry sight every winter when the roses on the vicarage wall would be dead but that uncovered the flint and brick so typical of Norfolk.

Everything in the garden was not lovely, however, nor was this strange male human being, and relations between them were thus very tense for several weeks that late summer.

"What is the matter, Oliver?"

"Who are you?" he replied.

"I am your wife, Charlotte. Don't you recognize me?"

"Oh, of course, Charlotte. But you died recently, didn't you?

"No, dear, I just went to London."

"That must be a sort of death, all that filth and noise. I want to grow oranges in the garden. How do you do that?"

"Oranges? They won't grow here."

"I have asked God to provide bananas."

The conversation continued in this vein for a good hour. The sky threatened rain as Oliver switched from topic to topic, each one stranger than the last. Finally, he said:

"I want you to know, Charlotte, I bedded Mrs. Hayhoe, the cook the other day and before that Belinda our maid. I have a plan for all three of us, too!"

"Really, my dear, that must have been a pleasure," said Charlotte, startled at first but then amused by this enlightening news.

Oh God, she thought, *he is living in a fantasy world. Given his previous eccentricities, what comes next? Nothing seems out of the question.* It had started to rain as he blurted out:

"You don't believe me, do you?" he said. "Well, I did."

"Very well, we will go and ask them," said Charlotte anxious to get out of the downpour.

She was also starting to feel angry with this delusionary husband of hers, so she led him straightaway into his study, sat him in his chair and then advanced to the kitchen where Mrs. Hayhoe and Belinda were preparing dinner.

Not beating about the bush, Charlotte said:

"My husband says that he has bedded both of you. Is this true?"

The women burst out laughing before Mrs. Hayhoe said:

"No, ma'am, but he has been pestering both of us and we just thought he was, if you don't mind my saying, going a bit barmy. He's got really worked up about them 'bishebarnabys' in his bedroom."

"You mean ladybirds, do you?"

"Oh, yes, ma'am, but we calls 'em "bishepbaranbys' 'cos we had a Bishop Barnaby here once that had a red cloak with big black spots on it."

"I see. Well, I do mind you saying he's barmy, though that may be correct. But why would he care about ladybirds? I suppose there is more."

"Well, we've both had to lock our doors at night, and he does touch us rather a lot during the day, but we would not dream of him bedding us. He's the vicar and vicars don't do that sort of thing."

"I believe you. How long has he been doing this? When I left, he seemed quite settled."

"It was just after Mrs. Longstaff came to see him, fussing about the arrangements for the Harvest Festival. You know her, a bit wanton I suspect. Not once did she come, but several days in succession and she was there in the study for an hour or more each time."

"Oh dear. Thank you anyway."

Charlotte decided that, for the moment, there was no point in conversing with her husband, whose mind was clearly very disturbed. He ate well; indeed, he gobbled his food like a turkey. His clothes were close to unsanitary, so she made him dress properly and had the maid clean them, though she had obviously tried to keep him in clean undergarments. Presumably he was managing church affairs and conducting himself properly there, but she needed to find out. She decided a walk into the village might yield a conversation.

The village was quite busy, notwithstanding the almost incessant rain which had plagued the country all year. There seemed to be a gathering of farmers' wives near the butcher's shop, but near the well, she spotted Mr. Dereham, a middle-aged sheep farmer who was the vicar's warden, talking with Mr. Graves, the people's warden.

"A very good afternoon to you, gentlemen. I have been in London on family business for a while and before that with my husband in Italy, so I have not been here a great deal. But I arrived earlier today and find my husband in some distress. Have you noticed any signs of that?"

"Yes, ma'am, and we have to discuss how to tell the Archdeacon. People that used to come regular have stopped coming to service."

"Why is that?'

"It is almost a scandal. He is shouting at individuals from the pulpit. The other day, he called my wife an adulteress," said Mr. Dereham.

"And he called Mrs. Longstaff a whore," said Mr. Graves, "and sermons are now all hell fire with these personal attacks thrown in, it seems, if he recognizes people."

"He's got the Communion prayers all muddled several times."

"I think he is very sick," said Charlotte.

"He is certainly very strange and and wild, you should inform the should inform the Archdeacon, his superior, for the Church has the responsibility for his bad behavior."

"We will go over to Norwich tomorrow and find him. He has a house in the Cathedral Close."

"Thank you; I hope matters don't get worse."

Gradually during the autumn, what was wrong with Oliver was not in remission. The Archdeacon had told the wardens that he would visit soon and matters could wait till then. The wardens reported to Charlotte that there was little they could do, and she was grateful as at least some sense of sobriety seemed to be returning to Oliver.

The investigating travelers eventually left for France in mid-September, and what with the weather, the length of the journey by train, boat, more train and a barouche incompetently driven by an old man in a beret, it took them several days to get to the village. The same was true of their return, with the result that Charlotte received a wire posted in Folkestone to say that they were now back on English soil, so she returned from Norfolk.

Honora went straight home on their arrival in London but came to Semper House shortly after breakfast the following morning. Charlotte got back mid-morning from Craynham, so the three of them sat together in Estella's drawing room to hear about their French excursion.

"I will have to go back to Craynham directly as Oliver seems to be going mad, but I am so excited to hear all about France first. I thought I would wait to select the investigator until you returned as what we asked him to do might have changed with your additional knowledge."

"I think Honora feels a great relief that she went with me, don't you, dear?" Asked Estella.

"Oh indeed. Let me tell you what happened.

"We stayed in a small hotel in *Argeles-Gazost*, but away from the *pension*. We settled in and the following afternoon went to that *pension*, ready to confront the Mitterands, only to find it was being run by a completely different family. When we asked for the Mitterand family we were met with stony silences and shrugs of the shoulder that indicated disinterest or secrecy.

"Estella and I then went to the police house to inquire. There we met the man who had questioned me, and he recognized me, obviously with some sense of shame.

"I asked where the Mitterand twins were now living, as I wished to speak with them. To our complete astonishment, he said they were both dead, killed in the war with Prussia and buried on some battlefield."

"That set us back," said Estella, "as he would not provide any more detail, except to say that a lady further down the street, a Madam Montaigne, might be prepared to tell us more. We were shocked and annoyed that we had travelled all that way and that all our preparations for confronting them were as naught," at which all three women laughed nervously.

"We ate an excellent dinner that night, didn't we, Estella, and we even had two glasses of wine, but agreed we must talk with Madam Montaigne the next day."

Honora continued: "She was a lovely delicate woman of about fifty years old, dark hair and deep black eyes. She must have been very beautiful as a young woman. She did not speak English, but Estella translated as my French is very weak. We knocked at the door and she answered."

"Madam, we have come from England, I said, and we are looking for Jean-Marc and Philippe Mitterand.

'Why do you want to meet with them?' She replied without inviting us in.

"Now that they are dead, I can tell you, I said as Estella translated for me.

"I came on a visit to Lourdes thirteen years ago and they raped me hideously and I later gave birth to twins.

"Madam then began to weep silently, her face in her hands.

'You too? She said. 'Please to come in.'

"You mean there were others?" asked Estella as we sat down.

"Madam M served us a glass of wine," Honora continued, "though I was as nervous as I have ever been, but Estella translated and this is the gist of what she said.

"The young men were the terror of the girls in the village. Her daughter Sybille was only thirteen years old, but they trapped her and did the most terrible things to her. People had reported them to the police for other instances, but nothing was done, partly because none of the girls had severe physical injury, though at least three had babies, and the policeman is a distant cousin of Madam Mitterand.

"It became so bad, said M. Montaigne, that public opinion demanded action.

"They were apprehended, but escaped from the cell in the village, and later that month they were found in a village north of Lourdes. They were tried and sent to prison on Devil's Island at the trial. Several other women came forward to attest that they too had suffered.

"But, three years ago, they were released early to go into the army as the Emperor needed as many men as possible. Jean-Marc, she thought, was killed at the Battle of Sedan and his brother in the Siege of Metz. Their parents have sold the *pension* and moved to Brittany, she did not know where, not that we were interested.

"So, Charlotte, she then inquired about me and I told her that I had given birth to twins, that they were taken away from me and that we planned to find out where they were. I am afraid I then started to weep, as did M. Montaigne.

"She also went very quiet," said Estella, "and said that she hoped they have not inherited their father's evil ways, and we all agreed. We left her expressing our thanks, hoping that Sybille would recover well. It was a much longer journey to and fro than we thought, but here we are."

Charlotte was engrossed in this story.

"What gets into men that they think they can treat us like that?"

"Extraordinary, isn't it, but quite common," said Estella, "think of all those women we are helping and the men who cruelly satisfy their lusts. Think of the young French girls whose lives they have destroyed."

"Indeed, but I must go to Norfolk tomorrow, and I will let you know how things are. I will then come back and get on with hiring the investigator."

Charlotte got back to Craynham Vicarage to find even more strange behavior, though no messages from the Churchwardens. These were very strange days coping with Oliver. Leaves were starting to fall as she walked back to the vicarage one afternoon through the churchyard after an unsatisfactory visit to the Churchwarden soon after her return.

Passing by the north transept on her third day back at the vicarage, she stopped in her tracks. Spread-eagled on the gravestones close to the church building lay Oliver, his hand full of wet leaves. Blood flowed from his head and he was obviously dead. She shouted for help, just as the Sexton came through the lychgate. He hurried over slowly as he was a man of some girth but also squeamish, for, on seeing the body, he looked as though he was going to faint, but he turned away saying he would get help.

Two hours later, Charlotte sat in the vicarage drawing room. The village constable had men take the body to the morgue in Norwich. Mrs. Hayhoe came in with a cup of tea.

"I s'pose there'll be an inquest, Mrs. Mudge,"

"Yes, there must be."

"I hears him mumbling t'other day about it raining on Saint Sebastian and how he must clean leaves from them gutters."

"He meant the stained-glass window, I suppose."

"Yes, that gutter he was clearing, that was above the window which has the Saint in it."

"He must have put up the ladder, scooped out the leaves from the gutter and lost his balance," Charlotte concluded.

"Long way to fall and them gravestones is very hard. I am so sorry, Ma'am."

"Thank you, Mrs. Hayhoe, but I think it is a good end. He had begun to lose his mind, poor man. What was his future? He would be disgraced. He would certainly have lost his place here, his living and, as he got worse, he would probably have had to go into a home."

"That's right, Ma'am, he was off his head, we thought."

"The sad thing is," continued Charlotte speaking as though no one was listening, "that he was physically strong, and he would only have a miserable existence in some home for as many years as God would give him."

"P'raps a blessing, really, but I'll leave you now, Ma'am, and you just call if you want for anything."

Blessing indeed, thought Charlotte as Mrs. Hayhoe bustled away. Henry was right. She should never have married this man and she wept for herself as much as for him. How much she would have loved a marriage of love and affection and, indeed, children. How weird were his recent extravagances, his perverse behavior with those choirboys, the man in the canal in Florence, the rows on the train, and now this foolish end.

The inquest had delivered a verdict of accidental death, nothing at all about being of unsound mind, though for a man of his age to climb a ladder and try to remove leaves from a gutter twenty feet above the ground without any help at all hardly suggested he was a man of balanced judgment.

She left the clearing of the vicarage for later. The funeral was a grim affair in the pouring rain with few mourners. The grave was under an oak tree in a corner of the graveyard, and she spoke to a stonemason in Aylsham about a stone. She also called on an auctioneer in the town to be rid of most of his property and a month later was surprised but gratified by the amount the furniture, china and other objects fetched, presumably as dealers county-wide had seen the catalogue. She told everything to Estella in a letter and indicated that she was anxious get back.

No one in his small family cared what she did with the property. She kept only a beautiful 18-carat gold watch made by Richard Hornby of Liverpool with a chain that had belonged to his father, a small mahogany writing desk of his mother's, and a round wall barometer, not shaped like a banjo that she always admired in the house. Charlotte had no need for the rest of his possessions, books, bookcase, furniture and other household stuff and none of it held any sentimental value.

1873
XVII

Honora was very restless on her return from France. The delay in finding an investigator to track down her twins was becoming a nightmare, though she appreciated poor Charlotte's problems. Charlotte was equally in despair about finding the right investigator on her return to London after her husband's funeral that October.

Charlotte promptly sent a message to Hamish in the belief that he would know of someone, though she concealed the real reason for wishing to hire one. She then received a letter from Adam on Hamish's behalf saying that their main man Sidney had an attack of severe rheumatism that prevented his travelling. Sidney suggested the name of another man, Heep by name, whom Charlotte rapidly met and with some reluctance employed. Heep indicated that the enquiry could take a month and a financial agreement was made.

Two days later Estella and Charlotte went to St. James Park in Estella's carriage.

"I am so sorry that my concerns with Oliver have so delayed our enquiries."

"Your duty to your husband came first."

"That trip to France must have been a very tiring experience for you," said Charlotte.

"It was certainly full of emotion, with Honora now coming out of her shell. We have met from time to time when you were in Norfolk and she is much more articulate, indeed, very good fun, though very anxious to get on with the search.

"You know, my dear, since my beloved Pip died my life has been remarkably full of many new relationships and Honora is certainly one. When Pip was quite young, he was said to be a man of great expectations, which was a way of anticipating his prosperity through an ambitious prediction. Maybe it was merely a prophecy?"

"That does not apply to you, my dear. You must be careful, Estella; try to moderate the pace you have generated for yourself."

"In some ways, I think, my coping with my grief has led me after his death to expectations which are better, perhaps much better, than they were that gloomy day of his funeral. Nothing can replace my Pip."

"I see," said Charlotte. "Better, but not great expectations. How sensible.

"What about Honora, though? Those dreadful twins were obviously very unpleasant young men, but to die in battle is always a case for sadness. I am perplexed by her situation. On the face of it, her twins should leave their adoptive parents and be brought up by Honora and Frederick, but it is not clear that Frederick would want them, or even that Honora would want them once she met them."

"True, but equally they might not be at all pleased to see their natural mother," said Estella, "so much would depend on their situation."

"Perhaps it will be enough for her drab life to be invigorated even by knowing where her children were, even if she could not care for them. She could write, surely, even have them to stay in London on occasion."

"I wonder what Pip and the lawyers would make of this complexity. Honora, poor woman, has no legal rights over her twins, yet Pip would also have tried to find out ways to change that."

"I think Frederick is the key. I do not like the man much as he seems something of a boor, yet he has given Honora a home and it was not he who had kept her on a short leash; rather, she had confessed to being frightened of the world."

"We both know what the ideal outcome is, don't we? Her boys living in the Brandram household."

It was three weeks to the day that a message arrived from Heep, the private investigator, that he would attend them that day, but if that was inconvenient he would arrange another time. It sounded like progress. They sent Honora a message but she was out visiting with her husband.

When Heep arrived, he appeared to Estella immediately all one might expect a person of his calling to be, greasy, slimy, probably untrustworthy, unctuous, but very clever. His name was Albert Heep, and Estella and Charlotte listened anxiously.

"Madam, I am here to present my findings in the case of twin boys who were born in Llanfairfechan twelve years ago and put out for adoption.

"The simple facts are as follows. They are Simon and Jude Jones. They were indeed adopted by a Mr. and Mrs. Jones, a childless Welsh couple who from all reports, led a very happy life in the village and were admired by all. However, sadness overtook them. Mr. Jones died suddenly from causes unknown; his wife was heartbroken, and she died six months later, leaving the twins without parents.

"Who told you this?"

"I knew their names. I heard they were dead, so I went to the cemetery and found their graves with the dates and details on them.

"With the death of their parents, the authorities sent the boys to St. Deniol's Orphanage on the Hawarden Road, near where Mr. Gladstone's house is. I was told that the prime minister visits every year to give the children a little present at Christmas. To my surprise the officials were quite friendly. I put on a Welsh accent and said I was a friend of the family and wanted to see how the boys were getting on. When we met, the boys immediately said they did not know me, so I told them I was bringing good news and they listened."

"How long were you with them? "

"About fifteen minutes. Poor boys, they were very sad and downcast. They seemed to be healthy and well treated, handsome children, so their life would not have been bad as far as orphanages go. I could not tell Simon from Jude! Oh, my goodness, are they identical! I took the liberty of asking them first about their parents.

"They knew they were adopted, but they had loved their Mam and Papa. I said that their natural mother had been looking for them and that I would go to London and tell her where they were. They then began to smile, though both said that they had no idea who she was or that she was still alive. I said I thought they would hear more once I had brought the news to you."

"Thank you, Mr. Heep, thank you very much. Let me give you a money order," said Charlotte. "How did you come to be in this business?"

"Oh, well, I am of 'umble origins. I felt for the boys because I too was adopted. Before I was born, my father was transported to Australia. My mother was a servant girl in a lawyers' house, and they were kind to her and arranged for my adoption. When I was a young man, I sought her out and discovered that my father was a man called Uriah Heep, so I changed my name to his, though, of course, I have no idea where he is over there or whether he is still alive. I am not of a mind to find out."

"A touching story indeed."

He left and Charlotte and Estella hugged each other with delight.

"We will get over to Chelsea forthwith and tell Honora. They will be back, I am sure."

Through the front window, Honora was thrilled to see Estella's carriage arrive and was at the door almost before they had dismounted.

"We have found them!" Charlotte called out from the carriage.

"You have? How wonderful," and she burst into tears.

"And no one has changed their names either," said Estella gaily, thinking of her own name change from her mother's Ruth to the Estella imposed by Miss Havisham.

"Come in, come in, tell me all," said Honora, clasping her mouth with her hands in delight.

"The important fact," said Charlotte, "is that they have been in an orphanage near Chester for almost a year as their adoptive parents died within a few months of each other. That makes it much more likely that you could get charge of them as I am sure the orphanage would be very pleased to have two less mouths to feed. The investigator said they were sad, but healthy and handsome."

"But now what do I do? Should I speak to Frederick? Write to the orphanage? Now my excitement is tinged with probable disappointment."

"Stuff and nonsense," said Estella.

"One difficulty," said Charlotte, "is how will you prove they are your natural children? You might just be anybody turning up claiming two boys."

"Let me think carefully. Hmm, how would I prove I gave birth to these two boys? I can see their lovely young faces, that's a memory I will carry to my grave. Something about them, what could that be?"

"It needs to be something you cannot possibly have known if you were not their mother."

"Estella's right," said Charlotte, "there must be something, one had a wooden leg or something," and they all laughed joyously.

"I know, I know, I know," said Honora with rising delight, "Just under his right shoulder on his back, Simon had a tiny birthmark."

"That will do. You won't need anything for Jude as he is so obviously a twin, we are told."

At that moment, the front door opened.

"Oh, it's Frederick, oh dear, what shall I do?"

"Tell him. Always better to tell the truth," said Estella.

"Ah, you have your new friends here for tea, I assume," asked Frederick, coming into the room.

"Welcome, Charlotte, Estella. I trust we have all recovered from our Italian trip."

"Yes, indeed," said Estella, "but Honora has something to tell you. It is something wonderful, quite wonderful."

"Go on, my dear."

"My twins have been found at an orphanage in Chester. They are healthy and handsome, so we are told."

"Why an orphanage? I thought they were adopted."

"They were, but apparently their parents died quite recently, so as they are only twelve years old the authorities sent them to this place, St. Deniol's Orphanage. What shall we do?"

"It is a great risk. We do not know them. I like children, provided I have nothing to do with them. I don't see how we could accommodate them easily."

"May I intervene?" asked Estella.

"I know something of the misery of being adopted, how it leaves a child rootless, however kind a guardian or an adoptive parent may or not be. My re-acquaintance with my mother turned my life around. She was crude, criminal and of the working class, but she was my mother.

"That natural bond is an inescapable tie. These boys knew they were adopted but, as far as we know, were never told their parentage, but they have recently been told of the existence of their natural mother.

"My suggestion is that you both go to Chester to meet them in the New Year. You, Frederick, can then assess what would need to be done. But if I may be perfectly frank with you, I do not see how in all conscience you can allow your wife's children to remain there."

"I see all that clearly. Thank you, Estella," said Frederick. "It is not as if they are babies either. It sounds as though they had a good upbringing before the parents died. All right, Honora, I am not committing myself until we have met them. Nor would I expect you to commit yourself. I told your parents I would care for you and while this is a distinct surprise, I am not averse to their coming to live with us."

Honora burst into tears, through which she said quietly, "Oh, Frederick, my dear husband, how generous, how kind you are."

"Don't fuss, please. I will make enquiries about the orphanage, but also write to them today and explain that we would like to meet your boys as we are considering offering them a home."

❧ ❧ ❧

The meeting of the sons with their mother was a magnificent triumph, one that would linger in the memories of the three of them.

The parlor at the orphanage had been set aside, and Frederick and Honora arrived from the Royal Oak Hotel in a carriage at exactly ten o'clock. The supervisor of the orphanage, also a Mrs. Jones, greeted them warmly. Frederick said he would wait outside in the hall and let Honora get acquainted. She went into the parlor where the boys, simply dressed and obviously washed with their hair flat on their heads, stood waiting.

The two boys looked at her with an instant sense of recognition, dragging up from their subconscious memories the sight of the face that had gazed at them in wonder as they sucked at her breast. She was overwhelmed by their beauty, that these were the babies she had surrendered, and how strong and healthy they looked. There was a long silence as they looked at her intently.

Simon broke the silence by rushing over and throwing his arms around her crying out: "Mamma, Mamma, Mamma." Jude was more cautious, but he too approached her, staring at her face, taking in her presence. She held their hands and sat down on a settee, pulling them down to her, one on each side, her arms tight around them, their arms round her waist, their heads on her breast. She nuzzled her face in their hair, each one in turn, speechless with joy.

Then she looked deeply into each face, realizing that not only were their eyes an identical color as would befit twins, but their eyes were an absolute replica of her own; hazel, more green than blue. Of course they would recognize her immediately! The twins had looked each other in the eye for twelve years, so when they looked her in the eye, each saw what he had always seen in his brother, eyes exactly the same.

Of course, she was their mother! Birthmarks mattered not a jot.

"How did you find us?' said Simon.

"I think you met that Mr. Heep we sent looking for you."

"Yes, we did. We did not like him much. Did you know our Mam and Papa had died?"

"Yes, we found that out from him."

"You see," said Jude, "we did not know what we would do.

"Before our mam died, she called us into her bedroom when she was very weak and told us all about you, how you loved us so much, how no one knew our father. She said she was dying and that we would go to the orphanage, but when we were grown up, we should go to find you, and she told us your name, Honora Brandram, though she did not know where you lived. She wrote it on a piece of paper that I keep."

"That was wonderful, so very generous of her indeed. She must have been a wonderful mother to you. I am so sorry that they died, but perhaps God intended for you to come back to me."

"When we heard from Mrs. Jones that you were coming, we did not know if we would recognize you," said Simon, "but when you came in just now, and looked at us, of course you are our proper mamma. Your eyes are like Jude's."

"I think we were just five," Jude interjected, "when our parents told us they were just looking after us, that they wanted to be our parents as best they could, but that our mother had had to let them bring us up. We knew we were adopted, but we clung together; we had each other, though not proper parents like other children."

"Now," said Honora. "you will come and live with us in London.

"Oh, my darlings," she continued, "I do not want you to stop calling Mr. and Mrs. Jones 'mam' and 'papa' when we talk about them, as they have been so kind to you. But then you also have me, your proper mamma, but also a new papa, the kindest of men, and he and I were married several years ago. Simon, please go to the door and ask Mr. Brandram to come in."

"Frederick, dear," said Honora, as he came in. "You have just met Simon, and this is Jude."

"Good morning, sir," said the boys in unison.

"Good morning, boys," said Frederick. "Your mamma and I have not had the pleasure of looking after two boys before, so it will be a new venture for all of us. But, let me look at you both. Oh dear, I am going to have a great deal of trouble knowing which of you is which, but I am sure your mother has no trouble at all."

"No indeed," said Honora.

"But the family resemblance is so striking. You are almost as handsome as your mother is beautiful," which made the boys laugh and cry at the same time, the relief sweeping over them that in such a short time, their lives had changed so dramatically from being the orphans of a poor but good family with a hugely uncertain future to the children of their mother in a well-to-do part of London.

Someone, somewhere, might just have told them they now had better, if not great, expectations.

Frederick, Honora, Simon and Jude came from Euston Station to Cheyne Row in a carriage to begin a new life. Honora's expectations of life had suddenly become much, much better—no, they have been transformed, she thought, as she savored this unspeakably lovely reunion. It seemed to be first fine day the sun had shone for weeks, after nothing but rain, rain. But how to tell them about their father?

The following day she wrote to Charlotte and Estella, asking them to call the next afternoon, and the two women immediately set out in a cab for Chelsea.

Over breakfast, the boys had chatted away about the house, how lovely the beds were, and how fine the furniture, and the piano which was much larger than the one at the Jones'. Honora had hardly slept that first night but left them to come down when they were ready.

They did not need to be told to wash for that had been part of the ritual imposed by the Jones. Frederick listened with amusement and then left for his office, kissing his wife warmly in a way he had never really done but to which she responded with great warmth.

"Mamma," said Simon, "who is our father?"

"He was a Frenchman, but we did not live together, and he died a soldier in the war between France and Prussia."

"Were you very sad when he died?"

"You know, I had not heard from him for a long time and I only found out recently about his death. I can see parts of him in you both, but I will tell you more about him later."

"Can you play the piano?" asked Jude, switching suddenly out of the conversation about his father with an alacrity typical of the boy of his age.

"Yes, and we will have you both learn if you would wish."

"I'd love to," said Jude.

⚜   ⚜   ⚜

"This is such a victory," said Estella to Charlotte as the cab rolled down towards the river. "We have managed to help dear Honora in a way she would not have believed when we were in Florence last year. You see, my dear Charlotte, it happened because we women worked together with common intent. She has been fortunate too that the adoptive parents are dead, and I have wondered these past few days what we might have done, had they been alive."

"I think about that too. It would have been enormously difficult for Honora to lay claim to them. Think of the hurt that might cause, the uncertainties of the reunion. Beggars the imagination, actually."

"Oh, my goodness, yes, could the children choose?"

The cab turned into Cheyne Row just as Pip and Susanna were walking from their home to visit the Brandrams. She looked as though she would give birth any moment. The Gargerys had not been brought into knowledge of what might be called the Honora Endeavor. They knew of course that Estella and she had gone off to France suddenly, but beyond that, nothing. Brandram always kept to himself, and they rarely saw him.

The two couples met at Honora's door, and before the maid opened it, Estella said to Pip:

"This is so exciting, isn't?"

"What are you talking about, Estella, what do you mean?"

241

She received no answer as they were all promptly standing in the hallway being greeted by Honora who, with tears in her eyes, said:

"Come into the living room and meet my children, Simon and Jude."

"Your what?" said Susanna as she came into the room.

"Goodness me!" she exclaimed, so startled on seeing the twins that she flopped down into a chair and winced as thought she was about to go into labor. Pip's eyes bulged with shock.

"Simon, Jude, these are all our special friends. This is Mrs. Mudge, who had the idea that we should send Mr. Heep to find you. This is Mrs. Estella Pirrip, who has also helped enormously, and here are Mr. and Mrs. Philip Gargery who live just three doors away with their two young sons, Lachlan and Malcolm."

The boys were standing up and walked to shake hands with these new adults. Estella was as overcome as Susanna. She looked at these lovely youngsters with tears in her eyes and told them how wonderful it was to meet them in their new home. Charlotte saw them and then had to leave the room to find somewhere to cry her heart out.

The boys then left, running up the stairs each to enjoy their very own bedroom, as Honora walked over and held hands with Pip and Susanna.

"Yes, my friends, these are my boys who were adopted soon after their birth. Their adoptive parents both died suddenly and sadly, and we were able to bring them to live with us from the orphanage to which they were assigned."

"I notice they have Welsh accents," said Pip, "where were they living?"

"The orphanage was at Hawarden near Chester, but they grew up in a small village on the coast, Llanfairfechan."

"How did they come to be there?"

"Oh, it's very long story which I will tell you sometime. But I am so grateful that their adoptive parents have brought them up to be very nice well-behaved youngsters and the orphanage seemed very good too."

"Ah, Hawarden," said Pip, "that's where the Prime Minister has a home."

"I like him," said Susanna, "and that reminds me, Pip, we must get going with the Liberal Party, I am sure they are the party for us."

"I would very much like to be involved too," said Honora, "and maybe I will get my boys interested in politics too."

"Politics?" asked Estella, "What sort of politics?"

"Now, Estella," said Susanna, "you are devoted through the Trust to helping people who are in distress, and that is wonderful, but, as you know with the laws on prostitution, it all comes down to politics and Parliament."

"Yes, I suppose so. Pip used to wonder whether he should have been more active but by the time he thought about it seriously it was too late."

"This is most interesting," said Pip.

"Here we have a group of friends who are interested in politics," said Susanna. "Maybe we could go together to important meetings and hear of ideas and plans. Of course, these days Parliament seems preoccupied with the Irish Question as it is called, which is enormously complicated, though I think Gladstone is not focused on that." Then with a sudden outburst, she squealed:

"Pip darling, we must go home and call the midwife. I think I am about to deliver your daughter."

With haste the couple got up to leave, but before they could, Frederick Brandram came into the room, and the Gargerys sat down together, Susanna's crisis being a false alarm..

"May I congratulate you, Frederick," said Estella, "on the acquisition of these two wonderful boys."

"I am surprised," he said, "by how much I am changing."

"We have had a difficult few years, but I have the sense that Simon and Jude are going to change us radically. To start with, we must now consider how they are to be educated. They went to a

Welsh school and are fluent in the language, and in English. They can read and write and do their sums, but we want them to be well schooled. I am looking at schools nearby. They have had too much upset to have to go away to a school for boarders."

"We have started to think about schools, too, Frederick," said Susanna.

"St Paul's School is very ancient and has a good reputation and it takes boys only between twelve and fourteen, so the times would be just ripe for Simon and Jude. And we hope we have a daughter on the way."

Hearing that everyone expressed their congratulations and delight and Pip beamed with a grin from ear to ear.

Then Frederick continued: "I have heard of the school. Of course, not having children, I am not well informed on schools, but that is an educational institution we should consider. The sooner the better for the boys, I think. They need to create friends of their own age, too."

Charlotte and Estella left for Semper House soon after this conversation.

"Is it not amazing, Charlotte, that the man I thought was cruel to his wife is in fact rather soft-hearted, and that she was the problem in their marriage being so completely deferential and thinking she had any sort of claim or right to say or do what she wanted without his permission. I can understand that now with hostile parents and the crippling loss of those two children."

"He seems almost ridiculously happy, almost as happy as she, a ready-made family, so to speak without all the trials of young babies."

"This has been the most interesting experience for me," said Estella. "I am sure I have told you that Pip and I were too old to have children. Well, let me say I was too old to have children, though we have Albert. This whole experience makes me slightly envious of Honora," she said laughing, "but now she can build on the basis the Jones had given her."

"Oh," said Charlotte, "I was never enthusiastic about children, I fear, and I would hate to think that Oliver's eccentricities might have been part of my child's make-up. You know my dear, we must not forget that whichever of the French twins was responsible for these children, they were both quite evil young men, obviously cruel and wayward, wayward in the sense that they came from an apparently sound family bringing them up well, but then losing their way, straying from the right path on which they had been led."

"That is such an important consideration and it had not occurred to me. I wonder how Honora will handle the question of their paternity when they ask, and whether indeed some of the father's characteristics will be manifest in either of them. I so hope not."

"What would you tell them, Charlotte, if you were Honora? I am sure she will consult us in the short or long run about the matter."

"I am too. I would not attempt ever to tell the tale of their conception. I would simply say something like 'I was in love with this Frenchman who was then killed at the Battle of Sedan.'"

"But wait. Do they not have the right to know their heritage?"

Estella demurred, but then said slowly.

"I think I would say this, not now, but when they are men. I was on a religious pilgrimage to Lourdes and a couple of young men, twin brothers, attacked and raped me. I became pregnant but they were both killed in the war in France. What you must learn from this is that men can be very cruel to women and I want you both to grow up, understanding your parentage, but also determined never to behave in any way like your father.

"And, I would add, it makes no difference but since both of them were involved, I do not know which of them is your father and it would be impossible to find out, even if they were alive."

"So, you'd go the whole hog, would you?"

"She should not accept any blame for not being married when they were born, for they might develop a romantic ideal of their father as a dead patriot soldier. She should certainly tell them he was in prison on Devil's Island. She should portray him—well, them—as real bastards, if you forgive the expression which sounds more like Nellie than me. They have to learn to fight against their father's worst instincts, not emulate or admire them."

"Well, as you said earlier, I am sure we will converse with Honora on the subject, sooner rather than later, I expect."

The cab stopped at Semper House. Dinner was prepared and was soon on the table. They retired to the living-room, each with a glass of whisky, their minds settling into a quiet harmony.

The following morning a message arrived to say that Susanna had been delivered of a daughter, Hannah Emily Gargery.

Guests arrived for the Partnership party at Crockett Grange in early June with great enthusiasm and the gardens looked glorious. It had been several months since Courtisone had mooted the idea, but the practice had begun to run very smoothly. At the rear of the house there were two large lawns, each surrounded by arbors of climbing roses, and on each of the lawn's perimeters there were roses in beds, the whole providing an exotic fragrance which the June sun brought out so brilliantly.

Finally assembled for dinner with Courtisone and his daughter Abigail were Hamish and Mary Macdonald, Philip and Beryl Hardyman, Adam and Ingrid Masterson, John Wemmick and Mrs. W. and Estella. Clarence Smythe and a young lady of great charm and beauty, Lady Emma Eustace, were also in attendance and, while there was clearly no formal engagement for marriage between them, it would have been a surprise had that not been in their futures.

The dinner was more than splendid with fresh salmon and carp, a roasted leg of mutton, three rabbits and four ducks cooked in cider, a cornucopia of vegetables of all shapes, colors and tastes, followed by various fruits from the garden, strawberries, raspberries, figs and grapes with a plentiful supply of madeira and port with claret or white wine, completed with coffee and brandy for those who wished it.

A toast to the new partnership was made by Hamish, very brief but well received. Courtisone would not allow the ladies to leave the table or the gentlemen to have their cigars, as all were summoned to one of the rose lawns where a small group had arrived to play a little Mozart and Haydn in the dwindling twilight of a summer evening where fireflies flicked among the roses and the candles sputtered. Fortunately, thought Estella, no one here is going to volunteer to sing.

After the music, conversation developed in various groups, though the Wemmicks retired to bed early. Clarence was taking the Lady Emma back to town in a carriage he had hired, so they too left.

XVIII

At breakfast the following day political discussions began in earnest. Courtisone and his daughter Abigail were down first, leafing through the newspapers.

"How do you define the Irish question, Father?"

"H'mm, there is the old joke that each time we English think we have answered the Irish question, the Irish change the question!"

Both father and daughter laughed quietly.

"I recall a speech made long ago by Mr. Disraeli which, though I was a young man at the time, still seems to be an accurate description. It went something like this.

"'Here is an island with a dense starving population,' Dizzy said, 'and it has been decimated by famine, 1.7 million in one decade!

'There is an established church, but it is not their church.

'There is a territorial aristocracy, most of whom don't live there, but who influence policy on Ireland hugely and from afar.

'The executive is very weak.

'In other countries the answer to this would be revolution.

'But Ireland is connected to England, and she could prevent that, and logically England is the real cause of Irish misery.'

"Now that is an accurate summation, I believe, except that since then some Irishmen, called Fenians, are playing with revolution."

At this juncture, Hamish and Mary came into the room.

"Are we talking about Ireland, then?" asked Mary, helping herself to kippers. "My family lived in Ulster for a while."

"And that is another part of the problem, Abigail," said Courtisone.

"King James I encouraged poor Scottish farmers to move to Ulster. They were all firm Protestants planted on a Catholic population and they gradually drove the Catholic farmers away from good fertile land into the hills. Protestants are now in the majority in Ulster, though not in the other three provinces, though it is not religious warfare, yet. And yet, poverty takes little account of such differences.

"There are plenty of Protestants – the revolutionary Wolfe Tone are examples, who wanted Irish grievances redressed, but, of course, the aristocracy has been driving a wedge between Irish Protestants and Irish Catholics to disguise the real misery of the average Irishman."

"Indeed," added Mary, "my family went there from Galloway at that early settlement time. But my grandfather got so tired of the problems of land, so he eventually left and bought a small cattle farm in Devon. He disliked the Catholics as lazy, shifty and with that 'terrible religion' as he called it, but then he disliked the Protestants there too."

At this point, Estella appeared and was listening as she helped herself to eggs and fish.

"Why is it," she demanded, "that people worshipping the same God can develop such religious hatred? I always understood that Jesus said we should love our neighbor."

"Politics, my dear Estella, and what Mr. Mill labeled the *odium theologicum*," said Courtisone sagely.

"Every institution, religious or otherwise, is a political organization. Politics creates rivalries, not common cause. Politics offer power over others, democratic or otherwise. Churches are no exception. Religions and sects ultimately connect their heritage back to Abraham and that includes followers of Islam and Judaism."

"Do you not think it might be because religions are dominated by men and, in most cases, women are not able to hold office? The idea of a woman Archbishop of Canterbury, for instance, is not possible, though it is not unthinkable, especially as we have a Queen. Women have exercised positions of power, Cleopatra for example, but it seems that most religions regard women as somehow ineligible for office."

Courtisone and the others smiled at Estella's fervor.

"Well," Mary remarked, "did you hear about those Ascott Martyrs in Chipping Norton?"

"No," said Abigail, "who are they?"

"A farmer dismissed those men who had joined an agricultural union and brought in labor from the neighboring village of Ramsden. Sixteen women in the village tried to persuade the Ramsden men to join the union and the farmer took them to court for 'obstructing and coercing' two of the men. Seven were sentenced to ten days hard labor and they went to Oxford prison, two with their infant children! Women are clearly capable of leadership at every social level;, they don't have to be monarchs."

"When was this? asked Abigail.

"A month or so ago."

"Here's yet another case for Mr. Mill. I don't know whether you saw his book on the subjection of women. I suspect Mill lost the election two years ago primarily because he suggested women should have the vote both in that book and in a speech to the House of Commons."

"That's right," said Estella excitedly. "Men came out in force to ensure that someone with such radical views should not be in Parliament. That should change. I have heard recently about the London Suffrage Committee, and I think it was my friend Charlotte who told me of a public meeting on women voting, too. I wonder whether these Liberals will help women get the vote."

"It won't be in my lifetime," said Courtisone, "and I would hazard guess that it won't be even in my daughter's."

"I am going to try to make sure it happens in mine," Estella replied.

"What about you, Abigail, are you able to work for women to vote?"

"I agree in principle, of course."

"And you, Hamish?"

"The problem for me about voting is that widening the franchise will include people who know nothing and care less about the problems facing our country. I am concerned by voters who are ignorant. I think the 1867 extension of the franchise was a sensible move, but that is as far as I would go. As for women, I am not sure how one would decide which category of women should be included. Of course, everyone we know would be included" and laughing gently, he continued, "the idea of one man or one woman, one vote, seems to undermine the system as we have it."

At this point, Pip and Susanna appeared for breakfast, both very cheerful as they greeted everyone around the table. As they stood filling their plates at the sideboard, Mary interjected with her usual candor:

"My dear husband, I have never heard such claptrap in all my life! You clearly think that voting is a privilege to be granted to others by people of your class and upbringing if, perchance, they were to bring themselves up to your standards which are, of course, quite arbitrary. Voting is a right which should be available to every adult. Only that way can we prevent tyranny."

"But my dear," countered Hamish, "just think of those poor women in the building, all of them leading lives of great distress, selling their bodies."

"The challenge, my dear, is to educate them to enable them to exercise their rights sensibly. You could do that by having them take part in the management of The Jaggers Building."

As the conversation went on, Estella's mind began to wander, and she excused herself and walked from the dining room to the library and then out into the rose gardens, which reminded her of Numquam and her mother Molly.

The more she learnt about the world, the more her emotions were in conflict. She bent down to smell a beautiful white bloom on a bush, reading the label 'peace'. Peace indeed, but what a change in her from her early carefree life. In that part of her life, she would have been no more interested in the lives of the maids in her employ as that of a dog roaming down the village street.

After her marriage she had become aware of the world's grievances. This conversation at breakfast, for instance: The problem of votes for women seemed obvious to her, not just as a woman, but in terms of a principle of liberty, a notion that had got into her consciousness recently. But then Ireland—*goodness me*, she thought, *how in God's name could the harm of six hundred years of history be remedied?*

I have a choice, she said to herself. *Think carefully about all this, or just ignore it and lead a life of leisure.*

Hamish stepped out from the library and walked across the lawn just as she noticed that the sun had started to open the daisies.

"Good morning, Estella. Deep in thought?"

"I was just considering the daisies greeting the sun and the tragedy of life."

"Oh, my word," he laughed, "that's hardly a topic for the early morning!"

"No, precisely the opposite; the clear blue sky, the beauty of the flowers, the buzzing bees and the tranquility of morning time are an excellent time for such a consideration."

"Which part of the tragedy are you thinking about?"

"My own, for at one moment my earnest desire is to retreat to my garden at Numquam, and lead a sedentary life, visiting London and friends occasionally. At the next moment, I am embroiled in trying to understand the Irish Question, to throw myself into our work with the Trust and expand the work on prostitutes.

"I swing like a pendulum between the two and have no way to resolve it. Yet, remembering my husband's youth as a person of great expectations, I am relieved to be able to manage my grief, but to expect that life will improve. Indeed, for all of us in this decade with our country getting wealthier, I suppose we have much better expectations than our forefathers had."

"How interesting. You see, the heart of religious belief as some people experience it in these days is what the theologians call 'salvation by works.' That, in the day of judgment, we will indeed be judged by how much we have contributed to the welfare of others, like the poor, the needy, our prostitutes and so on."

"Without the religious gloss, I am impelled to help others from which I get great satisfaction. Yet I also want to just sit in my garden, reading or listening to the birds, or selecting flowers for my living room, or chattering with the gardener, anything but this troubled world with its tragedy of living.

"Perhaps my expectations of life will diminish as I get older."

Mary had been smelling the roses but returned to them during this conversation.

"Of course," said Hamish, "especially at your age, you can properly spend time in your garden and combine it with your charitable work and thinking about how to answer the Irish Question. Yet you are certainly a remarkable woman, you know."

"More than that," said Mary, intervening. "Since I have known you, Estella, I have been in such thrall to your character, to your honesty, to your courage, to your passion for life which makes you something of an inspiration to those who know you, certainly to me."

"Oh, my dear Mary, fine words butter no parsnips, as they say. No, my earnest desire is to help those poor women who must sell their bodies. That kind of life seems to me to be the ultimate in moral degradation."

"I agree, of course," said Mary. "Yet is it not interesting that when young women are obliged to take for a husband someone who is selected primarily for his wealth or station, that almost amounts to a highly sophisticated form of prostitution, a different form of a woman selling her body to a man."

"That happened to me," said Estella, "but it seems too much of a leap for me to think of my marriage to Drummel as making me a whore, even though I felt inveigled into it."

"Exactly, so the sophistication arises in that the parents or guardians are the sellers, and it is usually for their own benefit, rather than the young woman."

"Perhaps, but that is a topic for another occasion. Reverting to our earlier discussion, however, it has expanded so much we should consider another project building in the west; the Victoria area for instance. We must talk to the Trust about that. But I have discovered recently, and I meant to talk to you about it before now, that areas close to my house in Soho are frequented by prostitutes.

"That will become a real nuisance, I expect as it will attract all kinds of villains."

"Yes, I suppose that what once was Mr. Jaggers' fashionable area is now much less so. Of course, the area is not *all* declining. I am told that there is now an excellent restaurant called Kettner's with a French chef."

"Really?"

"Indeed, and we should visit it, but when one always travels in a cab or a carriage to avoid one's clothes being soiled, it can be quite illuminating to walk. I set out from my home on a fine evening recently, down Gerrard Street. I turned into Wardour Street and then out on to Shaftesbury Avenue. I went toward Piccadilly Circus and there were women in doorways, and I am sure they were not just waiting for their husbands to return."

"I did not realize you lived so near that avenue," said Hamish. "I am sure some of the women in the building will have worked that area. Pip was telling me of one quite recently."

"Really, who were they?

"Fairly new arrivals. Emily Collins, I think one was. She was quite amusing as she said her mother had the attention of Mr. Gladstone when he was younger."

"What, the Prime Minister?"

"Yes, we've mentioned this briefly before, thinking it was a rumor. But she and one of the others said he used to walk around there. But she never knew of anyone he had, how shall I put it, used for his pleasure. He apparently seemed to enjoy the thrill of talking to them, while also urging them to give it up."

"I am not very surprised. I would not be at all surprised if one or two other politicians and lawyers frequented the area."

"I do not understand," interjected Mary. "What is it that drives men to use these women? Presumably adulterous men have women of their own class to befriend."

"I suppose so. I wonder. A thought has just occurred to me. You both know my Semper House, do you not? Charlotte and I are on our own there with Albert, though I think he is on and off to Paris. It is a large rambling sort of place with several rooms, and my husband and I spent several very happy years there, courtesy of Mr. Jaggers."

"Of course, I had forgotten that part of the legacy."

"Perhaps we should move west, find a smaller house in Mayfair or even as far as Kensington perhaps, and use the Soho house as our second building for prostitutes."

"That would be exceedingly generous. Come to Cheyne Row!"

"I might. Now I am comfortable financially, my dear, but not to that extent. The Trust could buy it from me."

"Now that is a possibility. We would need Courtisone's legal consent for the Trust to commit a capital sum, but not at his party."

After the party Hamish and Mary were excited by their argument about women voting and returned to their home in Walworth, not a stone's throw from the Wemmicks. In the carriage to Watford Station, Mary took Hamish's hand and said how much she was looking forward to getting home and resting. He turned and kissed her lightly, saying how wonderful it is to have a son. He was in a mood of happy contentment that he was established as a leading partner in *Courtisone and Jaggers,* and that the merger had gone so well.

In his office was an unkempt man with a straggly beard, of medium build, brown hair, an almost toothless mouth but wearing quite fashionable clothes: a frock coat, a waistcoat sporting a watch and chain, and carrying a hat which could well have come from one of those smart new shops in Oxford Street.

"What can I do for you, sir?"

"The name is Pennyfeather, Robert Pennyfeather. My wife, Margaret, is in a bit of trouble and we was told that Jaggers was the lawyer to go to."

"Mr. Jaggers has been dead these many years, sir, but we would be interested in helping you. Perhaps you could tell me what the problem is."

"Well, my missus was in a shop, all on her tod, and a gang burst in and started snatching all kinds of goods from the counters and then disappeared as fast as they come in, like she said."

"So, why does she need advice?"

"You see, it's like this. When the peelers arrived, they arrested my wife as an accomplice and she's in jug down there."

"When does she come to court?"

"Tomorrow in Bow Street."

"I will be there to talk with her before she is in the dock."

Wemmick came into Hamish's office immediately after the gentleman had left, and Hamish briefly explained what he was after.

"I am not sure whether you are aware of this," said Wemmick, "but there has been a growth in recent years of such snatches, though Mr. Jaggers never had any customers associated with such practices.

"A month or so ago, Sidney told me of an all-female crime gang coming from the Elephant and Castle area of the city. They have been engaging in stealing, shoplifting they call it, and their raids are called 'smash and grab' raids. They seem to work with a group of male criminals from that area."

"That's very useful information."

"I think we should be on our guard with this woman Pennyfeather. She might well be a scout for the gang. I was alerted to that possibility by the clothes her husband wore as he was leaving just now. It is unusual for a man of his class to have such fine clothes and be so dirty."

"Invaluable as usual, John. I will bear that in mind."

The following morning, Hamish went to Bow Street where Mrs. Pennyfeather was being held. Like her husband, she looked as though she had not washed for some months, but she was wearing an expensive dress and a bonnet that would not have originated in the Old Kent Road. She was a small woman, the sort that would go unnoticed but for her clothes, blue eyes, and dank, greying hair.

"Lor', bless you, Mr. Macdonald, you will save me when I come up before the beak, won't you."

"Tell me, Mrs. Pennyfeather, how did you come to be in Mr. Lewis's shop?"

"That's right, sir. Well, I was come over to see these new shops. I's from south of the river, see, near the Elephant and Castle, well, it's Lambeth really, and I thought I'd do some exploring."

"Do you have children?"

"Cor' blimey no! I've had a tragic life, you see," she said starting to sniffle into her handkerchief. "I lost both my babies to that cholera disease when we was living in Soho."

"Oh yes, I remember something about that outbreak."

"Yeah, it were terrible. The water from the pump, they said, but that was too late for us. Well, anyways, I was just doing a bit of looking around the shop when these men rushed in and started grabbing everything they could. I was so frightened, I tell you."

"Ah, well, we will just tell that to the court. Now, I will charge you a small fee of ten shillings for my appearance. But tell me, that's a very fine dress you have, and I noticed your husband was similarly well dressed when he came to see me."

"Oh yes, we keep our fine clothes for very special occasions, like going to church, shopping and going to court."

"Is going to court a regular occurrence then?"

"Oh no, I just meant for occasions like today."

"I see, and is Mr. Pennyfeather employed?"

"No, he works for himself, you know jobbing and selling."

"He's not in the court then."

"No, he don't like courts at all."

They parted and Hamish went up into the court where the magistrate, Mr. Thomas Fielding, seemed in a relaxed mood and, certainly to judge by the unexpectedly slow pace of the proceedings, to be in no particular hurry to shuffle cases off his docket. Shortly, Mrs. Pennyfeather appeared from below, and Hamish moved to the place reserved for defense counsel.

"Read the charge," said the magistrate.

"That the defendant did wittingly conspire with person or persons unknown to rob the emporium the property of Mr. John Lewis, on the fifth day of October 1872."

"Proceed please, Mr. Dobson."

"I appear," said Dobson, "on behalf of the Crown.

"The defendant was in the shop at the time of this robbery. My first witness will testify that she went to the door and signaled to a man outside immediately before the incident. A second witness will testify that, during the raid, she stood without any sense of alarm at the back of the shop, whereas other customers were terrified by the noises and the fierceness of the men doing the raid."

"Thank you, Mr. Dobson, you may call the first witness."

"Please state your full name," said Dobson as a very well-dressed woman stood in the witness box.

"Mrs. Helena Dorothea Antonia Robertson, your Honor."

"Please tell the court what you saw."

"I was in the store looking for a gift for my mother and noticed the woman over there," she said, pointing to Mrs. Pennyfeather. "She did not seem to be interested in the shop at all, you know how women look at everything available. She looked as though she was just waiting for someone. Then I saw her go to the window and raise her hand as if in a greeting. There was then this terrific commotion as the raid started and, of course, I lost sight of her and when the raid was over, she had disappeared."

"I have a question, Mrs. Robertson," said Hamish, "if it please the court."

"Carry on, Mr. Macdonald."

"When a woman raises her hand, how do we know what she is doing? Is she merely raising her hand, sending a signal, getting ready to adjust her hat, waving to a friend? Can you swear that the defendant was without any doubt making a signal?"

"Well, no, I cannot be certain that her raised hand was a signal."

"Thank you, that is all."

The second witness was called and again Hamish raised doubts about the woman's testimony by asking whether individual people might not react very differently to being present at a raid. Flimsy defense, he thought, but maybe enough to convince the beak that a sentence might be reduced.

"Mrs. Pennyfeather," said Mr. Fielding.

"Your actions seem to me to be clear, and although your counsel has thrown doubt on the evidence of the witnesses I am still finding you guilty. You will not go to prison but I am binding you over to keep the peace for a period of three years. If you commit any offence in this period, your sentence in this case will be taken into account."

Hamish walked out of the court with Mrs. Pennyfeather and she paid him for his services. She thanked him profusely and said she would be a good girl from now on.

"But" said Hamish, "you were a part of the raid, weren't you?"

She smiled and said with a laugh: "Now why would you think that?"

When Wemmick heard about the proceedings, he congratulated Hamish and said:

"We have heard bits about this gang, but we are going to hear much more, I know. I also know that your success this morning will certainly put more business our way. If you can sow even a little bit of doubt in the mind of a fair-minded judge that will be enough to mitigate a sentence. These women were obviously terrible witnesses, but, of course, it was a low-level crime, suspected involvement in a raid. The burden of proof would be great where only suspicion is the core of the matter."

"Yes, but my real concern is that as these raids have been successful, they will become more common. On the other hand, if the Pennyfeathers were involved, I suspect we may find ourselves being asked to act as their counsel."

"It is a problem though, Wemmick. Am I trying to serve justice, in which case, Mrs. P should have gone to prison, or am I just serving my client? The two are often in conflict and I am still find-ing it difficult to accommodate it to my conscience."

"Now don't you go about your conscience like Old Pip did. You are not the dispenser of justice but the person who presents a case so that others may judge. The Pennyfeathers are the kind of client we have not represented since Mr. Jaggers died. There's more where they come from.

"Mind you, I'm glad you were at the Old Bailey and not the Courts of Justice. That must be pandemonium there."

"Why?"

"Well, it's this Tichbourne Claimant case, isn't it? He is going to get done this time. I'd bet he knew Magwitch."

"Why?"

"Well, this Orton man comes from Australia claiming he's Roger Tichbourne, the vanished heir to considerable property, not mainly portable I should add."

"Oh, of course, I've read about it. It's been going on for years, hasn't it?"

"Yes. I have always had this inkling that everything that comes out of Australia is bad, like that man Unworthy. Do you remember how clever Estella was in dressing the man down? I never thought a woman could be so clever."

Estella got back to Semper House from Crockett Grange with a renewed determination to move her home somewhere much smaller. Albert was waiting there, anxious to talk to her.

"Estella, I have learnt as much as I can from the Kensington school. My eye is much recovered, and I am to have the plaster on my leg removed shortly. I will then need a month or so here to get it back to something like normal and stop using my crutches. I'd like to go to Paris again as soon as I feel I can."

"Good, but I have an idea to put to you. This house is far too large for us, even with Charlotte living here, but especially if you are going to be away. Soho has declined as the fashionable area it used to be. I walked along Shaftesbury Avenue recently and saw several what I think were prostitutes sheltering in doorways. How would you feel if we sold it and moved west to say, Mayfair, Chelsea or Kensington?"

"But who would buy Semper House?"

"The Trust, I hope, for use as a center for these poor women or men, though we will have to guard it much more carefully than we did with the building."

"We must start looking around at properties. Perhaps, if we find the right place, we might even move in before Christmas."

"That sounds good. I have to break the news to Charlotte when she returns. She might decide she wants to share the cost, not that it matters. I should have mentioned this to you earlier, but I was waiting to tell Charlotte as well. Mary, Hamish's wife Mary, is expecting another baby."

"Hmmm," said Albert. "I remember my father telling me all about men like him and I talked with Hamish about his desires once. He can't be that much of a mollie though," and they both collapsed on the settee in their mirth.

1874

XIX

"Charlotte, I want to talk to you seriously about our future together. I have done nothing about moving house since the Courtisone party last June. I talked with Albert about it and he is keen on the idea. I had hoped it could be accomplished before Christmas, but my desultory searches have found nothing.

"This house is far too big for either my or Albert's needs, and we should search for something more congenial. This part of London, especially where it links to Shaftesbury Avenue, has become degenerate with prostitutes in doorways and much else. Albert will want to go to Paris once he is confident about his leg, but he and I want to look directly for a home on the west side of London. I think the Trust will agree to buy this house and it will become a refuge like our other building, perhaps for men of the street."

"Goodness me, that is so sensible."

"Now, we would like you to join us in acquiring a house where we can both be together but separate, details of which we can discuss further if the idea appeals to you."

"Gracious me, I need to take all this in. The Diocese of Norwich claimed back the vicarage for a new parson, so I have no regular home. I have been so happy here these many months, but it is true I am in dire need of something permanent. My staying with you while I cleared up Oliver's mess has been a boon. I will need to think about this carefully."

"But you would like to do this in principle?"

"Of course, my dear. Though you are older than me, I feel we are kindred spirits, and I would anticipate that if we were to live together, we would find enjoyment in such pastimes as the theatre, concerts and so on."

"I am sure of it. I would like to travel a little, too. We would be good companions, I think."

"But, Estella, I am not sure how much I can contribute financially until Oliver's estate is wound up. Much would depend on the amount we would have to pay."

"I am not at all clear how much money would be involved. I am very comfortably off both with Miss Havisham's legacy and with my husband's excellent successes at the law, though appropriately Albert has inherited a good part of that estate. There will also be money from the Trust's purchase of this house. But we must temper the wind to the shorn lamb."

"I just don't know how much I might contribute, yet. One must think to the future, too. What happens if you were to die? If we share the ownership, won't that be very complicated with Albert's claim? Would I have to sell the house?"

"I had not thought about that. You wouldn't want to move your home in that eventuality, would you?"

"Oh dear, I wish I could be better informed about Oliver's estate. I think I must go to his solicitors in Norwich to get some idea of what there will be before I commit financially. Would it not be easier for us to rent a home? This is what most people in London do, after all, since the big estates that own the land on which all these new houses have been built want to keep control of their investments in property."

Warming to her idea, Charlotte continued, "If we owned a house, what if you or I were to marry in our old age? How might that affect matters? Would a husband not then have rights over the property? Leasing a home obviates that."

"Fiddlesticks, I wish I had been trained as a lawyer, but leasing is the obvious choice. We will have to consult Hamish. You are then agreed that we should set up a home together."

"I can think of nothing more delightful."

At that they got up from the table, gave each other a brief hug and walked arm in arm into the living room.

Estella later went to the Building, glad to be in her carriage out of the rain, contemplating on the way how she felt about Charlotte. She liked her openness, her care for Elizabeth and her friendliness, and she would make a good companion if they could arrange separate quarters in a house, though with a common living room, dining room and library.

Of all the women she knew, and there were not many, Charlotte could be a companion in pursuit of cultural enjoyment as equals. When she arrived back at Semper House, there was a post letter on the hall table which she opened with some curiosity as she did not recognize the hand. It read:

> 'My dear Mrs. Pirrip:
>
> We met briefly in Florence two years ago. I have been in Italy writing and studying but am now returned to London. I would value the opportunity to meet with you as, from our briefest of conversations, I thought that we might become acquaintances and perhaps friends."
>
> Your humble servant,
> Harriet Middleham February 8, '74.'

Estella sat down on the settle in the hall, quite astonished by this letter. She had certainly seen great charm and intellect in Harriet, but she did not know whether she knew that Pip had confided in her that she had been his lover.

If she met Harriet, might it be regarded as disloyal to Pip and more so to Susanna to foster such a relationship?

Or, for that matter, why should her mild interest in Harriet be curtailed because of her knowledge of Pip's behavior?

Returning home in the late afternoon, she found Charlotte reading *Middlemarch*, which she was especially enjoying because it was written by that scandalous woman Marian Evans. Precisely what her male pseudonym showed about the status of women was quite uncertain to Charlotte. Estella saw that she was obviously enjoying it greatly, as it took her a short while to distract her with the news about Harriet.

"Do you remember that woman we met in the Uffizi?"

"The one who was drawing but suddenly left us?"

"Yes, and she said she would call on us, but didn't."

"That's right, a handsome woman I thought, very English too."

"She has written a message asking if we can meet."

"Really? How interesting."

"Now, Charlotte, if we are to live together, we must try and keep secrets to an absolute minimum. Otherwise, we will make blunders we would have been able to avoid."

"Quite so, Estella. But go on."

"Pip confided in me several years ago when my Pip was alive that he had had an affair with a woman who was a free lover while he was a preacher. It appears at some point he resumed that relationship for a very short time. It was the Uffizi woman and that is why she left the Botticelli room in a hurry when Pip and Susanna came in."

"Oh, my goodness, how exciting! No, I should not say that. I didn't know he was a scoundrel and him a former preacher, too," she said, laughing.

"I need your help. Should I then make her acquaintance? Would it be disloyal to Pip and Susanna on the one hand, but, then why should we curtail our friendships for that reason?"

"We shouldn't," said Charlotte firmly, "we cannot let Pip's extramarital activities influence our decision, or any other philanderer for that matter. Who knows, we might be frightfully radical and have them all to a dinner party!"

At that they both laughed long and loud.

"Oh, dear how quaint men are! The more you get to know them, the odder they seem. But after Pip died, I realized that widowhood might give me a sense of freedom I had not had."

"Unlike you, I was not in love with my husband, who turned out to be really very strange. I too am beginning to feel a great sense of freedom now I do not have to worry about his indiscretions, for I do think he was on the way to complete madness and that makes me sorry for him."

"Well, I am not one to judge that, I am afraid," concluded Estella.

"However, we do know that Harriet is a free spirit in more ways than one. Perhaps we will form a coterie of free women, or should it be a gaggle? Mary Macdonald and Honora Brandram might join us."

"'A League of Free Women,'" said Estella. "Now there's an idea! Let us start by inviting Harriet to lunch with us. I am told there is a new restaurant quite near us, Kettner's, I believe it is called. I think I'd prefer to meet her first on neutral ground."

The half-yearly meeting of the Jaggers Trust took place in the *Courtisone and Jaggers* offices in the city later in the month. The Trustees knew each other well with their past and present connections, so having Estella as chairman was approved by acclamation. She was duly humbled and expressed the wish that the board members would help her when she was in error as she was bound to be. She welcomed Philip Hardyman from the Courtisone wing of the newly merged practice into board membership.

There were two main items on the agenda apart from the reports, and they were interlinked.

Pip delivered a report as manager of the Building Project.

"I have looked very carefully at Estella's informal suggestion for a building in the Soho area. I have talked with police and was astonished by a senior officer's remark that there were probably about twenty thousand prostitutes in London and that anything to get them off the streets would slightly relieve a pernicious social situation.

"Inspector Cooper told me that he had been responsible for the Soho area for several years and had noted the movement of the gentry away from the area and that it was gathering an insalubrious reputation, notably for prostitution, pickpocketing, burglary and assault in Shaftesbury Avenue and adjoining streets.

"I recommend that the Trust examine buildings in the Soho area to replicate that in Clerkenwell."

There were murmurs of approval round the table.

"We will certainly need additional supervisors," said Susanna. "Perhaps on the Trust's behalf, we could also look at other possible philanthropic activities and ask such people as Octavia Hill about supervision."

"The second item is a formal proposition that the Trust purchase Semper House for the purposes of the Trust's work with prostitutes," said Pip, at which Estella withdrew from the meeting.

"I have been a guest there," he continued, "but the board must create an inventory of the exact composition of the rooms, and then get an estimate of what the costs will be of using it for the purpose intended."

"Probably twelve rooms would be available on the two top stories with conversions, so I am sure the house is large enough," Wemmick said, and Susanna added that she thought the plan was excellent but that the Trust should not be blind to the expenses to come.

All agreed with her comments, but there was a sense that nothing should be delayed.

"I see no reason to object in principle, as the terms of the Trust allowed for capital expenditure allow it," said Courtisone. "I propose that, provided the costs of house alterations did not exceed one third of the price of the house, the board instruct Pip to move ahead without referring back to the board.

"An independent valuation will be needed, and I propose the appointment of two men, William Cheeseman and Arthur

Muschamp, independent of each other who can each be relied on to conduct such a valuation. If the valuations are similar, so much the better and if not, then the Trust should split the difference."

Pip was very pleased that Courtisone's stature in the legal community enhanced the work of the Trust, and the distinguished lawyer's proposals were accepted. Estella was then invited back into the room and Courtisone informed her of the decision, which she thought very sensible.

As usual lunch was taken at The Cheshire Cheese. Wemmick spent some time talking with Estella and telling her what a splendid idea selling Semper House was.

"I never liked the house, but Mr. Jaggers did not seem to mind the gloom."

No, I suppose not, but it was so generous of him to leave it to us as you may recall my husband fussing about finding a home before Jaggers told him of the legacy. He was concerned as much about Pip's status succeeding him as he was about our married welfare."

"You know, of course," said Wemmick, "that the owner before Jaggers was a rich madman who took his wife out into Gerrard Street one morning, stripped her naked and threw her under a passing carriage."

"Why on earth did he do such a shocking thing?"

"He thought she was having an affair with his butler. She was a sprightly young thing, married him for his money without knowing he was crazy. In fact, the butler was a very old man, an elderly retainer of the family, so the accusation was sheer nonsense. But they sent the owner to Bedlam where he died shortly thereafter. The butler outlived him."

"And what of the wife?"

"Oh, she recovered, I was told, and of course became quite a rich woman. She moved away, to somewhere in the Lake District, Ullswater if I recall correctly. I don't know whether she married again. Mr. Jaggers got the story from the newspapers and thought the house might be less expensive because of the notoriety, and of course he was right. It was going for a song."

"Is it not amazing, John," said Estella, "that men think they can get away with murder?"

"Nothing is a surprise with regard to human behavior to me with my life in this business, but maybe these new fellas, psychologists I think they are called, can find out why."

Since their marriage, Pip and Susanna sought to become involved in politics. They had much admired their member of parliament, Mr. Mill, defeated three years earlier in an election though he had continued to give public speeches. They had put behind them their quarrels about sodomy as they agreed that there were far more important social matters to attend to, notably the education of the nation's children.

In 1869 Mr. Forster had shepherded a bill through Parliament providing elementary education for all. The topic was a continuing matter of serious contention, notably at a dinner party Susanna hosted where she invited Sir Charles Dilke, one of the Members of Parliament for Chelsea, and his wife, Lady Katherine Dilke.

Susanna's experience with Sir Charles had initially been unfortunate when he had made unwelcome advances to her at a reception, but she decided that she could put aside that indelicacy in favor of having a rising Liberal star in her home. He was a good eight to ten years older than she, but an impressive man, tall, bearded in the contemporary fashion and a striking presence at any dinner table. When the guests arrived, Lachlan and Malcolm were introduced before being whisked away by their nanny.

As the soup dishes were cleared away, Sir Charles asked:

"Susanna, how do you plan to educate your children? They are fine-looking young boys."

"Thank you," said Susanna. "Like all parents of our class I suppose we are torn between having them board at a school, which is the modern fashion or go to a school nearer home.

"Talking of education," said James Bollaerts, "I must say I am not a supporter of the Parliament's decision to get every child into a school. It is likely that children who learn to read and write will get ideas above their station and then become dissatisfied with their lot in life."

"That has certainly been a viewpoint expressed in both Houses," replied Sir Charles, "but as our industrial might increases we are going to need men and women in factories who can read instructions and operate machinery more complicated than a plough."

"Oh," said Sarah Bollaerts, "Sir Charles, would you not like children to learn something of the arts, even to learn to paint in these new schools, not just the 3Rs?"

"Not if they make the market too crowded and I cannot sell my paintings," crowed Bollaerts to the enjoyment of the party, enabling Sir Charles to avoid an answer.

"I suppose my objection," said Charles Meggison, "is that I don't think government should be involved in education. We could get what they plan to have in France where the minister will know what every French child is studying in every school in France when he looks at the clock on the wall. I foresee regimentation of learning."

"Correct me if I am wrong, Sir Charles," Pip volunteered, just managing to avoid seeming unctuous, "Forster intended that control be local with boards running schools funded by government, but not controlled by them. Is that not right?

"Indeed," said Sir Charles, "that is the intention."

"I hear that the government is not going to give free education to the people," grumbled Frederick. "I understood these boards will charges some fees."

"Pip and I," said Susanna, "have been most exercised over how this so-called Conscience Clause operates. Maybe there are problems about government being involved in education, but it is a far worse situation to have the established church dictating what should be done by way of religious instruction. If I am a Jew or a Catholic or even a Buddhist or a believer from Islam, I do not want my children taught some other religion, so it is right that parents can remove their children from religious instruction."

"And if they are atheists, I assume?" said Honora, now such a proud strong woman after her twins had come to join her. "My children have been brought up as non-conformists, and I am going to support them in that, though I want them to make up their own minds."

"We are not considering send our boys to a boarding school," said Frederick, smiling at Honora, "but I would prefer them to have a religion-based education, though I have heard good things about Quaker schools. I am never sure whether Quakerism is a religion or a cult."

Ignoring that remark, Charlotte said, "I wonder whether we should not prosecute public education much more purposefully. As a nation can we afford not to have all our children in school at least to the age of fourteen and perhaps further, following what I am told is the Prussian example?"

"I agree," said Estella. "I have listened to this conversation with great interest. The core difficulty I find in such discussions is that we tend to think in terms of our own interests or from the standpoint of our own political perspectives.

"I think it was Mr. Disraeli, in perhaps an unguarded moment, who said: 'What a parent wants for his children, a nation must want for all its children.'"

"Yes," said Sir Charles, looking carefully at this older but obviously highly intelligent woman, "Dizzy did say that."

"The implications become clear," said Estella. "If the churches want to educate their flock in their religious beliefs let them do it, but the nation must provide the best and the longest education for its children first. Churches can do what they want on Sundays or in times when schools are not working.

"Moreover, I see in my stepson just how painting is transforming his life. What the children learn must be the cumulative wisdom and experience of civilization, not some dreary set of mechanical tasks designed just to provide fodder for industry. I would go further and suggest they be encouraged to take part in political debate and activity."

"Good heavens," said Pip. "I always thought you were a bit of a radical."

"I take that as a compliment, Pip, but I have suffered in my own life from a lack of education and in my philanthropic work with prostitutes, I also see how education might have helped them build a better life for themselves."

"Prostitutes?" exclaimed Lady Dilke. "What on earth are you doing with fallen women?"

"Just when we thought that was Mr. Gladstone's area of expertise," said Dilke, at which there was prolonged laughter around the table."

"I will explain our philanthropic work later," said Estella to Lady Dilke.

"Returning to education in politics," said Honora, "I read a short pamphlet the other day called 'Mr. Mill's Ideas.' I was most struck by his idea that our politics should be governed by what will bring about the greatest happiness of the greatest number. That might be difficult to work out but the idea is sound, I think."

"Yes," said Bollaerts. "There are numerous fantastical ideas around these days, but the fact is that our political economy is governed by the marketplace, in which government has no right to tread, except in so far as it is a buyer or indeed a seller."

"I don't disagree," said Sir Charles, "but if that is the case, then the government should not support institutions that bring no visible wealth to the country. I know I am unpopular in having suggested we abolish the monarchy, but we rarely discuss it in terms of its market value.

"Rather, we allow monarchs to accumulate great wealth and the present queen seems to think she can retreat into her widow's weeds and limit her public responsibilities without a thought to that fact that she is a serious cost to the nation while still keeping that wealth to herself. As for the Prince of Wales..."

"On that remark," intervened Susanna as the hostess, "I think we ladies should retire and leave the men to contemplate the place of a very powerful woman in our nation."

After the board committed to buy Semper House, Estella wrote to Albert, now in Paris, saying that Charlotte had agreed to join her in a new property and if he wished to have a say in the selection, he should come home promptly, then see the move through and go back to France.

Albert had been back for a week and they had seen two houses neither of which commanded much interest. One morning the three of them, Charlotte, Albert and Estella, took the carriage down from Soho in the direction of Westminster to view a house Charlotte had heard about. The carriage went around Trafalgar Square so that they could view the four lions placed around Nelson's column, itself completed in 1844.

Whitehall was crowded with horses and carriages veering toward Westminster Abbey but the carriage avoided that and drove close to St. James Park where Charlotte had heard that a house in New Queen Street might suit them. The carriage rolled up to number 29, a fine, tall, classical building, decorated in the Georgian style with four stories and a basement for a kitchen and other services with its own entrance. A housekeeper let them in. The house was light and spacious, belying its narrow front as it stretched back to a charming private walled garden. It was substantially different from Semper House.

"How light this house is compared to our home in Soho," exclaimed Estella as they went into the main hall.

"What a splendid dwelling," said Albert. "We can have a floor each: the ground floor for our drawing room, dining room and library. Estella would be on the first floor, Charlotte on the second and me on the third, with accommodation for staff on the fourth. I love it, and it is in a such a wonderful position. A short walk to

St. James Park and accessible both to east and west of London and Westminster. What do you think?"

"It is quite charming," said Charlotte. "We need not look further, provided the financial arrangement will be satisfactory. It is available on a long-term lease. It is immensely fashionable, you know. London is growing so fast; have you seen the shops in Oxford Street these days? Quite extraordinary for what was once a road where ancient Britons tramped in search of wild animals."

"This is an excellent find," said Estella, "we could spend a very long time finding the best house we can, but we only need to find a house that suits us, and this is it. I don't know what the cost will be but that should not be a problem for both of us to share, Charlotte, as we do not have to lay out huge sums from our capital."

"It is certainly more convenient for me, and it is splendid for the kind of entertaining we will wish to do, including the garden."

"How about decoration and furnishing? Do we know the identity of the previous tenant?"

"The agent told me it was a diplomat and family who were posted to America," said Charlotte. "They did a good job of decoration, and they were only here eighteen months."

"What good fortune then. No need for the endless decoration process I suffered, as I now realize, at Semper House. Let us settle on this house as our home and move as soon as possible. Then the Trust will have to think about the rebuilding needed in Soho and we can contribute from the peace and quiet of this home."

"I love it," said Albert. "The thoroughfare is not widely used, and the house is tucked away from the hustle and bustle of the city, unlike Gerrard Street. No whores on the street either," he said, laughing.

"But I will be back from Paris after our furniture is moved. I will leave most of my possessions here as I will probably live in Klein's garret until unless Elizabeth and I come together."

At this both Elizabeth and Charlotte stayed silent, looking at each other searchingly, though Charlotte's eyebrows moved dramatically heavenward.

"That is settled, then. We shall soon be the occupants of 29 New Queen Street in the City of Westminster. Hamish will handle the details, I am sure."

In the landau on the return to Semper House, Estella said:

"What did you make of the remarks Sir Charles made about the monarchy? I was deeply shocked to have my loyalty trampled on like that."

"I uphold the conventional view that the queen is the historically fortified rock around which Britain is gathered, whatever her present distress. What might be the alternative?"

"There has to be someone as Head of State," said Albert, "and in America they have a president, which seems to suit them."

"I don't find that attractive even if it were Dilke," Charlotte said with a smile.

"I certainly hope our dear queen would not then be subject to Marie Antoinette's fate if the idea were to gain any credibility," and they all laughed.

"I came away from that dinner," said Estella, "with two impressions. First that Sir Charles' extraordinary suggestion makes one think. In my case, it makes one strengthen one's commitment to examine everything, to be sure that where there is doubt, there lies the need to examine."

"And the second impression?"

"That Lady Dilke said little of consequence at dinner, another example of a woman being unable escape her husband's shadow, losing her independence and her somewhat unworldly inquiry. I must say also that I didn't like the man."

With the purchase completed, Albert hurried back to Paris, knowing that his home and his possessions in England were safe and sound.

XX

It was a shock to the inhabitants of Cheyne Row to discover one Friday morning later that month that the body of their Italian tour guide, Rizzio Campanile, had been discovered in his bed. He had missed various teaching assignations over a few days and one of his pupils had suggested to the police that he might be ill. No foul play, said the police, and natural causes was the coroner's conclusion.

A carriage arrived at the Gargery house in Cheyne Row on Saturday morning, and Estella and Charlotte stepped out. Pip went to the door to greet them and they went into the drawing room.

"Have you heard the news?"

"What news?"

"Rizzio has been found dead in his bed. We are told that there is no reason to ascribe his death to anything other than natural causes."

"Oh, I am sorry," said Charlotte, clapping her hand to her mouth as was her mannerism, "He coped so well with Oliver's eccentricity, I thought."

"Yes, indeed he did," said Estella. "He confided in me in Italy that he had a terrible tragedy in his life several years before he came to London, but he did not want anyone to know, as he had at the time been so overwhelmed by sympathy in Italy.

"His family were all killed in a fire that ravaged the Tyrolean house where his grandparents had a farm: his wife and his two children, her parents, her newly married elder brother and his wife. A terrible story, and I could scarcely bear to listen to the account of his journey to bring back the remains of his family for burial."

"Where was he when this happened, then?" asked Susanna.

"At an audition for the La Scala orchestra in Milan."

"Oh dear, oh dear," said Susanna, starting to weep. "Those children! Just imagine, waking up in their beds to a fire raging through the house."

"And the adults," said Pip. "Imagine them trying to find and help the children. He was truly an excellent guide."

"Indeed, my dear, I don't think he was more than forty years old."

"Let us think about Rizzio, poor man," said Charlotte, "It must have been a very great effort for him to handle our trip. I suspect he could not bear to return to Italy without something to preoccupy him. At least he was able to tell Estella his story, but then she is an excellent confidante," she concluded with a slightly ingratiating smile.

"That is true, I suppose," murmured Estella.

"This sadness apart, to what do we owe the pleasure of your company?" asked Susanna.

"We came to speak with you, not with Pip."

"In that case," said Pip, "I will walk up the row and see if I can be of any help at Rizzio's," and he went eagerly into the hall to collect his hat, coat and stick, which he was no longer using at home.

"Susanna," said Estella, "Charlotte and I are thinking of starting what we are calling 'The League of Free Women.' To begin with we just want to meet together and include Honora, Mary Meggison and Mary Macdonald, even Sarah Bollaerts if they are each interested. We thought we might begin with a dinner at what will be our new home in New Queen Street."

"I'd be delighted, of course. I do find I very much need conversations with women as we have so much in common to think about these days. Bringing up two boys and a baby girl is a challenge in itself. I cannot imagine what it is like for Honora and the twins, but I see her from time to time and she is blissfully happy. I even suspect she is pregnant."

"What did you say? I thought he was almost like her guardian," said Charlotte. "On the other hand, of course, their marriage will have been completely renewed with the advent of the twins. Oh, I do hope so, and I hope she will declare herself to us shortly. How wonderful for her and for her twins if they have a baby to dote on."

"Indeed," said Estella abruptly, "that must be a delight, but now Charlotte and I must depart as we have a lunch appointment. We must discover the date of Rizzio's funeral, too.

The two women headed off to Kettners Restaurant where they were to meet Harriet. It was almost two years since the meeting in the Uffizi, but for one reason or another, the acquaintance had not developed. Now however, Harriet was there sitting in the small foyer, immaculately dressed, with splendid hat and clothes that looked as though they were made from an Italian fabric. She is really very beautiful, thought Estella, with just a slight twinge of envy. The restaurant had a very French feel in its décor and in the menu.

"Perhaps I should explain," Harriet began, "why I hurried away from you in the museum those years ago so quickly and broke off our conversation, and indeed did not come to your hotel. A man had just come into the room whom I did not wish to meet for a variety of reasons. I apologize but hope that we can now renew our conversation."

"Of course," said Estella, "we will be delighted, I am sure.

"However, we both know the gentleman in question very well as he was closely connected to my now deceased husband. He has told us of your relationship with him, and I am glad you concluded your relationship as I am very fond of his young wife Susanna, who is quite a brilliant star in the firmament of our friendships."

"That is such a relief," said Harriet totally without embarrassment, which surprised Charlotte. "Between ourselves, he has completely spoiled me for any other man. I have tried twice to find someone his equal, but they were both great disappointments. Italians, of course."

Charlotte blushed deep at this confession and frankness of talk, and she pretended she knew what Harriet was talking about, although the experience of ecstatic love was outside her ken.

"You see," Harriet continued. "I determined when I was quite young that I would never ever be attached to a particular man as I saw enough danger in the way my father behaved."

"Why was that?"

"I thought him the kindest of men until he looked at me when I was eighteen in that way men have. I told my mother and she sacrificed herself for my sake to his lust, I think. But I also read Mary Woolstencraft about that time, and I do now believe that free love will make more people happier if we all feel free to pursue it.

"I am financially independent, thank goodness. Pip did impress me with his concerns for the poor, but I have recently been even more egotistical in my recent pursuits.

"I suspect we all might like to pamper ourselves more than we do," said Charlotte with a very slight grimace.

"Well, tell me about yourselves."

Charlotte began by telling Harriet of her marriage to Oliver, especially on the Italy experience, and his recent demise. Estella went over her life in enough detail to take Harriet's breath away.

Estella concluded by saying:

"We are anxious to gather together a group of women, Harriet, young and old, all of whom have distinctive experiences which provide us all with support for each other, but also will enable us perhaps to advocate politically for good causes relevant to women. We will be a very diverse group, I think."

"Briefly, who are 'we'?"

"There's Mary Macdonald, married with understanding to a man who loves men and is a lawyer. There's Honora Brandram who had twins because of a rape by twin brothers when she was on a pilgrimage to Lourdes. They are now back with their mother. Mary

Meggison is married to a well-known artist, but we do not know her that well. There is Charlotte and I, and then there is Susanna Gargery, Pip's wife, and you would have to decide whether you wish to let her know of your identity," she concluded with a broad smile.

"That sounds very exciting. Missing from my life which I intend to remedy is discussion of poetry. People say we have had some very fine poets in this century, some of whom are still alive. It would be marvelous to discuss them and read poems to each other. I have been writing poetry for some time and more recently in Italy, inspired by Robert Browning, and I hope to publish.

"But that apart, I will have to consider carefully whether I will join if Pip's wife will be there. At this moment, I would simply wish you good fortune but must decline."

"I think I should ask Susanna for her attitude to your attendance at an appropriate moment," said Estella.

"That would bring it out into the open," said Charlotte. "I don't know what she would say, but we will see. I adore your idea for poetry discussion which you could lead. However, might the three of us meet together for lunch from time to time? Next week Albert, Estella and I are moving to a house near St. James Park.

"My husband's son Albert lives with me," said Estella. "He spent some time in the Paris Commune where a bullet grazed his eye, and he broke his leg which is now recovered, but the eye will take much longer."

"Ah, Paris. I was there early in 1870. I experienced one of those interesting coincidences. I met a woman by accident in a small cafe, Katherine Bradley, who has aspirations as a poetess. I knew her because her father manufactured tobacco in Birmingham where my father also had a factory, and we lived almost next door to each other in Edgbaston.

"Of course, when I lived there she was much younger, but when we met in Paris, the age difference seemed to matter little. Perhaps I should get in touch with her if this group wished to meet with her. I know she is caring for a little girl, her niece I think, whose mother is an invalid."

"She sounds most interesting. We will be in something of a turmoil starting tomorrow, but where are you living as I must have your address?"

"Here is a card, Estella. I have resumed living at my lodging in Long Acre."

After lunch, they shook hands and departed. Once again it was raining. Charlotte wanted to do some shopping, so Estella went on alone to Semper House. Turning the corner into Wardour Street she felt a sudden blow in her back that sent her sprawling in the street and though she was not hurt, she got up, helped by passers-by and dusted herself off.

However, she was deeply shocked, and a constable happened by as she was recovering and helped her back to Semper House. Her handbag had been stolen.

"I'm sorry about that, ma'am. I hope you have not lost anything of value."

"Only a few sovereigns. I use the bag more for keeping notes, gloves and things. But I am glad to be moving away from this district soon."

"Very wise, I am sure."

She mounted the steps to the house slightly dazed by her fall, threw off her wet coat and hat and went to rest in her bedroom, and promptly fell asleep. When she awoke, she realized her right hip and shoulder were bruised where she fell, but then she smiled to herself that the volumes of clothes and coats women wore those days, especially in winter, had saved her from serious bruising.

Moving to New Queen Street could not come soon enough and when that was over, she would retreat for a while to Numquam for Christmas. She held back her tears as she remembered when Fletch sang "Drink to me only," and Pip and she had sung the second verse together. What a treasure that Christmas celebration was! She hoped it could be repeated.

❀   ❀   ❀

Although Estella felt a little groggy from time to time after the attack, she endured the move to number 29 which, when all was said and done, went very smoothly. Both women supervised the placement of their furniture, though Charlotte had recovered little furniture from Norfolk, and Estella was able to provide some supplements. Albert was an excellent help, shifting furniture around as earlier decisions were revoked. Closing the door on Semper House brought a sense of relief, as it had become an encumbrance after Pip's death now almost three years ago.

They decided to broach the subject of Harriet with Susanna today, but Charlotte mentioned a letter from Elizabeth which had arrived that morning.

"She is obviously very worried about her father who has been taken ill several times. They are coming back to Norfolk for Christmas if her father is well enough to travel."

"I am sure we would love to have her, and I'd still like to meet your brother when he is here," said Estella. "And Albert's leg seems quite healed but his eye has continuing problems, he says. Apparently it looks alright as he sees it in the mirror, but he can't get much sight out of it."

"It will improve gradually, I am sure," said Charlotte.

"Today I really must go to see Susanna about the League and Harriet."

"Do be careful, my dear. She can be very prickly, you know."

"I will be the soul of tact and discretion," said Estella with a smile.

Two hours later, she was at Susanna's door in Cheyne Row.

"Susanna," she said, after the usual pleasantries, "Charlotte and I have been planning a big Christmas at Numquam, and we hope you and your family will come."

"I am sure we will as we have no other obligations, and Pip loves his native countryside."

"On another matter, and I hope I am not being indiscreet. I am sure Pip will have told you that he had a long affair with a woman called Harriet Middleham before he met you.

"Yes, indeed it was almost the first thing he told me when we started to walk out together. These were just his wild oats, however unusual for a preacher, but why do you ask?" she said, bristling slightly.

"Charlotte and I have made her acquaintance."

"Oh, really, and is she as pleasing as I assume Pip thought? And why should I care?" she said rather crossly.

This is not going to be easy, thought Estella.

"Yes indeed, why. Oddly we began talking to her in the Botticelli Room in Florence, and we have met since, but she scuttled away at that time when she saw you both enter the room."

"Oh," exclaimed Susanna, "I knew it, I knew it! That was why Pip behaved so strangely. I have had this occasion in my mind for almost two years. I remember we walked into that room in the gallery and suddenly he turned around as if he had seen a ghost and could not bear to look at it. The ghost must have been that woman."

"Presumably, but she seems a highly intelligent and interesting woman and she might prove an excellent member of our new group."

"I suppose you want to include her," said Susanna acidly.

"She is disinclined to join us unless you are aware that she is who she is, not just another woman in the group."

"I might have born that," said Susanna with steel in her voice, "just in terms of their friendship in Salford, but now I learn that she was the cause of Pip's odd behavior in the Uffizi even though it was some time ago, I would say no to her joining the group.

"Why did he not want to meet her once he saw her there. After all their relationship had ended long before he married me. He could easily have introduced me, given my knowledge of her.

"Now I am beginning to put together what is happening. Before we went to Italy, I had this vague sense that he was seeing or had seen another woman. There was something about his behavior that suggested he was concealing something, and the obvious matter to conceal would be a relationship he did not wish to share with me.

"He is not a regular philanderer, Estella, nor is he prone to other male vices. But this odd behavior in the gallery was quite different. Of course, for me those months have simmered quietly in the background of my mind and now you have provided a missing piece."

"I have not had this kind of experience so I am of little help, except," and here Estella hesitated, "but if it worries you, you should confront him even though it is some time ago. As secrets of this kind fester, they promote distrust. But let me be clear. Our priority does not lie with her. We will need you to say you would be comfortable with her."

"But how can I be?" said Susanna angrily. "Oh, how distressing. I will now always imagine her with my husband in the height of their passions. No, I cannot do it, even if their relationship was just long ago, because I am now seriously wondering whether it is also more recent.

"Oh dear, oh dear," she said, starting to weep, "now I understand too why he was so eager to go to Florence and avoid Rome."

"Do take care, Susanna. You seem to be jumping to conclusions about him and her. If you raise this matter with Pip, it might undermine your marriage. What would be gained by an inquiry?"

"I am astounded by what you say, Estella. As to jumping to conclusions, I had a strong intuition which you have all but confirmed, and do you think if it was a wife who had an affair, the husband would not demand to know everything, or that he would not say anything to avoid any indelicacy?

"Yes, that is true, male superiority. Talk about it and damn the consequences."

"I will indeed."

"Whatever happens, I do hope that you will all eventually come for Christmas."

"I am sure we will, though whether it will be enjoyable is another matter. The children will enjoy it, no doubt."

Toward the end of that July afternoon, Pip returned home from his new office. With the creation of the *Courtisone and Jaggers* practice, the Trust had now to be accommodated in Little Britain in an office where Pip could handle the Trust's business.

When he hurried up the steps and into his house, he was surprised to see Susanna standing in the hall as if waiting for him.

"Pip, I need to have a serious discussion with you. I have sent the children upstairs with their nanny, so we can be alone."

"Let me put my hat and coat away," he said. Leaving his hat, coat and stick in the hall, he followed her into their drawing room where they sat side by side on the settee.

"This is very difficult for me, Pip."

"Don't hesitate, my dear, say what you have to say," he said quietly, with that look of suppressed terror that appears on the face of someone who is about to be accused of a deed but cannot determine which is the deed in question.

"Alright, just one question.

"Have you been consorting with Harriet Middleham?

"What do you mean, dear? I told you before we married that I had had a long relationship with her," he said, the palms of his hands now beginning to sweat slightly.

"I know that, but I have the sense that was not the end of it and that you have been seeing her recently."

"But where does this so-called sense come from?" he said, adopting a more aggressive tone.

"Estella called this afternoon. As I told you the other day, she wants to form a group of women and she called today to ask if I would find it difficult to have Harriet in the group, given your earlier relationship."

"What did you say?"

"Initially I said I would find it difficult, but then I asked her how she knew Harriet and learned that they had first met in the Botticelli room when we were all there two years ago, but that Harriet ran away when you and I appeared. Then I remembered your strange behavior at that time. You must have seen her, didn't you?"

"Who? Harriet or Estella?"

"Don't prevaricate. You know perfectly well I mean Harriet."

"Yes, I only saw the back of a woman leaving and I wondered if it might have been her, so I was not certain."

"Rubbish, Pip. You are dissembling."

"No, my dear."

"Then explain to me why you behaved so oddly."

"I don't know."

"Alright, now we get to the nub of it. After you went to see Biddy, I had this strong sense that you had not only seen Biddy, but some other woman, though I don't know whether that was Harriet or not."

"Why would I do that?"

"I don't know, do I? Were you tiring of me, then and now? Because if you are, I am going to find a lover forthwith."

"Of course, I am not tiring of you, that is ridiculous.

"Except that you are now different when we are intimate. I clearly remember the night that change occurred."

"What do you mean?"

"When we are intimate, you always used to call me darling without fail, and I reveled in your talk. Then you suddenly stopped, and you have only resumed calling me that lately when we are intimate and, of course, with the baby, we have not been as close that way for some months."

"What on earth is the significance of that?"

"Oh, dear God, you really are just a man like any other! Don't you realize how these small things matter to a woman as they are constant reminders and clues. Like every other man you just treat making love as a release, nothing more."

"I resent that, my dear. You know our love-making has always been a great treasure for me."

"It is time we brought this to a close, so just one question and I expect an honest answer from you, my preacher. Since we married, have you ever been intimate with another woman?"

Pip was now very disturbed, his ankle beginning to hurt viciously as if it housed his conscience. He hesitated. He knew if he said no, at some point he would be discovered. Secrets like this just cannot be kept. Estella knew about Harriet, damn her eyes, so Charlotte probably knew too. His marriage was hanging in the balance, but he felt he had to be honest, come what may. He tried to look away first, but then turned to look her in the eye.

"Yes," he said quietly.

Susanna leapt up from her seat and instead of the assault he anticipated, she jumped on to his knee and kissed him.

"I hate you. I hate you," she cried, "I hate you, but I love you for being honest enough to tell me. Now we can simply move on, though I want you to promise me you will not involve yourself with Harriet anymore."

"I promise. I hope now you know it all, you will find it easier to meet with her."

"Why would I want to do that?"

"Because she is highly intelligent interesting woman and I think you would find her company desirable."

"Pip, oh Pip," she said half in anger, half in disappointment, "if I had had an adulterous affair with a man, even if it were in the past, and I told you that I would like you to meet him because he is a man of such intellect and charm, can you imagine yourself saying 'of course darling, anything you say darling, let us all have dinner together darling.'

"My hope is that you would go round to his house and punch him on the chin, and then the nose. If you wouldn't, then our marriage is definitely over and done with.

"Understand this Pip, that woman is my deadly enemy."

The boys came down for dinner. Pip and Susanna spent the evening reading and then went to bed with merely a little peck on the cheek. Susanna wondered whether anything had really been settled, whether her attitude to her husband was now changed for good. Pip lay awake too, thinking he must get back to regular attendance at chapel, to try to live his life religiously as images of Harriet's body and the sounds she made in ecstasy could not be erased from his mind.

It was Estella who had brought all this old business to a head. Confound the woman.

Estella and Charlotte were pleased to arrive at Numquam after Estella's hazardous conversation with Susanna. Nellie had received a message to say they were returning, so the house was spotless and the following day, she arrived in the Fletcher cart to greet them.

"Welcome home," she cried, as she walked through from the kitchen.

Estella got up from her chair, eyes gleaming, hugged Nellie tightly, and they kissed each other on the cheeks. Charlotte approached Nellie, and not to be outdone, hugged her without a kiss.

"Oh, you look so well, Nellie. Now, before we go any further, I want your family to all come here for our Christmas celebration and perhaps we can persuade your husband to sing again."

"Oh, I am sure we'd love that. And there will be a nice surprise for you, too!"

"Then I cannot possibly wait for Christmas to come."

XXI

Early in August in Little Britain Hamish received information that Masham was to be released the following week, so Clarence asked Estella to go with him to Wandsworth Prison to meet the young man, as she had previously indicated that she badly wanted to see inside this gaunt edifice. The warders at the entrance had to be convinced that a woman should be allowed in, but as Masham was a non-violent offender and due to be released shortly, they grudgingly allowed her in.

Masham looked more cheerful than he was on Smythe's previous visit.

"Wot d'you want now and who is this fine lady?"

"I am Mrs. Pirrip and I want to explain something to you and then ask you a few questions."

"Waddya gie me for it?"

"Would a half-sovereign do?"

"Let's see the color of your money, first," he said with a smirk, so Estella rustled in her new purse for a half-sovereign.

"We work on behalf of a Trust. Our major project has been on behalf of women prostitutes and we have bought a building in Clerkenwell for twenty-four women where we supply medical advice and help as well as accommodation. We want to do something similar for men, but would somewhere near Moorfields be sensible?"

"Oh, no, ma'am, that would be terrible. There's so many mollies in that area, they'd be breakin' in and causing trouble if they wasn't given a room. You need somewhere up west or south of the river."

"You see," said Clarence, "you have already been very helpful. How about Soho, would that do?"

"Anywhere a good way from Moorfields. Soho would do."

"Tell me," said Estella, "how did you get into this life?"

"Like I told Mr. Smythe here when we met last, I was used by other men, and then I didn't know what to do, 'cept what I was already doing."

"How about other men and boys you know?

"Cor, I don't know. I suppose I know three of 'em fairly well as we always got together up in Moorfields waiting for our turn. Sid, I know well, he's much older. He was a cabin boy on a ship going to India and he got done by men in the crew every day and sometimes more, captain, first mate and all. When he got back, he was so accustomed to it like me, he didn't know what else to do and it was easy money.

"Now, Joe's different. He's crazy, he is. He'd dress like a woman all the time if he could and he could get trade like that, but he is obsessed, I fink that's the word. He likes it as many times in the day as he can. He is just a gay, plain and simple."

"What's a gay?" asked Clarence.

"Oh, it's another name for a whore, man or woman."

"Really, I've never heard of it."

"Not likely you would, really. See, I don't see myself as a whore at all. I cannot find a job, except ones that are dangerous or pay so little money it's not worth the struggle."

"If the building we are thinking of could provide jobs, men might come?"

"Oh, yeah. But there's Ted. Now he is another nutcase. He's married with three kids and he comes for one turn each night and he always gets a good 'un."

"How do you mean, a good 'un."

"Oh, a man with money, like I thought that Twaddell man was."

"What's he got that is so appealing?" asked Estella. "Is he very good-looking?"

"Not really. It's difficult to say with a lady present."

"What about the men who use you?" asked Clarence.

"Most of 'em is just that way inclined, not interested in women for whatever reason. And there are all classes, you know, some real gents, and lots of them are married too."

"Alright," said Clarence. "Now if you were found a job and a room in your building, would you stay there?"

"Oh, I would love to save up some money, perhaps get a job in a shop somewhere, even think about getting married, and I think lots of us mollies would too. Just for what we'd hope would be peace and comfort and, of course, a free turn every night," and he laughed. "But you see I don't have a trade, do I? I'd love to lay bricks or be a joiner, but I never had the chance."

"All right," said Estella, "thank you for your time. Come and see us," she said, handing over her card, "at this address and we will give you enough money immediately, so you don't have to go back on the street. We won't be opening the building for a while yet, but we will ask you do things for us as we fix the house."

"I never heard, Mr. Smythe, wot happened to that man?"

"Two years in prison, so they probably sent him to Dartmoor.'

"Oh Christ, that's got a terrible reputation for rape, y'know. Not like here where most of us are short-term and there's lots who are in and out, on trial, on remand and so on. Poor bastard."

"So, you have not suffered here."

"No, even though, and you have to laugh sometimes, some of the lads get sent here for Her Majesty's Pleasure. Cor, imagine that!"

Estella rolled her eyes and got up to leave.

In the carriage back to the office, she sighed and said:

"I am not sure I can cope with such stories, Clarence. They are so disgusting, so very depraved. That some human beings are so degraded presents those of us who are civilized with a choice, you know. Do we treat them with compassion or censure?"

"Yes," Clarence replied, "I am afraid it is the case that many people would regard people like Masham as sub-human and would be glad to see them along with the undeserving poor consigned to outer darkness. The more I have learnt about the life of sodomites, I wonder how on earth these boys can get like that.

"If a man cannot get a job, he cannot get any self-respect. He is just the offal from the body politic. It really is a scourge, and the Trust must do its bit to help."

"I agree," said Estella.

"Clearly there are men across the social spectrum who just prefer men, either by nature or something in their upbringing.

"Ah, well," said Estella, "we must get on with Semper House. I am supposed to call on Frederick Brandram this afternoon before the league meets in our new home this evening."

"Do you like your new accommodation in New Queen Street?"

"Yes, I do, but my country house in Kent is really my home. You must come for a visit and bring your lady. How is that progressing, by the way?"

"Very well. Frankly, Mrs., P. I am totally besotted with her and she is returning my affection. Any advice on how I can get her to marry me?"

"Shower her with love, letters, flowers, surprises, that sort of thing, not material gifts so much. And of course, you know her father and her brothers. If you are past that stage, get yourself a ring, go down on your knees in some romantic spot and, here is an incorrect aphorism for the matter at hand, let the devil take the hindmost!"

Both Clarence and Estella collapsed with laughter in the carriage at that remark.

"It is such a pleasure to know you, Mrs. P. Thank you."

Late in the afternoon, Estella arrived alone at the Brandram's house in Cheyne Row. Honora opened the door and the voices of the boys singing came from the living room.

"How delightful it is to see you again, Estella. I have something to tell you before you meet Frederick, and I am starting to make it public with you because you were the inspiration of my rebirth. Frederick and I are going to have a baby."

"Oh, my dear girl," said Estella, giving Honora a hug, "how wonderful."

At that moment, Frederick appeared from his library, grinning like a Cheshire Cat, clasping his wife around the shoulders and saying: "Is this not the event of the year?"

"Absolutely," said Estella. "And I need not say 'look after yourself,' as I am sure you have three men here to wait upon your every whim."

"That is true. I am so blessed. But you came to see Frederick, I know."

"You are welcome to hear what I am asking."

"No, I want to hear more of the boys singing. They have joined the church choir and are loving it. The choirmaster even suggested that they might audition for Westminster Abbey choir, but we will see. Their voices will break quite soon, I am sure, but they might do it for another year."

Frederick led Estella into the library, leaving the door open so that she could hear the concert, and she sat down in a comfortable chair while he stood at his easel.

"It is quite simple, Frederick. You know we have a building in Clerkenwell where we house prostitutes. We plan to have a similar property for men, and we have been diligent in our enquiries about that activity in London, so we are getting to know what we are talking about."

"To get to the point: the Trust has agreed to buy Semper House from me. It is a large, rather ugly house actually, but capacious, but we wondered if you would take on the project, create it to our specifications, and oversee its transformation."

"It would give me great pleasure to do so. I am just finishing a major project for a new enclave of sixty houses west of here on Beaufort. I finish that this week and hand it over. So, I will be free and while I have been offered two other commissions, I will delay those until I have looked at Semper House. And, by the way, I will not charge a fee as it is a charitable assignment."

"Oh, Frederick, you are so kind. I thank you from the bottom of my heart. I am sure we can establish an excellent partnership. As time goes on, we may build a housing estate for the poor, so, if that happens, we will anticipate a fee. And now, I must be off to meet my friends at the League of Free Women. I hope Honora is coming to our get-together."

"Yes, she mentioned it earlier."

Honora appeared and they then rode in Estella's carriage to the first meeting of the League of Free Women, which comprised the stalwarts: Estella, Charlotte, Susanna, Honora, Mary and Sarah Bollaerts (a late invitation). Estella thought it would be a quite short meeting. Once everyone was gathered, she asked everyone what they thought the purpose of such a league might be.

Mary spoke first with her usual candor. "I want my sex to have the same privileges as men do in our society. I do not care how we get there, or when, but I want to vote. I want my own property completely. But most of all, I want women who are wives to have equal responsibility with their husbands for their families and equal rights over the distribution of resources, however they are acquired."

"I could not have expressed it better myself," said Susanna, "but I would add that we must put as priority the state of the poor women in our society, not become a group of rich women anxious just to further our own ends. We are all women of wealth and position, not duchesses or marchionesses of course, but we do not have to worry too much about our financial resources. I wonder, just wonder, whether we can find a way to have poor women in our league. At some point, I'd like to see whether we could attract poorer women into the group."

"Now that also means," interjected Sarah, "close attention to the education of women and to their health."

"But" said Honora, "while I am fully in support of all that has been said, we cannot do this without male support. For the danger is that we create a kind of war between men and women which we would not win, and we would have lost opportunities."

"Bravely spoken, all of you," said Charlotte. "It is fascinating that Honora, Mary and Susanna are younger women, if I may describe them as such while Mary Meggison, Sarah and I are in middle age, and I know Estella will not mind being put in a category of older woman."

Estella laughed gaily at this, which gave the others permission to laugh with her.

"My goodness, we have the makings here of a powerful group and we must expand it on Charlotte's age analysis by seeking to recruit women in each of these age bands. I will write a record of this discussion or, perhaps as some kind of manifesto.

Animated discussion of topics close to the social and politics interests of this diverse group of women continued for another two hours.

The gathering eventually drew to a close, goodbyes were said, but Susanna stood and asked if she could have a private word with Estella.

"Of course, my dear Susanna."

After this meeting Estella led Susanna into the small library which looked out over New Queen Street.

"I have thought about our last private talk and I am now thoroughly disappointed in you, Estella," she began.

"My dear, whatever is the matter?"

"I thought you were my friend, and you have betrayed me. My marriage is now a sham."

"I am not sure what you are talking about, my dear."

"Of course, you do! Harriet, or whatever her ghastly name is."

"What about her?"

"You have been meeting her, knowing she was Pip's whore before we married and worse still, they have been consorting again."

"How do you know?"

"He told me. I am so deeply angry at him. I am considering taking a lover. Two can play that game. He lies to me and spends time in bed with that woman. How can you be her friend? Just because you chose a wanton life with some young whore does not mean that marriage is not sacred, and you knew all about it, didn't you?"

Estella was deeply shocked by this onslaught and did not really know how to reply. Susanna's blood was up.

"Why did you not come to me earlier with this accusation, Susanna?"

"I managed just to control myself so far, though God knows it has been difficult."

"I cannot tell you how sorry I am that you felt that way, as for me it was such a joyous occasion."

"Joyous be damned. My husband, for all his preacher ways, is a cad and a scoundrel. If I could, I would leave him. Now I must put up with him moping around the house saying how sorry he is. Does he really think that his sorrow is enough to heal the chasm he has created in our marriage? How typical of a man! Let us kiss and all will be well. Well, it damn well won't."

"Oh, dear, I am sorry."

"Don't you start being sorry, too," she shouted, "How could you do this? How could you befriend that woman?"

"They did realize their mistake, you know."

"Wait. You have had intimate discussions with this woman about her relationship with my husband, and you did not tell me? Shame on you, Estella! Shame on you! I will take no further part in your League of Free Women, and presumably Charlotte knows this, too."

"I fear she does."

"Then maybe the whole world will know of his treachery before long," and she howled in dismay, such that Charlotte came hurriedly into the room, for Estella to indicate her presence was not required.

"Let me say this, Susanna. Charlotte and I thought about whether we should meet Harriet, but we felt that we should not be constrained from getting to know her because of your marriage situation."

"Ever heard of loyalty, Estella? I gave you my word, madam, that I would not tell anyone about your young whore. Well, my commitment be blowed!"

"You cannot threaten me with disclosing that, my dear. To begin with it is over and I am proud of it and I don't really care if the world knows it."

"That is no defense, Estella. You have wronged me cruelly."

"No, my dear, it is at Pip to whom you must direct your wrath, not me."

"I know, I know," she said, downcast. "But here I am, with two young boys, a new daughter and a man I used to love to the depths of my being, and he has cast it to the four winds. Now, I must go, and it may be for a long while before I come to terms with this betrayal."

Immediately she left, Charlotte came into the room.

"What on earth was that about?"

"Susanna regards it as disloyal for me, and you by implication, to be friendly with Harriet as Pip's relationship with her had undermined their marriage. She's withdrawn from our group."

The next morning early, there was a hammering at the door. Estella had just come down for breakfast, and an irate Pip was shown into the room.

"Do sit down, Pip, and have something to eat."

"Thank you, no. What have you been telling Susanna? She questioned me the other day and said you had met Harriet and somehow she got to know I had recently been with Harriet again. Why did you tell my wife my secrets? What right did you have to do this?

"We had a long conversation and she dragged out of me my recent liaison with Harriet. She came home last night in a furious temper and would not talk to me at all. I have been banished to the guest room, too."

"Calm down, Pip. I saw Susanna to ask her whether she would tolerate us having Harriet in the group, and she asked me how I knew her. I told her about the Uffizi, and she connected that to your behavior at noticing Harriet there, so that presumably led to her confronting you."

"But how could you risk such a thing? How could you ask a woman if she minded if her husband's present or former lover came to join a group you were forming? This was an intolerable intrusion into our marriage and an extremely unfriendly act on your part and one that I regard with great dismay. As a result, I am not sure that my marriage can ever recover. Divorce is totally out of the question of course, though she has the wherewithal to pay for one."

"Oh, dear me, I have obviously done you both a terrible wrong without having the foresight to envisage the consequences of what you rightly call my intrusion. I can only apologize."

"Don't say you're sorry, Estella. It is too late for apologies, as I am finding with Susanna."

"Yes, she told me as much last night."

"What?" His anger rising again, "so it was you she saw her last night?"

"She came to our meeting and then attacked me afterwards in much the same way as you have done. I think you are both attacking me as some kind of scapegoat for what at the end of the day is your affair with Harriet, Pip.

"I am partly blameworthy but my unwise participation was the symptom, not the cause. Don't scrape around for someone to blame other than yourself."

"I see that, Estella. Quite where that will leave us, not just in terms of our former friendship but also in terms of the Trust, I do not yet know. I will bid you good day."

Once she heard the door close, Charlotte, who had been listening from upstairs, came down, smiling:

"All you need now is for Lachlan to come round to tell you what a naughty lady you are!" at which Estella smiled, though she was very upset, not being used to such virulent criticism.

"I can see why they are both irate, Charlotte, but you know there is a much more profound problem in that marriage. Susanna is much more, intelligent is not the right word, but you know what I mean, and I think Pip dallied with Harriet again as a protest at his inferiority."

"I would not be surprised if Susanna did not take a lover out of revenge, spirited young woman that she is."

"She said as much, too. Pip will certainly blame me for that!"

Two weeks later, Susanna came out of her house without the children to talk a walk by the river to continue the process of calming herself. On a bench along the river side sat James Bollaerts, one of the neighbors who had been with his wife Sarah on the Italian trip, but they had merely exchanged only pleasantries then.

"Ah, Mrs. Gargery, taking the lovely spring air like me. Come, sit awhile."

"Mr. Bollaerts, how nice to meet you. Do you often walk along the river?"

"Not often, I prefer the London parks for inspiration, but I was considering asking if I could paint your portrait. I have a studio in my house, and forgive me, but you are a beautiful woman who deserves to be captured on canvas."

"I am delighted by your offer and your chivalrous remarks and I will sit for you provided that you will also make portraits of my children."

"Not your husband?"

"No, he would not be able to sit still for long enough," she snapped.

"That is a rather tart observation. Is all well in the Gargery household?"

At this, Susanna suddenly felt the need to unburden herself, albeit with a relative stranger, but a man who seemed kind, gentle and of an understanding nature.

"In confidence, my marriage is in somewhat of a crisis. My husband had a long affair with a woman before we met, and recently he took up with her again for a brief time and I am devasted and angry."

"Oh, dear me, I am sorry. Be patient, confide in me if you wish and I will try to help. I think we know each other well enough for you to call me James, too."

"Of course, James, thank you, and I would be pleased for you to call me Susanna. Please let me know when you are ready to start the portrait."

"Ah well, let us see, I usually do portraits of two kinds, one a full-length and the other head and shoulders of the model. I'd start with head and shoulders to give me a sense of how the full-length drawing would work out. I would imagine three sittings would be enough. Come on Wednesday afternoon. Sarah usually goes shopping then so we will not be disturbed."

"I'd be delighted."

She continued her walk along the river, waving him goodbye.

James lit a cigar and continued to sit for a while, smiling to himself and stroking his beard. *Talk about a gift horse, Marriage on the rocks, eh? What an opportunity! Every woman I have bedded, married and unmarried, has found me not merely irresistible but addictive, so skilled am I at the arts of satisfying women, especially those in distress.*

Susanna smiled with pleasure at the thought of a portrait as she walked home. *James is a pleasant enough man, older, and quite handsome. If all goes well in the sittings, I will certainly consider him as a lover. What a sweet revenge. I won't tell Pip about the portrait but if he behaves himself, I might give it to him as a present, but only if James has been my lover.*

Estella told of her love—why should not I? Indeed, if Estella can do as she pleases with her body, married or not, why should I assume my dalliance would be somehow wrong? I had thought of her as this great shining light of a woman, devoted to good works and then that thunderbolt of her telling of her sapphic love with that Nellie woman.

By comparison, what I am considering is not unnatural like her relationship, it is just, well—what is it? I am punishing Pip and showing my independence in these awful times when women are so put down. I think if James asks me, I will and what's more it will be exciting and stimulating that this very attractive world-weary man of considerable talent should want me in his bed. I see myself seducing him but I will let him think he is seducing me.

Those who knew her would have been astonished by these thoughts running through the mind of this rich, beautiful and upright Presbyterian lady. How dare she, some would say, grasp at her independence in such a tawdry and deceitful way?

And yet: Others having an ear to the way she was thinking would be put in mind of Mr. Congreve's couplet:

'Heav'n hath no rage like love to hatred turn'd,
Nor Hell a fury, like a woman scorn'd.'

XXII

Frederick Brandram came to Little Britain where the Trust had its small office to discuss Semper House. Pip got up to welcome him and Brandram suggested they go there first.

"You seem out of sorts this morning, Pip. Anything wrong?" Brandram asked as they got into a cab.

"No. Well, yes actually. Susanna and I are hardly on speaking terms. Indeed, we have had a thundering great row sparked by Estella's intrusion into our marriage."

"Really, I am sorry. Especially when my expectations of marriage have become transformed in the past months."

"Yes, I congratulate you on the recovery of your twins. It is quite remarkable."

"Indeed, it is and it has made our relationship quite different. But I can't believe that Estella would do something to harm you intentionally. It must have been accidental."

"From one point of view, she is just an interfering busybody with no concern for others. From another, she is trying to do her best to make everyone happy. This time, it is a deadly serious mistake."

"But what is the reason for this animosity?"

Pip then told Brandram of all the circumstances, ending by saying:

"Somehow Susanna worked out that I have seen Harriet again and all hell has broken loose."

"Surely, that Susanna worked out that you had an adulterous relationship is nothing to do with Estella. She was doing her best to make sure everyone was happy. The fact is, Pip, that you have made the mistake that has caused this conflagration in your marriage; do not heap blame on Estella. However, here we are, let me look at this house. I am going to need a precise list of your specifications."

"Of course."

They dismounted. Brandram went to the other side of Gerrard Street to take a good look at the house. It was indeed very large, neo-Georgian but with only a couple of windows on each side of the door. It was tall, four stories with dormer windows behind, where generations of maids will have slept, but the houses on the other side of the street made it feel dark, almost as if the street was a tunnel.

They went inside and Brandram admired the Morris decorations, exclaiming that they must have been very expensive. The white paint on doors and wainscotting offset any gloom, but it was not what might be called airy or spacious. The hall was long with three rooms on each side and the walled garden was not very long, but the tall houses behind it made it very dark. Brandram wondered when sunlight penetrated the house; probably only in summer, true of many a London street.

They went inside. The ground floor rooms he saw needed no attention, but Pip was keen to establish the need for as many small rooms as could be created on each floor.

"Each room must have a window, of course," said Brandram.

As they went from floor to floor, he could see the possibility of creating six rooms out of three on each, making possible eighteen in all.

"With so many persons in a house like this, it is essential to have fire protection.

"I have been much exercised with the problem of escaping from a house fire, and I am using a variant of the design by Abraham Wivell. Each window must have a chute, big enough to hold a man and long enough to reach the ground. It will be attached to the window in such a way that, if there is a fire, a person opens the window, pushes the chute through the window which then unravels so the person can climb into it and slide down to the ground inside it, using the sides with his feet as a brake to control the fall."

"How ingenious and how simple. I must have them installed in my home. At least that would be a way to escape from a different sort of blaze," grumbled Pip.

"You would need to train the men how to use it, but thank you, Pip. I can see how to create the rooms. Manifestly you will have your own plans for the kitchen and rooms on the ground floor and the basement and I can help with any structural needs there."

They walked out into Gerrard Street.

"Let me give you some advice, Pip. Repair this breach with your wife. The sooner the better or the wounds will fester."

"I wish I knew how."

"There I cannot help you," he said climbing into a cab to go home to Cheyne Row, leaving a disconsolate Pip who decided to walk back to Little Britain. The thought occurred to him that if his wife would not talk to him, Harriet might, and with rising enthusiasm he walked to Long Acre.

Elizabeth was in Athens where her father was now head of the legation, and Albert was in Paris. Their original plan was that he would join her for the summer, but everything depended on Henry's health, which was now approaching a critical stage. Albert meanwhile had willingly accepted the use of a room from 'Steep' Klein and they went out to dinner at the *Maginot Bistro* nearby.

"And how is England?" asked Klein.

"Excellent. Estella has taken a house in a street near St. James Park and her friend Charlotte lives there too. You met Hamish, of course. He is married to Mary—you knew that, I think, and they have a baby boy."

"That astounds me, as I thought he was a lover of men."

"It surprised everyone, but they have an understanding, and he seems very happy with his son, and with his wife. She has a withered left arm you know, so he has much to do with a small baby, notwithstanding the nursemaid. Estella tells me there is some turbulence in Pip and Susanna's marriage, but I think they will weather the storm."

"Why the turbulence?"

"Pip has had an affair with a woman he also knew long before he married."

"Oh, you English! Of course, a man should have a mistress if he wishes, and women should be free to be someone else's mistress. We French have no problems about love!"

"Yes, I know, but we British think it is somewhat uncivilized, a belief honored more in the breach than the observance."

"Shakespeare, I assume. All right, what are your plans, Albert?

"I am going to seek out certain painters and will try once again to find the elusive Gustave Caillebotte whom I got to know slightly during the siege of Paris two years ago or so. Estella has promised to come to Paris too, and I want to introduce her to some of the painters, but I first need to get to know them."

"We will find out this afternoon where the studios of these painters are."

"I have Gustave's address. It is *77 Rue de Misromesnil* in the 8th arrondissement. He may not live there anymore as he has qualified as a lawyer. He is four years older than me, but we were quite friendly for a hectic three weeks and he took me to one or two cafes where painters congregated. Let us start there."

With regret, it had become clear to both Pip and Susanna that they needed to keep out of each other's way. Pip became more conscientious than usual about going to work in the Trust's office, overseeing the building and starting discussions with Estella following Frederick Brandram's visit to Semper House, as indeed a good manager should.

Susanna was glad of his absence, and today was her third visit in September to the Bollaerts house along the row for James to continue the drawings for her portrait. As usual, she explained to the nanny that she would be out visiting, an opportunity only available because the three children were clearly very well served by this new young woman.

She was slightly nervous, but the first and second meetings had gone well with no indication on his side that he would welcome her as a lover, though she was ready if he was. She suspected that he was an accomplished seducer of woman and that his stealth so far was just a tactic. Occasionally he had asked her to move her head and then, when she did not get it right, he touched her face with his right hand to move it with a gentleness that made her shiver. The second session was much the same.

That Wednesday morning, however, was quite different. First, when she arrived, he took off her hat and coat, remarking how lovely she looked and what a fine portrait it would be, though he would not allow her to see it. He laughed heartily, took her by the waist and turned her around, praising her figure and her beauty again. He then had her facing him, his hands now on her shoulders.

She had wondered how exactly how he would handle her seduction, for that she now knew was exactly what she wanted, so she looked at him enticingly. Moving his hands to her cheeks, he drew closer and whispered:

"I think you are beginning to feel that you would not be averse to my making love to you. Am I right?"

Putting all her Presbyterian sentiments to one side, she turned up her face to him and he kissed her, gently at first, but then with an abandon which surprised her.

So that was how it was done. He picked her up and walked to a curtain at the far end of the studio and, pulling it back with his left hand, she saw it contained simply a large low bed. He put her down on it, fondling her body, gradually removing those clothes that hindered intimacy. At first, it was as if she was in two places at once, one as the observer, the other as the participant. Then she engaged with him, knowing that she wanted the man urgently, not because it was *this* man but because her thirst for revenge had now been displaced in favor of an assertion of her independence as a woman.

Sated, she lay in his arms. He did not speak. So, without having to converse, her thoughts were again focused on Estella's independence. *If that woman could be so wanton, so free with her body, why should she not be? If a man could seduce a woman as easily as this, she could seduce a man. In her mind she had now become the seducer, not the seduced and she did not exclude other prey. No guilt, no remorse, just silent pleasure at being handled so expertly, and repaying his sensual energy in kind. This was what it was like to be a mistress, not a wife.*

For him, she was a real treasure, a catch if you like, and he would not have cared about any argument as to who was doing the seducing. He smiled to himself, congratulating himself that he had been sure earlier that immediately she agreed to a portrait, she was looking for much more. He did not expect to tire of this one easily.

"I think I would like to paint you naked as your body is so beautiful."

"Perhaps."

Later, it was time to adjust her clothes. Her whole body tingled with pleasure as she walked back to her house down the row. She passed Sarah Bollaerts on her way back from shopping.

"How is the painting coming along?"

"Very well, I think, but he won't let me see anything till it is finished. I expect he does the same with all his subjects."

"Oh, yes, he is a very severe man in that respect."

She got home, smiling again, without a care in the world. Did Sarah know of his affairs? And, if she did, did she care? Probably not, but I will ask him. Pip was in the living room playing with the boys. He did not ask and she did not say where she had been.

She picked up a message from the table in the hallway. It was Estella, pleading with her to rejoin the group. Of course she would, now she had something to tell! Maybe, if the group was to be a gaggle of wanton women like Estella and herself, Harriet should be invited to make three of them. Who knows what might follow?

But that afternoon sparked in her a thought she had somehow never had before.

Could I have just been a substitute for Harriet?

Surely not, Pip, please not.

That damn woman! Curse her to hell.

Pip had finally screwed up his courage to visit Harriet, who was completely oblivious to the diverse ructions that had dominated recent relationships between Estella, Charlotte, Pip and Susanna, severally and plurally. She opened the door of her lodging at his knock and stood looking at him.

Dear God, he thought, *she looks even more beautiful.*

Oh goodness, she thought, *what now?*

"Come in, Pip. I was sure that we had decided on not seeing each other, but I suppose a short chat will not count as a breach of that agreement."

"Oh, Harriet, it is terrible. Susanna has found out about us and she still banishes me to the guest room, and we are hardly talking to each other. I am staying out most of the day, and I have no idea what she is doing."

"Oh, my dear, I am so sorry. Am I to blame for her finding out?"

"No, as I understand it, Estella went to Susanna to ask her permission to invite you to a group she is forming, and it emerged that I had seen you in the Uffizi and Susanna put two and two together and has been incandescent with rage since."

"You must save your marriage somehow, Pip. I can offer no advice but that. How you achieve it is up to you. As I told you before, I know you well enough to know that you would be so unhappy if it broke down, even with me."

"Right now, I doubt that. I am inclined to suggest we live together."

"Do not be so stupid, Pip," she replied in an exasperated tone.

"Susanna is a very strong woman and you married her for that. She is reacting as any woman scorned so she is furious. I am now going to ask you to take your leave, both because you must, but also because I have a friend, Katherine Bradley, coming to lunch. This must be the end. We are breaking up for my good name as well as yours. I do not want to be regarded as just your mistress."

She got up and showed him to the door.

He was tempted to throw his arms around her, but he didn't. Rather he slunk away from her lodging, his limp exaggerated as he walked along the street. He felt very sorry for himself. If both Brandram and Harriet were right, he had to find a way out of the cauldron of his marriage. Perhaps Wemmick would have some sage advice. Yes, he would try Wemmick.

But when he got to Little Britain, everyone had gone over to the old Courtisone office to discuss allocation of briefs, which were coming in faster following the merger, so the clerk told him. Perhaps Mary Macdonald would help? No, she would be involved with her children. He must work it out for himself.

He would have to talk with Estella. She was not to blame as she had pointed out, and she was a woman of wisdom, presumably in matters of the heart as well, or so he hoped.

Charlotte and Estella puzzled over the events of the last few weeks. Both thought that Pip and Susanna were blaming Estella as a way of not facing up to Pip's adultery. They were concerned by Susanna's wrath, which Estella thought might turn out to be self-destructive. As usual, it was at breakfast time that their lives and those of others were discussed.

That April morning both were reading their newspapers quietly. As it was now into spring, Estella had mooted a return to Numquam for two weeks to see spring arriving, but no decision had been made. Charlotte suddenly exclaimed through tears:

"Henry, my brother Henry, is dead!"

"Henry? Henry Fitzroy? Elizabeth's father? Let me see."

Estella read the news item. Charlotte broke down and moved to an armchair to weep.

"Why have we not heard it from Elizabeth?" Charlotte asked.

"I expect she is in great distress and I am sure the embassy will be overseeing arrangements," sniffed Charlotte. "I doubt whether he can be brought home. I will send her a wire directly expressing our sorrow."

"I must also get a message to Albert," said Estella, "as he will want to know about Elizabeth."

Such thoughts about what must be done tumbled through Estella's efficient mind. What influence would this have on the young people's relationship? Perhaps now, his death would enable them to marry.

Estella decided she would like to take the opportunity shortly to see Albert in Paris, especially as Elizabeth would now come back to be with him.

"Let us go to Numquam now and enjoy a week or two out of London, and then let us both go to Paris, as I am sure Elizabeth will go there from Athens."

"An excellent idea," said Charlotte. "It will be such a comfort to see Elizabeth."

Nellie came to the house shortly after their arrival later in the day. Estella regaled her with the difficulties for Susanna and Pip. Her response was crude, candid and to the point:

"Silly buggers. They don't know what they're missing. Tell that Mr. Pip to get his arse back to his wife."

At this, Charlotte could not stop laughing.

"What's so funny?" asked Nellie aggressively.

"Oh, it's nothing Nellie, but your advice is so frank and so clear, whereas we meander around the problem. Please don't be offended. I love it!"

"Well," said Nellie, "it's true, ain't it. A lot of poncing around.

"They should be so lucky with their money and background. They should compare themselves to some of the folks I've seen with bad marriages. Blimey, they're bleeding idiots. All right, he had a little 'how's your father' with that other woman, but so what? Makes me angry, it does."

"Oh, my dear, don't you be angry too," said Estella, laughing too. "We have had enough anger with Susanna."

"Wot I can't work out with you rich people is this," said Nellie, shaking her index finger at both of them. "You treat a bit of sex as if it were strange. It's just sex, not murder, it's what people do, thank God."

"Now, I do know why I love you," said Estella, "if I didn't know before. You are so straightforward, so unique. You're wonderful. You have said exactly what my mother Molly would have said and in the same tone."

"No, I'm not that good, Estella, I just call a spade a spade, as they say."

"When I see Pip, I will tell him what you said."

"Good, now that's settled and I've spoken my mind, what you'se up to?

"Elizabeth's father has died," said Estella, "so we are going to meet her in Paris and see Albert there. We will probably be there a month or so."

"My brother was to be buried in Athens where he was working, but I am hoping they will bring his body home for internment in the family grave in Wymondham," said Charlotte, holding back tears.

"Oh, Charlotte, I'se so sorry. I'd forgotten he was your brother. Forgive me. Give her my love, she's such a pretty girl and so friendly. Cor, you ain't half lucky going to all these fancy places."

"You'll go one day, I'm sure."

Nellie gave Estella another hug and then went to the dining room to polish the candelabra.

Several delightful sunny days were spent in curative walks enabling Charlotte to talk about her grief.

Then one lunchtime Pip appeared as they began getting clothes together for Paris.

"Oh goodness me," cried Charlotte as she saw the trap arriving. "I will leave you to Pip," and hurried away to her room.

Estella went to the door and had him come in as the maid took his hat and coat.

"How is Susanna, Pip? Is she recovered?'

"Recovered? I have no idea. We do not speak. I spend all day at the Trust office and goodness knows what she does. I saw Harriet and she sent me away. I must talk to someone or I will go mad. I just got on the train at Charing Cross hoping we could talk."

"What do you think Susanna is doing all day?"

"I have no idea."

"She is hardly the woman to sit at home sewing, is she? I would say that you must stop this separate existence, or you will never recover your marriage. Who knows, maybe she has taken a lover."

"Come now," said Pip, shocked at Estella's candor, "that really is highly unlikely. She is a Presbyterian Scot."

"That's a maybe. But a woman scorned?"

"I didn't scorn her, for God's sake. I make a mistake. That's all."

"But that's not how she sees your infidelity."

"But it was hardly anything. Harriet and I were just ending our relationship."

"You sound like the maid who has got herself pregnant and when the child was born her father got very angry with her, and she said: 'But it's only a little one.'"

"Let me tell you what Nellie said about you both, sounding exactly like my mother. 'Silly buggers,' she said, 'They don't know what they're missing.' And then she went on to wonder why rich people get so upset. 'It's only sex, not murder.'"

"That's all very well for her, she grew up differently from us."

"Look, you did not marry Susanna because she would be good in bed, did you? Maybe you did? What Nellie means is you are lucky to have such compatibility in your marriage, and I agree. I would bang your heads together if I could.

"Just start talking to her, beg her forgiveness and so on, and see where that leads. Ask her if she really wants to end your marriage, even if you continue to live under the same roof."

"You're right. Thank you. I was going to ask to stay the night, but I will head back to the station and go back to London to talk with her."

"We will be out of touch. We go to France shortly. By the time I get back, I expect you to be settled back with Susanna. You must do whatever it takes, my dear. You know what your dear father Joe would advise, don't you?"

The next afternoon, Estella and Charlotte were on the boat to Dover, and both were pleasantly surprised that the crossing was smooth. They sat on deck discussing the question of their wills. Charlotte was still unclear how much Oliver had left her, and Estella was anxious to leave money to Nellie and her family, but she was aware that money had spoiled her husband's life, so she was confused on what to do.

"Goodness me," said Estella later as the train rumbled towards Paris. "Look at the destroyed homes, farms and spoilt fields."

"That's what war will do, I suppose," said Charlotte.

The train duly arrived at the *Gare du Nord* and Albert met them.

"Good Lord, no station either," said Estella as they dismounted, amid the clamor of re-building.

"At least the rail tracks and the platforms seem capable of hosting a locomotive and its carriages," Charlotte replied.

"Wonderful, there's Albert."

Albert's leg was healed, but he still had a patch over his eye which made him look piratical. He was now tall and obviously a young gentleman with his fashionable hat and the fine cut of his coat. They all got into a barouche and Albert chatted on:

"I have found a lodging for you both which I think you will like. I have taken it for a month, but you can extend the lease if you wish to stay longer. As it happens, it is in the *Rue du Vezelay,* close to the street where my friend Gustave lives. He is older than me by five years or so and I met him first in Paris just before the end of the war. But you will meet him.

"He is going to take me to some studios. He is already a lawyer, but he is going to become a student at the *École des Beaux-Arts,* which is like the institute I went to in Kensington but much more rigorous, requiring an entrance examination, if you please. It shows how seriously the French treat painting and the fine arts."

"Would you be able to attend?"

"Oh, I doubt whether I could pass the examination as my spoken French is by no means perfect and my writing worse still. The *École* is quite close to the Notre Dame Cathedral, which you must visit.

"It is such a tragedy that so many of the fine buildings of Paris were destroyed by the commune: The Tuileries, the Hotel de Ville and you saw the ruins at the *Gare du Nord, la semaine sanglante.* Terrible. But let us get you both settled. Madame Esterlay, the concierge, is a good woman, not corruptible I hope."

"That will be wonderful, and we will see how long we stay. Interesting, is it not? This barouche is very comfortable compared to some of the London carriages."

"Yes, Paris is gradually recovering from the commune in every way, and a major effort is being made by the government to restore every building."

"But where are you living?"

"I have a room over Nimrod Klein's shop, which he lets me use without payment, I think, because he is desperately lonely. I am to meet Elizabeth the day after tomorrow. She has travelled by steamer to Marseilles and will come on to Paris by train."

"You must be very excited."

"I am, and the embassy has offered her a room for as long as she wants."

"I too am longing to see how my niece is faring after her father's death. Was there any news of her mother?"

"I don't know."

After organizing themselves in the lodging and asking Madame Esterlay to find them a maid as soon as possible, Estella and Charlotte took a *fiacre* to the Café des Anglais where Albert promised to meet them. He appeared again immaculately dressed and very excited.

"Gustave is going to take me to Leon Bonnat's studio next week and he asked me to come to the *École* to meet some of the painters there. My ambition is to watch technique, learn from the perceptions of painters in this new development."

"What is the development, dear?" asked Estella.

"It does not have a name, really, though some are calling it *Impressionisme*, though I am uncertain why. From what I have seen, I love the colors they use and the objects, not the historical or classical topics like Samson and Delilah, but farmhouses, fields, buildings, people doing ordinary things."

"It sounds fascinating. Perhaps we may be able to visit some studios and to buy one or two paintings if we like them. We need some bright colors in New Queen Street, though I am still anticipating the portrait of your father."

"I know, but I cannot get it right."

"We will not see you for a few days as you will want to be with Elizabeth. But send us a message when you would like to have lunch."

When they returned to their lodging that evening, Charlotte said:

"I can see how much Albert is devoted to you, Estella. He is a fortunate young man, financially in good shape from his father's legacy, enjoying his painting adventure, in love with a beautiful young woman, which is rather different from his father at that age."

"Indeed, his great expectations are not at all clear," Estella replied. "I hope he does not turn out to be a wastrel. In my heart, I do not think much of his painting, but I don't have the courage to tell him what I think."

"Why?"

"I don't know. I suppose I am fearful of putting a distance between us, probably because he reminds me so often of his father."

XXIII

Life was changing in Cheyne Row, at any rate in the homes of the Gargerys and the Bollaerts. On her way to the final portrait sitting, Susanna met Sarah Bollaerts walking on her regular outing to the shops.

"Good afternoon, my dear," said Sarah. "I do not want you to feel discomforted on my account by your relationship with my husband. If you are not already lovers I assume you will be soon. He has not yet told me though he usually does and with you I am sure there would be some good stories to tell.

"You see, I have never been interested in the physical side of marriage at all whereas James is precisely the opposite. We tried a few times, but I was so bored. All I ask is that it does not engender any scandal. Just as my husband and I have an understanding, your relationship should be agreeable to your husband."

Susanna did not physically reel back in shock to match the shock she felt inside.

"Thank you, Sarah, I will think carefully about your advice."

"Well, you don't want yourself talked about as a common wench, do you?"

"Of course not."

"One thing you should know about my husband, which you will eventually discover. He can quite suddenly tire of a relationship. He always does, so be warned."

She continued up the row to James' studio for a final session in a state of profound disbelief.

He will finish with me suddenly, will he? Not if I have any say in the matter. How dare he? My reputation would be in tatters? In my anger I had not thought of that possibility properly. How can he and his wife have reached such an understanding? Could Pip and I have that?

All this was tumbling through her mind as she was admitted to the home.

They greeted each very affectionately, his hands straying over her body.

"How long will this take? When will you finish it?'

"I will be honest with you, my dear. I have the sketches of you when you have rested here after we are done. I have completed the portrait and I have been pretending I have been working on it as I want you to keep coming for our mutual enjoyment."

"Wait, do you think it is just the portrait that makes me come here? Not at all, I come to satisfy my lust, to expend my innermost desires on you. I give not a fig for the portrait. I will have it, of course, and give it to my husband. But tell me, does Sarah know about us?"

"Of course not," he replied, surprised at her tone, "she would be mortified, which is why we are together when she is not here."

"Really?"

"And the other women?"

"Of course not."

"Do your affairs distract you from your wife?

"Oh no, we have a wonderful time in bed. She is a very good lover, even though she is, how can I say, physically well-built."

"I see. Well, now that you have completed the portrait, I would now like to see it."

"Of course, come and see it."

He threw the cover off the easel. The canvas was forty-eight inches high and thirty-six wide, and she saw that while it was her in a crude sort of way it was astonishingly incompetent. The perspective was wrong, the colors were awful, the textures were crude and not offset by any account of her character, which was nonexistent.

It was the work of a bad artist, a paltry amateur, someone who had no artistic talent or temperament. What a trickery! He obviously preyed upon women to flatter them by offering to paint their portrait, then get them into bed with them, and be paid for an object they would consign to a fire as soon as it arrived in their dwellings.

"Do you like it?"

"Of course. I'd like to take it with me now as I am only four doors away." He wrapped it in brown paper in silence. Then excusing herself with a whisper about the time of the month, she kissed him on the cheek as a goodbye.

She left and he did not try to recall her, carrying the despised portrait.

As she walked to her home, she was suddenly taken by the enormity of her mistake: *Soiled, dirty, sullied, disgusted, filthy and angry at the depth of her degradation. What a catastrophe*: She was running of out adjectives to describe how she now felt.

I can hardly feel betrayed, gullible perhaps, because it was all my initiative. Yet this man was an imposter, a scoundrel and a prodigious liar, however good he was in bed. Would it have been different if he was a great artist? No, no, no, I must get home and burn the portrait before it is uncovered. My revenge-filled wantonness has burnt itself out. I have soiled Pip, too. After all, Harriet was a genuine love of his and they would have married if she had wanted children. That was true of Estella and Nellie too. It was love they shared, not this... not this... not this what?

She arrived home well before Pip, went straight to her bedroom, telling the maid in the hall to burn the package immediately. She threw herself on the bed and cried her heart out. Later she had the maid run her a bath to try to wash herself clean of it, as she looked out of the window at the smoking embers of the portrait at the other end of the garden.

Albert sent a message to Estella a few days after they arrived, saying he would be delighted if Charlotte and she would join Elizabeth and him for lunch at the *Café des Moulins* on the street leading to

Montmartre. Elizabeth was looking exceptionally radiant such that, when they met, Charlotte hugged her for what seemed ages.

"How are you, my dear?"

"Delighted to be here. Let me just say something about my father and mother before we continue. My father had not been well, as you know, but he developed a serious lung complaint in the dust and heat of Athens, which led to a fever. It all went rather quickly. When he became ill, I sent a wire to my mother who replied that she was very busy but would come if he was in any danger which meant she did not want to come. What a selfish woman.

"Then, when he died, she wrote to me a very long involved letter, but the heart of it was that as he was now dead, there was no point in coming. I was so shocked that my mother, this stranger, was so heartless. I am over it now. I have my aunt for comfort."

She reached out and held Charlotte's hand which brought tears to both their eyes.

"So," said Albert, "we need say no more about her, but we will both remember Elizabeth's father with immense love and affection.

"However, we have news. We have become engaged to be married, neither of us really needing anyone's permission and both of you are such modern women that you would not expect to be asked!"

"You are quite right, Albert," said Estella. "The first time I saw you both together at that dinner party, I hoped you would fall in love. How wonderful."

"We owe you a great debt, Estella," said Elizabeth.

"You gave us more freedom to get to know each other than most other young people get. There is no stuff and nonsense like dowries involved. We are both comfortable financially, though not rich, and that is how we would wish it."

"Well," said Estella, "when do you expect to marry?'

"This is so difficult," said Elizabeth. "Albert needs to spend a year or more here in Paris where all the new developments in painting are taking place and he does intend to become a painter. I have been reading my father's diaries and I want to write a memoir of him based on that."

"Oh, what a source of interest that will be to our family and relatives," said Charlotte.

"Did you know Elizabeth's uncle is the Earl of Camberley, Estella?" Asked Albert.

"No, I did not know that. You are marrying into an ancient aristocratic family, obviously."

"I know," said Albert. "I will clearly be marrying above my station," he said, looking lovingly at Elizabeth. "However, we are going to Bonnat's studio tomorrow with Gustave. It is Saturday so he does not have to be studying."

"We assume," said Estella, "that you will live together before you marry."

Albert and Elizabeth smiled at each other but did not respond to the comment.

In the month of October, Nellie had been at Numquam on her own doing her chores, and as she rode the cart through the rotting iron gates of the house, her idea of a surprise present for Estella for Christmas came back into her mind.

"Fletch, do you remember my idea about the gates?" She said when she got home. "I've twice heard 'er say to herself 'I must do something about those gates.'"

"Too right, they're in terrible condition, always left open and the iron's rotting with rust."

"I suppose the house being at the end of a lane, no passersby if you see what I mean, them gates is no protection, is they? I was wondering if you'd make her some for Christmas."

"Crikey Nel, what an idea! I could do that, I'm a good blacksmith. Shoeing horses and repairing carts or traps is good business, but I've always had the urge to create something interesting with iron. I'll make 'em tall and grand and light as a feather," he said, pulling himself up to his full height and putting his tree-trunk arms around her and lifting her off the ground, to which she squealed in delight.

Making the gates became a family event. Each of four Sundays, they drove out in the cart around north Kent looking at gates to big houses, how their hinges worked, what sort of designs there were, whether they looked light or heavy, though they would always be heavy and it would be a matter of balance. These were always very joyous family occasions as Fletch had them all singing songs: *Boney was a Warrior, Early One Morning, Ten Green Bottles* and *The Lincolnshire Poacher.*

"Now I know what I want," he said, puffing on his pipe one evening. "They must open at a touch, more like a welcome than a protection if you see what I mean, not pushed and shoved. I could put E.P. in a scroll like lettering on one gate and P.P. on the other, not any sort of coat of arms."

"You really are a clever bugger, ain't you," said Nellie. "We's all so proud of you."

It was mid-November before there was the design fixed in his mind and he set to draw it, calculated measurements, acquired the right sort of iron and set to work.

"We'll have to think how to get them up before she sees them, darlin.'"

"Too right, Fletch," she replied.

Susanna got out of the bath, her face still a complete mess with her crying, so she went to her dressing table and looked at herself in the mirror. Then she pulled herself together, dressed and took a cab to go to Mary's house to share her distress.

Mary greeted her with surprise.

"What brings you here, dear Susanna? You seem downcast."

"I have been such a stupid woman," she said.

"That I very much doubt," said Mary, leading her into the drawing room.

"No two ways about it, I'm afraid. Oh, Mary, I have just finished with a lover and I was exhilarated by the bodily passions that he found in me. I wanted that kind of independence. I offered myself to him to seduce him. I was not paid in sovereigns or shillings, but I now feel like a whore."

"You have not yet explained why you undertook such a perilous course, although taking a lover can be at the core of a woman's independence from her husband," Mary replied, anxious to conceal her surprise at this earth-shattering confession from such a woman as Susanna.

"I know, but this was just out of revenge. Pip had been back with Harriet and I was furious."

"I see, and the revenge has burnt itself out?"

"Yes, because the man was such an impostor. I can't bear to talk about him, but he was not my lover in anything more than the physical sense."

"That is different from Pip and Harriet, I assume."

"Yes, they met by accident and resumed their intimacy."

"Does Pip know of your affair?"

"Not yet, but should I tell him? Though I am mightily disgusted with myself if I am honest, I did enjoy it. I suppose I want to feel able to do it again if I ever found that I loved another man, though that is unlikely."

"I know you well," said Mary, "and all the hurly-burly of deceit is not truly within your character. Of course, Pip might agree that you should both be free to love others, though I would doubt it. Yet you seem to realize how much you have hated what had happened."

"More than my disgraceful behavior I have hated the weeks of hardly talking, the children neglected, the joyful home becoming so gloomy. What a muddle and I know I am partly to blame."

"You must go right back to Cheyne Row and reconcile yourself with Pip this very day or your marriage will become an open sore, bleeding when touched.

"The fact not to be avoided for women like us is that an effort to claim more independence is as subject to failure and mistakes as any other human endeavor."

"That is at least some comfort. Thank you so much, dear Mary, for listening," and she hurried out to find a cab.

Pip had returned from Kent a chastened man. Estella and Nellie's comments were uppermost in his mind as he determined to try to heal the breach with Susanna. He was most worried by Estella's suggestion that she might have taken a lover. As he thought about that on the train, he realized he could hardly take her to task for that. Silly buggers indeed.

The question was whether such a lover was a replacement for him. If he would have been quite content to have both Susanna and Harriet as his lovers, why could not Susanna feel the same and want what he had? But then, it's just sex, not murder.

As he entered the house, she came out of the drawing room. She had obviously been crying, however much she tried to conceal it. She came to him and they embraced and kissed. He took her hand, and they went upstairs to their bedroom and sat on the bed in silence.

"I am so tired of this breach in our marriage, Pip," she said.

"So am I, my darling. Let us now just have a quiet dinner and talk about it all later."

"Yes, let us just go play with the children first."

Later they lay in bed, both lying on their backs and just holding hands.

"I am so sorry about my connection with Harriet, darling, even though it has long since passed."

"Yes, but you obviously did love her before you met me. You told me you might have married her if she had wanted children. Loving someone is not to be spurned outright, you know."

"I suppose so, but what about you these past few weeks? Estella said you might have taken a lover out of, well, I don't know what, but have you?"

"I did and I am now so full of regrets, I feel like hiding away somewhere, the shame is so great."

"But I understand, Susanna. I know your character, the odd thing is that your intense fury showed that you loved me, or at least that you had loved me."

"We both need to be truthful about this," she replied, "especially me. I very much enjoyed bedding another man. It was different, exhilarating, adventurous, fulfilling in its way but it made me feel sordid, soiled, used and ultimately disgusted, because the man was such an impostor. But I have decided that I do not want the freedom to engage with someone other than you, even if I loved them.

"You bedded Harriet when you met recently because there is still a place in your heart and in hers for each other. I am sure that renewal of love was not a replacement for me, whereas my affair was but a false addition, if you like, because there was no love or admiration, just revenge."

"Revenge? That's not like you, Susanna. It was Harriet who insisted that we stop. She felt that our relationship was a threat to my marriage and yours, and that it would lead to unhappiness all round and she did not want to feel that responsibility. Though a free lover, she has immense integrity. I never really felt there was a choice to be made between you and her."

"I did not love the man I was with. Indeed, in my mind I seduced him, though he is of such a character that I am sure he felt he did the seducing. But it is now all finished, utterly and completely.

"I am glad, so glad. The sense of peace in our home is returning. We still have many things to talk about. Let us go away for a week together, somewhere quiet and peaceful, where we can walk on a beach and no one knows us. Cornwall, for instance— there is now a train to Penzance and we can walk together at Land's End."

"I am thinking of something more distant. We discussed once joining a mission to Africa with you as its preacher. Some time, we should reconsider that, when the children are a bit older. I would love to get away, though.

"Pip, let me ask you this. Are you not curious to know the identity of my lover?"

"Darling, if you loved him, I would want to know. As you clearly did not, I see no point in my knowing."

"You know I love you, don't you? You know I want another daughter, don't you? Two boys and two girls would be exquisite."

Christmas celebrations always began well before Christmas Eve and neither Estella nor Charlotte wanted to stay in Paris and miss the festival at home.

"Now we are back here for a while," said Estella, "I want to take the carriage and walk along the beach near Whitstable, which I have never done."

"It is some time since I saw the sea," said Charlotte, "so I would love that."

"Good, then we can lunch at The Sportsman Inn there, a hostelry famous for its oysters."

Nellie arrived later much to Estella's delight. They hugged and kissed each other and Charlotte also welcomed Nellie with an embrace but with more restraint.

"You now must tell us all that has been going on."

"Oh, our lives are very quiet. My Fletch is doing ever so well so he has had to find a journeyman laborer, Josh, to help before young Horatio can be a 'prentice. He's a surly devil, but he does good work. He comes on Thursdays and Fridays as Fletch could not keep up if he didn't. Old Mr. Buzza in the stables now uses him for his horses and his business has grown too."

"That is wonderful."

"Yeah. I s'pose there's other fings since you was here. I found out from a man wot came to the Bargemen that I could buy books through the post, 'cos there ain't no bookshop nearby. They sent me a notice and a list of other books I might like which was nice of them.

"I saw one book just called *Emma*. I've always liked that name, so I got that. Blimey, is that a good book? I ain't finished it yet, but it's about people like you only many years ago. I just hope she marries Mr. Kingsley."

"H'mm, Jane Austen, I will order all her six books for you for Christmas."

"Talking of Christmas presents," said Nellie, "we might have one for you."

"There is really no need for you to bother about that."

"It'll be a surprise but Fletch and I's been talking a lot about what Mr. Pip said after Fletch killed that Whistler man. When you kill someone and see his blood spurting everywhere, it's not some-fink you forget, whatever the beak says. Anyway, we's been to All Hallows Church a couple of times and we're sending the children to Sunday School. It's all new to us and most of it we don't under-stand, except when the vicar tells us what we have to do."

"I am very happy to help you both understand it," said Charlotte, "indeed I will come with you when you go. My deceased husband was a vicar."

"Really? That must have been a wonderful life. Was he like that lovely Mr. Pip wot was married to Estella?"

"No, I fear he wasn't."

"Well, that's enough chattering. I must get on with my chores," and she hurried away into the kitchen.

"Now," said Charlotte to Estella, "I understand you. She is this lovely sparkling diamond in the rough, isn't she? A frightful back-ground but redeemed by you is the way to put it."

"Redeemed is too religious, my dear. Transformed perhaps, but it is of her own doing. You see the initiative she has taken with her reading. I doubt whether I will come to church with you. I went on Miss Havisham's instructions, but thereafter not at all."

"Welcome, welcome," Estella called out as the trap bringing Pip, Susanna and their three children arrived just as Nellie was leaving and they exchanged greetings.

Estella crouched down to talk to Lachlan, asking:

"What have you been up to, Lachlan?"

With great confidence, the youngster said politely:

"We went to a great big hall, Albert I think it was called, and we heard people singing Christmas carols."

"And there was this big noise from the organ," added Malcolm.

"Well," said Estella, "it is nearly Christmas so we can sing some carols here too if you would like."

"They are beginning to sing beautifully," said Pip.

"Unlike their father," said Susanna seemingly with humor, not malice which Estella saw as a good sign.

"I wondered if we could borrow your carriage to go to Chatham on Christmas Day and go to the chapel where we met, as we need to take our religion more seriously," at which Pip turned to look out of the window.

Clearly, thought Estella, the wounds of Pip's infidelity are not quite yet beginning to heal properly, so she changed the subject:

"Who would like to go and see the sea?"

"I would, I would," shouted the boys almost in unison.

"Then we will organize an expedition across the marshes."

"They would enjoy that," said Pip.

A carriage was heard outside later and Hamish, Mary and James arrived after being met at the train station in Rochester by Albert acting as a chauffeur for guests.

Everyone, including the boys, looked lovingly at the baby James, his eyes flickering from face to face, searching for recognition where there was none. The MacDonalds retired immediately to their allocated bedroom to feed James, who was now nine months old. This was a task Mary was quite unwilling to delegate to anyone else, however distinguished or reputable.

Not an easy matter, she lay on her paralyzed arm, nestling the child against it so that she could use her right hand.

"You are just so beautiful," said Hamish, abashed by watching his wife suckling his child.

"I am as proud as a peacock, and I now see my purpose in life was to shield, protect, and love my son and his darling mother who are giving me a joy I have never imagined. Now we must have a second baby to enjoy."

"I love you too," murmured Mary as James was suckling off her.

Downstairs, Susanna asked, "who is the painter?" as she looked at a large canvas with a recognizable view of Numquam. Molly's stone could just be seen in the right-hand corner, and the house visible through leafless trees. Estella could be seen at the door with a trug in her hand.

"That is Albert's work," said Estella. "He has seen plenty of examples in Paris of painting *en plein air*, so he took the opportunity of being here in the country. He worked at it for what seemed like four whole days."

"H'mm," said Susanna, and to Estella's surprise said: "It is not altogether satisfactory, is it? The textures are awry, and the perspective is very ambitious," and Estella immediately cut in, anticipating further destructive remarks, given Susanna's aggressive mood.

"It is his own and he is a novice, and I am monumentally proud of it, so I have hung it in pride of place in the dining room."

"I am sure he will do better when he is more mature." Another snide remark, which Estella ignored, though privately she agreed wholeheartedly.

Shortly thereafter Albert arrived back from the station with Elizabeth, at which there was great delight, especially from Charlotte who hugged her without stopping.

On Christmas Eve, the Brandrams came over from the Blue Boar. Honora's twins, Simon and Jude, had been educated in Welsh music traditions, and sang together a few Welsh hymns and carols in which everyone joined where they knew the words. Neither of their voices had broken so they sang often with great Welsh ambition, and the more they sang, the more the company demand of them.

Frederick whispered to Honora that he had never heard them singing quite like this, and perhaps their twins might join the choir at Chelsea Old Church, which was near them in Cheyne Row, the Abbey Choir not being a realistic choice.

Wednesday, December 25th dawned. The Fletchers arrived early in their cart on the way to church. Fletch had summoned a couple of friends to help him install the new gates during the night. Nellie went into the house just as Estella came down for breakfast.

"Happy Christmas, darlin' but put on your coat," she said, giving her a hug and a kiss. "I want to show you something outside."

"Great heavens, Nellie dear, what are you doing here so early?"

"Ask no more questions, just come with me."

Estella put on her hat and coat hurriedly, perplexed by Nellie's insistent tone, and she took her arm and holding hands they walked at a good pace down the drive.

"Fletch and me wanted to give you a nice present for Christmas."

"I told you, you don't need to do that," said Estella as they rounded the corner, and the gates came into view.

"Happy Christmas," shouted the Fletcher family as Estella got her first glimpse of the gates.

"Oh, my goodness, oh my goodness," said Estella breaking away from Nellie and hurrying to the gates, holding her skirts up to avoid falling.

"Did you make these, Fletch? "

"Yes, ma'am. We knows you needed new gates."

"Come here," said Estella, taking him by the hand and putting her arms around him. "You are such a clever man and such a good husband. Thank you, thank you, thank you."

"Well, I'm pleased you like them, but now we mustn't be late for church but we'll open them for the others."

"No, let me," said Estella, clicking the latch. "Goodness gracious, they are as light as a feather. How wonderful, how wonderful! Oh, wouldn't Pip have been thrilled! Off you go now, and we'll see you later in the morning."

Estella, Albert and Elizabeth remained at home, while the others fulfilled their religious obligations. They all walked down to the gates, Estella for the second time, and Albert the artist was astounded by their elegant beauty, and how easily they opened and shut.

"Such craftsmanship, such a splendid design and look. Did you notice your initials in the small medallions?"

"Oh, my goodness, and Pip's on the other gate. How thoughtful! How generous!"

"No more than you deserve, dear Estella. You are loved and cherished by so many people. I am so proud of you. I admire you so much."

"Stop, please stop, Albert, or I will spend the morning in tears which is not appropriate for Christmas, is it?"

They returned to the house, and Elizabeth retrieved her music from the bedroom and played Beethoven's *Pathetique* Sonata on the piano with its mournful second movement. She was now clearly very accomplished, but the playing of the sonata reflected her memories of her father.

Charlotte rode with the four Fletchers to church instructing them in the liturgy of the Anglican Communion Service on the way. She always found it a moving experience, being herself quietly devout. Sometimes she thought her devotion was why she married Oliver. The Fletcher children were old enough to be well-behaved and seemed quite taken with the rhythms of prayer and watching the consecration of the bread and wine followed by the congregation taking communion.

On the way home, Nellie said:

"Amazing, when you think about it, I mean, you know the history. Christians celebrating for hundreds of years and not just here in Norfolk but across the world. I loved it. What about you, darlin?"

"Don't know really, but it made me feel quite peaceful, you know, just listening and thinking about what was being said."

"What I liked," said Nellie, "was that prayer about mercy. I hope God is merciful, 'cos I've been a right sinner."

"It is a wonderful prayer, isn't it?" said Charlotte. "That is what is called The Prayer of Humble Access, and she recited quietly:

"We do not presume to come to this Thy table, oh merciful Lord, trusting in our own righteousness, but in thy manifold and great mercies. We are not worthy to gather up the crumbs under thy table, but thou are the same Lord whose property is always to have mercy..."

"That's the one," said Nellie. "That was a real poem, wasn't it? When I think of all the sinners I've known, I'm sure they would want God to be merciful. I know I do."

"Well," said Charlotte, "it's been a real pleasure to take you, and I do hope you'll go again, not just at Christmas or Easter but regularly. I'll tell you all about becoming a member being confirmed as it is call, some other time."

"What's that?" said Fletch.

"It's when you become a member of the church through a special ceremony."

"I think we'd like that, wouldn't we, Nel, and the kiddies."

It was indeed a Christmas Day to remember as friendships between the families were further entrenched. All the children had full days and sleep-filled nights: the Brandram twins, Lachlan and Malcolm with Albert in his role as host accompanied by Elizabeth, leading the way with games and charades. The sea expedition did not take place as the year ended, much as it has been throughout the year with intermittent rain, a cold wind and grey skies.

Estella found Susanna in the small library in the late afternoon, clearly wanting to be left alone.

"Are you well?" she asked, at which Susanna burst into tears.

"Pip and I have patched up our differences and all is well," she said, drying her tears with her linen handkerchief, "but I am utterly dismayed by my own behavior."

"Well, you have been a bit of a curmudgeon these few days."

"I know and I am sorry. We women have been talking for so long about the need for our independence, especially at the league meeting. But, Estella, one can be deceived into thinking what one is doing is an achievement of independence, when it is despicable, sordid and uncharacteristic, a betrayal of one's own instincts and who one is."

"I suppose one can make mistakes."

"Mistakes, mistakes?" she cried. "Oh no, violations of everything one thought one held sacred in the name of independence. Terrible, terrible."

"What did you do, then?"

"You may as well know that I took a lover to assert my independence from Pip and, I suppose, to take revenge. I went against all my core beliefs and I am deeply ashamed."

"I understand, Susanna. Try to put it behind you or it will continue to upset your marriage. Just return to who you were beforehand."

She moved over to the woman weeping in the chair and kissed her gently on the cheek.

"Think of all those poor women we work for and realize your good fortune."

XXIV

All his life John Wemmick had followed passenger ships that sank, especially those with extensive loss of life. When he was two years old, news reached his Walworth home that the *HMS Blenheim* and the *HMS Java* in convoy had disappeared en route to India in 1807 with the loss of 870 lives. One explanation given at the time was that the *Java* went to rescue the *Blenheim* but was herself caught in a storm.

Little John Wemmick grew up with this story, as his uncle Harry was a mate on the Java, and for every year on the day, there had been a family lamentation that somehow, sometime, on some unknown shore, Harry would appear. But Aged P, John's affectionate name for his father, got older and the old man no longer remembered what it was all about.

John's list was immense, filling several carefully constructed notebooks. Not only were there frequent fatal accidents in the Thames, but he recorded sea-born catastrophes like that of the *HMS St. George* in 1811, where only 7 of 730 were saved. The *HMS Defence* tried to come to her rescue, but she too was sunk with only 14 out of 597 survivors. In 1852, the *HMS Birkenhead* carrying troops and their families hit a rock off the Western Cape, but only 193 out of 694 were rescued.

The age of newspapers enabled him to collect cutting for his scrapbooks. Their voluminous entries and newspapers cuttings later included such tragedies as the *RMS Tayleur* on her maiden voyage out of Liverpool in 1854, with only 280 survivors out of 650 passengers and crew. Then there was *Royal Adelaide*; only 7 out of 57 crew and passengers were saved. That was interesting too for what happened afterwards, as he once told Hamish. The ship was off Portland, then tried to shelter in Lyme Bay but her anchors failed her, and she ended up on Chesil Beach. But the wreckers arrived to salvage all the bottles on board and four of them died of exposure, dead drunk on the beach.

Britannia ruled the waves—at a cost.

On April 1, 1873, an ocean liner the SS Atlantic hit an underwater rock off Marr's Head, Nova Scotia, Canada, and sank with the loss of between 535 and 560 lives but with 371 survivors. The sinking was a chapter of accidents, of human error, a major storm and misreading charts leaving the ship twelve miles off course when she hit a rock. It would have amused John Wemmick to learn that a crew member who had completed three journeys with the ship was drowned, but 'his' body was found to be that of a woman. 'He was a good fellow,' said a surviving member of the crew. 'I am sorry he was a woman.'

John Wemmick had constantly discussed marine insurance with Old Pip and the wisdom or lack of it. Hamish had taken Old Pip's place as a partner to such conversations, and it had become clear to Hamish that this stalwart man was in decline. He had mentioned the fact to Estella at Christmas and, typically Estella wanted to do something to help. Yet Hamish felt with some alarm that he was no more than a polite listener that April morning as John seemed to be getting more and more excited, even incoherent as he spoke.

The anniversary of the sinking on April 1, 1875, brought it again to Wemmick's mind so he was discoursing on the topic with Hamish a few days later to put off his intention to tell Hamish that he was now finally going to retire.

Then he stared with wide eyes at his companion and said, "Hamish, I've got a terrible pain."

Quite suddenly, he clutched his chest with his right hand, his face turned as red as a sunset, his body started to wobble, and his knees gave way and he crashed to the floor of the office, knocking over a chair as he did so.

Hamish leapt to his feet, crying out "John, John, what's with you? John, John," getting quickly to his knees to pat his head in a vain attempt to bring him back to consciousness.

Then, "Robert, come here," he screamed, loosening the cravat around the dying man's neck.

Robert came rushing in to find Hamish with his head on Wemmick's chest, trying to find out whether he was breathing, but his face was gradually turning grey as his trembling lips went still.

"I think he's dead, sir," said Robert, unable to hold back his tears.

Hamish sat down heavily at his desk as Robert straightened out the body, putting the dead man's hands over his chest. Wemmick's face at first seemed contorted but then his cheeks fell in, slightly giving him a more peaceful appearance.

Hamish wept profusely at the sight of this man of wisdom, probity and friendship who had not obviously had any warning he was about to die which, for a man who prided himself on insights he described as inklings, was a sorrowful ending.

Four days later, the sun shone weakly through the stained-glass window on the south side of the nave at St. Peter's Church, falling in dappled colors on the pews in the south transept. The pews were packed with mourners. Mr. Courtisone was visiting friends in Glasgow and sent Mrs. W his condolences.

Hamish Macdonald began his eulogy, recalling his friend's fascination with such wrecks as the *Atlantic,* and of his talks with Mr. Jaggers about the tribulations of marine insurance investors. With the elder Mr. Pirrip, known as Old Pip, the discussion between the two was more intent on answering the moral question:

When a ship is sinking, who should be the priority for rescue?

Should it be 'women and children first? as with the *Birkenhead,* or 'every man for himself?'

Neither was satisfactory to John, Hamish recalled in a softer voice. Mrs. W. could not hear properly so the eulogy was punctuated with Mrs. W. asking Estella "Wot did he say?" in a voice loud enough for most mourners to hear, enhanced by the nave of

St. Peter's renowned for its echo. "John thought that 'women and children first' was too generous," he continued, "but 'everyman for himself' far too selfish and cowardly. If choice were possible in the circumstances of a sinking, he was a pragmatic man. As sea water cascades into a hold, he would say that was no time to be ferreting out women and children, but just to save as many as possible without regard for a select group.

"We talked about this subject on innumerable occasions and it exercised his mind wonderfully. His eyes would flash, he would walk up and down, stopping to make a point, as many of you will recall his mannerisms. Yet he always reached the conclusion that it was a matter of moral luck as to who would survive, but he had little admiration for a captain who decided to go down with his ship.

"My friends: You may find my rehearsal of his interest not proper for a eulogy. But you see, this matter is one we can all understand and contemplate, unlike some complicated legal case. His interest in it reveals that here was a man of great wisdom and perseverance, a man who diligently pursued a problem through to a conclusion and was generous enough to change his mind, a superlative human characteristic which was revealed in the way he discussed his inklings, a phrase that has made its way into the lore of our legal practice."

Mrs. W, the former Miss Skiffins, sniffled through these tributes, assuming them to be effusive. Although it was inappropriate to applaud such a speech many were tempted to do so, as Hamish had captured the deceased so well.

Hamish was followed by others who knew him. As he spoke, Estella thought how mature Hamish now was, a fact she attributed to his marriage to Mary. She herself was in two minds about whether to contribute as it was most unusual for a woman to speak on such occasions, conventions being what they were. Indeed, in some parts of the country, such as South Wales, only men followed the cortege to the graveyard by custom, which, to a cynical observer, seemed more like an arrangement for the women to get on with preparations for a hearty wake.

Overcoming her reluctance, she then rose to speak of her deep affection for John. In addition to comments about his character, she described how sympathetic he had been to her anger and emotion on meeting her mother in Mr. Jaggers' office all those years ago.

One or two people among the mourners who did not know Estella were aghast a woman could be so presumptuous, but she was not a follower of convention and those who knew her expected her to speak, for she had become such a formidable presence in their lives.

The wake at the Wemmick home in Walworth was a continued celebration of his long life of service, for which Mrs. W. was most grateful, though in a small house, the noise created by admirers gave her a headache. None of the many villains Wemmick had helped to bring to justice attended, as their movements were restricted. Of his extensive cadre of informants, Sidney was the only one there, he who had tracked the blackmailing lawyer, David Twaddell.

"Mr. Macdonald," said Sidney, sidling up to Hamish as mourners began to leave. "I wanted to say how sorry we are all about Mr. Wemmick, but I have a card here if you should ever be in need of my services."

"Have we met, sir?" said Hamish.

"I am Sidney, sir, who traced that Twaddell fella."

"Oh, you're Sidney. Well, well, I am pleased to meet you and I will let John's successor know of your talents, and your address."

"Thank 'ee, thank 'ee, Sir, I'm very glad to be of service."

Whether Sidney was mourning the man or the loss of a source of portable property was a conjecture that crossed Hamish's mind.

Yet John Wemmick left several important questions for *Courtisone and Jaggers*. Everyone knew he was irreplaceable. The lawyers and the clerks felt the loss of his wisdom deeply. Those of a religious bent would have an inkling that, like Mr. Standfast, the trumpets would be sounding for him as he passed over on to the other side.

That month Susanna could hardly keep up with the changes in Cheyne Row, alert as she was as to who might grace her dinner table.

The Bollaerts had suddenly cancelled their lease the day after Susanna parted company with James and disappeared to their Thetford house, which occasioned brief comment from neighbors, though Susanna kept the reason why to herself. Their lease was taken by Randolph and Eliza Culpepper and their three children, Timothy, Japheth and Margaret, none of whom had yet passed their majority.

Charles Meggison's paintings were selling well, so they decided to lease his house and move to *Breu-Auriac,* a small village in the French countryside not too far from *Aix-en-Provence.* The move had been considered for some time, but as Charles told Pip when they met in the row one afternoon, they had no children, and it was the light in that area of France that fascinated him, compared to the grey and dank of London.

That Cheyne Row house was now leased by a recently married couple, Aubrey Penoyre and his young wife Antonia and, after Rizzio's untimely death, the tenancy of his house passed to another Italian, Angelo Bonaccorso. Susanna told all who would listen that the house was far too capacious for a single man, and she disliked the man immediately on acquaintance.

To complete the changes in the row's inhabitants, Charlotte's brother-in-law had recently been summoned to South Africa where his regiment would be based for some time. Charlotte briefly considered moving back there but was very happy in New Queen Street. A brother and sister, Clive and Celia Enticott, took over that house.

All these changes kept Susanna somewhat breathless, as she appeared to have put her troubles behind her and now saw herself as the lynchpin of society in the row.

"I'm arranging a dinner party for our new neighbors and we hope you'll both come," she said after she had arrived at Mary's door one morning.

"Of course, and I will try hard to keep my opinions to myself," and they both giggled.

"Please don't stop talking or I would be bored. Remind me when you are due; your baby's arrival looks imminent."

"Let me be frank, Susanna," said Mary.

"Oh no, I anticipate an avalanche of criticism now," and she laughed.

"In your marriage, Pip is an earnest, well-intentioned man blessed with considerable virtues. You are far sharper than he is. You must stop trying to outwit him. You must become cautious in what you say. Be a Socrates, deftly asking questions of him yielding the answer you have spotted long before."

"I do understand that difference and I do try, and it makes me wonder whether our distinctive personalities will become reflected in our children."

"I am sure they will."

"Lachlan, my seven-year-old, is more like me. If I can say this without embarrassment, he is quick-witted, funny and a little temperamental. He was excited about his new school, starting to learn Latin, whereas Malcolm, my younger boy, is physically much more like his father with his shock of red hair, and he has not taken to reading under my instruction as easily as his elder brother. Hannah seems to have a mind of her own, but it is too early to tell."

"Will you have another child? Hamish and I are delighted by this baby."

"I'd love another daughter, so if I become pregnant again, it must be a girl as I will then have two of each."

"Let me know what you do to bring about that when you find out," said Mary with a smile.

The following day, Susanna called her maid to deliver the dinner invitations she had just completed to Randolph and Eliza

Culpepper, Aubrey and Antonia Penoyre, Angelo Bonaccorso, Clive and Celia Enticott, and Frederick and Honora Brandram of Cheyne Row. She also sent the cards by post to Estella Pirrip and Charlotte Mudge, and Hamish and Mary Macdonald.

The union of the *Courtisone* and *Jaggers* practices looked to be promising. Hamish was collecting some valuable briefs through the former Courtisone side of the practice. Adam Masterson was proving an exceptional senior clerk, not John Wemmick exactly, but with insight, connections and knowledge of the law that made him invaluable to Hamish.

Three of the Courtisone group of lawyers left for different reasons. Michael O'Grady had been so shocked with the Irish Famine twenty-five years earlier that the merger provide him with a reason to return to Dublin. Hector was too old for change, or so he said. Jonathan Greenberg and his wife went to South Africa to explore life in the colonies. Philip Hardyman seemed satisfied, though he kept his distance from the others.

Clarence Fotheringaye-Smythe, Hamish's junior lawyer, was worth his weight in briefs. He formally announced his engagement to the Honorable Emma Eustace on Easter Sunday. It promised to be what his mother called a splendid match, for it was founded in love. Her parents were delighted, Lord Eustace's ennoblement coming from his status as a Justice of Appeal. The Fotheringaye-Smythes were after all an ancient family of breeding, they thought, and it was sad that Clarence's father Hugo had fallen on such hard times, unable to resist the lure of the gaming tables.

The couple was together whenever possible. It was now May, and they were sitting on a bench overlooking the Thames during the Moseley Regatta. Friends of Clarence from Cambridge had joined a rowing club and were entered in various races, so they had accepted an invitation to watch. Yet as this was a serious couple, the hoopla around them was not a distraction.

"Emma, do you see yourself as an independent woman?"

"Oh, my dear man, I love you so much and I want to raise a large family with you. But I want to have the kind of life my mother has had being deeply involved in her husband's work and life. My parents are partners in everything, I think, and I want that with you. If that is independence, so be it."

"I have been musing recently on other people's marriages," said Clarence. "Hamish and Mary are so balanced not just because they love each other but because he supports her so cleverly and is never taken aback by her outspokenness or ashamed of it. I have the sense that Pip and Susanna's relationship is unstable, but that it is because they have no shared interest beyond bringing up their children. Estella is widowed but unique, and you will find her a fascinating study, I know. I don't really know her step-son Albert well, though he seems a bit of a rake to me, and I hope he does not cause her any trouble. She seems besotted with him, I suppose, because he reminds her so much of her husband."

"She sounds formidable indeed, but let me put another topic to you, Clarence. I know enough about the law growing up in a legal family. I would be very disappointed if you did not share your work with me, the details of your cases. If you did not, that would cut you off from me regarding a central part of your life. Partnership in bringing up our children, of course, but also in your work to the extent I have described."

"I see that clearly, Emma. We are very fortunate in that you are interested in what I do, as I suspect many a wife has no interest whatsoever in her husband's work, which must be a weakness in the life of a marriage. I think we are off on a good footing with a partnership in my work, and we do talk a great deal about serious matters, politics, religion and so on, do we not.

"I have been much influenced by the women I am getting to know. They are all strong and independent, even powerful. Each has a marriage of equals, some of which had to be won. It is a constant struggle to achieve that, and I want that for us."

"I agree wholeheartedly, and I do want to develop interests of my own, both philanthropic and political. This League of Women is an attractive venue for working those interests. I love those conversations, and I am delighted by your thoughts, but at this moment, darling Clarence, we need to think about our wedding. Here we are in May already, but are we serious about the autumn, say early September?"

"Indeed, I should hope so, but it is a matter for your parents really, in particular your father's commitment. It cannot be in law terms obviously, but I have no prejudice for any Saturday in September. It would then still be warm in Nice if that is where you would like to honeymoon."

"I think sunshine would be more enjoyable than a walking tour. All our relatives will come, I am sure, so we need not travel around, as so many couples do after their wedding, introducing themselves to families."

"We do also need to talk about my long-term future, darling."

"I have a yen to get into politics and as things stand that would be as a Liberal, though my family have been Tories from time immemorial."

The cheers from the banks indicated that the main race had begun. The sun shone and an observer might have sensed a golden glow above the heads of this couple as they sauntered toward the river and began cheering themselves.

"You can certainly join the party, "said Emma, "and I will be excited to support you. I think my father may be able to help you find a constituency as he is well-connected. That will take a few years, I am sure."

"Oh, indeed," Clarence replied, "I need to amass some money of my own before I venture into political waters.

"That will be necessary for while my father is obviously quite rich, the demands of my three Eustace brothers will surely outweigh any discrimination on our account."

"I am not so sure. The noble lord your father said quietly to me at our engagement celebration that he wanted to talk to me soon."

"Good, then he might invest in a political son-in-law, don't you know?"

"We must wait and see. I feel very comfortable at *Courtisone and Jaggers*. It is now such a splendid team and I am fortunate to admire everyone I work with, though I am sure it won't be long before Courtisone retires and then, presumably, Philip Hardyman, whom I am not particularly fond of, will become senior partner. A queer fish."

Estella realized that with John's death, there was now no one alive who was personally acquainted with her past. Elizabeth came over from Paris and stayed for a night with them in New Queen Street before Charlotte and she took a cab to Bishopsgate Station for a train to Norwich. Henry Fitzroy's remains had finally arrived from Athens at the Camberley mansion near Wymondham.

Estella was lonely with no one else in New Queen Street. The Jaggers Building was not causing any disruption, Semper House was not yet ready for occupation by male prostitutes and the meeting of the Trust was not until the autumn. Before going to Kent, she took a cab to go Pip's grave. It was a mild day, so she bought daffodils outside the cemetery to lay on the stone.

As she walked to the grave, she could not erase from her mind how he looked when she last saw him before the coffin was closed. He had looked quite at peace, the dear man, and almost with a smile on his face.

As always when she went to his grave, she had to fend off the vision of what he looked like at this moment, the wood beginning to rot, maggots getting into his decaying flesh but, when it was her turn, she only wanted proximity. She had not done this before, but she could not help herself talking to him, though she had always ridiculed the practice when she witnessed other people doing it.

"I have not talked with you before, darling. There is no one here but me. It is a splendid spring day so I bought you daffodils, not from Numquam, I'm afraid, but still daffodils. I want to tell you first about our Albert. He is such a splendid creature, brave too. He was badly hurt in Paris but recovered with determination. You'll remember how he wanted to paint and how we had to get him to stay in his room? He still has not finished your portrait, which bothers me.

He's been telling me to read about some French painters he knows who are doing quite new things with their art. So, if he continues with his present ambitions, he will become well-known. I worry whether I am enough for him, but he now has a young lady friend he intends to marry, so maybe my task as a mother will be less than it was.

This young lady Elizabeth is equally splendid, beautiful beyond comprehension, his height, perceptive, independent and full of grace and charm. I know you would be so delighted for him. But I am doing my best for your son."

She stopped and looked around her and sighed, wept a little, and got up from her haunches where she had imagined herself peering through the dirt at her man.

"This is ridiculous," she whispered to herself. *"I do not need such antics as pretending he can hear, it is demeaning. These semi-hysterical pantomimes to express my love and grief are unlike me, Estella. He is dead. He cannot hear me. His soul, whatever that is, is not there either."*

She walked away from the grave in silence and wandered along some cemetery paths, seeing large mausoleums, statues of weeping figures, the kind of sentimentality she detested though it was becoming increasingly common.

Was Miss Havisham a sentimentalist? She wondered. Many might have regarded that crumbling home as a monument to sentiment and grief. *True, that was how it started, but it shortly thereafter became this vigorous, cruel, unbending hatred of the male sex which she laid on me. How fortunate I am to have that curse finally broken by my mother Molly and by my lovely Pip.*

Odd, she thought, *that at my age in these private moments I think so much about physical love. I sometimes wonder whether my guardian had erotic thoughts or dreams, but I cannot imagine it. Nowadays, while I am by no means the woman I was when I was with Drummel, I am somehow not attracted to other men than Pip, for he has spoilt me.*

The gentleness in which Nellie and I have indulged has spoilt me too. The nature of intimacy with a man cannot help but be one of aggression by the male. Pip could be very aggressive, pain being a constituent of male-female intimacy whereas that was never the case with Nellie. Merely tender loving softness.

"Hey ho," she sighed as she reached the cemetery gate and called a cab to take her home to New Queen Street, shrugging off the memories of the fulfilled life she discovered with Pip. Later in the afternoon she caught a train to Kent and arrived in the twilight at Numquam, her other home with its unique attractions— the house, the gardens, the countryside and, of course, not far away in the Gargery's old cottage Nellie, her beloved friend and companion.

END

Appendix A: Contextual Notes

1. Highgate Cemetery was opened in 1839, fifteen acres for the Church of England and two for dissenters.

2. Henry Fitzroy is modeled on the life and career of the Hon, Henry Wodehouse. The letters are taken from *Letters from the Hon. Henry Wodehouse*, a free ebook.

   https://books.google.com/books?id=j1wIAAAAQAAJ&
   pg=PA51&lpg=PA51&dq=Henry+Wodehouse+papers+a
   nd+letters&source=bl&ots=D5fg7uor9w&sig=ACfU3U
   3nGqmdQ8fjvKaZ9flAIpybVscvvw&hl=en&sa=X&ved=
   2ahUKEwjn7rr46ezvAhXjUjUKHVS3ApE4HhDoATAI
   egQICBAD#v=onepage&q=Henry%20Wodehouse%20
   papers%20and%20letters&f=false.

   The letters quoted are in general verbatim, though amendments are made for chronological or literary reasons.

3. Courtisone's description of Jaggers ancestry cites the experience of Jews in Weisbaden.

4. The account of Pip's visit to St. Paul's is a reconstruction of the author's childhood experience.

5. The descriptions of the Franco-Prussian War and the Paris Commune are generally available through such books as Michael Howard's book on the war and Alastair Horne's book on the Commune as well as through various online sources.

6. Other historical figures mentioned include Sir Charles Dilke, Bt, MP; John Stuart Mill, MP and philosopher; Edward Nettleship, FRS, FCS an ophthalmologist working at the Moorfield Hospital in London; Octavia Hill a well-known Victorian philanthropist, and Gustave Caillebotte, an Impressionist painter, and Lord Lyons, ambassador to France.

Appendix B: Chronology and Primary Characters

*Estella Pirrip:	1804:	Born to Abel & Molly Magwitch. Guardian: Miss Havisham.
	1855:	Married to Old Pip.
	1870:	Widowed.
	1872:	Chair, Board. Jaggers Trust for Relief & Education of the Poor.
Albert Pirrip:	1853:	Born. February: Son of (Old) Pip and Beatrice (née Pocket). Stepson of Estella.
Pip (Philip) Gargery:	1837:	Born. Married, 1865, to Susanna Urchadan.
	1854:	March. Crimea. Wounded Battle of Balaklava. October.
	1856:	Itinerant Preaching.
	1857 – 1864:	Preacher Salford: Affair with Harriet Middleham.
	1865:	Marriage to Susanna Urchadan.
	1866:	Manager/Director of the Jaggers Trust.
Susanna Gargery:	1843:	Born.

	1865:	Married to Young Pip,
	1868:	Son: Lachlan Finlay
		Joseph Gargery.
Hamish Macdonald:	1841:	Born.
	1865:	Junior Lawyer to Old Pip:
		Appointed March.
	1871:	Married Mary Hamilton.
	1869:	Son: James Irving
		Macdonald, born 1872.
Mary Macdonald:	1839:	Born.
	1871:	Married to Hamish Macdonald.
John Wemmick:	1805:	Born. Senior Clerk to Jaggers.
		Married: Miss. Skiffins.
	1874:	Died.
Harriet Middleham:	1838:	Born. Affair with
		Young Pip, 1857.
Horatio Fletcher (Fletch):	1837:	Born. Pip's farrier companion in the Crimea.
	1861:	Married. Nellie Mosscrop.
	1865:	Takes over the Gargery Forge.
	1869:	Kills Whistler.
Nellie Fletcher (née Mosscrop)	c.1850:	Born. Young whore in Chatham.
	1870:	Affair with Estella.
Charlotte Mudge:	1815:	Born. Wife to Vicar of Craynham, Norfolk.

Reverend Oliver Mudge :	1812:	Born.
	1872:	Died in an accident.
Elizabeth Fitzroy:	1854:	Born, Daughter of Henry Fitzroy, Niece of Charlotte Mudge.
The Hon. Henry Fitzroy:	1825:	Born. Head of Chancery, British Embassy, Paris. British Embassy, Athens.
Mary-Lou Fitzroy:	1830.	Born. American wife of Henry.
Nathaniel Courtisone:	1790:	Born. Lawyer. Counsel to the Jaggers Trust.
Philip Hardyman:	1832:	Born. Lawyer, Courtisone and Jaggers.
Clarence Fotheringaye-Smythe:	1839:	Born. Lawyer, Courtisone and Jaggers.
Lady Emma Eustace.	1840:	Born.
	1873:	Fiancée to Clarence Fotheringaye-Smythe.
Frederick Brandram:	1820:	Born. Architect, living in Cheyne Row, Chelsea.
Honora Brandram:	1838:	Born.
	1858:	Mother of twins: Simon and Jude Jones.

Married to Frederick Brandram.

Nimrod Klein:	1830:	Born. Jeweler from Paris.
Biddy Gargery:	1815:	Born.
	1835:	Married: i) Joe Gargery,
	1862:	ii) Harry Shoreham,
	1872:	Died.
Rizzio Campanile:	1873:	Died. Tour guide and Musician.

Minor Characters

Robert Smith: Junior Clerk.

Residents of Cheyne Row:

            Sarah and James Bollaerts, artist.
            Giovanni Fantana, sculptor.
            Mary and Charles Meggison, painter.

Stuart Twaddell: Lawyer, Applicant for post at
Jaggers Practice. Imprisoned for
soliciting male prostitutes.

Jack Masham: Male Prostitute.

Algernon Pocket: Grandfather of Albert Pirrip, Father
of Beatrice 'Old' Pip's first wife.

Walter Mackenzie: Student Acquaintance of
Hamish Macdonald.

Other characters:

Lord Lyons: British Ambassador in Paris 1870-1872.

Sir Charles Dilke, Bt. M.P.
Lady Dilke.

Herbert & Clara Pocket: Old Pip's friends.

Mr. Justice Comely: High Court Judge in Twaddell case.
Humphrey Godspeed
    QC: Prosecuting Counsel in Twaddell Case.

George Holditch: Security in The Jaggers Building
                           (the home for prostitutes estab-
                           lished by the Jaggers Trust).

Ethel Coldheart: Prostitute, residents in The
                           Jaggers Building.
Maud Armstrong: Prostitute, residents in The
                           Jaggers Building.
Fanny Filby: Prostitute, residents in The
                           Jaggers Building.

Edward Nettleship: Eye surgeon at Moorfields Hospital

Mrs. Hayhoe: Cook: Craynham Vicarage.
Belinda: Maid: Craynham Vicarage.
Mr. Dereham and Mr. Graves: Craynham Church wardens.